TRAVELS of
Sir EDMUND de MONTGOMERIE
1095 — 1099

Silver Leopard

by F. van Wyck Mason

SILVER LEOPARD
TWO TICKETS FOR TANGIER
BLUE HURRICANE
GOLDEN ADMIRAL
HIMALAYAN ASSIGNMENT
DARDANELLES DERELICT
CUTLASS EMPIRE
SAIGON SINGER
PROUD NEW FLAGS
THREE HARBOURS
STARS ON THE SEA
RIVERS OF GLORY
EAGLE IN THE SKY
CASTLE ISLAND CASE
SPIDER HOUSE
CAPTAIN NEMESIS
"THE ADVENTURES OF HUGH NORTH
AS CAPTAIN AND MAJOR"

SILVER LEOPARD

BY

F. van Wyck Mason

DOUBLEDAY & COMPANY, INC., GARDEN CITY, N.Y., 1955

Library of Congress Catalog Card Number 55–10514

To ELIZABETH and EDWARD E. YAGGY, Jr.,
than whom none could be more loyal
in adventure and adversity

CONTENTS

FOREWORD   xi

BOOK I: *Sanseverino*

   I   *April the Thirteenth, 1096*   1

  II   *Castel Agropoli*   7

 III   Au Secours!   17

 IV   *On the Road Towards Pesto*   25

  V   *The Assembly*   31

 VI   *Lord Spear Warrior*   33

 VII *Pesto*   37

VIII Dieu lo Vult!   39

 IX   *Count Turgis*   49

  X   *The Feasting*   54

 XI   *The Wild Boar*   58

 XII *Baron Drogo Entertains*   66

 XIII *On the Battlements*   71

 XIV À L'Outrance   80

 XV   *Bohemund, Duke of Otranto I*   90

 XVI *The Offer*   94

 XVII *The Intruder*   101

XVIII *Hunted*   107

XIX	*Città Potenza*	111
XX	*Judgment*	115
XXI	*The Jousting*	122
XXII	*Bari, August 1096*	127

BOOK II: *Byzantium*

I	*The City of Constantine*	133
II	*Gideon of Tarsus*	142
III	*The Courier*	151
IV	*Diplomatic Banquet*	155
V	*The Library*	163
VI	*Intelligences to the Maritime Palace*	169
VII	*Street Brawl*	176
VIII	*In the Street of the Winged Bull*	181
IX	*Count Leo*	187
X	*The Recruitment*	198
XI	*The Duke of Otranto II*	205
XII	*A Scroll of Vellum*	214

BOOK III: *Jerusalem*

I	In Nomine Deus	223
II	*Imperial Headquarters*	229
III	*Private Conversation*	237
IV	*River Sangarius*	246
V	*Dorylaeum I*	251
VI	*Dorylaeum II*	260
VII	*Victory Bells*	267

Contents

VIII   *The Chronicler*   272

IX   *Before the Walls of Arkah*   281

X   *Saturnalia*   288

XI   *The Dry March*   290

XII   *Sir Outcast*   297

XIII   *The Plain of Ramlah*   301

XIV   *Commander of the Turcopoles*   307

XV   *Port of Jaffa*   310

XVI   *Rear Guard Action*   314

XVII   *The Beffroi*   319

XVIII   Jerusalem Victum   325

XIX   Christus Regnat!   334

FOREWORD

In undertaking this tale of the First—and only truly successful—Crusade the challenge of re-creating accurately the times and motivations of that epoch-making adventure was at once fascinating and appalling. So little remains of the scant literature and contemporary records of that day that hardly any major new facts have been incorporated in this account despite arduous research.

The author journeyed to Constantinople, Nicea, Sanseverino and many other places described in this narrative; he consulted a great majority of the eleventh- and twelfth-century manuscripts preserved in the Vatican Library and in the British Museum. Studies, often quite fruitless, were conducted among the museums and armories of Italy, England and Belgium in an effort to examine contemporary costume, weapons and armor. Alas, practically nothing of such a nature has survived since the dawn of the twelfth century.

There remain, however, the massive, inspiring and infinitely instructive ruins of such great fortresses as Sanseverino, high on a hill not far from Monte Cassino, of Istanbul's mighty bastions and the scarcely less imposing walls of Nicea and Antioch.

The First Crusade I have attempted to describe was the result of the personal exhortations and ambitions of that most able churchman and shrewd diplomat, Pope Urban II. He preached this Crusade primarily to unite Christian princes in a common cause and so make them desist from an internecine warfare which was threatening to obliterate in Europe the last sparks of political order, culture and learning.

The Seljuk Turkish threat to the glittering yet hollow Byzantine Empire—at that period reduced to a fragment of its once great dominions—was the pretext seized upon by Pope Urban II to unify the warring lords of Western Europe. It was a further ambition of this great Pope to reunite the Latin and Greek Churches—under the sway of Rome.

Considerable care has been taken to temper descriptions of the almost incredible brutality, ignorance, poverty and filth prevalent in the Europe of those times. If at times my characters appear overly barbaric and uncouth they nonetheless remain but pale counterparts of their prototypes.

The Franks—a generic term for all Western Europeans—particularly the Normans, were indeed iron men, whose physical strength has never since been approximated. Their powers of endurance, their bloodthirsty quick temper and sublime singleness of purpose also have remained unequaled.

When one considers that such men wore a hauberk—a long shirt of chain armor stitched to a leather backing—a hood of mesh steel and an iron casque weighing together close on forty pounds day after day under the torrid sun of Syria and Palestine, one can only marvel over their stamina. Usually they battled lacking adequate food or water and suffered terrible wounds from which they recovered, more often than not, without even the most rudimentary medical attention.

It is difficult to determine just how many of these adventurers—for adventurers they were in the purest sense—were inspired by an overwhelming religious fervor and how many were moved to depart on the Crusade through ambition or a sheer inborn restlessness. The Normans, both Northern and Southern, probably were the participants most activated by a persistent innate yearning for far horizons and bold adventures in unknown lands.

Possibly the followers of Duke Godfrey de Bouillon and Raymond of Toulouse may have been more often activated by true religious zeal and a burning desire to punish the Unbelievers than the other Crusaders.

Chronicles about the First Crusade introduced so many fascinating, strong and devious characters among its leaders it was difficult indeed to be forced, through the limitations of length and plot structure, to portray so many of these paladins only in passing.

The de Montgomerie family, of course, is fictional and although Castel Sanseverino still survives, its lord did not bear the name of Count Turgis de Bernay nor was there a Baron Drogo of Cetraro.

In describing various Byzantine characters I have employed the names of certain illustrious families of that day, but the various titles of the Emperor Alexis and the names of his generals, councilors, governors and such are exact, as are the names of the various Moslem Emirs, Sultans, Khans.

I owe debts of profound gratitude to Monseigneur Montini, Papal Secretary, to Miss Margaret Franklin for her assistance at the British Museum, to Miss Katherine Coplan of the Enoch Pratt Free Library of Baltimore and to Mr. Robert H. Haynes of the Harvard College Library and their staffs. Mr. Faysal Targan of Istanbul and Mr. Hilary Sumner-Boyd of Robert College in that same city, greatly facilitated researches in Turkey. I also wish to acknowledge the cheerful and able assistance of my secretary Mrs. Jane West Tidwell.

F. van Wyck Mason
Gunners' Hill
Riderwood, Maryland

BOOK I: *Sanseverino*

CHAPTER I

April the Thirteenth, 1096

For a long while Sir Edmund de Montgomerie, former Earl of Arundel, lay upon a stretch of wet gray sand weakly retching up quantities of seawater. In his ears sounded the incessant thunder of waves relentlessly lashing the shore. Continually sheets of spray drenched his chilled and all-but naked body. Another paroxysm of nausea set the castaway's powerful frame to shuddering and left him so spent and confused that, for the moment, he could not even open his eyes in order to determine the nature of this purgatory into which he had been plunged.

Monks cloistered in a Benedictine monastery near Arundel Castle often had described and in infinite detail the various circles of Hell. These grave instructors had dwelt upon the torments of eternal fire, mutilation or of freezing cold, but it was curious that never once had they described a watery circle similar to this in which he had been immersed for countless aeons it seemed. Of only one fact could he be at all sure: he still lived. But what fate had befallen his twin sister? Undoubtedly Rosamund must have drowned like all the rest of the galley's company.

Sluggishly Sir Edmund's consciousness rallied until he recalled struggling to support his sister upon an empty wine keg by gripping her long, red-gold hair. Since neither of them could swim and the Genoese galley in which they had fled England had commenced to break up with terrifying rapidity once she had impaled herself upon the reefs, that little barrel undoubtedly had preserved him. Even now in his ears rang the despairing howls of slaves who, shackled to their benches, saw themselves doomed.

Rosamund? The giant Anglo-Norman retained only confused impressions of his sister's lovely features streaming and dimmed by spindrift. Even the fear of death had not marred that perfection of feature which had been sung about through the South of England and as far north as London Town. Curious. It was such an eulogy which had brought about the disaster which had befallen his twin and himself.

Once Sir Edmund had regurgitated a final measure of seawater enough strength returned to permit raising his head from amid a slimy festoon of rockweed. The first thing he noted was that life-preserving wine cask; under the impulse of a breaker it would be flung far up the beach then rattle back over the pebbles towards the sea only to be hurled landward again.

At length a particularly vicious comber propelled the little barrel sufficiently high to leave it stranded. Only then did he notice Rosamund's body lying right at the high-water mark. Her long and shapely white legs were yielding limply to the swirling waters and her red-gold hair rippled like seaweed upon sand.

Only through a supreme effort did the former earl finally succeed in sitting up and become aware of how shamefully weak he was. Undoubtedly this was attributable to the fact that he had been unable to keep food in his stomach since the tempest had pounced upon the luckless *San Giorgio.* It had been a week after she passed between the fabled Pillars of Hercules that a gale had come screaming out of the west as they were passing a rocky island which the Genoese captain had been unwilling or unable to identify.

Panting, the big young man stared dully at his sister's inanimate form and noted that Rosamund de Montgomerie's pallid, slender and yet supple figure, under the sea's buffetings had become exposed save for a sodden undershift bunched uglily about her hips.

Much like a wet dog Edmund shook water and sand from tangled shoulder-length hair the color of dark red copper. Listlessly then he noticed his sister's long fingers flex themselves. Then very slowly, her right arm commenced to inch toward her. Rosamund was bleeding in two places; slowly from a shallow cut across her shoulder and much more rapidly from some wound in her scalp. The sand beneath her head swiftly was becoming scarlet stained.

Still too weak to move, the castaway for a while remained helpless, but when a meandering trickle of blood commenced to streak the sheen of his sister's back and collected in the long depression created by her spine he attempted to call out. Only then did the former earl discover that his throat had become so raw and swollen from seawater that a mere croak escaped him, a feeble sound which instantly became lost amid the roaring of wind and surf.

When the Lady Rosamund presently struggled up onto an elbow the discharge from her scalp wound changed direction, sketched vivid lines down her cheeks. The tall young woman suddenly arched her back like a frightened cat and commenced to vomit. Edmund somehow rolled onto all fours and began laboriously to crawl in her direction.

As the spasm ended Rosamund must have noticed her twin's approach for she attempted to clean her face, then picked weakly at her shift in an instinctive, but ineffectual attempt to conceal her breasts. The effort proved too great, however, and she collapsed onto the sand while Edmund continued his painful, crab-like progress.

The former earl rearranged Rosamund's shift then gathered her into his arms and awkwardly pillowed her head against his chest. Chilled by this on-shore gale and stung by flying particles of sand they crouched thus an undeterminable period. Edmund meanwhile squinted through the gradually brightening dawn. He needed to learn as soon as possible on what coast they had been cast up. It had been pitch-dark at the moment the *San Giorgio*, in fearful violence, had been hurled upon a reef rising so near and yet so far from certain friendly lights which, bobbing low to the water, had suggested a haven for the storm-racked galley and her exhausted rowers.

Presently he made out that he and Rosamund had been cast up on a little sand-and-gravel beach carved by the sea from a bold and rocky shore line. Next he noticed the bodies of several drowned men being tumbled about by the waves—much as had been the wine cask.

Of the *San Giorgio* only a dim and shapeless tangle of timbers remained impaled upon the reef. Over them giant combers continued to spout and soar in pale fury and scatter over the nearby shingle sizable pieces of wreckage and jetsam of every description.

Weakly, Edmund mumbled an *Ave Maria* in gratitude for the miracle which just had occurred; apparently, he and his twin were the *San Giorgio's* only survivors.

Next he bent to reassure himself that the gash on his sister's shoulder indeed was less serious than it looked. At his touch the girl stirred and moaned so he patted her cheek and croaked encouragements in Norman-French. Sufficient strength presently returned to permit his raising the girl to a sitting position and slipping her arms back into the bloodied shift. At the sound of his voice the girl's dark eyelashes stirred and she stared dazedly up into his angular brown features. Large and of a clear blue-green, her eyes suggested the hues of a fine greenish tourmaline as they widened at hearing him chuckle.

"Why laugh?"

"Could our Most Noble King Rufus first have beheld you in your present state the Royal Lecher never would have sent his constables to fetch you and we would not have been hounded out of England."

The ghost of a smile curved the girl's wide mouth. Although lavender-hued through exposure, her lips' curve remained subtly provocative.

Gradually the day brightened enough to reveal endless squadrons of tattered, gray-black clouds charging furiously in from the sea. If this storm was about to abate there was certainly no indication of its doing so. While chafing Rosamund's wrists Edmund became aware that he retained no garment beyond a white woolen breeching cloth the tie strings of which miraculously had remained knotted.

Presently the red-haired girl faced him as they rested upon the cold gray sand. "Where—we?"

"St. Christopher alone knows; God send the waves have not spat us up on the shores of some Infidel kingdom." He deliberated a little. "Come to think on it, just before we struck, our Captain mentioned a place called Sardinia—then another named Sicilia or something similar." Frowning he shoved sand-caked and sodden hair from his forehead. "For aught I know this may even be the coast of that land from whence came the ancient Romans. In any case——"

He broke off for, from the corner of his eye, he thought to detect a stealthy movement among sand grass whipping wildly along the crest of a low bluff rising almost sheer above them. Breath went hissing into his lungs when he recognized the outline of a spear-point and the indistinct silhouette of a shaggy head protected by a close-fitting leathern cap.

The instant the head drew back Edmund heaved himself erect then half-carried, half-dragged his sister towards inadequate concealment afforded by a group of slimy and barnacled rocks. Soon, clearly visible in the brightening light, heads to the number of seven or eight lined the bluff above them. Then raising shrill whoops the swarthy, wild-appearing natives of this unknown land came bounding down a goat path and fanned out over the beach.

At once they waded into the surf and hauled ashore those corpses rolling, log-like, amid the wash. These apparitions, mostly clad in cloaks of coarse furs, bared long daggers and used them to hack off fingers adorned by rings afterwards they fell to stripping the dead. Others of their number appeared and occupied themselves by dragging above the high-water mark casks, chests, sailing gear and all manner of jetsam.

Clenching jaws in an effort to still the violent chattering of his teeth, the tall young Norman vainly attempted to guess the nationality of these strangers in rough *byrri* and goatskin cloaks. Uniformly they were shock-haired, painfully thin and short of stature—not at all like those stalwart Norman liegemen and sturdy Saxon kerls he once had ruled in Sussex. Of their speech Edmund could comprehend nothing at all.

Inevitably these shaggy brutes must notice his tracks. What then? The only weapon within reach was a section of broken yard lying almost at his feet. Although this clumsy club was encumbered by a length of line and a shredded section of sailcloth, he caught it up bemoaning a mortifying and quite disconcerting sense of weakness.

"Are they Moors?" whispered Rosamund peering up through lank and sandy strands of hair. Bloody streaks still dribbling aslant her face furthered her eerie aspect.

Edmund gestured for silence and crouched lower. Fresh cause for anxiety appeared in that a horse's blunt head now had become silhouetted against the livid and lead-hued sky, its mane streaming straight out. Its rider, to Edmund's amazement, was wearing a conical steel headpiece equipped with a nasal or noseguard while over a shirt of rusty mail a dingy, dark-blue surcoat snapped furiously in the storm. God's love! This ill-favored stranger for all the world resembled a Norman serjeant.

Still etched in bold relief the horseman swung his head about then cupped gauntleted hands to bellow some command downwind. Next, he guided his coarse-limbed mount down the goat path and rode out onto the beach.

As increasing amounts of flotsam continued to be spewed up the helmeted man directed his shaggy retainers to put down their weapons and heap this sea-spoil well beyond reach of the boiling surf.

The mounted figure's every gesture somehow suggested an arrogance and contempt of his underlings which, to the lurking Anglo-Norman, seemed familiar. From where he crouched, racked by forebodings of disaster Edmund noted that the rider must stand at least a head taller than the rest of these natives and was carrying a whip composed of a wooden stock equipped with a long lash. When his followers proved tardy in carrying out a command he kicked forward his horse and lashed these spindle shanked creatures who only cringed and made no effort to defend themselves.

Since this rider wore a hauberk, or steel shirt reaching from neck to knees, and a pointed casque Edmund guessed he must be Norman. But of what sort? Perhaps even by this poor light Edmund glimpsed a flash of steel, not gold, on the rider's right heel so deduced, that this was indeed a mere serjeant and not a knight, no matter how arrogant his bearing.

The Anglo-Norman shrank flatter beside his shivering twin for the horseman now wheeled his ribby mount and splashed knee-deep through the sea.

Cloak flapping furiously from clasps securing it to his shoulders, the serjeant rode forward. Bent over his pommel he scanned the sand until, inevitably, he discovered those telltale tracks left by Edmund in struggling over to his sister. The unknown at once roared a command which brought a half-dozen dark-faced spearmen racing up to him. Without bothering to unsheath a long, straight sword jammed under his left knee the horseman commenced to scrutinize that jumble of rocks which, during the ages, had fallen from the cliffs.

While hefting his piece of broken spar the former earl briefly considered bashing in his sister's head. Thus surely would be preserved the honor of Sir Roger de Montgomerie's tall and stately daughter. After that he would make so good an end that people hereabouts would speak of it a long while. He was granted no time to take action for a pack of spearmen shouting in high-pitched voices, closed in and quickly their bright spearheads ringed in Edmund's refuge.

Wide-set blue eyes dangerously a-glitter the red-haired and half naked giant raised his club. If only he could wield "Brainbiter" these pitiful churls could be made to scatter like chaff. A spearman leaped in when Edmund pretended to sway, whereupon the castaway whirled up his piece of spar and, after beating aside the threatening spearpoint, clubbed the fellow's sheepskin-clad shoulder so hard that he shrieked and reeled back, his right arm dangling limp and useless.

"St. Michael!" Edmund's blood stirred as, thickly he attempted to raise his war-cry. "St. Michael for Montgomerie!"

Before his other assailants recovered from their astonishment he had dealt a second native so shrewd a blow on the head that the rogue staggered and crashed upon the shingle to lie there, shuddering like some pole-axed bullock.

Barely in time Edmund ducked as a javelin hissed over his head. A moment later he had beaten its caster to his knees. The mounted man, in Norman-French, emitted a volley of curses and spurred forward, a gauntleted hand upraised.

"Hold hard, you who speak the Norman tongue. Who and what are you?"

To Edmund's profound disgust he found himself too exhausted to make immediate response. How incredible that so brief a bicker should even have quickened his breath.

"Are you a knight?" demanded the swart horseman bending low in his brass-studded saddle but even while Edmund sought breath to reply three natives leaped from behind and bore him, outraged and weakly struggling, into the sand. Even so, the Anglo-Norman might have won free had not someone dealt him so vicious a clout on the head that his legs gave and he collapsed helpless.

"Do you yield yourself?" the dark-bearded horseman roared.

Edmund, his head ringing like a beaten anvil, could only nod. Blood in warm trickles was coursing freely down his back.

"Tie them up," directed he in the steel headpiece. "And if you value your filthy hides do not let yonder red-haired vixen escape. I've a fancy for long-legged wenches."

Perforce Edmund responded to the tugging of a rope which, noosed about his neck, was secured at its other end to a ring set into the serjeant's cantle. He stumbled miserably along behind the serjeant's mount, only half aware that his twin, swaying like a birch about to be felled, trudged by his side.

Waiting at the rim of the bluff a dozen or so hairy villeins, or churls, as his Saxon mother would have termed them, were herding a few horses and mules about the scrawny necks of which yet dangled crude lanthorns some of which still burnt smokily. These, Edmund realized in bitter anger, must have been those shifting lights which, simulating vessels at anchor, had lured the storm-driven *San Giorgio* to her destruction.

CHAPTER II

Castel Agropoli

Leaving a majority of his followers to collect wreckage as it drifted ashore, the thick-bodied serjeant—he answered to the name of Nissen—proceeded at so rapid a walk that his half-naked and blood streaked prisoners were forced to dog-trot at the end of their lead ropes.

Edmund, although a trifle revived thanks to a sudden rain squall, lurched along and winced because of sharp stones nipping at his bare feet. Poor Rosamund! Certainly she could be faring little better. At length he sufficiently regained voice to inform their bullet-headed captor that he and his sister were both of gentle blood and that he was not only a knight, but also a belted earl. Edmund de Montgomerie would have continued to protest had not the rider signaled a spearman to jab his weapon's point into that gigantic young man's sinewy buttocks.

"Silence, you lying dog! The two of you more likely are an escaped galley slave and some mariner's trull." Serjeant Nissen by his speech sounded like an adventurer but recently arrived from Normandy.

For some distance the straggling column followed a sandy track paralleling the sea where harsh-edged grasses whipped at the prisoners' ankles and wind-driven sand stung their eyes.

Soon Rosamund commenced to limp badly and her lithely muscular figure again had become bared to the waist through the slipping of her sodden under-*tunica*. Nonetheless she still held her coppery head defiantly high.

During a lull in the storm's uproar Edmund demanded in an undertone, "How much further can you travel?"

"Not far. In whose domain are we?" The girl gasped and quickened her stride to ease the lead lines' vicious tugging at her tight-lashed hands.

"Mayhap in Sicily or among the Lombards. At least we seem not to have fallen into Infidel hands—for all those natives look so dark-skinned."

"What next will befall us?" Rosamund presently inquired.

"God alone knows," he growled. "Truly, we remain in the hollow of His hand as surely as when that accursed galley struck the rocks."

The coast road, after winding among bold cliffs and tumbled heaps of rock, emerged at last upon a bare plateau bereft of all trees and high vegetation and led past the fire-scorched remains of what once must have been some stately temple or palace. Only three of six gracefully fluted white marble columns remained erect before a crumbling façade. The rest lay broken, lichen-stained among bushes and coarse weeds.

That the soil along this coast must once have been fertile was attested by the existence of so many ruined habitations; in all directions they dotted the landscape. Nowadays the ground had become so bereft of topsoil through over-cultivation and senseless deforestation that only bare rock, clay ridges and gravel-filled gullies remained. Nowhere on this desolate seashore were to be seen herds, crops or occupied habitations.

Eventually the sea road rounded still another battlement-like crag and Edmund vented a grunt of relief for situated on a rocky pinnacle rising sheer from the sea, loomed what must be either a small castle or a large watchtower. This gray-brown structure consisted of a tall keep on the stronghold's landward exposure and a curtain wall separating it from a lesser square tower fronting on the sea.

To the hollow-eyed captives it differed in no particular from those watchtower forts William the Conqueror's men still were constructing to guard the coasts of Kent, Essex, Sussex, Dorset and

Hampshire against marauding Danes, Saracens and other sea raiders. He could see a narrow road winding up to the stronghold.

In fact an almost identical stronghold situated some six miles below Arundel Castle, guarded the Arun River's mouth. Now as he swayed weakly along the prisoner recalled its harsh outlines as seen by moonlight when he, Rosamund and a handful of loyal retainers had fled downstream to board the *San Giorgio*. Along a road paralleling the Arun had sounded the hoofbeats of King William II's mail-clad pursuers grimly intent on the capture of the late Earl of Arundel, Sir Roger de Montgomerie's heir.

Dully Edmund reflected upon that disastrous sequence of events which had befallen his sister and himself since Rufus the Red's burly Constable had ridden into Arundel Castle bearing Royal commands. The Lady Rosamund must present herself at Court with all haste whilst the new Earl of Arundel was to raise his levee and forthwith join an expedition to suppress a serious Saxon rebellion in Somersetshire.

With regard to Rosamund the King's intent had been unmistakable —far too many lovely ladies thus had been summoned to London where, soon or late, they became still another royal concubine. Report had it that King Rufus was uncouth and so little pleasing physically that force often was required to ensconce these luckless maidens in the royal bed.

For Edmund there had been no choice save to defy King William so, in a bloody little encounter which took place some weeks later, the young earl and a few followers bold enough to take arms against the Conqueror's son had defeated a posse dispatched by that choleric and outraged Norman.

That skirmish had been won, but to what purpose? Never in the world could Arundel Castle hope to hold out against the powerful expedition immediately dispatched by the Royal Lecher. For the defiant red-haired earl and his twin there had remained no course save immediate flight and abandonment of that great stronghold built by their father.

At the lower end of a stony road which climbed to the castle's gate a wretched, straw-roofed village straggled down towards a tiny harbor amid festoons of limp brown nets. Through the rain was visible a bent old man attempting to plow behind a skinny little donkey and employing the crudest imaginable wooden plow.

When Serjeant Nissen's column skirted the village not a soul peered out of its glassless windows but numbers of fierce, hungry-looking dogs rushed out to snarl and bare their fangs.

The serjeant turned a broad face over his shoulder and frowned to behold his prisoners stumping along with heads held high despite hands bound tightly behind them.

"Sir Volmar will bend those stiff necks of yours," he predicted then reined in and spat into Edmund's long, powerfully-moulded features.

"For that, someday I will surely kill you," the Anglo-Norman promised in a deadly monotone.

The serjeant uttered a rasping laugh then kicked his mount into a jolting trot which caused his prisoners to struggle along at the end of their ropes until Rosamund tripped and fell. Correctly calculating that their combined weight would prove too much for the serjeant's wretched little horse to drag, Edmund immediately flung himself flat enforcing a halt until both could regain their feet. Lord! How cruelly those cords were skinning Rosamund's wrists muscular though they were through years of hawking and riding to the hounds.

Presently captors and prisoners commenced to climb towards that ugly little stronghold strategically situated upon a crag and ringed on three sides by water which still boomed and frothed in relentless fury. Furthermore this watchtower was accessible only by a narrow road which followed the spine of a rocky ridge finally to become dominated by the tall donjon.

"Help—I—I—strength going." Rosamund's blue-green eyes rolled dazedly behind the tangle of hair masking her blood-streaked features.

"Rally!" hoarsely pleaded Edmund, trying to forget the anguish stabbing at his wrists and head. "'Tis only a little further."

It was fortunate that the serjeant's weight was so great that his undernourished mount could struggle upwards only slowly panting and with head held low.

Edmund forced himself to observe his surroundings and perceived that this compact stronghold was indeed a rugged affair, devoid of graceful lines or ornamentation of any sort. Its square donjon tower was unroofed while its walls lacked either stone crenellations or wooden mantlets and its only entrance appeared to be a small gate let into the landward wall. The portal itself consisted of massive oaken timbers liberally studded with spikes and strengthened by rusty iron bands.

A tern, driven inland from the sea, skimmed past Edmund's head shrieking as if in pain—prophetically perhaps.

The little column's arrival had been observed for immediately could be heard the hollow *click-clock!* of bolts being drawn back, then the gate was swung open by a pair of towering rascals in rusty mail shirts and unornamented conical headpieces.

To the prisoner's growing astonishment, these men-of-arms cursed in perfectly recognizable Norman-French while holding steady the door against the wind's mad buffetings. Through force of habit, Edmund estimated that this stronghold's donjon rose sixty feet above the rock upon which it had been constructed, that its landward curtain wall, extending to a second and smaller tower facing the sea, was not over eighty feet in length and about ten feet in height.

Shivering and sodden to the skin, the wreckers and their captives tramped beneath a low arch. The wall at this point appeared to be easily five feet thick and rough dressed, but of excellent construction. Serjeant Nissen jerked his prisoners to a halt in the center of a muddied and dung-splashed courtyard above which bluish streamers of wood smoke veered furiously away from a chimney flue climbing the bigger tower's courtyard side. What appeared to be a small, dun-colored barracks occupied half of this courtyard's far side and a pent-shed the rest. The latter structure's red tiled roof not only kept dry stocks of firewood and fodder but also sheltered a trio of thin, sad-faced cows and a number of geese, ducks and chickens. A brace of shaggy watchdogs had been chained to either side of the donjon keep's entrance and made the courtyard ring with their savage clamorings.

Heavily, Serjeant Nissen swung down from his horse and wiped moisture from his features ere he ordered his retainers to drag the prisoners under the pent-shed.

Once the Anglo-Normans had caught their breath they gazed dully about while becoming aware that no matter how great the pain in their bound wrists it nonetheless was a relief to escape from icy wind and pelting rain. Presently the former Earl of Arundel noticed that much of the masonry composing this stronghold's walls must have been used before. For instance, the lintel of the shed in which they crouched was supported by two beautifully sculptured marble columns. These were of differing lengths but this inequality had been equalized by the builders in lengthening the base of the shorter shaft.

Near the donjon's base showed a slab of perfectly dressed snow-white marble which had been set among roughly hewn blocks of gray stone and bore, neatly engraved upon it, part of some handsomely carved Latin inscription. Presently Edmund recognized another section of this same inscription built upside down above the gate. Visible here and there were Roman capitals, sections of cornice and entablatures—even sections of purple or green marble columns. All had been utilized to rear the ugly and uninspired ramparts of Castel Agropoli.

To encourage his sister the big-limbed young knight summoned a smile. "There is still room for hope. Surely, this Sir Volmar must be a Norman and if indeed he wears a knight's spurs, under the laws of chivalry he is bound to befriend us and set us free since I was not overcome in battle or worsted in trial by combat."

The tall young woman only nodded and bit her lips to suppress moans prompted by bound wrists aching almost beyond endurance. It came as some consolation that Rosamund's scalp wound and the shallow cut across her shoulder had ceased to drip and stain her ragged undershift. A wry laugh escaped her when she pictured the present appearance of her who once had acted for her widowed father as chatelaine of Arundel Castle. She had presided over the great domain graciously and modestly, too, for all that beauty which had won the admiration of every knight within three days' riding.

Now she crouched half-naked, pallid as a ghost, and muddied to her knees. Her glorious, red-gold hair had become tangled into a veritable mare's nest.

Would it not have been just as well if she had slipped away from that life-preserving keg? She would have drowned quickly, painlessly. Neither she nor her brother could swim—very few Normans could. In fact the only good swimmers along the coasts of Sussex and Kent were Saxon like young Gerth Ordway, whose father had been Penda, Thegne of Sussex. He had ruled over Arundel before William the Conqueror had won at Senlac—and later had caused his execution. Could her brother's esquire Gerth possibly have survived the shipwreck? Probably not. Even if the Saxon had won his way through the surf he most likely had been killed among those jagged rocks studding this wild and dismal-appearing coast.

Edmund recalled her to the present by silently indicating a truss of straw. Although a stunted and shock-haired spearman on guard over them scowled he did nothing to prevent his prisoners from sinking onto the straw and huddling together for warmth from that raw wind which, swirling down into the courtyard, caused puddles to shimmer and ruffled feathers on the fowls.

Rosamund commenced to weep, but very quietly as became the daughter of tough old Sir Roger de Montgomerie. When had she last partaken of hot food? Not in three days at least. How her throat ached and burned from seawater.

Pondering the fate awaiting her in Castel Agropoli Rosamund gradually lapsed into the semi-stupor of extreme fatigue and Edmund also dozed after fighting down futile fury over this unprecedented and wholly ignominious situation. If, as he was beginning to suspect, the lord of this bleak stronghold proved to be a common

pirate, then his future and that of his sister seemed sinister indeed
since he could not promise so much as a single gold piece by way of
ransom. Did not King Rufus the Red's bailiffs hold Arundel Castle?
No doubt a new earl long since had taken possession of his domain.
Worse still, the small personal treasure he had brought away had
gone down with the *San Giorgio.*

Voices roused him to the realization that into the courtyard was
clumping a swarm of wreckers and a pair of wains, heavy laden with
jetsam. Solid wooden wheels screeched on ungreased axles like souls
in torment until these ungainly ox-drawn vehicles came to a halt.
Almost simultaneously there swaggered through a narrow door at
the base of the donjon keep a burly figure wearing a mantle of dark
blue silk trimmed in mangy-looking fur. Undoubtedly this must be
Sir Volmar, lord of Agropoli.

The rain ceased and a sickly-yellow sun began sketching patches
of brilliance among mud-puddles dotting the courtyard. A knot of
sinewy, hard-faced men-of-arms slouched out of the barracks to lean
on their pikes and watch a throng of brutish serfs unload the wains.
Legs straddled and tugging at long and drooping blond mustaches
the lord of Castel Agropoli directed his villeins to expose sodden
bundles of loot for his inspection.

Very little of value was displayed, Sir Edmund decided through
half-opened eyes. Certainly there was no sign of that small, leather-
bound coffer which had contained his hoard of silver cups, bracelets,
brooches, rings, hairpins and gold chains extorted by grim old Sir
Roger from certain luckless Saxon nobles back in 1068.

The spoils in fact proved so meager that the Serjeant Nissen
cringed before his beetle-browed lord, a plump, yet muscular individual whose pale hair streamed untidily down to his elbows from
beneath a greasy leather cap. Flinching under a series of cuffs the
serjeant hurriedly indicated the pent-shed. The lord of the castle
whereupon wheeled and glowered at that unprepossessing couple
crouched upon the straw. He snarled a series of commands, then in
a rage of disappointment jerked from his belt a short-stocked whip
and with it lashed everyone in reach. Bellowing disappointment, the
squat figure turned on the heel of strapless chausses and disappeared
within the donjon keep.

Presently a quartet of Norman men-of-arms in rusty mail hauberks
draped over leathern shirts ignored Sir Edmund's protests to jerk
the prisoners erect and haul them over towards the donjon tower.

Outraged to the very depths of his being because common men
were defiling his sister and himself by their clutch, Edmund heaved
and struggled in vain for a disconcerting and quite unfamiliar weak-

ness caused his head to spin and his knees to slacken. Characteristically it had never occurred to him that his feebleness was the result not of hunger but of prolonged seasickness. Why, during a campaign against Saxon refugees holding out in remote parts of Cornwall he had subsisted for days at a time on an occasional bowl of dilligrout —a thin gruel made of oatmeal.

The donjon itself proved to be gloomy and not even arrow slits admitted light or air below the tower's second tier. The atmosphere in its guardroom was indescribably foul with the mingled stench of stale sweat, garlic, damp leather and the sour reek of mouldy cloth.

Ten or twelve unkempt men-of-arms lounged or squatted on their heels about a small fireplace drinking and using their hands to shovel a midday meal out of a common pot and into their mouths. From iron spikes driven into the walls hung a haphazard array of shields, spears, axes and other weapons, while in a far corner were heaped loosely tied bundles of darts and arrows.

"God's Splendor, Nissen," belched a pimpled, red-nosed fellow. "That's a bedraggled pullet you've snared. She the best you could find in such a fine, big galley? Best be wary. So ill-favored a doxy won't please our master."

"Aye, that she'll not," chuckled another. "It's two to one she'll be flung to us within the hour, so ready your dice, Hubert."

Seized by one of those blinding gusts of rage which, more than once, had cost him dear, Sir Edmund hurled himself towards the speaker but, of course, only earned himself a spear butt in the pit of his stomach.

"Up, you filthy foreign pigs! Up!" Serjeant Nissen used a dagger's point to prick his prisoners up a wooden stair so steep it resembled a ladder.

On the keep's second floor another fire blazed, dimly illumining an apartment perhaps twenty by twenty-five feet in dimension. Here to the walls had been nailed fragments of once-beautiful tapestries, while from wooden pegs hung clusters of capes, robes and all manner of garments mostly stained by seawater.

Upon a pair of handsomely inlaid curule chairs sat Sir Volmar and his lady—if so hawk-faced, graceless and angular a female might be thus dignified. Obviously far gone with child, she lolled back behind a round and swollen abdomen that strained fearfully at her soiled gown of green-and-yellow brocade. The woman's mouse-colored hair had been plaited into two loose and lusterless braids secured near their ends by heavy silver rings. Like pale serpents they coiled about her shoulders.

Volmar of Agropoli leaned hunched forward bellowing, "On your knees, insolent dog!"

Edmund's voice suddenly deep and strong again rang out. "Go to, you ill-mannered churl! I kneel before none saving my liege lord and God in His high Heaven! Be you, as yonder gilded spurs would indicate, a gentle man, I require you to treat a distressed fellow knight with the courtesy due him and to his sister, the Lady Rosamund de Montgomerie."

This Italian Norman's bloodshot, yellow-blue eyes narrowed. "You call on me, the Seigneur of Agropoli, as a fellow knight?"

"I am one and if——"

"—Who is your liege lord?"

"The King of England. I am, or was, an earl of his realm."

"Cease to lie, you graceless oaf. 'Knave and villein' is written all over your miserable carcass."

Sir Edmund surged forward but the men-of-arms beat him back with brutal eagerness.

"How dare you, a dirty hole-in-the-wall wrecker of innocent voyagers, give a de Montgomerie the lie?"

"Silence, dog!" roared Sir Volmar. "One more piece of insolence and I'll have that impudent tongue of yours cut out and fed to the dogs."

There was no restraining the red-haired giant. "Be damned for a recreant knight! No true Norman gentle man would question another's word or heap indignities upon a lady of gentle birth."

For a space the Master of Agropoli appeared impressed. "By the Lord Christ's tender toenails! You *have* a 'cursed haughty way with you. If I spare you what might you offer by way of ransom?"

Edmund held his head high, stared unwaveringly into the Southern Norman's ruddy features. "Nothing. My lady sister and I have been forced to flee England and what little wealth we brought away lies on the bottom of the sea—thanks to you."

"Oh-ho! So you were forced to flee? No doubt, you ill-savored rogue, you murdered your father, raped a nun, or desecrated some church?"

Only by effort was Edmund able to rule his always uncertain temper and fight back an outburst which must have proved disastrous. Being forced to explain his sorry state to this crude robber knight roweled his pride beyond expression.

Said he coldly, "The King of our land would have seized my lady sister, here, for a concubine. When he sent his Constable and a posse to fetch her to him I raised my levee and drove off King William's men, slaying many of them. He then proclaimed me rebel and ordered so powerful an array against Arundel that my liegemen and I could have no hope of a successful defense."

The tall prisoner's scratched and naked shoulders lifted in a weary shrug. "Nothing remained for me but to take ship and flee anywhere save to Normandy—or here, it would seem." Sir Edmund hesitated, loath to become indebted for even the least favor, yet he must learn the fate of his esquire. As the Saxon's master it was requisite that he should make inquiry. "Sir Knight, has aught been seen by your people today of a sturdy, yellow-haired youth who is my armiger?"

Sir Volmar merely scowled and spat into the crudely-designed hearthan affair built into that same flue which served the guardroom below. The hissing of damp logs sounded surprisingly loud as the wrecker cast his bloated spouse a questioning glance. Her face, weather-beaten to a raw red, was streaked by wrinkles that showed dull white about her eyes and mouth. In ungainly fashion the Lady Aldebara only shifted on her seat. Deftly, however, she cuffed one of several tangle-haired brats rioting about the floor and sent it screaming into a corner.

Again tugging at his drooping mustaches Volmar of Agropoli swung over to survey the disheveled girl with care. In obvious distaste he turned away and confronted his other captive.

"I think that you have spoken only lies so I shall hold you and someday sell you to the Infidels. They pay well for Frankish soldier-slaves. Serjeant, this hag is yours until you tire of her. Then she's for the guardroom."

Edmund's restraint snapped. Wrenching free by a circular motion from the hips upward he kicked at his tormentor's groin, but Volmar of Agropoli turned quickly aside so that the prisoner's bare toes only struck him on the thigh. An instant later all the stars in the heavens seemed to explode and swim before Sir Edmund's eyes.

When the former Earl of Arundel regained a measure of consciousness it was to discover that he lay upon the donjon's greasy flagstones with the heavy chausses of several men-of-arms pinning him down.

Only dimly did Edmund realize that Aldebara had risen awkwardly to her feet and now was confronting Rosamund. His twin had been shoved over to the fireplace where her superb and supple figure could be effectively silhouetted against the flames.

"My serving-nurse died in child-bed last week so I will have you attend my children," she was announcing in harsh Norman-French. "Yonder damned rutting boar gets every wench in my service in farrow." She cast her spouse a vicious look.

Rosamund's head snapped back. "*I* swaddle your run-nose whelps? Never. It is beneath my station. I will not——" Rosamund got no further because the Chatelaine of Agropoli had dealt her a resounding blow across the face. All the while hissing obscene maledictions the beldame then caught up a faggot and despite her heavy figure commenced to belabor the prisoner.

"Too proud to tend my children? Well, by the Rood, *I* can humble the proudest draggle-ass bitch as ever trod this earth!"

Under blows thudding across her wounded back Rosamund shuddered, then collapsed like a bundle of wet clothing to lie with long white limbs outflung and shimmering in the firelight.

Sir Volmar thrust aside his wife. "Eh! Look at that! The hussy has a rare fine figure."

"Let the slut be, you accursed jack ape!"

In shrieking rage the Lady Aldebara commenced to belabor him with both fists until Sir Volmar dealt his wife so shrewd a buffet that she went lurching across the room amid delighted screams from her unkempt brood.

CHAPTER III

Au Secours!

During two seemingly endless days Sir Edmund de Montgomerie alternately raged in helpless fury or brooded sullenly in a small and miserable cell facing the castle's courtyard, or inner ward, and situated directly opposite the donjon tower's entrance. The prison was indescribably foul. There was not even a heap of straw upon which a prisoner might sit or lie. Worse still, the Anglo-Norman was forced to share this dim hell-hole with a semi-lunatic, who, because his tongue had been torn out, could neither identify himself nor explain why he was held prisoner. Obviously, this stark naked, gaunt and long-haired wretch had been confined a long while. When addressed he would roll his eyes and gabble incomprehensibly while scratching lice with fingernails grown long and curved as claws.

At first the other prisoner had gibbered and cowered in terror but, gradually, he had become apathetic and resigned to the presence of a companion in misery. Although inured to mephitic atmospheres prevalent about camps and castles, Edmund never ceased to sicken over the dreadful stench of this cell. Since no provision existed for disposal of a prisoner's excrement, of necessity a corner of this living tomb had to be utilized as a latrine to the satisfaction of dense swarms of flies.

Only once in twenty-four hours did a member of the garrison open a panel let into the door and pass an earthenware bowl of water and dump onto the stone floor some unidentifiable mess he called food.

To listen to the gabble of geese and the cackle of hens in the court-yard became a refined torture so easy was it to visualize them brown and smoking on a spit. These *prud'hommes* paid not the least heed to Edmund's demands to be granted opportunity of proving the justice of his claims in trial by combat. At times his soul re-volted by this hopeless, deadening confinement, he wrenched wildly at the little window's bars and shouted himself hoarse.

Eventually the former earl lapsed into semi-stupor in which he was afforded ample leisure to review the past. Slumped all-but naked, filthy and unshaven against a slimy wall he saw himself again as a gawky red-headed lad of ten—a so-called "bachelor." Then he had taken his first steps in that long and arduous training which, eventu-ally, might end in the glorious honor of knighthood. How fortunate he had been that his father grim old Sir Roger, who had more than once sustained William of Normandy's personal banner in battle, had sent his only heir and son to learn the art of war and the code of chivalry, still in its very infancy, under one Baron Richard de Dom-front, Seneschal of Dover Castle. This knight once had been a savage and merciless campaigner but through many wounds and the passage of years, he had gentled and had become great of patience.

Head sunk between knees, the former lord of Arundel again saw himself playing at war games against the other little bachelors. All of them had been equipped with miniature shields, wooden swords and had ridden gentle or aged palfreys. Other Norman barons who had received nearby fiefs and castles from the Conqueror, privately had considered the first Earl of Arundel to be eccentric and roaring over their cups had gibed at his insistence that his heir should learn to read and write—a most ignoble accomplishment. Further, Sir Roger sternly had required that young Edmund receive instruction from the monks of a nearby abbey in Latin—the only common language of Christendom and the sole means of communication among any num-ber of vague dukedoms and principalities. Later he had insisted upon his heir's acquiring a smattering of Greek—perhaps because he had heard rumors of rich pickings to be won in certain lands lying some-where far to the eastward. One of these realms was called Byzan-tium, or sometimes Romania, and was fabulously wealthy, or so a wandering friar had insisted.

Piercing howls raised by some helpless serf squirming under Vol-mar of Agropoli's ever-busy whiplash no longer sent Sir Edmund rag-ing to that tiny window which afforded a view of all that transpired in the inner ward. At the start of his imprisonment he had lingered hour after hour at this aperture hoping for at least a glimpse of his twin. But she had never appeared—at least while he was on watch. What fate could have overtaken her? Was she even alive?

Again he permitted his mind to travel back over the years, reviewing his service under often brutal and always exacting Baron Sir Richard de Domfront as an armiger or esquire. Since the old baron, crippled by wounds, no longer himself could take the field in more-or-less continual expeditions against rebellious Saxon clans or participate in minor but savage wars of extermination against the Welsh, Edmund perforce had done his first fighting under Sir Richard's brother, one Tibault of Rennes.

Monotonous, often tiresome weeks had been commoner. His day commenced before dawn with the feeding and grooming of his master's favorite destrier, or great warhorse; next he had had to clean, repair and oil the Baron's weapons and saddle gear. This accomplished, he next had devoted long hours in perfecting himself in the employment of such knightly weapons as the lance, mace and above all that heavy three-foot-long Norman sword which, in battle, had proved all-but irresistible.

To strengthen shoulders and arms young Edmund de Montgomerie had, on his own initiative, exercised with clubs so heavily weighted that a twenty-pound iron mace afterwards had seemed light as a reed and a knight's sword little heavier than a cudgel. To his satisfaction eventually he had become able to wield for hours on end weapons more ponderous than any armiger or many a knight garrisoning Dover Castle could manage. Too, he had become able effortlessly to support the weight of a chain mail shirt that covered his body to the knees, a hood-like coif of the same material and a pointed helm in all weighing thirty pounds at the least.

When not studying language, penmanship or, much more happily, practicing warlike arts the red-headed youth had been required to serve Sir Richard at table, standing at his elbow ready to pour the Seneschal's wine or with his dagger to carve a tough chunk of meat— a task he had abominated.

With all his heart he had loathed the fulfillment of another knightly requirement—the ability to play upon a lute and to sing verses composed by himself. His efforts in those directions must have been appalling for, invariably, Sir Richard had endured them as briefly as was consistent with courtesy before beckoning some other armiger to raise his voice in song. Before he might retire, heavy-eyed, to a hard pallet in a draughty cubicle his master's destrier once more must be fed and watered. He and the other esquires then had been required to make a round of all sentry posts about the stronghold in order to make certain that sentinels on duty were indeed alert.

No armiger ever was allowed to wear a Norman sword or use one, even in battle, until he became a knight. A single important exception to this rule existed. If, in battle an esquire managed to beat an enemy and so capture his sword, then he might wear it—but only into another battle. He had taken advantage of this exception during a foray to the Isle of Wight upon which a noble pirate, Sir Tête de Loup, had had his stronghold.

The captive raised a disheveled head to peer through buzzing swarms of insects at his fellow prisoner and saw the wretch lying as if dead, so oblivious was he to flies drinking at his eye corners and crawling in and out of his mouth.

Blankly the big prisoner stared upon his broken and black-rimmed fingernails. Could these be those hands between which a knight's sword once had been placed?

How well he could recall even the least event on a certain glorious June morning. All the night before he had lain prostrate and with arms extended, cross-like, upon a cold stone floor before the altar of Dover Castle's Chapel. At sunrise close friends had appeared, soberly for once, and had conducted him into a chamber in which he had bathed and had combed his copper-colored hair before clothing himself in robes of spotless white.

In solemn silence the youngest knights owing fealty to Sir Richard de Domfront then had escorted the candidate to Dover Castle's great hall and into the presence of the Seneschal, of his father and of many another famous knight and champion.

To one side of the knight-to-be had moved the Seneschal's eldest daughter. In reality she was a very plain young woman but on this occasion, she had appeared more beautiful than one of God's own angels. Smiling, the Lady Ermengarde and her tiring women had brought forward plain wooden trays supporting a knight's hauberk, coif and leggings; gloves and shoes of cunningly joined iron rings.

Then the old Seneschal's great voice had rung out, perhaps as it had during the second Norman rally at Hastings.

"Do you, Edmund de Montgomerie, swear to faithfully honor and serve Holy Church and be ever obedient to your undoubted sovereign, King William II? Will you swear always to keep your pledged word and to respect the laws of chivalry? Will you champion the weak if their cause be just? Will you aid fellow knights in their distress, no matter how great the cost to yourself?"

Edmund recalled that after swearing to honor all these requirements he had been told to kneel before the fiercely proud old Earl

of Arundel who, thereupon, had tapped his heir upon the nape of his
neck with the flat of one of those long Norman swords so feared
throughout Christendom—and beyond. The Earl then had cried out
in a great voice, "In the name of God, I make thee knight! Arise, Sir
Edmund de Montgomerie!"

After that, his former master, Baron Sir Richard de Domfront,
Royal Seneschal of Dover, had assisted him to his feet, and placing
hands upon the new knight's shoulders, had cried urgently, "Be
proud! Ever be proud!"

Next Sir Richard had buckled to his war belt, "Brainbiter," as Edmund had christened that sword he had won while an armiger from
Tête de Loup. Other knights then had strapped on spurs of gilded
steel and finally, Sir Richard had presented him with a long, kite-
shaped Norman shield upon which someone had painted, crudely
enough, a leopard rendered in silvery paint.

Often as a small boy Edmund had wondered concerning this bla-
zon's origin but none knew anything save that the device was as old
as the de Montgomerie clan. In later years he had deduced that some
remote ancestor among the dense forests of central Normandy, must
have encountered and slain an albino leopard. For a long while
various doughty lords had caused to be carried before them such
standards as stuffed eagles, bears' heads or the effigies of griffins and
camelopards that their followers might the more readily identify
their lord upon the field of battle. Recently they had caused these
creatures to be painted upon their gonfanons or war flags—they being
so much easier to handle than standards.

Last of all accoutrements to be presented to the new gentle man,
was a Norman helm. This heavy iron headpiece was unornamented,
conical and equipped with a heavy strip of steel designed to protect
the nose.

Sighing, the long-limbed prisoner scratched at a particularly hungry louse. Would he ever again in this life recapture the exquisite
ecstasy of that moment when, in Dover Castle's exercise yard, he had
vaulted in full mail into the saddle of a "great horse" to receive the
ten-foot lance of chivalry? How deafeningly knights, serjeants, men-
of-arms and other onlookers had roared when, shouting "St. Michael
for Montgomerie!" the new knight had tossed this ponderous weapon
high into the air, then caught it and thundered about the courtyard in
a series of mock charges.

Knights, warmed by the Seneschal's hospitality had bellowed war
cries, as if in battle, lovely ladies had blown kisses and trumpets had
blared.

The prisoner blinked, the joyous picture faded. What? Edmund's

head rose uncertainly. Could he be dreaming? Had a real trumpet
sounded somewhere? A trick of his imagination? *Par Dex!* A real
trumpet was sounding before the gate to Castel Agropoli!

Two more brazen notes reverberated imperiously against the donjon's sides. Edmund lurched to his feet in time to watch Sir Volmar's
frowzy garrison come swarming out of the keep's dark entrance like
wasps from a disturbed nest.

The *prud'hommes* still were buckling on swords and adjusting their
helms when Sir Volmar appeared. He screamed orders while tugging
to adjust a red cloak bordered with fox fur. The garrison lined up in
a poorly dressed rank facing the portal while a quartet of serjeants
made haste to unbar the gate.

Bright yellow sunlight drenching the inner ward dazed Edmund's
eyes but he continued to peer out, for in his ears sounded the familiar
trampling of steel-shod hooves. Tall and erect in the saddle there
rode into the courtyard a grizzled cavalier who over his mail wore a
dingy white surcoat upon the breast of which had been stitched a
glaring red Latin cross. If the new arrival with the aquiline profile
held Sir Volmar of Agropoli in respect, the fact was not noticeable;
his bearing was at once arrogant and aloof.

In this sinewy knight's wake clattered a quartet of mounted serjeants, big, leather-faced fellows whose chain mail and steel caps
glistened in glittering contrast to the garrison's dull and rust-flecked
accoutrements. When the stranger's supporters reined aside it was to
disclose, framed in the castle's entrance, a white-bearded figure in
black—a monk whose features for the moment were concealed beneath a cowl of the same somber hue. At arm's length he carried
before him an ebony crucifix bearing an image of the Saviour beautifully fashioned of ivory.

Behind this monk then appeared men-of-arms, sunburnt, dusty and
some twenty in number. Meanwhile the knight in the white surcoat
dismounted and prepared to surrender the brass-studded reins of his
great horse.

Edmund drew a deep breath and, as loudly as his weakened condition permitted shouted the appeal of a knight in dire peril, "*Au Secours! Au Secours!*"

When the hawk-faced knight's head swung sharply about, Edmund perceived that not only was his left eye lacking but that whole
side of his face had been crushed under some terrific blow.

Once more the Anglo-Norman raised his call for a rescue, then quivering in anxiety, he heard the newcomer demanding who had raised
the cry.

" 'Tis an idiot prisoner who fancies himself a gentle man."

"He speaks French. I will see him."

"Pray waste not your time, Sir Toustain. The rogue is mad, quite mad."

"Fetch him out. I would behold him who cries like a knight for succor."

The stranger, a veteran judging by the iron-gray hair which escaped from beneath a peaked leather cap, came swinging across the sunlit court with the long white surcoat curling about his legs.

Scowling and red of face, the Master of Agropoli sent for a key then directed two of his most powerful retainers to lead the prisoner out into the beneficent April sunlight.

"What is your degree in life? Why did you call for rescue?" The new arrival stood almost as tall as the prisoner and his single eye glowed in its cavernous socket bright as polished steel.

Holding himself erect Edmund curtly described his lineage, his former title. The monk shuffled forward, raised the crucifix that now dangled from a belt of knotted cords.

"Will you swear upon this Rood that you speak well and truly?"

"Assuredly. But to do so is unnecessary, Holy Father. Already I have given my knightly word that I speak true."

Watched all the while by the stronghold's ill-favored people, the one-eyed knight strode forward, ungloved his right hand. "I am Sir Toustain de Dives, presently Constable to Count Turgis II of Sanseverino. I am thankful to have been accorded the honor of succoring a gentle man in distress."

Sir Toustain then turned and, with long sword asway over his left hip, stalked ominously over to the lord of Agropoli.

"Damn you for a perjured rogue!" he growled. "How dare you imprison one of gentle blood without first bringing him to trial before your liege lord?"

"He is my prisoner," came the sullen evasion.

"Then you defeated Sir Edmund in knightly combat?"

"He is my prisoner."

"Bah! You cannot even give a straight answer."

Mail formed by interlaced iron rings descended to Sir Toustain's elbows. It gleamed when he turned to the prisoner at the moment reveling in the sun's wonderful warmth. "How came you, Sir Knight, to this sorry pass?"

Succinctly Sir Edmund de Montgomerie described the matter of the false lights, the loss of the *San Giorgio* and the brutal capture and imprisonment of his sister and himself.

Color deepened in a long purplish scar slanting Sir Toustain's bronzed countenance. "Sir Volmar, when my lord of Sanseverino hears of this spurs will be struck from the heels of a low-flung scoundrel. You have not sent in your lord's share of spoils taken upon his coast!"

Sir Volmar scowled. "Nonetheless, this stranger is my prisoner and since he cannot pay ransom he remains here."

"By the Glory of God! He shall not!" roared the Constable.

Grimly, Sir Toustain ran an eye over the Anglo-Norman's gaunt frame, noted his sunken stomach and announced acidly, "Sir Edmund is in much too poor a case to fight a trial-at-arms, therefore I here and now do constitute myself to be his champion. Go don your mail, you perverted dog."

"I thank you, noble sir, but ever I have done my own fighting." Edmund shook off his guards, grinned savagely. "Lend me but your sword and your helm, Sir Toustain, and my strength will return."

Sir Volmar apparently had no stomach to engage even the wasted figure before him. Therefore he turned aside. "I yield to the lord Constable's demand. The rogue is yours."

"Rogue, eh?" In two swift strides Edmund cleared the space and dealt his yellow-haired captor a blow on the jaw which made the fellow's teeth rattle. Volmar lurched back grabbing his sword handle but as quickly released it.

"Where is the Lady Rosamund?" demanded Edmund. "If her honor has suffered even the least hurt Satan will claim you."

"Nay! Nay!" babbled Volmar of Agropoli. "The lady's virtue has not been violated—for a very personal reason," he added hurriedly. "Upon my oath, she has suffered nothing worse than sundry kicks and blows from my wife."

So it came about that, a little later, the Lady Rosamund wearing a simple gown of coarse gray wool was led out of the donjon tower, pallid and sadly in need of bathing. Her waist-long red-gold hair, however, hurriedly had been braided. Oblivious to curious stares from the onlookers, she fell into the arms of her twin and clung to him while Sir Toustain cursed the now thoroughly apprehensive Master of Agropoli in a mixture of Italian, Norman-French and, of all things, Greek. He offered no reproaches at all concerning the deliberate wrecking of vessels off Agropoli, only that Sir Volmar had failed to forward the Lord of Sanseverino's half-share.

"Harken to me, you unsoldierly swine and learn the purpose of this visitation," growled the Constable, his one eye balefully surveying the crowded inner ward. "Brother Ordericus, here, is a most reverend monk from the Monastery at Monte Cassino. He conveys tidings which may win salvation for even such rogues as you."

His long and snowy beard gleaming like newly polished silver,

Brother Ordericus, advanced to the center of the court and raised
his Crucifix on high.

"As you fear the flames of Hell," cried he in a ringing voice that
penetrated even into that cell from which the tongueless man was
peering, "I charge you and all others inhabiting this countryside, to
assemble in a village called Pesto on the second morning following
this." The monk's deep-set brown eyes glowed with an almost unearthly luminosity. "I charge you, Sir Volmar, to dispatch mounted
messengers throughout the length and breadth of your holding and
have them assemble in Pesto to hear me preach the solemn call to
arms raised by His Holiness, Pope Urban II!"

CHAPTER IV

On the Road Towards Pesto

Riding at a comfortable jog-trot along the pitted and pud-
dle-filled length of what once must have been a magnificent Roman
highway Rosamund de Montgomerie drew deep breaths of sparkling
air streaming in from a sunlit sea. Happily she smiled while watching
varicolored pennons flutter from the lanceheads of Sir Toustain's
mounted followers.

How glorious it was thus to be riding along the shore of a great bay
which, blue as had been her Saxon mother's eyes, swept grandly
northwards around a succession of rocky cliffs. As became the daughter of a hardy Norman earl, Rosamund rode astride and managed the
reins of a gentle, sad-eyed palfrey with skill.

To be removed from the discomforts and malodorous meanness in
Castel Agropoli to Rosamund de Montgomerie was a boon past all
description. How debasing, how humiliating had been her experi-
ences these last few days! Imagine the late Earl of Arundel's daughter being forced to submit to abuse from an ill-bred virago like the
Lady Aldebara!

Her lips shiny as oxblood cherries compressed themselves when
she recalled having been forced to go about barefooted on the keep's
icy-cold floor, clad in a gown so coarse and ragged that at home she
never would have inflicted such upon even a swineherd's drab. The
fireplaces had seemed always to smoke no matter what the wind's
direction. No wonder Sir Volmar's wolfish brood suffered from perpetually inflamed and swollen eyes. Her bed in a chilly corner of
the donjon's third story she had contrived of a blanket stretched over
a heap of mildewed sails salvaged from various wrecks.

In lively interest Rosamund gazed out over a broad, sandy and
almost treeless plain stretching back from the Bay of Salerno and rev-
eled in the melodious song of thrushes, skylarks and the liquid trill-
ing of blackbirds in the little marshes all about. Under this warm
April sun even this harsh stone-studded countryside appeared gentle,
softened as it were by vernal greenery. What manner of people willingly would inhabit such a denuded and oft-ravaged stretch of coastline? The few peasants she had noticed were small dark-skinned and
black-haired people. They seemed invariably to dwell in some ruin
or other when not tending flocks of sheep and goats.

The little cavalcade's mounts seemed to sense the presence of
Spring, and playfully curvetted and snorted whenever big white
gulls came planing by a few feet above them. The tall destriers
stretched their necks and snatched at fresh green grass sprouting between the road's disjoined paving stones.

Rosamund's fingers tightened upon her reins when still another
covey of small, blue-gray quail evidently on a northward migration,
flashed over the road on roaring wings and startled the horses no little.
Far away to the cavalcade's left could be discerned a series of ponds
bordered by dense banks of shimmering reeds. Above these wheeled
dark clouds of waterfowl.

Sir Toustain, grimy, erect and proud in his high-peaked saddle
rode foremost in the column with the faded yellow and green checkered gonfanon lashed to his lance head curling slowly above him.
Next came the veteran's armiger leading a sumpter mule upon which
had been loaded Sir Toustain's battered, kite-shaped shield. Four-
feet-long and triangular at its top, it sloped downwards and inwards
into a smaller triangle at its base. Sir Toustain's mace, helm and coif
rested in one of a pair of wicker hampers, his precious hauberk and
the balance of his fighting gear, with the exception of his long sword,
reposed in the other.

Following the leather-faced armiger Brother Ordericus and another monk trudged along on sandaled feet with staffs swinging and
heads bent. As the clerics walked amid clouds of sifting white dust
they endlessly recited their rosaries. At the monks' heels rode the
Lady Rosamund and her brother, big and square-shouldered and
clad in a tunic of mulberry-hued wool. For the moment his dark red
head was bare since he wore neither cap nor helm. She experienced a
profound sense of relief to note how color was returning in those dear
features.

What miracles a few sound meals and a single night's good rest
in the pavilion of Sir Toustain de Dives could accomplish! The former
Earl of Arundel rode in silence. He was sorrowing more bitterly than

ever that his shield bearing the silver leopard and his sword, "Brain-biter," lay at the bottom of the sea, together with that small treasure chest the contents of which might have gone far towards outfitting the modest following he must have if he were to conquer a new do-main.

Rosamund fetched several more deep breaths before glancing over her slim but muscular shoulder to view the serjeants—*servientes* as the ancient Romans had termed such—the men-of-arms, and the foot soldiers. They were swinging along, some under pikes, others car-rying *franciscas,* short handled axes or a bow and quiver of arrows in the fashion most comfortable for them.

Not too many of these liegemen—they all held land lent to them by their lord in return for service—wore shoes, but their broad feet, like those of the common folk back in Sussex, had become callused to such a degree that even the sharpest of stones would not cause them to flinch.

Occasionally a wretched, straw-thatched village became visible in the distance, clustered untidily about some ancient watchtower. Cowherds at their first glimpse of the cavalcade's dust and twin-kling lance points always drove their charges as far away from the road as possible and in frantic haste. So also fled the few farmers, woodcutters and weavers of willow withe baskets encountered in this bleak and sparsely inhabited countryside. On two or three oc-casions the severe outlines of some minor stronghold very similar to Castel Agropoli, were to be seen crowning a high hill or rocky crag.

The Italian-Norman overlords hereabouts, Rosamund decided, must cause their villeins a most miserable existence. Only once did the increasingly dust splashed column pass an inhabited place. Among the ruins of a Roman fort a handful of shaggy, wild-looking peasant bowmen manned the weed choked summit of a turret still in defensible condition. They neither waved nor called out, only gripped their weapons and scowled sullenly down upon the passing cavalcade.

At intervals Sir Toustain identified certain structures lining the Via Salerno as of Roman, Byzantine or Gothic origin, but only a very few of these appeared to be inhabited as indicated by the presence of domestic fowls, yapping dogs and a few dirty and stark naked children who dully followed their hunger-distended bellies about in the sunlight. Otherwise this littoral appeared depopulated, as if recently ravaged by a plague.

Riding along between ragged olive groves Rosamund sighed on recalling similar misery amongst those stubborn Saxon serfs whose fathers had fought—and failed—at Senlac. Bitterly but in vain those

poor churls had sought to defend their ancestral homes. Now many
of them and their families also lurked in squalor among crumbling
villas, temples and watchtowers, relics of the long-ended Roman occupation.

In Sussex, also, wild, half-naked men and women roved the forests and swamps, furtive as hunted game. Scarcely better off were
survivors of the Saxon aristocracy; yellow-headed Gerth Ordway, Edmund's armiger, was an example. The boy, unlettered and untrained
in gentle ways had been working as a blacksmith's apprentice when
the Lady Matilda de Montgomerie, herself of Saxon origin, had discovered him by chance and, learning of the big lad's descent from the
Thegns of Sussex, had taken him under her protection.

Poor Mamma! Never had those dark and cruel Norman noblewomen of the countryside permitted Matilda Godwine to forget
her Saxon ancestry nor that grim old Roger de Montgomerie had lost
considerable favor with the Conqueror—"the Mamzer" as he was
known to his Saxon subjects—because of his marriage with a noblewoman from the conquered race.

Yes, it really *was* glorious to find herself once more astride a horse
and watching tall lances sway beneath twinkling points. How rhythmically the riders' sheathed swords were swaying to their horses'
stride. It was enjoyable, also, once more to be treated with a deference which had not been hers since that fearful day, nearly a month
and a half ago, when King Rufus the Red's levées had invested Arundel Castle. Alas that an earl might not alone hope to hold out
against the King of England, no matter how heartily the latter was
detested by a majority of his subjects!

Edmund had permitted only a handful of his followers to follow
him and herself in flight towards the unknown East, for to the West
lay only water and the wilds of Ireland. Gerth Ordway, only surviving son of Penda, last Thegne of Sussex, had been among these.
Rosamund sighed, shifted her feet in the stirrups. Poor, cheerful, yellow-headed Gerth! His body now must be feeding lamprey eels off
Castel Agropoli or rotting on some beach—a feast for ravens and
foxes.

What a storm of criticism had been aroused among the Norman
lords of Sussex when her brother of all things had selected *a Saxon*
to be his principal esquire. No doubt memories of their mother
must have persuaded him to such an unpopular course. Oddly, it
never had occurred to Sir Edmund's straight-backed twin that she
must have inherited her own lithe beauty from the Lady Matilda
rather than from her raw-boned and black-browed sire, he who had

been listed in the Conqueror's Domesday Book as Sir Roger de Montgomerie, Earl of Arundel.

Again the tall young woman sighed and shifted in her saddle her back and buttocks being still discolored by very painful bruises suffered at the hands of Lady Aldebara. Someday, Rosamund grimly promised herself, that frowzy virago in Castel Agropoli would suffer in kind and with interest.

This sparsely populated and long-ravaged province of Calaloria, the Anglo-Norman girl gradually had ascertained once had formed a part of the land of Italy from whence Roman legions had marched to conquer the known World and, for centuries, to rule over it. Everywhere evidences of the Ancients' engineering genius remained in the form of endless-seeming aqueducts, magnificent broad roads and sturdy stone bridges such as the one the cavalcade even now was traversing.

Abruptly Edmund reined to her side and pointed to the right. "Look yonder, sweet Sister. I can scarce believe my eyes."

"What do you see?"

"*Par Dex!*" he chuckled. "Some gentle folk are flying hawks in yonder meadow."

Along the further border of a green plain bright with flowering almonds and scarlet Judas trees three horsemen were riding slowly along the border of a reedy pond. They carried hooded hawks balanced upon well-padded gauntlets.

"Would to God, I had here my sweet Lilith," grunted Edmund, "I'd teach yonder fellows not to ride downwind ere making their cast. Ha! See? The tall rider is slipping his falcon. Look! His bird looks like a nailor to me—makes a clean strike and falls at the mark. Good. Now she waits on above. God's love! Does that fool *have* to ride in so fast? He'll surely make her rake off."

The falcon did just that. Startled by the rush of her over-eager master's mount the nailor released her prey and went circling back up into the softly blue Spring sky while the big Anglo-Norman cursed under his breath.

"Patience, Edmund. This is not England, remember," she smiled then, in her turn pointed off to their left where on a hilltop gleamed the ruins of a magnificently proportioned and white-columned structure. "I say, Sir Toustain, to what use was put that building on yonder rise?"

"I have been told," Sir Toustain informed, "that that was once a famous pagan temple raised in honor of a Roman god called 'Neptune' by the Romans and 'Poseidon' by the old-time Greeks. The village lying below is called Pesto—our destination."

For some moments Rosamund rode along in silence with clear, tourmaline-hued eyes feasting upon the beauty of those soaring pillars and the battered statues still decorating the ancient structure's pediment. At length she cried softly, "I think I never before have seen anything even half so inspiring. What think you, Edmund?"

His attention still on the distant falconers, the former earl shrugged absently. "Why, 'twould make a good site to build a keep and the stone is already there."

Rosamund frowned. "Does not yonder structure move you, Sir Toustain?"

"Aye," grunted the veteran. "I've often thought it a pretty sight, but wait until you spy the city of Constantinople and the great churches there."

Rosamund glanced anxiously at black clad Brother Ordericus and his dust covered companion, and observed loud enough for them to hear, "I know I shouldn't admire a heathen temple, for, really, our chapel in Arundel Castle was much handsomer." Yet she knew this was not so. What could there be so strangely inspiring, about that mute and desecrated structure? Perchance yonder ruin, even after all these centuries, was an expression of Man's eternal yearning to comprehend the Infinite?

"When do you suppose yonder temple was built?" she inquired of Edmund.

"Possibly a hundred years ago," her brother returned carelessly. "What boots it?"

Sir Toustain de Dives reined in the palfrey he bestrode—his war-horse, riderless, was being led along by an esquire growing hot and weary through continued efforts to control that vicious and spirited beast's cavortings.

"Dear my lady," said he his one eye bright in the battered brown expanse of his face, "permit me to inform that yonder temple most likely was built several centuries before the birth of Our Lord."

Rosamund's eyes flew wide open. "Then it has stood for over a thousand years?"

"—And more. Soon we will come upon relics of another such temple. It was raised in honor of Demeter, goddess of Fertility and Marriage. The old Byzantines would have named her Ceres."

Flattered by Rosamund de Montgomerie's patent admiration of his knowledge, Count Turgis' constable beamed like a friendly wolf upon this stately young female who rode so well and lent to the coarse garments she wore a distinction. They might have been fashioned from the finest of camlet and trimmed with sables.

"But Messer Toustain," the girl burst out, "how could these pagans

—unbelievers that they were—build so well? Surely God did not inspire them?"

The knight's hideously scarred features relaxed still further. Said he quietly, "I have observed that the Arts can be made to serve Christian and pagan alike. This much I learned when, as a youth, I rode with Sir Roussel de Ballieul in the service of Romanus Diogenes, a most ill-fated Basileus of Byzantium."

He slowed his horse to a jog. "Yonder lies the other temple I mentioned. No need to frown over this one, my lady, for when the Byzantines ruled over this land their Patriarch caused the temple of Demeter to be consecrated as a Christian church and such it remained for near four hundred years until Arab pirates, God's blight upon them, burnt and defiled it."

The veteran slapped dust from his sleeve then bent forward to brush a gadfly from his palfrey's neck as he informed his guests, "My lord, Count Turgis of Sanseverino, has commanded his vassal knights, liegemen and every quality of villein to assemble tomorrow morning at yonder village by the sea in order to hear the venerable Brother Ordericus and the other *excitatori* preach the Journey of God."

"—And then?" prompted Rosamund infinitely relieved that at last the straggling straw roofed and rubble-built village of Pesto had appeared in the offing. Her body ached, it seemed, in its every joint.

"—And then we shall ride to Sanseverino, principal stronghold of Count Turgis de Bernay."

"To what prince does he render homage?"

Sir Toustain hesitated, pulled at his drooping mustaches. "That, my lady, remains presently a matter of some dispute. Duke Bohemund of Otranto and Roger 'the Counter,' his half-brother, who is Duke of Sicily, both claim the allegiance of Sanseverino."

"Roger the 'Counter'?"

"Aye. For 'tis that sly prince's custom whilst in earnest conversation, to delve into his purse and count over and over such coins as it may contain."

CHAPTER V

The Assembly

In Pesto, ancient Paestum, which must have been a considerable town in Roman days the inhabitants surprisingly neither ran away nor hid themselves among the ruins.

Here was to be found the outline of a large market place and
the remains of not a few imposing villas over which towered a typical
Norman citadel. About its base clustered the usual collection of pent-
houses, huts and hovels. Already in the vicinity, jackmen and villeins
were pitching tents for their lords among groves of olive trees or
under dark green umbrella pines.

The tents already erected, Sir Edmund estimated, must number
about twenty but more were going up and, even as the dusty cavalcade from Agropoli drew rein, similar little columns could be
descried approaching along the remains of Roman roads which
converged upon Pesto.

Gratefully the Lady Rosamund dismounted to accept a leather cup
of water fetched from a roadside spring by a cheerful young serjeant
whose looks were not improved by the loss of all his front teeth.

She now was beginning to regret her refusal of Sir Toustain's offer
to force the chatelaine of Agropoli to produce raiment suitable for
the sister of a Norman earl. A plague upon her over-hasty disdain.
For certain local seigneurs surely would be accompanied by their
ladies. The opportunity to attend such an assembly was too precious
to be missed by well-born females forced to exist for months, if not
years, amid dull and squalid isolation similar to that prevailing in
Castel Agropoli.

Surreptitiously she considered her brother. His shoulders had resumed their arrogant squareness for all he remained without followers and was utterly penniless. Small wonder that well-born
maidens inhabiting fiefs in the vicinity of Arundel had sighed and
had gazed on the young earl with melting eyes.

How curious that although several of these females had been of
surpassing beauty Edmund had accorded them at best a courteous
tolerance. Privately, Rosamund suspected that, like most young Norman nobles, her brother took his pleasure often forcibly, no doubt,
among red-cheeked and blonde girls to be found among the huts of
his Saxon serfs.

True, for a while he had paid desultory court to Elaine Molyneux of
St. Leonard's. How rapturously that beauty had sighed when, wearing her favor in his belt he had battled a whole morning in one of
those often fatal tournaments which, far removed from the gaudy,
formalized jousts of later years constituted nothing more nor less than
a prearranged battle fought between a number of knights who de-
sired to lose none of their proficiency at arms through prolonged in-
action. As always, blood had flowed freely, bones had been broken
and more than one combatant later had died as the result of this
miniature battle which could only be distinguished from actual war-

fare by the proviso that a knight, pressed too hard or failing in strength, might in honor retire outside the lists and forfeit neither his arms nor his destrier.

Sir Toustain's armiger planted his master's gonfanon amid tender young grass beside a clear-running brook to inform all and sundry that the puissant Constable of Sanseverino had selected this spot for his encampment.

Slowly Rosamund's dark red lips contracted and she grimaced for yonder several ladies, obviously of gentle blood were staring at her while they awaited the pitching of a patched and faded green pavilion. Gaily their white kirtles and long-sleeved gowns of bright blue, yellow and red, stood out against the meadow's blue-green hay grass.

Lightly, for all her soreness, the Anglo-Norman girl dismounted amid a swirl of skirts which momentarily delighted onlookers by a glimpse of bare legs. She smiled at her brother. "Dear Edmund pray not to appear too ashamed of my ill-tended locks, grimy hands and this horrible, shapeless gown."

CHAPTER VI

Lord Spear Warrior

Gerth Ordway, whose name in the Saxon language meant "lord spear warrior," knew even less concerning ships than did his master, but all the same he sensed that the *San Giorgio* was about to break up. Accordingly, he released those shrouds to which he had been clinging, dashed spray from his eyes and fought his way across the canting, spray-lashed deck in search of his lord. The young Saxon—he was approaching twenty, last had glimpsed Sir Edmund and his twin sheltering in the lee of bulwarks just forward of this Genoese galley's double-bladed steering oar.

On a particularly stormy passage that oar had guided the *San Giorgio* down the coast of Castile and then past an Infidel kingdom which, so the Genoese officers declared, was a part of a great Moslem realm known as the Caliphate of the Almoravides.

This inhospitable-appearing domain, the shores of which seemed studded with watchtowers, extended all the way to the Pillars of Hercules, known to the Infidels as Gibraltar, where the cold and dark blue waters of the Atlantic joined the warm and sapphire-hued Mediterranean.

That same steering oar safely had guided this galley past the pirate-

infested Isles of Pithyrusa, past similar perils off Cape Nao, and on
past to that port which Roman conquerors centuries ago had known
as Cartagena or "Little Carthage."

Favorable winds then had propelled this blunt-bowed craft into
the Gulf of the Lions and up to the wicked port of Marsala. Two
days after leaving that place a great storm had risen. Screaming out
of North Africa, the mistral had sent the luckless galley reeling southward past some great island dimly seen through flying spindrift. It
might have been either Corsica or Sardinia for all he knew the Genoese captain had quavered.

"My lord! My lady!" Gerth shouted over the thundering of waves
upon the reef. Then he glimpsed the former earl and his sister clinging desperately to a length of rope looped about a cask. It kept rolling uncontrollably about in water sluicing over the deck. Knowing
well that neither could swim, he called out reassurance, then, panting
a prayer to St. Olav, he jammed his favorite *francisca* or short-handled battleaxe into the back of his belt and started wading towards
them.

His intention had been to tow the pair to a not-too-impossibly-dis-
tant stretch of rock-free beach, but an extra vicious billow had
vaulted the sagging bulwarks and had carried the Saxon, half strangled, over the opposite rail and into the sea. Although Gerth battled
furiously to find his lord it required all his strength and skill to keep
his own yellow head above the raging waters.

Doubtless through timely intervention on the part of St. Olav, his
patron saint, the armiger finally fought his way, bruised and breathless onto the sandy beach of a small cove.

To win clear from the backwash of incessant breakers required the
last of Gerth's strength and he just managed to crawl out of the
reach of the boiling surf to lie gasping on cold and slimy pebbles.
His first concern was for the safety of his axe. All praise to St. Olav!
his belt yet held the heavy, double-bitted and razor-edged weapon
pressed against his loins. Deprived of it, he foresaw that he might
fare badly once he started inland.

On recovering breath Gerth Ordway, only remaining son of Penda,
last Thegne of Sussex, scaled a rocky cliff and stood viewing his surroundings with a warrior's care. The *francisca* now dangled ready,
suspended from his wrist by a thong.

The young Saxon found himself viewing as bleak and forbidding a
shore line as he had ever beheld. Upon it the storm waves were beating with a white fury that drove spray far inland. Come to think on it,
this wild land was not unlike certain parts of Cornwall observed during a raiding expedition of the previous year.

When he noted that the *San Giorgio* had all-but vanished and that only broken spars, sections of bulwark and other wreckage were being driven ashore, tears welled into the Saxon's wide-set and light blue eyes. Certainly valiant Sir Edmund and his stately twin must have perished long since—even a fair swimmer would stand no chance among those thundering billows and rocks sharp as a badger's teeth.

He mourned aloud. They were the only Normans who ever had befriended him—but, of course, that was because they were not whole Norman. In the veins of their mother, the Lady Matilda Godwine, had run the blood of one of the most ancient and famous families in King Harold's realm. Even as Gerth stood there with sodden locks still dripping over his naked shoulders, he blessed the Lady Matilda's memory and that day she had chanced to ride past the thatch-and-wattle smithy before which he was swinging a heavy hammer without apparent effort. Certainly, he must strongly have favored his sire for at once the beautiful lady on horseback had reined in to call out to learn whether this dirty, barefoot youth with the tousled yellow hair could be related to the late Thegne of Sussex.

When she had learned the apprentice's lineage what a wonderful change had ensued! No longer did Penda's son snore upon a bundle of rushes in a draughty shed shared by the smith's cow and half a dozen goats, no longer was he clad only in a kilt and cloak of sheepskin. Best of all he now tasted meat at least twice every month.

The stables of Arundel Castle, cold, draughty and comfortless though they were, yet had seemed a part of God's paradise, and the endless tasks and arduous training to be endured by a hopeful esquire, trifling.

Casting therefore a final glance at those boiling reefs upon which the galley had broken up the Saxon dashed tears from his eyes and, following a sheep track, started warily inland.

To stalk and surprise a pair of hairy, wolfish herders sheltering from the gale behind some rocks with their flock had proved ridiculously simple. When these answered his challenge in an outlandish tongue and grabbed up spears his *francisca* had hewn them down in a matter of seconds. These fellows had been very dark of skin and black of hair so he guessed they must be Infidels. Back in England everyone had heard that followers of Mahound, the Arch Anti-Christ were dark complected like Satan and that they spoke the queerest of languages.

Ignoring the limp figures draining their blood away among the sand grass roots Gerth caught and methodically butchered a kid. He

cooked a haunch over that same fire beside which the herders had
been warming themselves.

"Such wild rascals undoubtedly were Christ-hating Infidels," he re-
assured himself while licking his hands free of grease. "I therefore
have gained merit in God's eyes as well as a sound meal and a pair
of spears."

Gerth began to feel better, but far from happy. Now that Edmund
de Montgomerie was dead he had become his own master—a responsibility he accepted with considerable misgivings. It was so much easier for a slow-witted fellow like himself to follow orders than to arrive
at decisions of his own. Well, since "Lord Spear Warrior" was what his
name meant, he'd have to try to live up to it—for all he preferred his
axe. Odd that the Saxon tongue still fell more readily from his lips
than the harsh Norman-French which, perforce, he had had continually to employ for over three years.

Rolling himself in the dead men's verminous sheepskins he curled
up on the sand and dropped into the leaden slumber of near exhaustion.

At dawn Gerth rebuilt his fire and over it roasted the kid's other
haunch. He appropriated such clothing as seemed useful and came
close to fitting his stocky, very white-skinned frame. He picked free
of lice a round and pointed felt hat then secured it in position by
means of thongs tied under his chin. To the young Saxon it was a
matter of regret that, during the night, the goats not unnaturally had
wandered off and dispersed. They could be heard blatting discon-
solately high among some rocky hills behind which the sun was rising.

Having breakfasted to repletion, Lord Spear Warrior shouldered
the deceased herders' spears and at a safe distance he commenced to
parallel a badly-pitted road which skirted the shore line. Like an endless pale yellow serpent it followed the rim of a huge bay. What
yonder body of water, serene once more and unbelievably blue, might
be called he had not the least notion. Such ignorance however troubled the armiger not in the least now that his belly was full and a rude
haversack was heavy with food enough to last another day at the
least. It proved reassuring also to be carrying a brace of spears over
his shoulder while his beloved axe—secretly he had named it "Penda's
Avenger"—swung to his hip.

CHAPTER VII

Pesto

More posses, invariably small and shabby of appearance, continued to arrive and profanely were warned from encroachment upon Sir Toustain de Dives' campsite. Situated near the source of a spring-fed brook and benefiting from the shade of grotesquely twisted olive trees the Constable of Sanseverino enjoyed a reasonable seclusion from the dust and tumult of camps pitched nearer to ancient Paestum's crumbled walls.

Shortly before sunset Sir Volmar of Agropoli and his raffish posse straggled up to the rendezvous and by dint of threats and curses cowed a weaker contingent into conceding a spot on which to pitch their tents.

Atop a pile of fresh cut hay-grass sat Edmund de Montgomerie. The sunset tinted his thick, shoulder-length hair a coppery red as moodily he watched the posse from Agropoli make preparations to encamp.

Ever more acutely the former earl was missing his young Saxon's unfailing good humor, his way with intractable horses and his skill as an armorer for all that Thegne Penda's son remained hopelessly inept in the matter of waiting on table and lute playing.

Several times during the course of a repast consumed beside a cheerfully blazing campfire, sounded the sudden clashing of arms, hoarse shouts and curses forcing the Constable of Sanseverino and his men to quell, at its inception, a dispute between feuding noblemen, or a brawl among drunken servitors. But, later in the evening, when a series of shrill, desperate and unmistakably feminine screams arose nearer Pesto, Sir Toustain hunched over to the embers glowing at his feet and calmly continued to savor his wine.

At a sharp, inquisitive glance from the Lady Rosamund, Sir Toustain showed badly gapped teeth in grinning like a friendly old stag hound. "Take no alarm, my lady. 'Tis only some *prud'hommes* having their pleasure with the peasant wenches." The one-eyed veteran raised a short drinking horn he customarily wore slung to his belt. "Here's to tomorrow, my friends, and may Brother Ordericus' preaching save many a poor, damned soul from the flames of Hell."

Edmund propped himself up on one elbow as he lay comfortably sprawled across a saddle blanket. "What is this preaching to be about and why has Count Turgis ordered all able-bodied liegemen assembled to hear it?"

Sir Toustain delayed replying long enough to toss a faggot onto the coals then demanded incredulously, "Can no word have reached England concerning the Holy Father's 'Journey of God'?"

"No. At least not in Sussex. What is this 'Journey of God'?"

"It concerns a great sermon delivered by His Holiness Pope Urban II, last autumn at Clermont, in the land of the Burgundians."

"Burgundians? What are they?"

Incredulity became written broad over Sir Toustain's mangled features. "Dear God! Do you know of *nothing* outside of Sussex or England?"

While bursts of drunken song and piteous wails for mercy arose behind the ruined walls of Pesto Rosamund looked up from mending by the dancing firelight a rip in her skirt, "Who is this Brother Ordericus who looks so frail yet seems so strong?"

"A learned monk from the famous Benedictine monastery at Monte Cassino," explained the grizzled figure while easing his sword belt. "Brother Ordericus is said to be among the ablest of those *excitatori* who now travel the length and breadth of Christendom bringing the Holy Father's message to his flock."

"And what might this message be?" Edmund roused from a somewhat discouraged consideration of immediate prospects.

"Tomorrow will tell you far better than I tonight," replied the veteran and yawned cavernously.

To Edmund's vast surprise, he did not immediately drop off to sleep once he had rolled himself in a blanket with hip fitted snugly into a depression scooped out of the earth. He glanced at his sister and saw her curled in feline grace within a spare tent. Sound asleep she lay with strong, yet delicate profile faintly outlined by moonlight beating in this travel-worn pavilion's open flap.

From all sides sounded the resounding snores, sighs and coughs of Sir Toustain's followers. From farther away came the sleepy snuffling of a horse and the even more distant howls of wild dogs which apparently inhabited those ruined temples above Pesto.

Again he studied his twin and wondered what Fate held in store for them. Even yet he entertained only the haziest notions concerning just where in Europe Sanseverino and Salerno might lie. Sir Toustain seemed to possess only limited knowledge about what domains lay to the north of the ancient city of Naples where Roger Guiscard, the original Norman invader of Italy had gained a foothold some forty years earlier, and, still further north lay the shell of Imperial Rome, the often-sacked, ravaged capital of Christendom. Um. What manner of reception would a pair of penniless wanderers be accorded by Turgis II, Count of Salerno and Sanseverino? Briefly the former earl wondered how many fiefs might be included within this Norman adventurer's holding? If the balance of Count Turgis' holdings were not richer or more populous than the rocky, barren and almost treeless strip of coastline between Agropoli and Pesto his, indeed, must be a miserable property compared to similar domains in Southern England.

Suppose Count Turgis found a pretext to hold him against a ransom which certainly would not be forthcoming? Again, and more likely, suppose this fierce old adventurer forced him to become a liegeman—a landless mercenary entirely dependent upon his lord for sustenance and a fighting man's equipment?

Now thoroughly awake Edmund locked hands behind his head and stared unseeingly into the star-studded heavens. Well, chance what might, he entertained not the least intention of remaining a landless fugitive for long. Um-um. What should be his first step? To secure arms and a mount, of course. Once this was accomplished it should prove easy enough to provoke some local seigneur into a trial at arms. If successful, as surely he would be, he thus might win a modest ransom. After that, it should not prove overly difficult to recruit enough men some gray dawn to take an unwary stronghold. Once lord of a keep similar to Agropoli, he should be able, after learning something concerning the local politics of this strange land, by dint of guile and hard fighting, gradually to extend his holdings. Had not other Normans been doing just that in Italy for going on half a century? Why not Edmund de Montgomerie?

An owl commenced hooting among the ruins of Pesto and maintained its eerie ululations until sleep descended upon him with the force of an avalanche.

CHAPTER VIII

Dieu lo Vult!

To the end of her days Rosamund de Montgomerie would recall to the least detail all that chanced upon that memorable morning of April the eighteenth, 1096. She would remember just how a rough cross, hurriedly fashioned of trimmed branches, had been reared upon the summit of a low hill, how Sir Toustain's tough men-of-arms had circulated the encampment warning all and sundry that, under pain of death, there must be no bickering or disorder of any sort until Brother Ordericus had delivered the Holy Father's message.

She judged it to be an hour after sunrise when nearly four hundred souls of all degrees congregated about that knoll upon which the cross had been erected. Behind the holy emblem Sir Toustain's yellow and green checkered gonfanon curled in a balmy breeze blowing in from the sapphire-hued Mediterranean. This banner was displayed there for two reasons, first to emphasize that this assembly had been convoked on orders from the liege lord of the domain, also to assure protection for such peasants as might venture to come in from the hills and marshes.

The tall Anglo-Norman girl stood in stately beauty beside her twin to the right of an altar hastily improvised from a section of broken column and a handsome Ionic capital. Openly she surveyed the handful of brown-faced gentle women in garish and often dirty finery standing beside their lords. To her astonishment these ladies conversed among themselves in Italian; obviously there was never a Norman among them.

To the number of sixteen the local seigneurs assembled together with their pages and esquires—every man armed to the teeth. They carried the usual kite-shaped Norman shield and wore ragged surcoats of varying hues over gray-brown hauberks of chain mail. Not a few of them affected linen pantaloons, cross-gartered in the old Norman fashion. Gradually a complete ring of ten foot lances displaying the pennons of serjeants and men-of-arms and the square gonfanons of knights encircled cross and altar.

Outside this ring of fighting men collected malodorous knots of villeins, serfs, fishermen, shepherds and farmers.

The gabble of conversation came to an end when the slight, black-robed figure of Brother Ordericus made its way through the throng and up to the altar. In his wake shuffled two tonsured monks, the one clad in a rusty brown habit and the other wearing robes of black and white. Their presence soon became explained for when Brother Ordericus threw back his cowl and commenced to preach in Latin, the monk in brown shouted a translation in Norman-French while his companion did the same in Italian. With the newly-risen sun gilding his gaunt and ascetic features the Benedictine raised both hands and pronounced a blessing when the assemblage knelt, bent heads and clasped hands. He then led the throng in reciting a *Pater Noster,* quite ignoring the snarling uproar of a dog-fight taking place on the outskirts of the crowd.

Brother Ordericus then stepped into the shadow of the cross and, for a long instant, intently surveyed the rows of upturned hairy and weatherbeaten faces. Long white beard stirring to his vehemence, he commenced to speak in a clear, ringing voice.

"Harken well unto me, my children, for I bring you tidings of vast importance.

"Know, then, that last year Our Holy Father, Urban II, received most evil tidings from the Emperor of the Byzantines. That Christian prince complained that a barbarous people, estranged from God, have invaded his eastern themes, or provinces, and are ravaging these with fire and steel. Know then that these pagans are numerous as the sands of the desert and are called Turks. They and their fellow Unbelievers, the Arabs, beat like a mighty sea upon the walls of Byzantium which is the last outpost of Christianity in Asia Minor. If aid does not arrive promptly, they soon will capture this city."

Brother Ordericus' voice, Rosamund decided, was most unusual for, without being loud, it carried over the warriors' pointed helms out to the furthest humble folk.

"The Empire of the East Romans, therefore, stands in dire peril. Its richest provinces have been so far overrun that today Turks pasture their horses before the gates of Byzantium itself. How many multitudes of our fellow Christians these Turks have murdered, enslaved or dragged away into cruel slavery no man can tell."

The frail figure's voice soared. "Listen well, my children. Know also that these impious dogs have pulled down churches of God after befouling their sacred altars with excrement." A horrified moan arose from the listeners. "By force these savages have circumcised Christian men and have poured the blood of such mangling into fonts of holy water."

At this a gasp of sheer outrage escaped Edmund de Montgomerie and a bandy-legged knight standing opposite him, commenced to curse horribly under his breath.

"These Children of Satan stable their horses in such churches as they leave standing," continued Brother Ordericus. "At this very moment these demons torture Christian men and women by binding them to pillars and so filling their bodies with arrows that they resemble hedgehogs. They slash the bellies of others and force Christ's children to walk about treading upon their own entrails, and Christian females of all ages are being ravished without mercy."

Rosamund, gazing upwards, in frozen horror, watched the old monk's cavernous eyes flash like newly lit torches. "The Saracens, another barbarous nation of Infidels who have conquered the Holy Land, despite solemn agreements to the contrary, rob and murder helpless Christian pilgrims on their way to pray before the Holy Sepulchre. Those poor souls who trusted in poverty as a protection

have had calluses cut from their heels by Infidels searching for coins.
When a Christian town is taken they cut off the women's breasts and
infants in arms are spitted upon spears of laughing Saracens. The
weak and the sickly this Spawn of Hell drowns in ordure and they
force dying men to devour their own private parts."

Something like the growl of many angry hounds circulated the knoll
and those clumps of lances upon it swayed like cattails stricken by a
squall.

"Who shall avenge these outrages? Upon whom shall fall the duty
unless it be you and your brother Christians?" Beard gleaming silver-
gold in the newly risen sun's radiance Brother Ordericus with arms
raised on high, circled the improvised cross all the while peering
down into faces growing dark with passion. At length he halted before the largest gathering of gentle men and sadly shook his head.
"You spurred and belted knights no doubt have proved yourselves
valiant enough upon the field of battle but, nonetheless, you also are
sinners puffed up with pride and arrogance. You dare to doubt this?
Do you not, day after day, delight in assaulting fellow Christians
and find glory in cutting them down? Is this Christian conduct?" The
excitator's magnificent voice rang out like a trumpet's blast. "Do you
call this fighting in God's name? Pah! You are but glorious makers
of orphans, doughty despoilers of the weak and brave persecutors of
helpless females! In all truth you are but bloody-minded killers who,
despite high-sounding words, seek battle in no matter how selfish or
ignoble a cause that you can rant about the land boasting of your
prowess. Whom do you slay? Only fellow Christians. And why? That,
in your shameful greed, you may seize their possessions!"

In impressively deliberate tones the black-clad Benedictine again
circled the cross fashioned of tree branches. He paused every few
steps to study with care each segment of this motley congregation.

To Edmund it seemed as if the *excitator's* blazing eyes were probing the most secret recesses of his conscience, reading, condemning
so much he had been taught to revere concerning the knightly code.

"Repent, O ye sinners!" cried the Benedictine in vibrant tones.
"Desist from this unholy strike amongst yourselves and battle rather
in the service of Christ our Master. The Holy Father, Urban, bids you
to abandon your feuds and plottings against one another and to direct your weapons against the hounds of Mahound, the Anti-Christ!"

Brother Ordericus' clear and penetrating tones then issued a summons which, for half a century, was to inspire imagination, faith and
valor of men to unbelievable accomplishments.

"*Dieu lo vult!* God wills it that you must march against the Infidels.
Who will be first to take service in the Army of God?"

Sir Toustain's deep voice rang out. "Holy Father, already I have taken oath to undertake the Journey of God. So have most gentle men to the north. Look, my lords, do you see this?" With a mailed forefinger he tapped that scarlet Latin cross which blazed upon the breast of his simple white surcoat.

"Well spoken, Sir Toustain de Dives!" Brother Ordericus cried. "Remember, all you sinners, that the Lord Jesus said: 'Where two or three are gathered together in My Name, there am I in the midst of them.' So, unworthy servant of God that I am, I bid you march against the Infidels, and win salvation for your miserable souls. Let your battle cry be, *Dieu lo vult!*"

The austere old man paused, afforded his interpreters opportunity to speak.

From where she knelt upon the stony ground atop the knoll, Rosamund de Montgomerie noticed that the white-bearded *excitator* had commenced to tremble violently, that a fine froth showed at the corners of his mouth and that his features appeared radiant, trans-figured.

"This, the Holy Father has empowered me to promise: Whosoever shall offer to go upon this journey wearing the Sign of the Cross upon his breast shall depart from his home without fear for the safety of his loved ones or for his earthly possessions. So let nothing detain you, neither fear for the future nor the love you bear wife, child or home.

"Take oath then, men of the Cross, set forth and turn your faces to-wards the East, towards the Holy Sepulchre. Wrest the Holy Places from the Evil Race and keep them for yourselves."

Brother Ordericus' shaggy gray brows straightened and, suddenly, his manner became suave and confidential. "Know, my children, that verily the land of Israel flows with milk and honey. Jerusalem, the Golden City, awaits you. Many cities, rich beyond description yearn for Christian masters again. Was it not there that our Lord Jesus Christ lived, *and died* for us? Depart on the Journey of God and fear nothing! Urban II, the Holy Father, has decreed that your poor pos-sessions here shall be safeguarded, even though you despoil the Chil-dren of Satan of great treasure and having won Salvation, return home wearing jewels and cloth-of-gold!"

Across the knoll Sir Volmar's thick lips glistened after his tongue had wetted them.

"Do not fear death, my Children, on the way to that land where Our Lord suffered for you. Welcome it, rather." The speaker's voice gained in volume until it sounded loud as any oliphant. "Hear me and remember well. His Holiness has ordained that should any Cross

Bearer, *on the way to Jerusalem,* by land or sea, lose his life, then he shall be absolved of all his sins. This dispensation I am empowered to grant.

"Therefore, fellow Christians, you are not to fear torture nor to deny yourselves the glorious crown of martyrdom. Verily, I say unto you that the way to Jerusalem is short, the struggle brief, and reward everlasting. Take up arms, O you valiant men of Christendom and go forth against the Infidel! 'Tis better by far to fall in battle than to leave Christ's sepulchre unredeemed and to witness the end of Christianity in the East."

The Benedictine again confronted the red-faced and palpably uneasy group of knights kneeling to his right. "Let the rich arm the poor," he thundered. "As for the rich, a Power greater than wealth shall aid them." The old monk's voice dropped so low everyone strained to hear his next words. "Lo! I see guiding the Cross Bearers, an Angel bearing a flaming sword. Though invisible this Angel will lead Christ's army to triumph and salvation.

"Listen well, you miserable sinners, you whose hands run red with Christian blood! How many among you dare to reject the hope of absolution from past crimes and the promise of an indulgence for such sins as you may commit during the next three years?" The *excitator* leveled a forefinger at Sir Volmar and then at Edmund de Montgomerie. "Dare you? Or you?"

A shiver descended Edmund's back. "No, Holy Father," he stammered. "I dare not."

"Can a poor man undertake this voyage?" A young, tousle-haired shepherd called upwards through cupped hands.

Brother Ordericus' stringy arms violently flung towards the clear Spring sky. "Have I not already promised that whosoever undertakes the Voyage of God shall be as born anew and cleansed of sin?"

Somewhere in the background several voices commenced to recite the *Confiteor,* or general confession of sin and the whole assemblage joined in. Many burst into tears and sobbed loudly.

Rosamund, kneeling once more in the shadow of the cross and the lance planted behind it, from the corner of her eye saw a tough, leathery-faced knight suddenly jerk out his Norman sword which, because its guard had been mounted at right-angles to the hilt, formed an excellent Latin cross. Once he had plunged its point into the ground and the weapon stood of itself, the gentle man bowed his brutal head over hands joined so tightly that their knuckles glistened in the morning sunlight.

When the three monks in unison began to chant, "*Dieu lo vult! Dieu lo vult!*" Sir Toustain and the other knights added their deep voices to the chorus. Even Sir Volmar of the rattail mustaches and all the other fighting men joined in. Louder and louder the cry of *Dieu lo vult!* rang out until pigeons and skylarks sped away in fright and tethered warhorses although inured to pandemonium of all sorts snorted and pricked their ears. Even the stupidest serfs who had understood little or nothing of what had been said, obediently added their voices to that slogan which was beginning to sound all over Western Europe.

Brother Ordericus gestured sharply for silence then called out. "Are you willing to die if need be to free the Holy Land?"

"We are!" yelled the multitude and brandished their weapons.

"Will you bear the banner of Christ unflinchingly against these Infidels?"

So thunderous was the assent that Rosamund commenced to tremble through the profundity of her emotion.

"Then go forth to this Holy war, my sons, and fear not. Your possessions at home shall be safeguarded under the terms of the Truce of God for whosoever molests even the least of your property shall be outlawed and anathema will be pronounced against any who dare to affront your womenfolk."

In Edmund's mind still was ringing that tally of atrocities committed by the Turks: the defilement and destruction of Christian churches, the torture and mutilation of pilgrims and prisoners, the rape and enslavement of Christian females. Before God, how *dared* this dark-skinned race of blasphemers so afflict followers of the gentle Lord Jesus? Certainly such intolerable outrages must end and swiftly.

Sir Toustain, meanwhile, from his esquire's haversack had plucked several long strips of scarlet cloth. These he waved on high while with his other hand he touched the emblem blazing upon his white surcoat.

"Which among you, my lords, will wear such a Cross? Which of you will join with the hosts from the lands of the Burgundians, the Provençales, from Normandy of the North, from Brabant and from Lorraine?"

Quite before he realized what he was doing, Edmund de Montgomerie had sprung up and was rushing forward to drop upon his knees and peer up into Brother Ordericus' fiery and deep-set eyes.

"Do you swear to march with God's Army?" thundered the Benedictine. "Will you vow never to swerve from smiting the Infidels until Jerusalem is won?"

"I do!" Edmund cried in ringing tones, then silently wondered why no promise of obedience to some leader of the Crusade had been exacted—as he would in time again wonder when disaster loomed near.

"Go then, my son, and fight valiantly in God's cause." The *excitator* amid excited cheering draped two ragged strips of red cloth over Edmund's left shoulder. Now all save two aged and obviously infirm knights came stumping forward after handing lance and shield to their retainers. Even Sir Volmar's brutal, brown features somehow appeared purified.

Once they had kissed the *excitator's* Crucifix these hard-bitten seigneurs who had lived in enmity for years, who had slain one another's fathers, brothers and sons, embraced and, weeping, implored forgiveness. The three monks then circulated the throng, bestowing upon these brutish folk the magical strips of red cloth in exchange for an oath of service. These, the common sort, accepted with pathetic eagerness. Why should they not? Whatever fate might await them in those mysterious lands beyond the sea *must* be an improvement over the fear-filled, hopeless and wretched existence they now endured. Besides, they would not be gone long. Did not almost everyone agree that Jerusalem could not lie more than a week or two's travel away?

A withered old man bent over a shepherd's crook, uttered a piercing cry and using a palsied forefinger indicated a marsh above which a few clouds of morning mists yet were eddying. "I see a vision!" shrilled he. "Look! Look! Yonder lies Jerusalem! Can you not see the Holy City's walls, towers and temples? Do you not behold great groves of fig trees and a river of honey flowing before it?"

"I see it!" "I see it!" various voices proclaimed.

While gusts of emotion swept the exalted and uplifted crowd Rosamund fancied that certain of those billowing mists momentarily at least, *did* resemble domes.

"Yonder I see the King of Hosts, ready to lead us on," Sir Volmar shouted and from under bushy brows stared fixedly into the sky.

"You behold Gabriel the Warrior Angel!" proclaimed Brother Ordericus. "He will lead you on to victory and ever fight at your side. His fellow angels will lift you to eternal bliss should you fall in battle or perish upon your journey."

Edmund, chancing to glance over his shoulder, saw Sir Toustain grinning, but because of his single eye it was impossible to tell whether he then winked or simply blinked.

"A good day's work, this," he chuckled, tossing the empty haversack back to his esquire. "By God's Glory, we have added quite a few really stout blades to the posse of Sanseverino."

Gerth Ordway reached Pesto just as Brother Ordericus and his companions were concluding their exhortations. He noticed of course, the crowd collected upon a nearby knoll and immediately set off to find out what was afoot. Before him limped his bound and weeping prisoners, two peasant youths he guessed might fetch a fair price in some slave dealer's pen—if so civilized an institution existed in this desolate, sparsely populated and unknown land.

He had surprised these captives watering cattle beside a reedy pond. To his astonishment they had not put up even the semblance of a struggle but at the first flash of his axe had flung themselves at his feet and begged for mercy in some outlandish tongue. In Gerth's estimation these prisoners weren't much; mere dark-faced striplings with skinny legs and narrow chests, but proceeds of the sale of these sniveling wretches might start him now that he was his own master, on his newly determined course—restoration of that power once wielded by the Thegnes of Sussex.

Ha! This, of course, must be a fair of sorts! Once or twice a year in Sussex, merchants and peasants would risk lives and goods to visit trade fairs held in Winchester and Horsham. There always had been dealers in slaves and serfs in attendance on such affairs, usually offering for sale poor devils of Saxons taken in rebellion or captured Danish, Irish or Arab pirates.

Shoving through a shifting crowd of barefooted peasants, unspeakably malodorous in sheepskin mantles and heavy woolen cloaks, Gerth tightened his grip on the captives' lead lines. When he drew near the knoll's foot he halted and strained his ears to catch what was being said. Of Brother Ordericus' Latin he comprehended less than nothing, yet when one of the monks shouted out a translation in Norman-French, he understood readily enough.

Presently he was listening in rapt interest, in particular to that part of the preaching which dwelt upon untold riches to be won from the Infidels. His curiosity soaring, Gerth Ordway pushed forward until he secured a clear glimpse of the knoll, the clumps of flaunting pennons and a number of armed knights grouped around a rough wooden cross.

Suddenly the curly haired armiger stiffened. By St. Olav! Yonder, the sunlight had caused a coppery flash very similar to that which he often had beheld in the Lady Rosamund's hair. Hastily he crossed himself lest he might be beholding a ghost. But no. The Lord be praised, *it was indeed* she of the straight back, stately carriage and high-held chin!

A ringing shout of joy escaped him but went unnoticed amid the general hubbub, for up yonder, towering half head taller than the

tallest knights about him stood Sir Edmund de Montgomerie. He
would have surged up the hillock weeping with joy—the Saxons like
the Gaels were never prone to conceal their emotions—but at that
moment the speaker's voice soared in his climactic call to arms, evoking a great shout of *"Dieu lo Vult!"*

All about him men and women began falling upon their knees and,
clasping hands, confessing their sins at the top of their lungs. Gerth,
too, became carried away by the *excitator's* promise not only of
earthly riches but also of salvation and the promise of much hard
fighting. In fact, he became so absorbed in his confession of sin that
both captives—unprincipled rogues that they were—took advantage
of this sacred moment to slip their bonds and so disappear.

Heart hammering, pale eyes shining the Saxon watched his liege
lord kneel and accept two strips of scarlet cloth.

Despite the gigantic former earl's lack of rich raiment or arms of
any description the figure he presented was nonetheless impressive.
How had Sir Edmund and his twin, unable to swim, managed to
survive the sea's white fury and those rocks? Not until the congregation commenced to disperse was the armiger able to advance—
through liberal use of his axe handle—sufficiently to confront his lord
and kneeling press a humble kiss upon his hand.

"By the Glory of God, 'tis Gerth!" Edmund, forgetting custom,
heaved the barrel-chested youth off his feet and hugged him de-
lightedly. "How came you here?"

"Inland and up the coast, my lord," the armiger smiled ruefully. "I
had taken a pair of rogues to sell as serfs but just now they escaped
in the crowd."

"What miracle is this?" demanded a rich, soft voice and again
Gerth knelt, this time to press his lips to the Lady Rosamund's hand.
While she patted his curly, straw-hued thatch much as she might
the head of a favorite hound the esquire's eyes peered upwards and
saw those shiny, dark-red lips part in that wondrously sweet smile
he had treasured ever since he first had beheld her in Arundel
Castle's innerward.

She murmured in deep, almost husky accents, "Dear Gerth, soon
I shall burn a candle in honor of St. Christopher because you, also,
have been spared from the cruel sea."

CHAPTER IX

Count Turgis

Count Turgis II, son of Turgis de Bernay, that doughty Norman adventurer who, with merciless efficiency had aided Robert Guiscard in overrunning Campagna, Calabria and, later, the whole of Sicily—took what ease he could upon a battlement of his castle of Sanseverino. Restlessly he gazed out over the hilly and sparsely populated valley spreading blue-green away on all sides and felt immeasurably bored. Grunting, he eased in its sling an ever-painful and permanently crippled arm. Stifling a groan, the old man settled back upon a folded bearskin that this benign Spring sunlight might the better bathe his wasted, once-powerful body.

Ever more impatient with his lot, the gray-haired and hawk-featured Lord of Sanseverino still again surveyed the familiar little fields of cereal crops, the flowering orchards and silver-gray olive groves. A few poorly tended vineyards terraced the slopes of the hills nearest at hand.

It was easy to see all that took place below for he had built Castel Sanseverino upon a steep and very rocky hill rising in strategic isolation from the floor of this valley through which meandered a slow little river.

Well, during his fighting years he had not campaigned in vain, mused Turgis de Bernay, keeping one eye on a wild falcon wheeling high in the sky. To the first Count Turgis' modest domain he added nine fiefs of varying size at the expense of two lesser counties, and at points of strategic importance further had caused to be constructed a number of minor strongholds such as Agropoli.

The only thorn remaining in his side during these declining years was the existence of an aggressive neighbor immediately to the north, a Lombard adventurer known as Baron Drogo of Cetraro. Thus far, to be sure—the Wild Boar of Cetraro—as he had become known during Duke Roger Guiscard's unsuccessful invasion of Thrace—had contented himself by extending his boundaries to northwards and eastwards at the expense of various Papal properties.

A shadow flickered swiftly over the battlement's sunlit parapet and, glancing up, Count Turgis noted that the hawk was circling nearer probably in quest of rooks or pigeons. Instantly he identified the bird as a rock falcon gentle, a female, for, as in the case of most hawks she was larger and bolder than the tiercel, or male bird. Ha!

He watched the falcon gentle strike down a pigeon, strayed from
the straw-roofed village of Sanseverino Mercato at the foot of this
hill, and bear it off to a crag opposite the castle. Good. Tomorrow
he would order his chief falconer to seek out its eyrie and perchance
remove from it a likely eyas, or nearly grown but still flightless young
bird, for training.

The fierce old warrior cursed under his breath that no longer could
he gallop the fields with Adèle, his favorite peregrine, balanced on
a padded leathern gauntlet, the scarlet hackles cresting her hood all
a-flutter under the rushing wind. Turning, Count Turgis cast a longing look at the mews of Sanseverino, a squat, round tower in which
were trained and sheltered all manner of hawks.

Perched upon their blocks in there, one would find peregrines
flown only by his sons, and, according to the usages of falconry, sakers
for various knights of the garrison, hobbies for esquires, a merlin for
Alixe, his beloved only daughter, and even a few sparhawks for the
use of any prelate who might chance by.

The old warrior's rheumy gray eyes then considered the Via
Salerno, that broad white road which wound southward towards
Pesto and Agropoli, outposts defending the southernmost boundaries
of his domain. Although his eyesight remained keen he still saw no
little clouds of dust down there, nor did a faint flashing of steel advise
that Sir Toustain de Dives, his Constable, might be returning.

Count Turgis accepted a wooden cup of spiced wine poured by a
little bachelor and, after swallowing hugely settled back again. Um.
What about this ever-increasing friction between Hugues, his eldest
son and heir, and Robert his next younger brother? Too frequently
of late his authority as head of the family had been strained to quell
their furious quarreling.

Indeed, Count Turgis reflected while watching a cart drawn by
two huge yellow-white oxen toil laboriously up a narrow and winding road which ended before Castel Sanseverino's barbican, if it had
not been for the intervention last night of Alixe, their devoted
young sister, blood might readily have flowed despite his most ominous threats.

The Count arose, limped over to a section of battlement from
which he could view the courtyard. Below, his burly son, Hugues,
was at exercise. Employing both hands, that young knight cease-
lessly was whirling about his head a training sword rendered heavier
than the genuine weapon through strips of lead clasped at intervals
along its blade. The old man's heart lifted. Verily, Hugues promised
to develop into a most formidable champion, one who might, when

that inevitable day dawned, wage successful war against the Wild Boar of Cetraro.

To Turgis' ears came the thrumming *twang!* of bowstrings. Good. His young archers were busy practicing at the butts. In another section of the courtyard a quartet of knights were sweating, red-faced, as they stamped about belaboring each other with padded maces.

On the castle's south tower top the Lady Alixe and a pair of her tiring ladies were appearing. They formed a colorful group as they set to work over tapestry frames fetched up by a number of spindle-legged little bachelors. Settling their skirts the ladies seated themselves upon three-legged stools, oblivious that this bright sunlight pitilessly was revealing various rents, patches and stains on their finery. Certain shadows would linger about their necks and ears, not quite disappearing until Spring grew mild enough to risk the semi-annual bath in a huge wooden tub.

Once in a while young Alixe de Bernay had pondered over the fact that in the vicinity of Sanseverino existed certain ruins containing curious arrangements. In them, or so tradition claimed, the ancient Romans had bathed not two or three times a year, but almost every day! Not that she would ever believe this. Everybody knew it to be definitely injurious for a person to bathe more than once a month at the very most.

Blunt embroidery needle poised for threading, Alixe cast a sidewise glance at the Lady Blanche, a silly but lively young thing whose father held a minor fief to the eastward of Malfi. Why wouldn't she quit casting sheep's eyes at her brother Robert? Papa had noticed and was not pleased. If she did not mend her ways Blanche would soon be sent packing back to the scrubby little town she had come from.

"Oh, Alixe," sighed Blanche stretching in feline grace, " 'tis such a glorious day can we not be sung to by your minstrel?"

The Lady Eleanor of Agregenza, younger of the two tiring ladies, made a little *moue* of distaste but seconded the suggestion whereupon a servant was dispatched in search of the musician.

Privately, Alixe felt convinced that, as troubadours went poor young Alain was no great artist. She would never have wheedled her father into retaining the lad had not the Countess of Policastro, their neighbor to the south, recently acquired a minstrel. Why should Sanseverino be cast into the shade by a lesser County? Best to retain Alain who, though he usually sang off-key, was better than no minstrel at all.

Her thoughts veered to Drogo of Cetraro, that other neighbor so soon to become a guest of Sanseverino.

Drogo. Alixe's needle hovered above her tapestry and the skin of her smooth and very white shoulders granulated. What was so frightening about the prospect of entertaining him? All the countryside knew the so-called Wild Boar of Cetraro to be handsome in a fierce and overbearing fashion but also it was said that when inclined he could display the most charming of manners.

No doubt this fearsome neighbor did cause troublesome enemies to be flayed alive or condemned to an agonizing death through being suspended by the chin from a sharp iron hook let into his castle's battlements. But then, nearly every seigneur did such things or worse. Possibly, mused the blonde young girl—she was about to enter on her eighteenth year—it was fortunate that this Drogo and her father owed a common allegiance to Duke Bohemund of Otranto and so for the nonce dared not invade each other's domains.

The minstrel, a weedy, black-haired youth appeared smiling diffidently and clad in a tunic several sizes too large. Profoundly he bowed to the assembled ladies then in response to the Lady Alixe's signal, seated himself, poised a battered lyre and raised his voice in song.

> "Of one that is so fair and bright
> *Velut maris stella*
> Brighter than the day is light
> *Parens et puella*
> I cry to thee
> thou see to me."

Poor Alain's voice was deplorable, Alixe decided, worse even than her brother Robert's. Eventually she would suffer no more so, when Alain had quavered to the end of a quatrain, she gestured him to stop and looked sharply upwards. The Lady Eleanor had sprung to her feet and was pointing down the misty valley of Sanseverino. "Is that not the Constable returning?"

Emerging from Sanseverino Mercato was a short column of armed men whose helms and lance points twinkled brightly in the sunlight. The day being clear it soon became possible to distinguish the colors of pennons and even Sir Toustain's green and yellow checkered gonfanon.

"You've eyes like a merlin," laughed Alixe bending again over her embroidery. "I had hoped to be the first to spy Sir Toustain's company."

Presently the sharp-eyed girl from Castel Agregenza uttered a small squeal of excitement. "Alixe! Alixe! A woman rides in Sir Toustain's company."

"A woman? Are you sure?" cried Blanche.

"Can you not see her gown billow? She rides between Sir Toustain and some strange knight who appears to be tall and seemly."

Blue, yellow and dark green, the three ladies' cloaks fluttered when they leaned over the parapet and their hair, plaited in each case into twin braids, swung out over jagged crags beneath Castel Sanseverino's soaring walls.

"How very tall that stranger is and how wide are his shoulders!" commented Alixe, absently adjusting a fillet of silver leaves clasped about hair white-blonde as a newly-minted solidus.

Slowly and amid a lazy haze of yellow-white dust the cavalcade commenced to toil up towards Sanseverino's barbican.

Cried the Lady Blanche, "Brother Ordericus has succeeded in persuading at least one knight to undertake the Voyage of God. See? The big stranger wears a scarlet cross at his shoulder."

Alixe de Bernay said nothing, her attention being concentrated upon a woman who sat so straight yet so easily in her saddle while with obvious attention, she studied the castle and surroundings. Just who might this damsel be whose copper-hued hair braids dangled at least as low as her own blonde tresses?

Count Turgis' daughter drew a slow breath then straightened, frowning. God send yonder female would not prove overly beautiful. Alixe de Bernay enjoyed to the utmost her role as the County's reigning beauty. Who *could* yonder creature be? She still was peering up at Castel Sanseverino's square gray towers, at the moment effectively outlined against billows of woolly white clouds sailing across a sky of brilliant azure.

Blanche of Malfi was good-looking, of course, in a silly, moon-faced fashion. Hers was a scarlet but too-small mouth, large and very pale gray eyes which she kept forever rolling about. Eleanor of Agregenza's features on the other hand, were regular but her complexion for a Norman was on the dark side and her mouth too big and, alas, her brows were joined into a single line.

Below the barbican, that massive outwork protecting the castle's gate, Sir Toustain's trumpeter sounded a flourish which sent *prud'hommes* and men-of-arms running to the armory while Count Turgis' half-red, half-yellow banner atop the donjon was dipped in reply.

Although her companions stared down in curiosity upon the dusty company halted for admittance Alixe held back pondering a sudden premonition that yonder lithe young female presence might inflame the discord already prevalent within Sanseverino's walls.

A ladylike restraint was no longer to be suffered so Alixe, too, sought the parapet. Her lips flattened themselves and she drew a

breath so sharply that it hissed between singularly white and regular
teeth, for this girl on horseback was not merely handsome, despite a
coating of road dust and the shapeless gown she wore, but beautiful
in a cool and stately way.

CHAPTER X

The Feasting

Gerth Ordway's eyes streamed because billows of acrid
wood smoke were backing down the flues of fireplaces occupying
either end of the Castel Sanseverino's great hall. A chill wind, beating over from the Apennines had sprung up during the afternoon to
banish the Spring's warmth. Now the breeze stirred into furious motion tattered cloths hung to screen very narrow and glassless windows, really arrow-slits.

The wind also created rustling noises among rushes scattered over
the hall's stone floor and set into motion gonfanons belonging to
Count Turgis II, his sons and their principal retainers. One and all
the ladies shivered despite thick robes and heavy woolen mantles.

At the dining board Gerth took care to maintain his position directly behind his lord. Nearing twenty, the young Saxon was too
old to act as cupbearer but since his master's page had drowned he
had no choice. Someone must be ready when the friendly brawls
broke out. Therefore he remained alert, tousled head glowing under
the glare of torches which, stuck into iron sconces, sputtered and
added resinous fumes to the strata of eye-stinging smoke drifting
about the great hall.

A table, T-shaped and consisting of boards placed across a series
of trestles only recently had been readied for, in inclement weather
the great hall was used as an exercise area. The day's only other meal,
breakfast, was consumed whenever the gentle folk sent varlets to
fetch wooden bowls of stew to their quarters.

Gerth with care commenced to consider the faces at this feasting
board at the head of which sat gray-bearded Count Turgis. Lady
Rosamund, ever serene yet warmly interested in all that transpired,
occupied the seat to his right.

The young Saxon grinned to himself. Gossip current in the armiger's
barracks claimed that a furor had arisen when this penniless foreign
female had been accorded the position usually reserved for the Lady
Alixe. At Rosamund's right, Sir Robert, Count Turgis' brawny second son, stolidly shoveled food into his mouth and spoke only in

monosyllables. During this phase of the meal there was little conversation, only belches, the smacking of lips and the champing of hardworked jaws.

Sir Toustain employed an eating dagger with which to hack apart a roast fowl pinioned by his free hand upon a trencher of hard bread. Next to him was Sir Hugues, then the ever-vivacious Lady Blanche and then a landless knight who had sworn fealty to Sanseverino in return for arms, armor, a charger and sustenance. Next in order sat dark faced Lady Eleanor and a hideously birthmarked gentle man who defended a small fief in the direction of Salerno.

To Count Turgis' left was his daughter Alixe, her pale blue eyes reddening from dense drifting smoke which often set the company to coughing. Beyond Alixe, and becoming pleasantly aware of the delicate way in which she licked her fingers free of sauce, was seated the former Earl of Arundel.

On Edmund's left the homely and hungry dame of a visiting vassal stuffed food into her mouth so fast that her cheeks bulged like a squirrel's. Deservedly she ignored the Captain of the Castle Guard. This brutish lout lacked most of his left hand and swilled stew and wine like the serjeant he once had been.

For that matter the entire company were preoccupied in cramming their mouths with coarse but plentiful viands fetched in by gaunt dark-skinned Saracen slaves. Every now and then a diner would toss a bone or a strip of gristle over his or her shoulder thereby precipitating a noisy tussle amongst favorite hunting dogs which customarily were kenneled in the dining hall. Not a few paused to lick gashes received during the boar hunt of that morning.

This day had been a long one, reflected the Saxon. First he had attended his lord on a wild boar hunt among dense oak and walnut forests blanketing the foothills, next on a long ride up the valley to inspect with Sir Hugues and Sir Edmund a watchtower under construction in the mountain pass leading to Cetraro.

Gerth was not astonished presently to see the Lady Alixe signal Alain to slash wings and legs from a pheasant. This done she picked up the carcass and gnawed at it with the simple earnestness of a hungry vixen. It was only to be expected that grease should gleam on the Lady Rosamund's delicately rounded chin. How else could she suck the last succulent tidbit from an ox bone, expertly cracked before the hearth by a sad-eyed slave?

Upon signal from his master Gerth ran over to a wooden bucket and dipped up a bowl of steaming hot water. This he offered to the Lady Rosamund who raised it and rinsed her mouth. Turning, she

quite daintily spat the water over her shoulder onto the rushes behind her.

At length the gentle men, stomachs filled to repletion, licked the
last drop of gravy from their fingers and loosened broad belts before
sheathing their table daggers.

Under a particularly piercing blast Count Turgis winced and
beckoned an armiger to rearrange the mantle shielding his crippled
arm. Reproachfully he then eyed his daughter.

"And, you lazy girl, when will you finally complete that wind-
screen you have been promising since Michaelmas?"

Alixe lowered her gaze. "I crave your indulgence, sire. Another
week should see it completed." Then she glanced sidewise at wide-
shouldered Edmund de Montgomerie appearing so subtly distinguished despite his lack of ornaments and the plain brown tunic he
wore.

Suddenly Hugues from across the bare, food-splashed board, demanded of Rosamund, "And what, my lady, did *you* derive from
Brother Ordericus' exhortations at Pesto?"

The Anglo-Norman girl dropped her gaze with becoming modesty.
"Indeed, the holy man's message was so telling, so moving, so inspiring, my lord, I am surprised to note that you do not, like Sir Toustain
and my brother, wear a scarlet Cross upon your surcoat." As his face
flamed she treated him to a swift and yet dazzling smile. "Possibly
I am being unjust? Surely you cannot yet have heard the Holy Father's summons to ride against the Infidel?"

Edmund shot his sister an exasperated glance. Plague take her for
an untactful baggage! During the past few days she surely must have
learned that Count Turgis' brawny sons were at daggers drawn
since both yearned to take the Cross, yet one must remain to hold
Sanseverino for their ailing sire. True, Pope Urban II *had* promised
security for the property of an absent Crusader yet it stood to reason
that, in this turbulent land of Italy, there would be many masterless
men who, believing themselves already damned beyond redemption, would not hesitate to pounce upon a weakly guarded stronghold.

Young Robert, as tall but not quite so powerful as his beetle-
browed elder brother surged to his feet. "Sire!" he called over the
snarling of boar hounds disputing a beef bone. "Since Hugues is your
heir, I implore your permission to depart and fight for the Holy
Sepulchre." An edge entered his voice. "Have you not yourself, sire,
often vaunted that Hugues is surpassing able in the management of
Sanseverino; that my noble elder brother can estimate a horse, a cow
or a fief's value to a maravedi?"

Hugues' stool clattered backwards. "By God's glory, you *are* an impudent puppy! How dare you name me as a *bon homme?* A huckster? You, who cannot even yet decently level a lance! Bah! The Turks would slit your weasand in your first skirmish!"

"You lie in your teeth, arrogant braggart!" snarled the younger of Count Turgis' sons and, lurching forward, wrenched out his dagger.

"Peace! Damn your souls." The old lord bellowed. "Be still, both of you, else you'll cool your tempers in my dungeons! Damn you, Robert, put away that blade!"

When Hugues lurched forward, growling like an angry bear, Edmund caught and held onto the young fellow's arm sufficiently long to throw him off balance and so allow a pair of knights to interpose themselves between him and his raging younger brother whom Sir Toustain was attempting to restrain.

"In God's Mercy keep them separate!" screamed the Lady Eleanor. All evening long she had permitted her gaze to linger upon young Robert's aquiline countenance.

The brothers strained, swayed back and forth through the drifting wood smoke, shaking off first one and then another of those who would restrain them while hounds set up an excited clamor. Such sudden, murderous and insensate affrays were commonplace among the always short-tempered Normans.

"Summon the serjeants!" roared Count Turgis in a flaming rage.

Rosamund sat quite still, tourmaline-tinted eyes intent upon Sir Hugues' dagger blade. She remained imperturbable, as if nothing more serious than a wrestling match impended.

"Let be, Sir Hugues!" panted the Constable. "In God's name save your blows for worshipers of the accursed Mahound."

Serjeants came running in, their casques and mail gleaming with rain and promptly formed a double rank to separate the would-be combatants. Count Turgis was catching breath to berate his sons when a trumpet's blast sounded in the twilight outside.

"What the devil does that mean?" the old Count demanded.

" 'Tis a herald, my lord," informed an officer of the Guard. "He demands immediate admittance to your presence."

" 'Requests' or 'demands,' fellow?" snapped Sir Robert, putting away his poignard.

"He *demands* admittance, my lord, in the name of his lord, Drogo of Cetraro."

"Bid that insolent dog *request* admittance else he'll linger beyond our barbican until he rots."

Still panting and red faced, Sir Hugues pushed heavy brown hair from his eyes. "God's curse upon that Lombard's arrogance. The Boar needs gelding and he'll soon get it done."

CHAPTER XI

The Wild Boar

During those days which would elapse before the arrival of the dread Lord of Cetraro, Sanseverino's garrison devoted long hours to cleaning arms, armor and saddlery that they might turn out refurbished, cap-à-pie, and so impress these fierce Northerners with their martial glory.

Because of youthful experience as an armorer's apprentice, Gerth Ordway found himself sweating from before dawn until the last flambeaux spluttered out within the castle's gloomy halls. His skill at the forge now was turned to good account since his earnings could, and did, discharge the most immediate and embarrassing obligations incurred by penniless Sir Edmund and his lovely twin. Mightily it grieved the young Saxon to witness the former Earl of Arundel's mortification that as yet he remained destitute of arms, armor or a warhorse. Nor could that young man perceive means of acquiring such warlike essentials.

In the matter of martial exercises Sir Edmund's cheerful, flaxenhaired armiger quickly had proved himself at least the peer of the hardiest esquires in Sanseverino's service. Although perhaps not quite as adept as some in the handling of a lance, Gerth's use of a blunted sword or a padded mace stretched many a powerful esquire stunned and bleeding on the courtyard's pavement. As for axe-play, none dared stand against him.

On the other hand Gerth Ordway admitted himself less skilled than these Italian-Norman youths in the training of horses. Therefore he earnestly set about learning everything possible concerning the intricate process of schooling those great destrier stallions which kicked, squealed and bit in the stables of Sanseverino. From enslaved Infidel grooms and a captive Byzantine cataphract, or heavy cavalryman, he obtained further specialized information.

He would long remember that evening when, after certain young warhorses had been bedded for the night, a sheep was dragged in by Moslem slaves and was butchered directly before their stalls.

"Since most horses instinctively despise and fear the smell of blood," explained the ex-cataphract, "they must be habituated to it, lest in battle they riot out of control."

The young stallions had gone white-eyed, snorted, reared, and tried to kick down their stalls. Finished destriers meanwhile stood stock-still, only shivered a little as they stared upon the tub of steaming and pungent blood.

Saracen grooms averred also that a foal destined to become a knight's destrier must be dropped within the walls of an occupied human dwelling. Arab tradition held that a foal so born necessarily would feel accustomed to the presence of humans therefore would not fear them and so prove difficult to tame.

To the young Anglo-Saxon, it was most instructive to observe how savage young stallions were trained, often painfully, to ignore the appeal made by a mare in heat. Many a good knight declared Count Turgis' grizzled Horse Master, had been known to lose his life through the amorous distraction of his mount during a critical moment in battle.

When broken to bit, poiterial, cingle and saddle, these great horses next were taught how to fight balanced on their hind legs so that they could with their forefeet strike out and smash down foot-soldiers and lesser mounts before savaging the fallen enemy with great tearing bites.

A measure of peace ruled within the de Bernay family after Count Turgis, following the singing of Solemn High Mass, announced to the garrison assembled in his inner ward that Sir Hugues would lead Sanseverino's levée to the Holy Land in support of Duke Bohemund's blood-red banner. For all that young Robert raged and vowed he would so cripple his brother in the lists that he could not ride forth Hugues merely laughed and continued to pay shy and manfully inarticulate court to Lady Rosamund de Montgomerie.

Whether or not she welcomed the heir to Sanseverino's advances that beauteous and self-contained young lady gave no hint whatever but, to plague him, she flattered Sir Toustain and made repeated efforts to draw from him colorful tales about the campaigns he had fought on the Rim of the World.

He had gone thither years ago as an adventurer-knight in the service of the celebrated Roussel de Ballieul. This Norman adventurer had been of the same audacious and avaricious ilk as William the Mamzer and Robert Guiscard and some forty years earlier, not only had made and unmade a Byzantine emperor, but he had conquered a great principality for himself. Later, however, the one-eyed knight related, de Ballieul's fortunes had failed and, after suffering a long imprisonment he had perished in agony, poisoned by certain politely smiling guests pretending to flee the wrath of the newest Basileus enthroned in Constantinople.

To the veteran's accounts of mighty deeds and of perils overcome Rosamund listened in rapt attention, silently goading Sir Hugues into a jealous frenzy.

Not so diffident concerning her maidenly emotions was the Lady Alixe. From the moment the red-haired Anglo-Norman first had smiled upon her, Count Turgis' slender daughter caught her breath, dropped her large and limpid blue eyes and blushed whenever he appeared. Seldom did she neglect an opportunity to be near him and to express a discreet interest in his past exploits and future plans.

As for Sir Edmund, he experienced at first amusement at this pale beauty's manifest admiration then increasingly he became intrigued by the pretty attentions paid by this lively damsel who could sing as sweetly as one of God's own angels. To his own astonishment he felt inspired to compose a roundelay in her honor and which she applauded warmly for all that his voice was even worse than poor Alain's.

It was Rosamund, however, who correctly evaluated the chances of this budding romance. Although Sir Hugues and his brother might sigh over her, then strut around one another like bellicose young gamecocks, she sensed that not the remotest possibility existed of Count Turgis' permitting any child of his to marry a destitute wanderer from an almost unknown land beyond the seas.

As she and her twin lingered on a tower top one afternoon she cautioned, "A word to the wise, beloved Brother. Waste not too much attention upon Alixe. It will come to nothing."

"Why?" he demanded sharply. "The girl adores me and I am beginning to love her, I think."

"That I do not doubt, alas," Rosamund said quietly. "But all the same you will not be allowed to wed her."

The former earl checked his stride and faced his twin. "If I wish to wed Alixe de Bernay why then I will have her to my marriage bed," he promised grimly. "Count Turgis and all his threadbare followers notwithstanding. Pah! These hungry Italian cutthroats should have seen the rich fields, fisheries and tall forests of Arundel."

"They know nothing of them and care less," reminded Rosamund. "No. Old de Bernay will permit no alliance with either you or me, even should we deign to marry into their Norman corsair brood. What lands would we add to his? No. 'Tis far better, O Brother mine, that you devote your attention to the problem of securing, no matter how, arms, mail and horses for you and Gerth Ordway."

On a rather green charger borrowed from Sir Hugues and wielding weapons lent by Count Turgis, Edmund whenever possible, participated in exercises at arms held daily either in the courtyard or on a level meadow below Castel Sanseverino where destriers could maneuver at top speed.

Gradually the Anglo-Norman's extraordinary strength and endurance became remarked upon, if not envied. How many of these Italian-Norman gentle men could lift a weanling colt clear of the ground and hold it so for as long as he pleased? How many could hurl a light battle-axe as far and as accurately? For hours this red-haired stranger would wield the heaviest procurable swords and maces and remain fresh enough to scale a high wall supporting a heavy shield slung across his shoulders.

After other gentle men of the castle had retired to their quarters, Edmund and his armiger were given to lingering in the exercise yard. Master to man, man to master, patiently they tossed and caught heavy stones until their muscles crackled and they drew breath in wheezing gasps.

Sir Edmund was sufficiently astute, however, to decline direct competition or a trial-at-arms with either of Count Turgis' sinewy sons. Privately, he felt convinced that, at any time, he could best powerful young Sir Robert—for all that Rosamund gazed upon him with increasing interest. But to prevail over Sir Hugues, growing dangerous in his desperate infatuation over Rosamund, might prove more difficult. He was experienced in the field through having done battle not only in Sicily but in North Central Italy as well.

At last came the hour when the sentry, posted day and night atop Sanseverino's donjon called down that a sizable cavalcade was riding south along the Via Salerno. Immediately trumpets, but not the oliphants of battle, sounded, sent the garrison to racing about in search of arms and panoply.

Watchers on Count Turgis' bastions drew quickened breath when they counted no fewer than fifteen belted knights and twice as many esquires following Baron Drogo's orange-and-black gonfanon. Also jogging along under a pall of whitish road dust at least sixty mounted serjeants and men-of-arms and a long train of bat horses were to be descried.

Like stars upon a still pond lance points commenced to twinkle along that narrow road winding up to the barbican and varicolored pennons flaunted bravely in the sunshine.

At this moment everyone on the ramparts could tell that Baron Drogo's jackmen were herding the baggage animals towards that exercise meadow which lay below the walls. There undoubtedly they would pitch the Wild Boar of Cetraro's camp.

Upon the barbican trumpets brayed a series of flourishes then
Sanseverino's two hundred fighting men altogether motley of arm
and garb, formed up in the courtyard. Their ranks, Sir Edmund noted,
were none-too-well dressed to his notion. How sloppy seemed these
Italian-Normans and their Lombard neighbors. If only he had not
been forced from Arundel! There, by God, had been a well drilled
garrison.

Sir Hugues and his brother, the former wearing for the first time
the scarlet cross of a Crusader, rode out to greet their distinguished
visitor. When the latter was perhaps a quarter of a mile from the
barbican, Baron Drogo clapped spurs to his destrier, a magnificent
dappled gray easily seventeen hands in height, and advanced, quite
by himself, just as Count Turgis' personal oliphant emitted an ear-
shattering blast. Wearing a mirthless smile Hugues spurred forward
to offer an ungloved hand in welcome to this rapacious neighbor.

Edmund, standing beside his sister upon the barbican, decided
that never before had he seen a countenance at once so vital, so
handsome and so brutal as Drogo's. The hulking lord of Cetraro's complexion was of a clear bronze-red. He affected neat mustaches and a
short black beard trimmed into a fork.

Rosamund de Montgomerie's impressions were somewhat similar.
This famous champion undoubtedly *was* pleasing in a coarse and
overbearing fashion. His was a thick, slightly hooked nose and a
well-formed red mouth disfigured by a small scar at its left corner.
The Baron of Cetraro's surprisingly wide-set eyes were penetrating
and of brilliant blue. This much at least proclaimed his descent from
those Teuton barbarians—the Long Beards—who, long ages ago, had
accomplished Imperial Rome's final destruction.

"Why do I not perceive Count Turgis?" She heard Drogo's complaint as his destrier's iron shod hoofs clattered into the courtyard.
"Is Turgis dead that he sends only his sons to greet a friendly neighbor?"

Young Sir Hugues flushed to the roots of his long light brown hair.
"My noble sire's wound has worsened of late," said he harshly. "Therefore my brother and I have been accorded the honor of welcoming
our valiant neighbor to Sanseverino."

The towering lord of Cetraro, Edmund reluctantly admitted to
himself seemed a very accomplished horseman so easily did he restrain the restless curvettings of his stallion.

There was nothing covert about Baron Drogo's appraisal of Castel
Sanseverino's plan and military strength. He even demanded, bra-
zenly enough, to be allowed to view the castle's armory, a privilege
which Count Turgis refused to allow.

For reasons best known to himself, Count Turgis delayed presentation of his puissant guest to the ladies of the castle. Therefore it was not until the midday following the Lombard's arrival and nightlong entertainment by a pair of luscious fourteen-year-old peasant girls fetched in, willy-nilly, that he was conducted by Sir Hugues to the south tower's top.

Rosamund at once was repelled yet oddly fascinated by this wide-shouldered figure in a surcoat of Venetian green silk shot with gold. So this was the famous captain of fortune, the merciless seeker after power and the renowned seducer of females, no matter what their age or station? All at once Edmund's twin understood why, if rumor was not at fault, this burly nobleman had found no difficulty in twice winning lovely and well-dowered brides. Certainly this man exuded an indefinable yet overpowering physical appeal. She cast a glance at Alixe to determine whether she had noted the guest's attention upon her. She could discern nothing at all. Alixe's eyes were expressionless while her small and regular features were as pale and rigid as those of some Roman noblewoman's marble bust.

"The Lady Alixe de Bernay," muttered Hugues. "Sister, this is our neighbor of Cetraro. Certainly you will have heard something of his—valor?"

"Of course. Who has not heard of our neighbor's prowess—in many directions?"

Clad in a simple blue camlet gown girdled by a zone of crimson silk clasped in silver, Count Turgis' daughter stiffly sat upon a settle, a mechanical smile gracing her lips.

"Welcome to Sanseverino, my lord of Cetraro," she murmured and dropped her gaze. "I trust you will enjoy your visit here."

His feet braced apart and with left hand fingering the golden guard of a long dagger, the Wild Boar of Cetraro stood staring down at the slight figure before him. "My lady, since I have every intention of enjoying this visit to the fullest, the more time I shall spend in your company, the greater will be my pleasure," he declared in a loud, but not unpleasant voice.

"This is the Lady Blanche," Hugues continued, "daughter to Sir Geoffrey of Malfi and this is the Lady Eleanor from Agregenza who unfortunately is without par——"

Count Turgis' elder son fell silent. Drogo of Cetraro again was staring fixedly, boldly upon Rosamund de Montgomerie as she stood looking out over the valley with puffs of wind lazily stirring the fine, red-gold hair over her brow.

"*Per Baccho!*" grunted the lord of Cetraro. "What astonishing beauty!" He turned abruptly to Sir Hugues. "Why do you delay in presenting me to so fascinating a lady?"

Everyone on the tower's top watched Rosamund's firmly rounded chin rise, saw her gaze unflinchingly encounter the Lombard's. Under the obvious lechery in his regard bright color welled into her neck and features.

"This is the Lady Rosamund de Montgomerie," growled Sir Hugues. "She and her brother, Sir Edmund, are my father's guests."

Drogo ignored his host's son and stepped so close that his scarred and robust features encompassed Rosamund's entire field of vision. "Where lies your family domain? In Burgundy? Lorraine? Normandy?"

"At present there is none," she replied tonelessly. "My brother and I are exiles—from England."

"Oh. He's the big fellow who claims to have been Earl of Arundel?"

"He was Earl until a short time ago," Rosamund spoke evenly, did not for an instant divert her gaze from those compelling, dark blue eyes now almost glaring into hers of tourmaline green. "We are landless and for the moment dependent upon the generosity of Count Turgis."

A small grunt escaped the towering black-haired figure in green and gold. "A pity. Beauty as great as yours deserves great wealth to adorn it. I fear you will find it difficult to contract a suitable marriage hereabouts."

"My lord, I do not recall having invited your opinion on the subject," Rosamund observed, then turned serenely aside to concentrate upon an unfinished bit of tapestry work.

Under the amazed glances of those present, the Wild Boar followed her across the tower top and placed a hand over her work. "Tonight, my lady, I will give a feast in my pavilion. For you I shall reserve the place of honor." He turned, revealed large and very white, teeth in a curiously winning grin. "I shall expect you other ladies, as well."

So crass was the slight to Sanseverino by this impressive ruffian that Alixe's fixed smile vanished and her brother commenced to finger his dagger's handle. After all, had the Lombard not journeyed here with the express intention of seeking a third wife, and alliance with Sanseverino? Together with Cetraro the two domains would equal a duchy at least as large as that which Bohemund had inherited.

It was just as well, Hugues was reflecting that Edmund de Montgomerie of the impulsive temper was not present. To the guest he suggested, "And now, sir, shall we repair to the tilting yard?"

"No. I will go hawking," Drogo stated. "Especially I desire the Lady Rosamund to accompany us."

Sir Hugues' voice sounded like a sword's blade dragged over a grindstone. "Hereabouts the best flying of hawks does not occur until late afternoon. You, my lord, should be aware of that."

"Should I really?" rasped the Lombard. "*Per Baccho! I* hawk when I've the mind to."

Alixe had never seen her hot-head brother more controlled. Did he really fear this fellow? Hardly. No. He was gaining stature in Rosamund's regard.

"My lord, none shall forbid your riding out whenever you desire —using your own hawks and hounds." He stared into Drogo's eyes. "In all Sanseverino there is not mewed a falcon worthless enough to be flown during the heat of the day."

"Indeed? My birds are stronger and can well fly at any time."

Hugues drew a quick breath but observing Rosamund apparently busy at her tapestry once more, he controlled himself. "My lord, my sire awaits us in the tilt yard."

Drogo hesitated, but then jerked a nod and followed Sir Hugues down a circular stone staircase.

Once the trampling of feet faded away Alixe leaped to her feet and cursed Drogo of Centraro's conduct with a pungent and picturesque fluency which astounded and then amused Rosamund de Montgomerie. When she caught her breath Alixe glared at the staircase.

"I pray my sire will realize that short of force I never will wed that Lombard ruffian."

"Really, now, I thought the baron rather splendid," Blanche's pale vapid features for once seemed luminous. "Did none of you notice Cetraro's proud bearing? To be dominated and protected by so masterful a man for any girl would mean——"

"—Dominated, and murdered!" corrected Alixe in a strangled voice.

"Murdered?" Rosamund demanded. "What is your meaning?"

"This arrogant bully, at thirty, already twice is a widower. Half and more of his great domain and lands were gained through his marriages. Is it not passing strange that both wives perished soon after this Wild Boar's claim to their dower-lands had been confirmed?"

CHAPTER XII

Baron Drogo Entertains

A swarm of Cetraro's jackmen had pitched his pavilion of glaring purple as near as possible to the base of that rocky monolith upon which stood Castel Sanseverino. Tents for vassal knights and picket lines for warhorses and baggage animals encircled Drogo's quarters, but without the least semblance of order. At sunset this smoke-veiled camp bestirred itself. Hairy, ragged menials bustled and sweated between the pavilion and a bed of coals over which the carcass of a young ox slowly was assuming a luscious red-brown.

Within the Baron's pavilion carpets covered the ground; although worn and soiled through use in many a campaign, they nonetheless were carpets which only the rich could afford. Benches had been arranged paralleling a double row of trestle tables.

The evening proved so mild and still that the barking of a herdsman's dogs high among the stony hills beyond Sanseverino Mercato distinctly could be heard. Backed up to the pavilion twin casks of heady Tuscan wine rested ready for tapping upon the tailgate of a two-wheeled wain. Barrels of less noble vintages already had been broached for the benefit of Cetraro's serjeants and men-of-arms. Villagers bold enough to venture near the Lombard's encampment found it significant that although most of these strangers were off duty they nonetheless retained their hauberks.

Tethered destriers stamped, whistled and snapped at each other amid gathering darkness when, on the road leading down from the castle now looming black and forbidding upon its hilltop, appeared clumps of flickering torches which commenced to descend towards the visitors' encampment.

Once the group of guests and numerous well-armed guards appeared upon the meadow, Drogo and his principal liegemen strode forward to guide them among the campfires towards the pavilion.

Sir Edmund de Montgomerie quickly became aware that considerable wine must already have flowed as he rode among the encampment's outermost tents. Not only the tall host but most of his retainers talked boisterously and bellowed with laughter over the slightest pretext.

As was only to be expected when wine flowed, taunts and veiled challenges could be heard among the tents and shadows. No clashes took place no doubt because the Wild Boar must have ordered his followers to restrain themselves; an elementary precaution since Count Turgis II's tough men-of-arms outnumbered his own by three to one.

Sir Hugues and his brother bronzed, and supple in their motions as young panthers, were anything but at their ease while handing the Lady Alixe and her waiting ladies out of uncomfortable litters borne by two mules each.

As for Edmund de Montgomerie he felt more than a little relieved that his twin, although appearing as fresh as the rose for which she had been named, had pleaded sudden indisposition and so had avoided the Lombard's encampment.

While dismounting and turning a borrowed palfrey over to his armiger the former earl glanced carefully about. "Well, Gerth, and what do you make of these Northerners?"

The young Saxon grinned at horseplay going on among the campfires. "Dirty and ill favored as usual, my lord, but I note never a rogue hereabouts but what seems stout and well armed." In an undertone he added, "I'd feel easier, my lord, were you wearing a shirt of mail beneath that mantle."

"Would to God I owned one! How it sore goes against the grain that the very clothes upon my back are borrowed."

The air inside the pavilion smote the guests' nostrils like a blow. Not only was it hot and smoky but also rank with the odors of scorched food and the stench of bodies long unwashed. Under rows of flaring torches a trio of servants plucked at harp-like instruments the jangling tinkle of which was all-but lost among the mournful howls of a boar hound chained to the pavilion's central support pole.

Surprisingly, Baron Drogo's banquet commenced in orderly fashion. Menials appeared bent under battle shields charged with chunks of beef and pork still smoking from the fire. Also offered were dozens of badly cooked quail, ducks and geese—all roasted whole and retaining the heads.

Occupying a gilded, well battered chair at Baron Drogo's right, sat the Lady Alixe, her delicate blonde beauty in sharp contrast with her host's massive bulk, restless eyes and powerfully modeled features. Cetraro for the occasion had donned a tunic of black and yellow-striped silk and had slung two long gold chains about his neck.

The other ladies from Sanseverino were flanked by towering Lombard knights. Most of them were scarred and to eat used hands from which fingers were missing more often than not. These bravos had donned knee-length tunics without exception trimmed in fur of some sort while their legs were encased by cross-gartered pantaloons of white linen. On their feet they wore chausses of soft leather, originally dyed red, yellow or blue. But now these were scuffed, dusty and stained by horse droppings.

The host called down to Sir Toustain. "I hear, Sir Knight, that you, also, have done some campaigning among the Byzantines?"

"Aye, my lord," the one-eyed veteran replied gravely. "Once I served under the banner of Messer Roussel de Ballieul."

"Then you must have fought at Manzikert?" eagerly suggested a young Lombard.

"No, my lord, we Franks were occupied with the siege of Chiliat when the Sultan Alp Arslan, aided by treachery on the part of the Turcopoles—Turkish mercenaries in Byzantine pay—routed the co-Emperor Romanus Diogenes. Thus were lost the richest themes of the Byzantine Empire."

"There lies the Byzantines' chief weakness," Drogo informed the Lady Alixe. "These bastard Greek-Romans hire barbarians—such as us," he threw back his head and roared with laughter, "to drive the Turks, Saracens, Sclavonians, and Patzinaks from the frontiers of their shrunken empire."

Alixe arched slender brows. "But, my lord, are not Turks and Saracens one and the same?"

Baron Drogo tossed a marrow bone back to his cup-bearer for cracking. "Nay, my lady. The Saracens are Arabs, of the same big-nosed and dark-skinned strain as the Jews and Armenians. The Turks, or Seljukis as they are known in Constantinople, on the other hand are white men like ourselves, very ugly but showing straight noses and, very often, gray or blue eyes. They are blood-thirsty savages; wily and very brave on occasion, but *per Bacco!* they cannot withstand the charge of Frankish chivalry."

"Their sultans seldom are foolish enough to attempt it," grunted Sir Toustain and his single eye kindled. "Only once do I recall their doing so and that was in 1072 during a famous battle—the Bridge of Zompi. At that we were only able to crush the Turks because we caught them in a defile."

Drogo laughed. "From what I saw of Turcopoles when I was fighting in Thessaly with Duke Bohemund I say that Infidels, no matter what their breed, are cowardly." Between muscular hands he tore apart a round loaf of hard baked bread. "All the same 'tis a pity the last of them have been driven out of Sicily, yonder was a fine proving ground for young knights."

After gulping a measure of wine he turned unsteadily to Alixe de Bernay and muttered something in Greek.

Gerth, standing behind his master, saw him smile. Sir Edmund, the armiger had learned, was heartily ashamed of his fair, though far from perfect, knowledge of that tongue.

"I trust what you said was a compliment, my lord?" murmured Alixe. "I understand not a word of what you said."

Sir Toustain grinned hurriedly. "I believe his comment on the perfection of your bosom was so intended, my lady."

Enormous quantities of viands constantly were lugged in by menials so awkward that frequently they spilled sauces over the table's bare boards and spattered the ladies' gowns. A sudden volley of curses resounded at the table's far end and steel glimmered under the flambeaux. A knight from Sanseverino and another from the North stood swaying, glowering at each other.

"Hold hard there!" bellowed Drogo. "Do your blood-letting outside—damned if I'll have you spoiling my carpets."

For the first time Edmund spoke. "They must not fight, my lord, here or anywhere."

"Why not?"

"Both wear the Cross on their shoulder. Such are sworn never to assault each other."

"The foul fiend fly away with such pious fools!" The Wild Boar of Cetraro glowered at Edmund. "Keep your advice to yourself, sirrah, as becomes a landless beggar!"

Features flaming the Anglo-Norman surged to his feet and would have lunged at his host with his dining dagger had not Gerth on one side and Sir Robert on the other gripped his forearms.

"Peace, my lord!" panted the armiger as they reeled across the pavilion. "He is drunk and means to provoke you. You are not Count Turgis' liegeman."

"Then let him better guard his tongue." Although shaking with rage, the Anglo-Norman finally reseated himself.

"Let be, friend Edmund," whispered Count Turgis' younger son. "This Drogo is the most dangerous swordsman throughout all this part of Italy. Single handed, he once held a bridge near Capua against twenty stout men-of-arms and slew six of them before the rest took to their heels."

"A plague on that Lombard braggart," growled Gerth. "Last year I saw my lord's sword, 'Brainbiter,' split an armored Danish pirate from neck to loins after he had by himself cleared the dragon ship's deck. In the lists I have watched him beat down or unhorse many of the best and bravest of knights in England. I have——"

"—Be still, Gerth," snapped the former earl. "My cup needs refilling."

In vain did a long-haired minstrel attempt to relieve the prevailing

tension through singing the ever-popular "Song of Roland." Nobody
listened. The ladies remained tense and big-eyed on their chairs
whilst bickering broke out louder than ever. Here and there a
drunken feaster would lurch over to vomit against the nearest tent
wall and then return to continue the wassail.

To complete the tumult a pair of stallions picketed nearby selected
that moment to commence a screaming combat among themselves
which, in turn, set all dogs in the encampment to raising so hideous
a clamor that the Lady Alixe clapped hands over her ears and cast
beseeching glances at Sir Hugues. That big, brown-faced young
knight, however, appeared oblivious to the uproar and continued
conversing with Baron Drogo's principal henchman.

When eventually a measure of order was restored, the host stood
up and began roaring for more wine. Only then did he seem for the
first time to notice the absence of Rosamund de Montgomerie.

"And where is your lovely guest from beyond the seas?" he rasped
at the Lady Alixe while tugging at his forked black beard. "Methinks
I invited her to attend this feast?"

Alixe paled, dropped her eyes. "The Lady Rosamund declared herself indisposed, my lord, and invites your forgiveness."

Baron Drogo's white teeth glimmered beneath his drooping mustaches as he snarled in Greek, "How dare that impudent whey-faced
English harlot defy me?" He spoke not loudly but loudly enough to
send Edmund, Sir Toustain and others who understood that language
to snatching at their daggers. A single great bound served to carry
Edmund over the table and to send villeins sprawling amid the food
and drink they were serving.

Before Baron Drogo could straighten on his semi-throne, the
knuckles of the first and second fingers of Edmund's right hand
clamped themselves upon the Lombard's aquiline nose and twisted it
so savagely to right and left, that his long earrings swayed like miniature pendulums.

"Peace! Peace!" roared Sir Hugues leaping up onto a bench. "Remember all of you that here you are within my father's law!" Since
Count Turgis' followers hopelessly outnumbered the Northerners,
daggers, one by one were slipped back into their sheaths while everyone stared with bated breath at the amazing spectacle of the Wild
Boar of Cetraro mopping a bleeding nose upon his cuff.

"Well, you foul-mouthed dog," Edmund rasped at Baron Drogo.
"Must I kick you in your parts to make you apologize?"

"What did the Wild Boar say?" Sir Hugues was yelling.

Sir Toustain called out above the tumult. "In the Greek tongue,
he named the Lady Rosamund a harlot."

Barely in time did certain of Count Turgis' knights restrain Sir Hugues and his brother.

"By God's Glory, you red-nosed Lombard pig, you shall answer to me!" roared Hugues struggling like a madman against a background of screaming women and overturned benches.

"Mine is the right to *combat à l'outrance!*" shouted Edmund, red hair aflame in the dancing torchlight. Everywhere sounded running feet and voices calling out to learn what had chanced.

Drogo, his features suffused and contorted by passion, suddenly spat bloody spittle full in the Anglo-Norman's face.

"Tomorrow, you landless dog, I will surely slay you."

"No!" Sir Hugues' big voice dominated the clamor. "I say this combat must take place two days hence if fought on foot, and five days if fought a-horseback."

"Why so?" shouted the Northerners.

The heir to Sanseverino glared about at those wine-heated faces crowding in from all sides. "This foreigner has suffered ill fortune and so possesses no arms, armor or destrier of his own. Therefore he requires a period to accustom himself to the horse and arms I shall lend him."

The Southern knights looked startled. Should this Anglo-Norman be defeated, as almost certainly he would be, then his borrowed armor, weapons and destrier, no mean investment, would be forfeit —along with his life.

"Sirrah!" snarled Drogo. "I deem it most unfriendly of Sanseverino to arm this landless dog from beyond the seas against me. I shall not forget the matter."

Eventually because of Drogo's insensate impatience to attack his enemy, it became decided that, although their respective mounts would be at hazard, the two champions would fight two days hence on foot.

Sir Toustain gloomily shook his head. Drogo, he knew for a crafty campaigner and a very deadly swordsman, while of the Anglo-Norman's fighting ability he knew nothing beyond certain observations made about Castel Sanseverino's tilting yard.

CHAPTER XIII

On the Battlements

Among the activities within Castel Sanseverino's walls those of the fletcher's shop and armorer's smithy stood as second to none in importance. In the former short Norman bows were shaped and arrows by the hundred were headed and feathered while in the other new pikes, bills and helms were forged or old ones mended. Count Turgis' master smith, Osric, though able, lacked the skill to forge and temper a knight's heavy three-foot sword, the blade of which was nearly as wide at the point as it was at the guard. In all Italy only certain pampered Saracen slaves possessed the art of forging tough and lasting blades like that of "Brainbiter."

Gerth Ordway, standing before the anvil, had stripped to the waist so his muscled shoulders gleamed with sweat as he paused to tighten a leather apron about him.

Rainulf, Sir Hugues' usually silent esquire and the master armorer meanwhile inspected Gerth's handiwork—a heavy, iron shafted weapon some two feet in length. Its head lay deeply bedded among coals glowing in the forge. In their ears sounded the monotonous wheezing and puffing creak of giant bellows worked by Master Osric's grimy apprentice.

This weapon soon would become a mace of wrought iron, the handle or the grip of which later would be wrapped with rawhide. Some two inches in diameter, this iron shaft at its other end terminated in the ponderous *clava* or head. Sometimes these striking edges were wrought into cinquefoil form or, as in this instance, into a heart-shaped, five-edged lump of iron which, in an instant, could crush a helm and the skull within it.

The weapon, now rose-hued half its length, weighed easily fifteen pounds and would become heavier still once Gerth had welded a heavy, well-opened hook to the shaft just below the mace's head. Both onlookers grinned derisively. Who had ever heard of attaching a hook to a mace? Undoubtedly, it must disturb the arm's balance. Humming to himself, Gerth used tongs to fish from a half-cask of water the hook he had beaten out during the afternoon. Once he had thrust it into the glowing charcoal he signaled the youth working the bellows to increase the draught until a small volcano of sparks erupted and went whirling up the flue.

Laughing, Gerth said in his halting Norman-French, "Wait and you will see that even you clever Normans can learn something."

Master Osric seemed not favorably impressed when the flaxen haired young foreigner kept the mace in the forge flame.

"Do not overheat your metal, fool," he warned. "You'll lose the edge to the *clava's* flanges."

Gerth merely wiped his hands on his apron then, using tongs, affixed the white-hot hook to the glowing mace shaft and hammered powerfully until the metal fused. He was not worried. In England

a sharp edge was not deemed important to the flanges of a mace—
only its balance and weight of the weapon's head. This, when
brought down with terrific strength of a Norman knight's arm, usually
nullified the protection afforded by shield, helm and chain mail and
crushed an enemy's bones and muscles into shapeless pulp.

At length Gerth hefted the mace, swung it experimentally in various arcs then nodded to himself. The weapon's balance had not been
appreciably disturbed.

"To what use will your lord put yon silly hook?" came Rainulf's
contemptuous query.

"You will learn, an you live long enough."

"Well, Sir Edmund will need every advantage. This Drogo is
stronger than Satan's self. Why, last year he was seen to hew off an
ox's head with but a single sweep of his sword."

"You have never beheld my lord rage in the battle line. His is as
the strength of ten." Gerth simulated a confidence that no longer
was entirely implicit.

Tomorrow, when Sir Edmund faced his enemy, he would not be
swinging his beloved "Brainbiter." Would the former Earl of Arundel
ever find another blade as heavy, as perfectly balanced and as beautifully tempered as that weapon now rusting on the sea floor?

Features glowing scarlet in the forge's heat, Gerth plunged the
still rose-colored mace hissing an instant into water and so sent clouds
of steam whirling up among blackened cobwebs festooning the
smithy's rough-hewn rafters.

Next the brawny young Saxon thrust his handiwork into a tub of
oil and a few flaming droplets glanced off his leather apron.

Once the master armorer had tramped off to consume his evening
meal of black bread and lentils stewed in olive oil, Rainulf fetched
a deep sigh and spat gloomily into the forge.

"Best not tell your lord that Sir Hugues now regrets having risked
his second-best destrier, arms and mail."

"He has no cause for concern."

"I hope not. Do you know, Saxon, those terms upon which my lord
has lent your master this equipment?"

Gerth shook his yellow curls.

"If your master is beaten and should the Wild Boar spare his life,
then he must swear to serve Sanseverino as a landless liegeman until
released from such an oath. But, of course, the Cetraro will kill him."

"My lord will prevail and damn you for a doubting Norman fox,"
Gerth burst out.

"But should he fall, what then, Saxon?"

"Why, I will take service in Sir Hugues' company." He said nothing

concerning his resolve to restore the house of Ordway's lost glory
and to conquer a fief of his own equaling those broad lands lost at
Hastings.

Before a pair of candles guttering on the altar of Castel Sanseverino's bleak little chapel Sir Edmund de Montgomerie groaned.
His knees had begun to ache intolerably as well they might at the
end of so long a vigil upon a stone floor. Two hours had he spent
imploring the Virgin and St. Michael to strengthen his arm.

Wind, sighing through a narrow and glassless window, extinguished one of the candles flickering before a fine old Byzantine
crucifix of gilded silver and a battered monstrance displaying the
black and withered thumb of some local saint.

Indeed, the barren chapel was of a piece with the utter lack of
comfort prevailing in this typical Norman stronghold. From what Edmund thus far had observed only the bare bones of Calabria, that
once-rich and populous Roman province, remained, thanks to recur-
rent plagues, earthquakes and ceaseless ravaging.

During the recitation of a final *Pater Noster* Edmund de Montgomerie remained with head bowed and hands clasped before his
Crusader's white surplice adorned by a Latin cross done in brilliant
red. All at once the suppliant became aware of a whispering of cloth
and, turning abruptly, he glimpsed Alixe de Bernay advancing amid
a graceful swirl of skirts and holding a lighted candle in either hand.

A step in her rear came Rosamund, by the candlelight lovely beyond belief in a stalwart, supple way. Beside her loomed Sir Hugues'
solid bulk. In silence the new worshipers knelt, bent their heads and
commenced to tell their rosaries.

While the four prayed, up from the courtyard drifted the voices
of villeins teasing serving wenches, the barking of dogs and, more
faintly, the resounding clang of some hammer upon an anvil.

At length the Lady Alixe arose, inquired softly, "You are now in a
state of grace?"

"Yes, my lady. The Father Angelo heard my confession. He departed whilst the third watch was being posted."

Sir Hugues grunted. "Your prayers, friend Edmund, should be
granted for 'tis cursed cold and uncomfortable amid the odor of sanc-
tity. Br-r-r! Let us onto the battlements until the bell summons us to
dine."

Narrowly Count Turgis' heir considered the Lady Rosamund's
brother and, to his surprise, noted an unfamiliar expression of seren-
ity dominating the usually turbulent former earl's ruddy countenance.

Never, mused Hugues de Bernay, had this girl from beyond the seas appeared more lovely than wearing this light-blue mantle above which swayed her waist-long hair. Bound with blue cloth, her braids glistened in the candlelight as if fashioned from pure red gold. The simple chaplet of Spring flowers gracing her brow seemed as if fashioned from jewels and silver. Verily, here was a demoiselle who really personified that purity and nobility of character which belted knights were sworn to defend—to the death if need be.

Upon a twilit curtain wall of Castel Sanseverino the four strolled awaiting a summons to the evening repast and admired shadows among the surrounding hills. All at once Rosamund halted, raised her hand. Then they all heard an ominous sound in the distance. On the exercise meadow jackmen were hammering into the ground rows of stakes designed to mark the limits of a rectangle which would constitute the lists for tomorrow's *combat à l'outrance*. Each blow of these axes sent a small shiver of apprehension to stab the heart of Alixe de Bernay. If only it could be anyone save the Wild Boar of Cetraro he must meet!

In the twilight Rosamund paused to let Alixe and her brother saunter on then peered up into Sir Hugues' blunt and squarish features. "In our prayers my lord brother and I forever will remember your generosity in lending him arms and a mount in his hour of need."

"I crave not your prayers, dearest lady, but you, rather." Hugues seized a cool and slim hand then, dropping onto one knee pressed his lips upon it during a long instant.

"But that, Sir Hugues—even if I wished it, would not be possible. Your revered father would never——"

"Should my sire refuse to accept you *sans* dowry, then, by the Splendor of God, my sword will win a great one for you!" The young Italian-Norman almost glared upwards and spoke in a voice thickened by intensity. "Oh, fairest Rosamund within a month I will conquer for you a fief and from this same Lombard swine your brother battles tomorrow. Upon our wedding day it shall be added to our County."

"You honor me far beyond my humble deserts, gentle sir, but do you not forget something?"

"How is that?"

"How could you conquer me a fief, Sir Hugues, when you have sworn to depart upon the Voyage of God?"

"A pox upon the Crusade," cried he bitterly. "Your beauty is so wondrous I had clean forgotten my Cross Bearer's oath. I—I will——"

"You will depart with Duke Bohemund, else I should hold you in no esteem whatsoever."

"But, Rosamund, Fair One, I can think of naught but you."

"You must, Sir Knight—in all honor you must! Later perhaps we will talk of winning a fief."

She turned away to place fingertips upon the parapet then raised eyes to the donjon about the summit of which belated rooks were circling and uttering their raucous cries.

"How many men think you, Messire, will follow the banner of Sanseverino on this Voyage of God?"

"Not less than a hundred well-armed knights, serjeants and men-of-arms and perhaps twice as many axe and pike-bearing villeins." The young Italian-Norman's heavy blond brows contracted. "A sorry business, this calling upon the rabble."

"And why? Have they not a right to win salvation?"

"St. John alone knows how many of my father's farms will go untilled, how many a rich field will lie fallow because a swarm of stupid, untrained louts have listened too well to Brother Ordericus' promises of salvation—and loot." He frowned down upon the courtyard. "Already the common sort on all the great domains hereabouts abandon their holdings to swarm like locusts over the countryside, purposeless and leaderless."

"Then Crusaders already are commencing to collect?"

"Aye. Only yesterday a friar from the monastery at Capua told Father Angelo that huge armies of Cross Bearers are gathering beyond certain mountains known as Alps." He seemed to be suffering from an inner struggle. His voice sounded taut, strained.

"Where?"

"The friar could say nothing concerning the names of these far countries or of their sovereigns. If he and other travelers are not great liars then all Christendom will be marching toward Byzantium ere snow flies."

"Byzantium!" Rosamund arched brows in surprise. "But is not Jerusalem your goal?"

Irritably Sir Hugues ran blunt fingers through shoulder-long brown hair. "It is, my lady, but before advancing the Christian armies must join together. Byzantium, or Constantinople, as some call it, is the proper place, so says Sir Toustain. He having long served the East Roman Emperors should know whereof he speaks.

"Dear my lady," young Sir Hugues' broad features became taut. "I have a suggestion I beg you to consider well."

"Of course. I should be less than courteous not to do so. Pray speak out."

"Will you ride with me on this Journey of God?" he pleaded. "Nay, do not look so astonished; it is said many gentle women have sworn to undertake this pilgrimage not only to save their souls but also as a comfort to their husbands."

Rosamund's fine eyes became ringed in white as she fell back a step. "'Husband'? Did you say? Has your sire heard you speak in such a vein?"

Unhappily, the future Count of Sanseverino's gaze sought the small orchards and fields below, verdant and flowering with Spring. "Nay, dear my lady. To him I have as yet vouchsafed nothing concerning the depth of my love for you."

"Nor had you better, Sir Hugues, for all that I hold you fine and upright. Consideration of a betrothal now is out of the question."

The strong oval of the girl's features gleamed faintly as she spoke.

"Yet," Hugues' voice deepened and his big jaw hardened, "you I *must and will have* and soon. Since first you came to Sanseverino your grace and loveliness have tormented my dreams."

Intently Rosamund peered at him through the dusk. "And what do you mean? Did I not deem you a valiant and an honorable knight I might become alarmed. One thing must never chance—that on my account you should defy your sire who has been so generous to my brother and me."

"My sire is ambitious and grasping beyond reason," growled Hugues looking aside. "Even now he plots to expand his domain into a principality. 'Twill be easy enough should your brother slay the Wild Boar." He loomed close and beating one fist against its mate, said, "Pledge me your heart, sweet Rosamund, and I will find a way for us."

"No. You must find patience, my lord," she reminded in a soft voice. "Remember much remains to be done ere you depart upon the Voyage of God so I beg you not to dwell overly upon your attachment for me."

"'Attachment'?" Hugues burst out. "I adore you—love you past all expression. Once this war against the Infidel is won you shall return to become Countess of Sanseverino and that within a few months. These Turks, no matter what old one-eyed Toustain claims, will never prove a match for Frankish chivalry!"

"A few months?" The alluring outline of Rosamund's lips parted. "Tell me, my lord, how long must you march ere you arrive before Jerusalem?"

Impatiently he shrugged. "A few weeks, two or three months at the most. We shall of course carry the Holy City by storm at once."

"Why so sure?"

"Did not Brother Ordericus promise that the Heavenly legions will fight on our side?"

"Yes, but all the same, would it not be wise to ready yourself against a long and difficult campaign?" Quietly Rosamund gathered her mantle. "Now my lord, shall we repair to the dining hall?"

She had started along the battlements above which numbers of bats had begun to flit on silent silken wings when Hugues de Bernay's hand closed over her wrist. Into his expression became written a sudden and violent suspicion, entirely characteristic of the Norman race.

"Do you put me off for the sake of another?"

"Release my wrist," Rosamund commanded coldly. "You demean yourself."

Hugues shook his big head and did not relax his grip. "Ha! So that is it! Often have I seen you and my brother, Robert, together. You even have sung to please that unwashed cub!"

In a sudden, surprisingly strong motion Rosamund freed her wrist. "Even were it so, I would not tell you. Step aside, my lord, the evening grows chill." Lifting her skirts she sped away and never once paused to heed Sir Hugues' breathless apologies.

Meanwhile, further along the parapet and on a spot not readily visible to sentinels the Lady Alixe halted with the fading sunset tingeing her ash-blonde tresses a dusky rose and pointed to the north.

"In that direction lie the holdings of your enemy." She commenced softly to laugh. "Merciful St. Mary! Will I ever forget the Wild Boar's expression when you seized his snout and tweaked it? Oh, Edmund, if only you could as easily win his barony."

The Anglo-Norman's hands spread themselves in a gesture of helplessness. "But how, my lady? For retainers what have I left? Only a single esquire and I cannot feed or arm even him."

Alixe pressed close and clasped his arm. Lord! How corded with muscle it was. Why, 'twas larger in circumference than the thigh of one of those miserable villeins who prostrated themselves whenever she rode over her sire's domain.

"Fear not. Soon you will win a holding either through hard fighting or the use of guile. That is how fortunes have been won hereabouts ever since the first Normans appeared as pilgrims. Being hired at first to defend various fiefs, they lingered and soon made themselves masters over them."

Alixe's light manner abruptly departed and her full lips quivered. "Oh, Edmund! Edmund! When you enter the lists I shall die a thousand deaths. Indeed, I shall pray for your success as I have never prayed before."

"And do you really fear for me? Why?" Edmund peered intently into features warmed by the afterglow from the usual pallor.

Spasmodically Alixe's fingers tightened over his forearm. "Had you but your own sword, mace and shield I would not be so distraught for I know that your strength and skill far surpasses that of ordinary men."

"Why say you that?"

"I would not be Count Turgis' daughter were I not able to tell whether a weapon is deftly wielded or a destrier well ridden." Her voice continued musical and thrilling as a low note played on a viola. "Many a time and oft I have seen you continue to swing a weighted sword after the strongest of our knights were forced to pause. I have watched you and your armiger toss great stones about as though they were pebbles."

"I shall do my utmost," he assured with a shy smile. "First, because I fight to sustain the good name of a fair and virtuous damsel. Second, because this Cetraro's manners are not those of a gentle man. Third, I would despise to lose the mail, horse and weapons your brother so generously has lent to me."

Alixe's great blue eyes flew wide open. "Horse? But—but me-thought you were to fight on foot!"

"And so we do, fair Alixe. Sir Hugues was right in insisting that I should not, against so formidable a foeman, risk fighting astride an unfamiliar destrier. But although we fight on foot, your brother's destrier remains at hazard, all the same." He moved closer, shielding Alixe within his mantle against a chill breeze beginning to beat down from the Apennines. "Last of all, my lovely lady, I have not the least desire to die on the morrow—too much remains for my accomplishment."

"Accomplishment?"

"Yes. Where the Infidels' lands may lie I have no idea," he admitted, "I know nothing of how warfare is waged out there on the Rim of the World but Sir Toustain declares it is vastly different from our mode of doing battle." The Anglo-Norman's huge frame seemed to expand against the evening sky. "Yet I swear this, dear my lady; somehow I shall find money and so raise a company which I shall lead to the rescue of Christ's Holy Sepulchre. Then, when our Saviour's banner floats once more above Jerusalem, I shall conquer from the Infidels a rich and fruitful domain for me and my heirs to come!"

Hesitantly her fingertips brushed the broad back of his hand. "You *will* accomplish all of this!" she cried softly. "In my heart I am certain

of it." She sighed, then turned to view the plain below where campfires in Cetraro's encampment were commencing to glow.

Silently, he reviewed varied items of information gleaned concerning his enemy's style of combat and knew that, beyond a doubt, he
was to engage an adversary far more dangerous than any he had
previously encountered. No longer could he be confident that his
own extraordinary strength would assure victory. What worried him
most was young Gerth's increasing and ill-concealed concern after
he had mingled with armigers from the Baron's camp and had
picked up tales concerning the Wild Boar's amazing powers of endurance and the fact that he could fight equally well with either hand!

It was just as well, brooded Edmund de Montgomerie, that tomorrow's *combat à l'outrance* would commence, at least, with the sword.
As for mace-play, he had no intention of permitting the contest to
continue until their use became unavoidable. The sword ever had
been his favorite arm, for all that he was reckoned equally proficient
with the lance.

He was recalled to the present by the pressure of Alixe de Bernay's
fingers. "I know naught of what you ponder, dear my lord, but know
this: should you fall tomorrow, which God forbid, I—I swear upon
the Rood I will spend the rest of my life in a nunnery."

His hand closed over hers and his harsh expression softened. "Say
not so. Many knights are more worthy of you than I."

"Nay, my lord, I am fixed in my intent," she insisted, then, before
he could divine her purpose, she slipped an arm around his neck and
in passionate intensity pressed her lips against his. "All night I will
pray, my lord, not only that you rid us of Drogo but that you survive,
able to ride against the Infidels and—that you will return to t-take me
to w-wife."

Alixe fled ghost-like along the battlement past a pikeman who had
appeared to stand, statue-still with the starlight drawing pale lights
from his pointed cap of steel.

CHAPTER XIV

À l'Outrance

The day, which promised to be a fine one, lacked a half hour
to sunrise when ironshod feet advanced down the corridor towards
that ill-furnished cubicle in which rested the former Earl of Arundel.
The Anglo-Norman lay stretched, wide-eyed, upon a pallet with fingers locked behind head and staring unseeingly at a series of rough-

hewn roof beams. Might this prove to be the last dawn he ever would
behold brighten? Or would he today take a first long stride towards
restoring the de Montgomerie fortunes?

In tramped young Sir Robert, armed cap-à-pie. "You are indeed a
cool one. Cursed if I could sleep so sound were I about to engage
the Wild Boar *à l'outrance!*"

Edmund swung legs from beneath a wolfskin coverlet and stood
up, his undershift of coarse linen heavy with the perspiration of deep
sleep.

Next Gerth Ordway appeared bearing a wooden bowl of steaming
soup and a great slab of bread. Then Sir Hugues arrived looking uncommon grave and followed by a pair of esquires bent under the
weight of the equipment to be lent.

"Our sire wishes you well," Sir Hugues reported, broad red-brown
features relaxing. "Also he bids me say that should you rid the countryside of this Lombard swine he will bestow upon you the fief of
Lucano—a small property, to be sure, yet it boasts a strong tower
and two prosperous villages."

"My earnest thanks to your most noble and generous sire," returned Edmund then, having drained the soup at two gulps he bent
forward and permitted Gerth to slip on a padded leather jacket to
be worn beneath the hauberk. Next he donned leggings of chain mail
which extended to his ankles.

In oily, gleaming gray-blue folds Sir Hugues' second-best hauberk
was brought forward by Rainulf. He would have assisted the champion in donning it but Gerth would have none of that.

"I, and no one else, arm my lord for combat," he growled and
eased on the shirt of knee-length mail which, to admit freedom of
movement, had been slit up nearly thigh-high on either side.

To the Anglo-Norman it felt infinitely reassuring once more to feel
those familiar twenty pounds of iron mesh dragging at his shoulders
and he grinned broadly when iron-toed shoes were lashed upon his
feet and a pair of gilded, long-shanked spurs buckled over them.

"Tighter, Gerth, tighter still!" he ordered while a broad, nailhead-
studded swordbelt was being secured. "I would not have my scabbard slew about and so trip me before a foe so formidable."

"St. Michael and St. Olav will aid you to conquer, my lord," Gerth
kept mumbling. "You will lay this Wild Boar low, even as you did
the giant Dane on the Isle of Wight."

Sir Robert then beckoned forward his esquire and offered a surcoat of pale blue linen. "My lady sister sends this and begs that you
wear it in her favor."

Uncommonly serious of mien the gentle men of Sanseverino

crowded about making certain that the borrowed mail fitted with
no hampering wrinkles.

"Methinks, young Ordway, you might trim your master's hair
somewhat shorter," Sir Hugues suggested. "At this length it will pull
and overheat him beneath his coif."

"You had best try to finish off the Lombard with your sword," advised Sir Toustain.

"Aye," agreed the Captain of the Guard, " 'tis reported that with
the mace this Drogo is supreme—remember also, my lord, that he can
wield weapons equally well with either hand."

Presently to the ringing tramp of steelshod hooves, the party
from Sanseverino rode out from the gate in full armor. The usual
coarse jokes and predictions were made, guffaws of deep-throated
laughter rang up to the ladies gathered anxious and excited upon the
barbican. All the riders carried lances topped by brightly-colored
pennons, and all wore long Norman swords slung ready for use—
full many a single combat had degenerated into a wild and general
mêlée. Those warriors in the pointed helms and nasals who did not
favor battle-axes, instead carried maces dangling from brass-studded
belts.

It was a grim, hard-bitten company that rode slowly down towards
the exercise meadow; there were no bright streaming plumes, no
billowing caparisons on the horses or ornate surcoats decorating the
riders. It was a company of tough, entirely practical soldiers intent
upon the deadly business at hand.

Sir Toustain, his one eye bright in the morning sun, rode at Edmund's left, Sir Hugues at his right.

"So long as your enemy fights with shield," the veteran was saying,
"little perfidy can be attempted by him but once he casts aside his
buckler and so finds both hands free—beware!"

Word of the impending *combat à l'outrance* indeed must have traveled fast and far for already about the lists milled a dark swarm of
onlookers. Present was the entire garrison of Castel Sanseverino saving a few invalids left to guard the gate and, of course, every soul in
Baron Drogo's retinue. Standing awkwardly about were also numbers
of brown-faced farmers and shepherds in woolly capes and wearing
round, pointed hats such as had been seen in the region for a thousand years and more. Various local knights and *prud'hommes* and
their womenfolk had ridden in, accompanied by throngs of shaggy,
ill-fed villeins who with their dogs plodded patiently along through
dust raised by their masters' horses.

Edmund alert and icily composed noted that a breeze was beating
up from the south strongly enough to set weather-faded pennons

and gonfanons to tossing. Um. A point to be remembered. Clumps of spear points twinkled at either entrance to the lists.

Count Turgis, although cursing sulphurously all the while had allowed himself to be fetched down from his castle in a horse-litter. Collected about it in a steel-clad knot stood the Count's foremost retainers, men who had ridden into many a battle at his side.

Together with Sanseverino's other gentle women, Alixe and Rosamund gathered on the barbican to watch from afar the impending duel. Rosamund's lips, full and richly red, compressed themselves when she distinguished her twin's tall figure dismounting at the lists' western entrance. Against the brilliant green Spring grass his azure-blue surcoat was not nearly so recognizable as the scarlet one, which, as was required of a challenger, was worn by Drogo of Cetraro.

An unfamiliar queasy sensation manifested itself in Rosamund's stomach. Why should she, despite herself, feel so unnerved on viewing yonder scarlet surcoat?

Above this crowded meadow pigeons out of Sanseverino Mercato's lofts wheeled and frolicked on flashing wings and, at a little distance, a skylark hovered, and sang its throat out in blithe disregard of the violence about to take place so far below.

His nerves yet under control Edmund bent to allow a close-fitting coif to be pulled over his head and thrilled to the sensation of those cool, well-oiled links pressing against his brow, neck and cheeks. Finally Gerth passed him a heavy helm complete with noseguard which because of dents in its surface must have seen considerable service.

"Best discard your scabbard," Sir Toustain advised in an undertone from amid a ring of scarred, red-brown faces crowding about the Anglo-Norman. " 'Tis heavy and of no use in this business."

Wide-set blue eyes gleaming, Gerth produced that mace over which he had toiled so diligently. Its grip now was wrapped in rawhide and a stout thong had been looped through a ringlet let into its butt. The wide hook he had added glistened evilly when the former earl flexed muscles by several times swinging this ponderous metal cudgel about his head. Eventually he suspended the weapon from his belt.

Sir Hugues, sweating with anxiety, presented a sword with heavy brass guards projecting at right angles above the handle. Although heavier than most such arms it lacked by at least three pounds the deadly weight of "Brainbiter." The blade, however, appeared stout enough and was counterbalanced by a big knob of iron on its tang. This was reputed to enclose the toenail of a certain St. Anselmo.

Finally girt and armed Sir Edmund de Montgomerie glanced
across the lists and noted his enemy similarly surrounded by knights
and esquires. How brilliantly the Lombard's surcoat blazed among
them. Cetraro's sable locks, beard and mustaches showed up sharply
until he donned coif and helm.

Sternly suppressing a sudden uneasiness Edmund looked steadily
about. Oh to see one familiar face besides Gerth's—Henry's, Hubert's, Osric's, Ralph's, any of those youths he had known as fellow
bachelors, armigers and young knights. Never had he felt so alone.
All the same, with God's help he would show these foreigners what a
champion Arundel could produce. Oddly enough he recalled his father recounting adventures as a knight-errant among the Burgundians, a savage race inhabiting the lands somewhere to the south of
Normandy. Well, old Sir Roger could never have been in more foreign surroundings than his son at this moment.

Praise God, very soon now the issue must become joined. Apparently today there was to be no fanfare preceding the combat, no
shaking of lances or brave caracoling of destriers. Now were any
ladies present to wave scarfs and shrill encouragements.

The lists, Edmund noted with satisfaction, was a green and level
square of turf approximately thirty feet on each side and enclosed by
close-set stakes of raw yellow wood. He drew a deep breath to quiet
a sudden pounding of his heart and glanced up to the ugly gray mass
of Castel Sanseverino.

From its battlements Rosamund and the Lady Alixe must be
watching. What were Alixe's thoughts now that the "Moment of
Truth" was at hand? On impulse he pointed his sword at the distant
stronghold then gravely kissed its crossguard.

Upon Count Turgis' signal a trumpeter raised the oliphant of Sanseverino and sounded such an ear-piercing blast that badly-trained
chargers snorted and reared, but made destriers paid no attention.

Once the oliphant's notes died away the knights attending Edmund hurriedly remounted and grabbed lances held ready by their
esquires. If this duel degenerated into a mêlée they intended, most
joyfully, to participate therein.

In many weeks Edmund had not felt so alive as when he saluted
Count Turgis and strode boldly into the enclosure with Alixe's azure-
blue present flapping about his knees. His shield's guige dragged re-
assuringly at his left shoulder.

A ringing shout arose when, stalking towards him behind a highly
polished shield adorned by a big *umbo* or brass boss at its center,
appeared Baron Drogo of Cetraro.

The Lombard's equipment, Gerth noted in an agony of apprehension, was identical with that of his master save that the former was carrying a heavy leather wallet suspended from his belt. What was its purpose? From the swarming mass of onlookers swelled a cry of intolerable excitement while the distance separating the scarlet and the blue-clad champions steadily diminished.

Exultantly Baron Drogo flourished his sword then raised his battle cry of, "Cetraro! À Cetraro!" Edmund shouted, "St. Michael for Montgomerie!" and commenced cautiously to trot towards his enemy. He judged himself to be not quite as heavily built as the other but probably he would prove the fleeter of foot.

Dark eyes shining to either side of his nasal the Lombard halted to meet his enemy's advance then whirled up his blade in a glittering arc. Edmund's momentum, however, was such that, before the Lombard could strike, the former earl raised his shield, sprang inside the blow and jabbed viciously, but without effect at his antagonist's face.

A breathless yell arose when, leaping backwards, the Lombard landed so terrific a blow that his blade sank deep into the upper rim of Edmund's iron-faced wooden shield. The Anglo-Norman countered savagely and he in scarlet emitted a startled grunt and fell back a step on realizing that his enemy's blade had cut in halves the *umbo* of his shield.

For Edmund the world became centered in Cetraro's gleaming, dark blue eyes and the small red oval of face left visible by a tight-drawn coif.

Edmund misjudged the Lombard's agility for, almost before he was aware of it, the other came leaping in again with sword upraised.

"And now—foreign fool!" Cetraro delivered a whistling cut which Edmund barely succeeded in parrying. The shock however caused the Anglo-Norman's sword arm to tingle as if it had been "asleep." The rasping, snarling clang of blade countering blade sounded loud over the meadow while the silent crowds watched in rapt attention.

Matters progressed evenly until Edmund's iron-shod foot lost purchase on an extra lush patch of grass and he slipped onto one knee. Instantly he in the scarlet surcoat emitted a hoarse bellow and surged forward to capitalize upon the mischance.

The Anglo-Norman's long shield rose barely in time to deflect what should have been a finishing blow. Staggered by the impact and with his shoulder pierced by shooting pains, nonetheless he rose, again leaped inside Drogo's next blow and jabbed under the Lombard's shield. This time Edmund felt encouraged. His swordpoint had jarred strongly enough against the other's chest to cause him to gasp and fall back, panting like a hard-run hound.

The Lombard charged again this time slashing horizontally. Edmund in turning to meet these cuts again went momentarily off-balance. A second stroke instantly delivered by Cetraro, now scarlet of face and panting loudly, slewed the Anglo-Norman's shield about so violently that its upper brace broke and it no longer could be balanced evenly upon his arm.

"Drop your buckler! Rid yourself of it!" Sir Toustain shouted over the crowd's clamor. Obviously, this was what must be done, if it could be managed without fatal consequences. Edmund therefore retreated slowly across the lists parrying a flurry of blows and attempting to discard his hampering shield.

When he in blue seemed to take flight with mace bumping awkwardly at his side jeers and piercing whistles broke out among the men of Cetraro.

"Stand, sirrah!" panted the Wild Boar, features now bright with sweat. Flecks of foam-like spittle burst from his lips to speckle his beard and dangling mustaches.

Eventually Edmund managed to disencumber himself then, raising his war cry, he gripped Hugues' sword in both hands and attacked but he moved not so rapidly as before because his breath came only in brief, searing gasps and perspiration was flowing so freely under his leather lined coif that it threatened to obscure his vision.

He landed a double-handed blow upon Cetraro's shield with such force that the big Lombard reeled back, palpably shaken and destriers lining the lists commenced to snort and paw the ground at this familiar clatter and clang of arms. Lances swaying violently the riders cursed and reined hard in attempting to restrain their mounts.

Fortunately Drogo proved slow to perceive the greater mobility gained by his enemy through discarding his shield. Gripped in both hands his adversary's weapon had become deadlier and was far more easily managed.

Sanseverino's men raised a ringing shout when a terrific slash delivered by their gigantic champion split Drogo's shield half its length and tore away its upper grip. The Lombard experienced none of Edmund's difficulty in ridding himself of his buckler.

At that moment came sorely needed encouragement as Gerth shouted, "St. Michael for Montgomerie!" and lent him reassurance that he did not fight alone in this foreign place.

In unrelenting ferocity tinged with new-won respect the combatants circled about the level turf slashing, stabbing and hacking at each other like tireless automatons. Brown faces lining the lists grew taut in anticipation of a decisive exchange. Mounted onlookers leaned far over their pommels tensely noting every cut and parry while villeins and jackmen yelled themselves hoarse in an ecstasy of excitement.

Sir Toustain on casting Gerth a questioning glance, perceived the young Saxon to have gone pale beneath his tan. "Surely my lord should have prevailed ere now," he muttered.

"Cetraro tires," warned the veteran. "Warn your lord he had best be on guard for a trick."

"He will be wary, my lord." The armiger nodded but began to finger that short-handled axe he could hurl with such deadly accuracy.

Shaken and wearied as never before, the former earl fought doggedly, skillfully. Such a duel should have ended long since with his enemy lying dead or pleading on his knees to be spared against ransom. Now breath came whistling in between his teeth and sweat in sticky rivulets was coursing down his arms and into the iron mittens, rendering treacherous his grip upon the sword handle.

Gradually the appalling realization arrived that this Lombard was tireless. Certainly his blows were becoming increasingly difficult to parry while his own arm muscles were commencing to burn and quiver.

Alixe, meanwhile knelt ashen-faced upon the barbican, sobbing promises of lavish votive offerings to Michael, Edmund's patron saint, if only her champion might prevail. As for Rosamund, she leaned as far out over the rampart as she could, lips compressed into a straight and bloodless line. Intently she followed on that green square amid the dark mass of onlookers the movements of those tiny red and blue figures maneuvering so far below.

"Oh, dear Lord—have mercy on them both!" she panted.

The Lombard had completed a series of slashes delivered in swift succession—cuts which called upon all Edmund's skill and strength to ward off—when Drogo suddenly shifted his sword to the left hand and retreated, at the same time fumbling at that heavy pouch suspended to his belt.

But for a sudden shout of warning from Sir Toustain, Edmund de Montgomerie would then have been undone.

"Stoop! Shut eyes!" yelled the one-eyed veteran. Edmund, readying himself for a final rally, saw the sky darken immediately before his eyes. Even as he bent over and slewed sidewise in desperate haste, myriad hard particles stung his cheek. As it was enough grains of sand penetrated between his lids instantly to cause stinging, blinding tears to form. But for Sir Toustain's warning he would have been blinded, an easy victim for the Lombard's trenchant blade.

He leaped back frantically attempting to dash away the tears. His mittens' iron links rasped at his brow but he managed to clear his vision sufficiently to permit glimpsing a row of stakes looming close behind him.

Fury over the trick surged into his being, restored a deal of strength to his arms and a measure of agility to his legs. All the same, experience warned that, until he could indeed see his enemy more clearly, his best chance was to crowd in upon him so, bracing a foot against the palings he lunged forward as the other, emitting a choking cry, whirled up his blade for a quietus. While Edmund parried he felt his wrists jerk oddly then heard a startled yell rise from Sanseverino's partisans. Not a soul among them but had watched the foreign knight's sword break halfway down its blade.

A yell of triumph escaped Drogo but faded as his tall enemy, helm flashing in the clear sunlight, charged like a maddened bull jabbing with the jagged stump of his weapon. His target was that small area of the Lombard's face left unprotected by his coif.

Drogo perforce yielded ground as Edmund struck repeatedly with his shortened weapon until, catching the Lombard's sword just above its guard, by strength alone he tore the weapon from Cetraro's grasp and sent it spinning high out of the lists.

"Mace, my lord! Your mace!" Gerth's voice called out in an agony of suspense.

If the scarlet-clad champion was dismayed by this sudden reverse he betrayed no evidence of it; instead he emitted a bellow of rage and circled, brandishing a ponderous mace equipped with a cinquefoil head.

When the two lashed out again with seemingly undiminished vigor Sir Hugues and Sir Toustain exchanged glances. Both were aware that should either man's weapon land fairly then the other's helm would be cracked and his brains spattered over the trampled turf. At best the loser's arm or shoulder would be smashed into perpetual uselessness.

At this moment Edmund yearned for his shield. He knew himself to be by no means as proficient with a mace as with sword or lance so in desperation he maneuvered to avert a sweeping impact from the Lombard's iron club. Would that he had better heeded warnings from the old Seneschal of Dover that if sheer strength were to be the measure of combat, a mace was best.

Oblivious to the crowd's continuous clamor the figures in the fluttering blue and red surcoats exchanged a succession of furious blows and counter-blows which brought only the shafts of their maces into contact and caused a dull clatter. Jeers arose from among the

Northerners when Edmund, now sickeningly aware that he must win quickly or not at all, feigned partial helplessness following a particularly savage interchange and reeled backwards.

Half blinded by sand and sweat, he ducked beneath a murderous blow, then spun sidewise and darted past his enemy. Once behind Cetraro the Anglo-Norman whirled and instantly drove the hook on his mace among links of the coif protecting the Lombard's neck.

Muscles a-crackle, Edmund heaved mightily and succeeded in pulling his enemy over backwards. As he struggled to rise, the former earl dealt a glancing blow on the other's helm but it proved shrewd enough to knock Drogo flat once more. The Lombard lay supine, limbs quivering like those of an ox stunned by a butcher's poleaxe.

Tumult rent the air as, drawing breath in painful, shuddering gasps, Edmund knelt upon his enemy's chest and leveled his dagger at the other's mouth.

"Slay him!" implored Gerth. "Slay the foul-mouthed swine!"

"Slay him!" howled the Sanseverino men and at the same time readied their weapons as the Lombard's followers began to shoulder shields and close up together.

To Edmund's great surprise Drogo had not been knocked completely unconscious. Although his bloodshot eyes appeared fixed and unseeing he managed to croak, "Mercy—lord—grant me grace!"

"You—admit—l-lied? You c-crave—la-lady's p-pardon?"

The Lombard's dark eyes rolled wildly as the dagger's point gleamed before them. "Aye, Sir Edmund—d-do not s-slay me—beseech you. I too—f-full of sin—d-die."

Through stinging sweat Edmund glanced at that point where Count Turgis' litter stood guarded by his two tall sons and noted the Cross flaming upon Sir Hugues' chest. "Your l-life I—will spare— one c-condition."

"Name it!" gurgled the prostrate champion.

"Swear—undertake—Voyage of—of God—and abide by—Crusader's oath!"

"As G-God is my judge, I—I will," choked the fallen knight.

Swaying, his head yet ringing like a hard-used anvil Edmund paused, staring down at the huge mail-sheathed body at his feet.

Edmund de Montgomerie only dimly was aware of bile in his mouth and of iron-clad men invading the lists from all directions, then, to an oliphant's imperious blast, everyone on the scene halted and their heads snapped about. In the moment of exchanging grips with Sir Hugues Edmund watched that individual's expression alter.

"*Par Dex!* Bohemund fitzTancred is here."

Men of both parties paused to gaze upon a small party of splendidly accoutred knights who had approached, unobserved, during the heat of the duel.

Sir Robert after tugging off his helm bowed deeply in his saddle while dismounted knights and serjeants fell onto their knees as into the enclosure rode a massive individual in a surcoat of scarlet and black velvet. Quite aside from his gorgeous attire this new arrival with the flaming red hair presented the most impressive figure the former Earl of Arundel had ever beheld.

"Welcome to Sanseverino, my lord Duke!" Count Turgis was calling through the gilded leather curtains of his litter. "Thrice welcome. Would to God I had perceived your arrival or had been granted warning of it."

Bohemund, Duke of Otranto, laughing hugely urged a splendid gray destrier to the litter's side. "God's splendor, Turgis, my rare old pillager, what finer reception could you have accorded than a contest so manfully debated? By the gullet of God! This has been the daintiest bicker I have witnessed in much too long!"

Sir Hugues and his brother after dismounting hurried to kiss the Duke's broad and freckle-mottled hand.

"Our humble service to you as always, my lord," cried Sir Robert. "Pray forgive our seeming incivility."

"And why not?" boomed their broad-shouldered suzerain. "Not one of you would have noticed the approach of a band of angels. Turgis! Pray send instantly for yonder valiant knight who has acquitted himself so featly."

CHAPTER XV

Bohemund, Duke of Otranto I

His eyes still watering due to sand particles lodged under their lids Sir Edmund de Montgomerie blinked as he peered upward and beheld the burly bearded figure astride a very tall destrier.

At first glance the Anglo-Norman perceived Duke Bohemund's thick and curly hair to be of an even brighter red than his own and trimmed uncommon short—on a level with his ears. From beneath the brim of a flat hat of sky-blue leather quite small but piercingly blue eyes considered him. Quite unawed, Edmund nonetheless became unhappily conscious of his sweat-bathed countenance and that his hands yet were quivering violently from his exertions.

Bohemund, Duke of Otranto, was sitting very straight in his saddle, but easy all the same. His stomach was flat, his hips narrow and his waist appeared inadequate to support such massive shoulders and a neck so corded by muscle. About the Duke's mouth showed many good-humored lines interspaced however by others suggestive of cruelty.

"They tell me, Sir Knight, that you hail from a distant island called England?" Bohemund commented in crisp, yet guttural accents. "There are many English, I hear, in the pay of my dear enemy, Alexis of Romania. Who do you own to be your liege lord?"

Still struggling to level his breathing, Edmund explained that at the moment he owed allegiance to no one.

"A good thing, eh, your Grace?" The Duke glanced at a rotund figure wearing the habit, ring and gilded cross of a bishop. To Edmund's eye he much more suggested a warlike baron than a prelate of the Holy Church. "Sir Knight," Bohemund continued, "I fain would reward a most doughty warrior for in sooth seldom have I witnessed a combat more evenly or more bitterly contested." He beckoned an esquire. "Giles! Pray present this gentle man with a certain dagger to be found in my traveling hampers. 'Tis the Saracen poignard which bears an amethyst set into its pommel."

Duke Bohemund seized the victor's hand in a bear's grip then spurred over to confront Drogo of Cetraro who still dripping blood from his mouth was being supported by his esquire.

"*Par Dex!* If it is not Drogo, my lieutenant from the old days in Thessaly. I vow I had never thought to see *you* overcome like this."

Still partially dazed, the Lombard dropped heavily onto one knee and kissed Bohemund's thick hand. "My lord, how greatly do I lament that you of all persons should have witnessed this, my only downfall." He raised congested, bloodstained features and actually managed a smile. "Yet, sire, I own I was fairly overcome."

"Ah, say you so? Well, old comrade-in-arms, this meeting is indeed fortuitous since for some time I have been minded to visit the domain you hold in my name."

Humbly Baron Drogo inclined his head. "I trust my lord Duke has not received lying reports casting doubt upon Cetraro's loyalty?"

The Duke's wide, thin-lipped mouth tightened. "Perchance. 'Tis bruited about that, of late, you wage unlawful war upon neighbors who, like you, are *liegemen of mine!* And why have you failed to take the Cross, once I set the example?"

Drogo, dark eyes uneasily a-glitter to either side of his bloodsmeared nasal, evaded the first question. "Nay, my lord Duke. I *have* sworn to undertake this so-named Voyage of God."

"Aye, quite willingly"—came Sir Toustain's dry observation—"with this English knight's dagger at his gullet!"

"You have taken the Crusader's oath? Well, when or how is of no moment." Duke Bohemund collecting his reins, suddenly grinned. "Now mind you that you keep your oath, Cetraro, else I'll see you and your fine stronghold leveled with the dust!"

Drogo spat blood and then wiped his chin. "As in Greece, my lord, I will ever serve you loyally and to the limit of my powers."

Frenzied were the preparations in Castel Sanseverino, it being no slight matter suitably to entertain the dreaded suzerain of Campania, Apulia and Calabria. He and a half-brother, Roger, acrimoniously had divided dominions wrenched by their father, cruel old Robert Guiscard, from the crumbling power of Arabs, Byzantines and sundry Italian states.

When Duke Bohemund and his principal lords settled down to feast in Sanseverino's great room Baron Drogo was among them. Although visibly battered and limping, he appeared surprisingly cheerful and affable of manner.

Among Duke Bohemund's hard drinking and leather tough entourage were to be recognized such celebrated champions as the brothers Richard and Rainulf of the Principate, Count William of Apulia and Girard, that lusty, big-nosed Bishop of Ariano who could with his mace slay quite as many men as if he had been permitted the use of a sword, a weapon forbidden to all churchmen. This scion of an ancient house was, as Duke Bohemund dryly put it, a very practical cleric, believing as he did that when preaching failed the use of a mace generally carried conviction.

Under the stimulus of a third cup of spiced Malaga Bohemund fitzTancred's humor grew expansive and his sallies at Cetraro's expense more obscene. What emotions his late adversary might be experiencing defied analysis since that coarsely handsome individual's expression remained inscrutable.

Certainly St. Michael himself must have inspired that impulse to force Drogo into joining the Crusade? Yes, Edmund's patron saint must be thanked for he himself had certainly been too near exhaustion, too shaken by his escape from death, to have seen that by this maneuver he not only had won a formidable recruit to the Army of the Cross but also had secured Sanseverino against encroachment whilst its men were away in the Holy Land—wherever that blessed country might lie. Only survivors of foreign wars such as Duke Bohemund, Sir Toustain and Cetraro possessed even the vaguest notions as to the location of Jerusalem and differed considerably on that score.

Throughout the repast, Edmund remained uncommunicative, not through innate modesty—never a strong virtue in the Norman character—but because he still felt queasy and thick-headed, thanks to the impact of Drogo's mace shaft upon his helm. Further, his shoulder and arm continued to suffer stabbing pains resultant from that terrific blow which had damaged his shield.

Despite all this Edmund felt vastly pleased with life. Did he not now possess Drogo's gray warhorse, a magnificent beast reported to be thoroughly trained, to say nothing of an excellent hauberk and weapons of the finest quality? Alas that his impoverished state had rendered it impossible to wager money on the outcome of the combat! A chestful of solidi certainly would have proved useful in recruiting certain free-lance knights and other masterless soldiers for a company of his own leading.

A rather tough haunch of venison was being served when Duke Bohemund hammered upon the board until the Bishop of Ariano reluctantly pushed aside the well-heaped wooden bowl to which he had been applying himself.

"Silence, you greedy-guts!" Bohemund heaved himself to his feet, jewels flashed in a necklace slung over his *tunica* of dark green, a garment gracelessly copied from some ancient Roman's sarcophagus. The Duke's leonine head swung to include the whole company. "I would have you learn that I am determined my levées shall not assemble at Bari"—for a number of reasons everyone hung on his next words—"until the month of August is spent and the harvests are made."

Cheers arose. This matter of not assembling until after harvest time raised the spirits of landed knights and *prud'hommes* alike, the latter being fighting farmers who, through service in war, repaid their landlord for the use of his fields, forests and vineyards.

Duke Bohemund frowned. "You must know, my lords, it is reported that a great band *already* has departed for Jerusalem."

"Under whose leadership?" demanded Sir Hugues.

"That of a saintly and eloquent, but I fear ill-advised, old man who calls himself Peter the Hermit."

"Why 'ill-advised'?" Sir Toustain wanted to know.

The prelate shrugged. "Because this Hermit's following is no true army but is composed of rabble: knaves, thieves, cutpurses, mock priests, whores and a multitude of runaway serfs. Surrounding Peter the Hermit are few leaders having even a little experience in the arts of war. The best of these I am told is one called Walter the

Penniless, a poor Frankish knight without a fief or following of his own." Under the flickering flambeaux the entire company listened in rapt attention. "When last heard of this band was straggling like lost sheep toward Byzantium along a great river called the Danube, but I think precious few of the Hermit's flock will ever reach the Emperor Alexis' capital."

A buzz circulated the long tables. So some persons *actually had departed* on the Journey of God!

Duke Bohemund set straight on his huge red head a gilded fillet which, to some eyes, appeared dangerously suggestive of a kingly crown, and once more arose. "Listen and understand why my levée will be among the last to depart on the Voyage of God. Ours is the shortest route to Byzantium so we must, in order not to arrive ahead of the other armies of Christendom, delay our departure from Bari until the end of the month of September or early in October."

CHAPTER XVI

The Offer

Because the Duke of Otranto's escort was small and he was traveling in haste he elected to lodge in Castel Sanseverino rather than pitch a camp in which to receive reaffirmations of fealty from vassals in the vicinity.

Edmund soon ascertained the wherefore of this hurried tour about Campagna and also the real reason occasioning the delayed embarkation at Bari. Before departing on the Crusade Bohemund, ever suspicious, intended ruthlessly to weed out from among his vassals such lords as might acknowledge his brother, rather than himself, to be their suzerain.

Although grunting under the pain of his old wounds, Count Turgis set the example by kneeling and reavowing his fealty, then all day long scarred and rapacious Norman liegemen rode in from lean fiefs and lonely castles and up the hill into Castel Sanseverino. A majority of these already wore a scarlet cross upon their well-worn surcoats when they placed both hands between Bohemund's huge, sunburned paws and acknowledged him to be their undoubted lord and suzerain.

Smiling and forthright in his farewells Baron Drogo of Cetraro rendered homage then marshaled his followers and struck camp. It came as a surprise that when the dark-browed Lombard humbly begged pardon of the Lady Rosamund he kissed the hem of her skirt and vowed mighty deeds in her honor, for all that she gazed upon him in a cool and distant manner. Ever an astute observer, Sir Toustain noticed this and resolved to remain doubly wary; unless the Wild Boar had changed overnight someday Sanseverino would be forced dearly to pay for this humiliation. He had been crafty also in feigning a profound enthusiasm for the Crusade's purpose while, with rough jocularity, he had recalled anecdotes connected with his previous service under Bohemund's red banner. He even made bold to inquire Sir Robert's advice upon the treatment of a young warhorse which, badly kicked by a neighbor on the picket line, must be left behind for a space.

The same morning Baron Drogo rode off to his domain, Edmund de Montgomerie, exhausted and aching in every bone snored on and on. It was almost noontime when Gerth Ordway shook him, announced that the Lady Rosamund was becoming concerned over his non-appearance.

"Bid my lady sister be patient and say that I am as well as ever I will be." Nonetheless he winced because of sundry heavy bruises. After splashing water on his face, he drew on an under tunic and was about to comb his hair when light footsteps sounded beyond the coarse hangings dividing his sleeping place from the rest of this long and draughty hall. To his complete astonishment the Lady Alixe appeared, limpid blue eyes wide with anxiety. She hurried over anxiously eyeing a purplish welt raised between his eyes by the helm's noseguard.

At the sight of her, radiantly beautiful today in a close-fitting red gown which, tightly girdled, emphasized certain delectable curves, his heart lifted. A vision of cool loveliness, Alixe hesitated, illumined for a moment by a shaft of sunlight penetrating an arrow slit. Seen thus, she appeared as wondrously fair and pure as had angels he once had seen depicted upon certain parchments illuminated by the learned monks of Glastonbury Abbey.

Edmund remained immobile, feasting his eyes upon the flawless pallor of Alixe de Bernay's complexion, upon the silver-gold sheen of her tresses and upon the allure of lips provocatively curved and of a pink-rose hue.

"My humble service to you, my lady, but I had thought my sister—?"

"She has departed to the kitchens with your bear of an esquire, to ready a breakfast worthy of so famous a paladin." Alixe stepped out of the sunbeam, hands extended. "Oh, Edmund! Edmund! Never can you comprehend the depths of my pride in your victory."

"But, but truly, my sweet Alixe, I do not merit a concern so deep."

He felt annoyed because blood came welling into his cheeks. Why had not one of the maids at home, many of whom must be as fair or fairer than Count Turgis' daughter, ever set his heart to hammering like this?

"Why so serious of regard?" Alixe was demanding lightly. "Have you forgotten, dear my lord, that no longer are you landless?"

"Landless? But of course I am. That cursed Rufus holds all I ever owned."

She made a little *moue*. "Nay, through your victory you are now lord of Lucano. Alas that it is almost the poorest of my sire's holdings. Oh Edmund, how wondrous clever of you it was to spare Drogo of Cetraro. Now he must depart on the Journey of God and cannot attack Sanseverino until Jerusalem is won! By then we shall be ready for him, you and I."

Forgetful of his being unshaven and that his dark red hair yet was a tangle, Edmund dropped onto one knee and pressed her hand to his lips. "To you, Demoiselle de Bernay, do I dedicate now and forever my loyal service, my sword and my heart."

"Believe me, *mon preux chevalier*, a Summons to God's Paradise could find no sweeter reception in my heart." She raised him then entered his encompassing arms as easily and gracefully as a doe enters a thicket. As her lips experienced the hard, almost painful, pressure of his her body surged against him so ardently that he became transported by pressure of firmly soft breasts and thighs.

Footsteps advancing along that stone passageway which led to his cell-like quarters caused them to step apart, flushed and quivering.

"Let us say naught yet of our love," she whispered, radiant and smiling. "I must gain time to win my sire to our intent." She made a wry grimace. "If ever that is possible—my dearest love."

Bohemund fitzTancred drained a goblet of gilded silver in a single thirsty gulp at the same time bracing a dusty boot on his varlet's bottom that he might tug it off. His gaze, however, lingered upon Celeste, his favorite gerfalcon, which sleek bird sat perched upon her *pertica ima* or portable block calmly preening herself and viewing this convivial group from bright, sherry-hued eyes.

"Giles, you may remove her back bells," directed Bohemund, whereupon the Master Falconer untied a trio of tiny silver bells secured to the top of the gerfalcon's tail feathers. These had been placed there lest Celeste be tempted to rake away and resume hunting on her own account. As usual, the stately gerfalcon hissed a protest and snapped halfheartedly when the falconer gently slipped over her head and tied into place her *capella* or blindfolding hood gay with a nodding hackle of scarlet and black feathers.

"A memorable day's sport. Why is more game to be found about a poor countryside like this than in a fertile one?" queried Girard, Bishop of Ariano. Putting down his cup, the prelate wiped his mouth and removed from his left wrist, protected by a scarred and well-padded gauntlet, a very swift hawk of medium size called a hobby.

Everyone present was aware, of course, that, as a man of God this big, full-blooded man had no right to be flying such a bird. He should have used a sparrow hawk just as Duke Bohemund should have contented himself hunting with rock falcon—the noble gerfalcon being reserved to a king's use, just as an eagle should only be flown by an emperor. Possibly Bohemund had usurped this privilege because he never had admitted owning fealty to anyone save the Pope of Rome?

Sir Toustain, Rainulf of the Principate and the rest of these hard-featured gentle men had done their hawking with sakers and simple knights with ranner hawks.

Sir Toustain uttered one of his rare laughs. "Sir Hugues, my lord Duke will be long in forgiving the fashion your Celeste crabbed his bird away from that hare during the last flight."

In high good humor, Bohemund clapped Sir Hugues on the shoulder. "Tell me, who first named that hawk of yours a rock falcon? By the Nails of the Rood she's no more a rock falcon than is that hobby of Girard's. She's a syrena."

"A syrena, my lord?" demanded Sir Toustain, certainly the least practiced falconer crowding about the wine bowl. "And what might such be?"

The Duke's wind-disheveled red head swung about as, gripping a long loaf of bread between strong but irregular teeth he tore it in half. "A syrena, Sir Knight, is a hawk belonging to some species unknown to falconry." Chewing noisily the while, Bohemund strode over to his hooded bird to conduct a careful examination for minor hurts or broken feathers. On finding none, he chuckled, drawled, "Take her to the mews, Giles, and take His Grace of Ariano's chickadee as well. Make sure their *alimenta* is both fresh and sufficient."

In handing over his bird, the Bishop suppressed a curse. He loathed this having to fly a hawk inferior to a gerfalcon and silently vowed that once the Crusade penetrated Asia Minor he would fly any bird that suited his taste.

Goblet poised midway to his lips, Bohemund from under bushy eyebrows, shot the one-eyed veteran a speculative glance. "And what did the Count of Sanseverino say concerning your undertaking an embassy for me?"

The Constable's ruined features tightened in a mirthless grin. "Why, my lord, he ranted and cursed like a madman over losing his constable, but, of course, a vassal cannot deny the request of his suzerain."

"I regret his reluctance, however understandable, yet you, my lord of Dives, are the very one who must undertake the difficult and dangerous task of estimating the Emperor's true intent toward me." He winked at Sir Hugues and his rasping laugh rang out. "Somehow I doubt whether our ally, Alexis Comnene, truly has forgiven our storming of Corfu, Avlona and Durazzo—Crusade or no Crusade."

A snigger escaped Bishop Girard. "—Any more than you have truly forgiven Alexis' hiring the Venetians to aid his Turcopoles in driving you out of Castoria."

"God's wounds!" roared Bohemund, suddenly thunder-browed. "How dare you mention Castoria?"

Rainulf of the Principate moved forward, ready to interpose between the Duke and the highly-amused and quite unfrightened prelate.

"Was it my fault that our native levées ran like hares?" he bellowed, small, bright blue eyes dangerously a-glitter. "Take care, Girard! Do not count too heavily upon your cloth and tonsure!"

Sir Toustain's harsh voice interrupted. "My lord Duke, may I offer a suggestion?"

"Out with it! Don't goggle like a damned, one-eyed owl!"

"With your embassy to Byzantium in mind I bethink me of a gentle man at present in Sanseverino. He not only speaks and writes French and Latin well but also," the veteran paused for emphasis, "he has a wide, if imperfect, knowledge of the Greek tongue."

"Well? And what of that?" snorted Bohemund fitzTancred as the color ebbed from his cheeks.

"Have I need to remind you, my lord, that the air of Constantinople frequently proves fatal to—er, visitors, from unpopular principalities? Suppose that I, your only emissary, were to drink from a poisoned cup or nibble upon the wrong pomegranate at some Byzantine feast? Who then would remain to collect intelligence concerning the best route for your army to follow across Thrace?" He paused again. "Or to carry out certain other of your designs?"

"Humph! You have a point there." Bohemund eased his topheavy body backwards upon a rawhide chair. Its lashings creaked in protest. "Who is this fellow? Surely so clever a linguist cannot be gently born."

"My lord Duke, he is none other than the victor in yesterday's duel."

"The red-headed Englishman? Now God strike me dead had I deemed him educated sufficient to count up to fifty!" Bohemund's bright little eyes fixed the veteran like dagger points. "Is this indeed so?"

"As I stand here, my lord. However this foreigner is much ashamed of such ignoble and clerkly accomplishments."

"Hum-m-m. Even though I'll probably not dispatch him to Byzantium, he should prove useful on the march as a linguist." Bohemund flashed a singularly winning smile. "Go, bid him come immediately, friend Toustain, and accept my thanks."

So it came about that presently Sir Edmund de Montgomerie was roused from a reverie in which he and Alixe sauntered arm in arm through fields of fragrant, flower-filled grass and lingered beside a spirited, crystalline brook.

He stretched and sat up. "And how did the falcons fly? I would I had accompanied you. I dote upon the sport."

"Well enough. A dozen-odd duck and perhaps twice as many herons and hares were taken." The veteran's mangled features hardened. "My lord Duke would have an immediate word with you, which may lead greatly to your profit."

Duke Bohemund's blunt fingers strayed through his short auburn beard while with care he studied the huge and muscular figure standing erect before him. At length he drawled, "I hear that you are liege-free, Sir Edmund, and are therefore able to accept the offer I am about to make. That is so?"

"That is so, my lord Duke."

"First you must swear fealty to me. Then, if I so determine, you will accompany our wise, trusted and experienced friend, Sir Toustain, upon a delicate mission to Byzantium. There is need to repair—er—my relations with the Emperor." He fixed the Bishop of Ariano with a cold stare lest that worthy be tempted again to mention Castoria. "I must make *certain* of the reception I can expect once I arrive before the gates of Alexis Comnene's capital."

At Edmund's attempted interruption the Duke raised a broad hand. "I am aware that you lack wealth and therefore am prepared to see you enrolled among that gentle company which guards my personal banner in battle. As one of them you will share in the choicest spoils. I would further——"

"—Your Grace is in slight error," Edmund broke in. "Since last night I am no longer landless, but have become the seigneur of Lucano."

Bohemund burst into that snorting laugh so typical of him. "Lucano! You term that overgrown pigsty a fief? Now by God's

eternal glory, in my service you'll win fiefs richer by a hundredfold."
He frowned. "You have rendered homage to old Turgis?"

"Not yet, my lord."

"That is well. You are not bound to his service. Well, what say
you, Sir Knight?" A broad smile creased Bohemund's squarish visage,
disfigured here and there by small livid scars.

"Speak up," snapped prematurely bald Rainulf of the Principate.
"To my memory precious few young knights have been thus hon-
ored."

Edmund's gaze flickered from the Bishop of Ariano to Richard
of the Principate and thence to him whom he counted his closest
friend in this strange land, Sir Toustain. As he stood confronting
Bohemund the Mighty's massive figure a vision of Alixe de Bernay
interposed itself. Alixe! Surely, before the men of the Cross departed
for Bari, Count Turgis could be won to consent? After all, his prospective son-in-law was once more a landed gentle man, if only lord
of a fief small as Lucano? Swiftly he intended to enlarge that small
original holding as had Count Turgis and many another Norman adventurer.

"Come, come, young sir," prompted Girard of Ariano fingering a
big, gilt-silver Cross dangling over his habit of dull brown wool.
"Speak up! You are ill-advised to keep your liege lord in suspense."

Stiffly, Edmund bent his head in the Bishop's direction. "I crave
your Grace's pardon but the Duke of Otranto is not my liege lord."
He drew a deep breath and faced Bohemund's penetrating little
eyes. "While I thank you, my lord, for the undeserved honor you have
paid me, I do not intend to quit Sanseverino until its levée departs
on the Journey of God. Therefore, my lord Duke, I cannot accept
your most generous offer."

Bohemund's chair crashed over and his goblet flew across the
chamber spraying ruby drops far and wide. "What?" he roared. "Do
you, a miserable, masterless fugitive actually refuse a place in my
standard guard?"

The two red-headed men glared at each other a long moment then
in level tones Edmund insisted, "I do, my lord Duke, for reasons
sufficient unto my conscience. However I——" His voice became lost
amid a hubbub aroused by this unprecedented crossing of the Duke's
will.

Bohemund had entered into so dangerous a rage that esquires and
varlets hastily sought far corners. "Now God smite you for a stupid,
insolent fool! Sirrah, know you that this advancement I offered is
one which many a valiant captain has sought for years?"

The Duke's rage subsided as quickly as it had flared and turning to a bowl of walnuts he fell to cracking them between horny palms. "Bah! Get you gone from my sight, Englishman. 'Tis well I uncovered your doltishness in good season."

CHAPTER XVII

The Intruder

A half-gale beating up the Sanseverino valley was driving ragged ranks of rain clouds across the moon alternately plunging Edmund de Montgomerie's cubicle into gloom and then flooding it with a pristine radiance. A lovesick hound chained in the courtyard below mourned from time to time and further depressed the former Earl of Arundel as he lay sleepless upon a cot of thongs stretched over a rough wooden frame. Fixedly he stared at ceiling beams high above him.

How sweetly warm and solicitous had been Alixe's manner during their accustomed twilit stroll along the battlements. It was fine to see the castle returned to its normal routine now that both its turbulent guests had departed. Bohemund, in taking leave of the old Count, had given out his destination as the walled town of Potenza, about which he owned several important fiefs.

While he lay ruminating the Anglo-Norman speculated on whether Count Turgis' manner towards him really *had* altered since his victory in the *combat à l'outrance*. Was it imagination, or was the ailing Master of Sanseverino indeed according him a more favorable consideration? Certainly at supper this night he had been surprisingly gay and good humored.

Rosamund as usual had sat straight and reserved. Her manner had seemed abstracted, as if she were occupied with secret speculations. In fact she had little more than tasted her slab of cold veal pie and apparently was oblivious of Sir Hugues, frowning and hunched over his trencher as he stared steadily at her. Several times Hugues had sighed while picking his teeth with a forefinger.

Robert de Bernay also had gazed hungrily upon her healthily glowing countenance. He had kept shifting upon his bench and laughing a trifle loudly while tossing bones to a favorite hunting dog crouched beside him on the carpet of rushes.

When moonlight again flooded the cubicle Edmund shifted and raised his head to cast an eye at Gerth wrapped in a cloak and huddled on a mat barring the threshold—as became a well-trained armiger.

The young Saxon heaved a little moaning sigh and rolled over; his yellow hair created a pale pool against his dark mantle of coarse wool.

Had he, the Anglo-Norman pondered for the hundredth time, been ill-advised so swiftly to reject Bohemund the Mighty's offer? Certainly this refusal to fight under the Ducal banner would not greatly advance his ambitions while at the same time he had earned the contemptuous enmity of a very puissant prince. *Par Dex!* How angry Bohemund had been! Veins had stood out like cords along the Duke's bull neck! Restlessly Edmund turned onto his side and at the same time silently cursed that dog howling below.

Had he elected to pursue the surest course towards a restoration of his fortunes? In retrospect he acknowledged to himself that real riches and notable gains could be won only through the Duke's patronage. How had Bohemund termed Lucano? "A pigsty of a fief." All the same were he to depart for Byzantium, what opportunity remained of winning the old Count's consent? But Alixe de Bernay he would win to wife, no matter what the cost.

To justify his decision he conjured up visions of Alixe's pale beauty graciously presiding over his domain, riding to hawk and hound with him, rearing a brood of lusty, tousle-headed children.

He must have dozed off for he flung himself violently sidewise when a hand pressed his shoulder. Gerth's voice was whispering urgently in his ear. "My lord! My lord! Rouse yourself. Just now I have been warned that Sir Hugues creeps in stealth towards my lady Rosamund's sleeping room."

"Impossible! Sir Hugues is a most honorable knight."

In deep distress Gerth muttered, "Perchance, but did not my lord mark at meat tonight how he sighed and stared so burningly upon my lady's beauty?"

"Aye. That I did."

Edmund sprang out of bed, tall, agile and naked save for the diaper-like loin cloth in which he slept during the mild seasons. "Who told you this?"

"An armiger who sped away ere I could recognize him surely," breathed Gerth. His eyes showed wide and white in the half-light.

From beside his cot Edmund caught up that same mace which had proved Drogo's undoing and on naked feet sped ghost-silent down a long, dark passageway.

Wary of raising an alarm which might forever besmirch his twin's name, Edmund hesitated, listening intently before that heavy leather curtain which shielded the entrance to Rosamund's sleeping apartment. Had the wind set it gently to swaying or the passage of some person? He heard Gerth padding softly up behind him. The Saxon was holding ready his broad-bladed throwing axe and would have come crowding in had not Edmund waved him back.

The Anglo-Norman drew a deep breath then parted the heavy curtain and stepped inside, mace poised.

As a dreamer senses rather than perceives doom pouncing upon him, Edmund whirled. The moon, abruptly unveiled, caught the flicker of a blade being driven at his throat. Barely in time Edmund diverted the stab with his mace, then brought his weapon crashing down. He knew at the same time that this prowler had closed sufficiently to avoid being brained by his mace's head and so had been struck only by the weapon's shaft. Its impact however proved sufficient to stretch the prowler senseless upon the rushes.

A brief tinkle caused by the intruder's falling dagger and the thud made by his body alone sounded over a sudden spattering of rain against the donjon's masonry.

While still bent over his enemy's figure, Edmund, from the corner of his eye watched Rosamund awake, slowly raise her head. Obviously she had remained asleep until this moment.

"Make no outcry. 'Tis Edmund."

The girl stirred, muttered something and then sat up, vaguely pushing a strand of hair from before her eyes. When she noticed the body sprawled at her brother's feet she pressed fingers convulsively to lips, but only expelled a sibilant gasp before she breathed, "Edmund, what evil thing is this that has chanced?"

"No time now to explain." Heart hammering and sickened beyond description, Edmund lowered his mace, bade Gerth guard the passageway and then dragged his assailant's body into a patch of moonlight. From the intruder's sodden scalp were dripping dark and deadly rivulets that quickly meandered away over the stone flooring. How *could* Hugues de Bernay have so far forgotten his knightly oaths as to attempt a deed so foul?

"Who—? Oh, Edmund, surely this cannot be!" Rosamund's eyes grew huge amid the semi-darkness.

The former earl straightened surprised to find how clearly he foresaw what must be done. One fact burned in his imagination like a flaring torch. No matter how extenuating the circumstances, the fact remained that he had slain the heir to Sanseverino. For him there would be no trial whatsoever. Either the infuriated garrison would cut him into gobbets or he would perish under slow and exquisite tortures.

"Pull on a dark cloak. Come at once," he whispered to the girl standing rigid and horror-stricken beside her bed. "We must flee."

"But why, Edmund? Your cause was honorable."

"D'you fancy the old Count will pause to weigh that?" For an instant he listened behind the leather hanging but heard only Gerth's excited breathing and smelt the sickish-sweet odor of blood creeping away from Hugues' head toward that dagger gleaming like a broad splinter of silver in the moonlight. Since, apparently, no alarm had been raised, all three retreated to Edmund's cubicle. There he gripped Gerth's wrist, directed sharply, "Hie you to the armory and fetch back a hauberk small enough to fit my twin, together with a small helm and coif—and a sword."

"Sir Robert's third armiger is slight," Gerth whispered.

Edmund spoke in swift undertones. "Good. Fetch them and his leathern breeches, too. Arm yourself, also—then we seek the stables. Should you encounter the watch say only that Count Turgis has ordered me to convey private intelligence for Duke Bohemund's own ear. Say also that I intend to ride accompanied by two armigers."

Once the esquire's footsteps had receded Rosamund advanced to his side. To Edmund it was not surprising that she should so steadily, quietly, await instructions; even when a small girl her poise, under all conditions, had been astonishing. He sought a crude clotheshorse supporting Sir Drogo's hard-won coif, hauberk and other accoutrements. Rosamund, although shivering in a night rail of coarse linen, deftly assisted in tying on her twin's leggings and shirt of mail, then bent to buckle his spur straps. Every once in a while Edmund would gesture for silence and stand listening intently, but save for snores from gentle men slumbering in adjoining cubicles all seemed still.

Now he stood, fully armed, with Drogo's sword slanting over his left hip and the victory-giving mace dangled over his right.

His features stiffened. "Rosamund, I know what I am about to ask is madness, yet I—I *must* have speech with Alixe. Do you think you could summon her?"

In the half-light Rosamund hesitated. "What you ask *is* madness! Must you indeed bespeak her?"

"Nothing in this life is more important."

The girl was gone almost before he realized it, clutching her dark cloak over her nightrobe. He waited, staring unseeingly out of the arrow slit upon Castel Sanseverino's moon-silvered courtyard, towers and battlements. He noted but a single light shining in the serjeants' barracks and there seemed to be no activity in the inner ward. Such sentries as he could discern obviously were dozing on the battlements with spears rested against the masonry beside them.

At a sound of softly padding feet Edmund spun about, hand on mace. Alixe de Bernay, very short by comparison with his twin, hurried in her long, wavy hair flying above the robe she huddled about her.

"Oh, my love! My love! What terrible thing has chanced?" Eyes wide and overflowing she flung herself into his arms.

Once he had kissed her tenderly he muttered, "I surprised a member of your father's household invading my sister's sleeping chamber. We fought. I slew him."

"But who? Who would attempt such villainy?" choked Alixe.

He raised her face, stared hungrily into her eyes. "I will not tell you, not at this moment, I say only that Rosamund and I must ride for our lives. Pray don't attempt to question me further."

"Must you indeed flee Sanseverino? My sire is harsh, true enough, but also he is just, when not found in ill-temper."

He clasped her to him. "We must go, my beloved. When you learn who the intruder was, try not to hate me."

"How could I hate you for once again defending your sister's honor?" she demanded fiercely. "Never could I blame you even though it had been my own brother who attempted to despoil your sister. Whither will you go?"

"We will attempt to come up with Duke Bohemund. When he hears the truth I trust he will forgive me and keep us safe from vengeance."

Alixe's mouth worked and she looked wildly about. "Then I shall ride with you."

"I have thought of that, too, but it is impossible," he gravely assured her. "Did I seem to abduct you I could have no hope of justice."

Sobbing the distraught girl flung both arms about his iron-clad waist and pressed herself passionately against him. "Edmund! Oh Edmund! What will become of me if you leave me behind?"

"Abide here till I send for you," the Anglo-Norman whispered. "I shall do so at the earliest instant. Trust in me, my dearly beloved and believe that every instant we are apart will seem as an eternity." He kissed her, gently loosened her hold.

She dashed away streaming tears and summoned a pathetic, tremulous smile. "I *shall* trust you, my soul, as you will trust in me. I call upon God and you, dear Rosamund, to witness that so long as I live, Alixe de Bernay will *never* become wife to anyone saving Edmund de Montgomerie. God keep you safe, my adored one."

From the entrance Rosamund pleaded, "Come quickly, Alixe. Quickly, quietly. I hear Gerth's tread."

Casting the tall and soldierly figure a final, heart-rending glance, the Lady Alixe darted across the cubicle. "No, Rosamund, do you remain here. An I encounter someone I will only have paid a visit to the jakes."

Once she had pattered away Edmund drew his dagger and gripped one of his sister's waist-long braids. "This I will shorten."

"Must you, really?"

"Aye. Such a mass of hair could never be concealed within a coif and God wots that it must!" Two swift slashes severed the golden-red hair level with the girl's shoulders. Steadfast as she was Rosamund could not restrain a burst of tears once her braids coiled snake-like upon the floor.

Barefoot, but wearing helm, hauberk and leggings, Gerth reappeared bearing the requisite arms and accoutrement. "What now, my lord?"

A silence fell for on the battlements could be heard the calls of sentries being relieved.

"During the false dawn, we will make our attempt," Edmund announced. "Meanwhile, Gerth, do you seek the stables. Saddle the destrier I won and strong palfreys to bear the Lady Rosamund and yourself."

The minutes crawled by while the two dissimilar figures in chain mail waited breathlessly in Edmund's cubicle. To quit it too soon would only prompt the guards' curiosity but for a knight and a pair of armigers to ride forth at dawn was a commonplace enough occurrence. Granted luck and the use of unmitigated effrontery this evasion might successfully be effected. Their attempt, Edmund calculated, must be made to coincide with a final changing of the guard. Then the courtyard would be crowded with yawning, coughing and spitting men-of-arms.

When the Anglo-Norman and his twin strode boldly into the stables sleepy-eyed armigers already were at work grooming and feeding their masters' horses. One tossed Gerth a ribald comment as he tightened the cingle to Stormcloud's heavy saddle—thus had Edmund named the tall, gray destrier won from Drogo.

"Ready the other mounts," Edmund directed and took his stallion's reins. All the while he kept an anxious eye upon shadows among which lurked a very slightly built armiger.

A milky quality in the sky had commenced to dim the stars' lustre when the horses were led out with the shields slung from the right side of the cantles softly clanking. Already Gerth had fetched three lances from the armory then, with casques dully a-gleam, the three horsemen mounted and found trouble in controlling the skittish rearing of beasts rejoiced to be out in the cool, clean air after the ammonia-tinctured stench of the stables.

When perforce the trio halted before the barbican to wait for its portcullis to be raised, the gatekeeper peered narrowly out the guardroom but saluted when he recognized the victor of the recent combat then ordered the gate to be opened. "Whither away, my lord?"

"Towards Venosa," Edmund informed and at the same time covertly pricked his stallion causing it to rear and so force the guard to leap aside. As he did so the slighter esquire spurred forward among deep shadows while the massive iron grille creaked ponderously upwards. God in Heaven, would it *never* rise high enough to permit passage?

Edmund's pulses quickened for from the main donjon voices had begun to call out and a hubbub of mounting intensity was rising.

When, somewhere upon the battlements, a trumpet commenced to bray an alarm Edmund lowered his lance point and, bending low over his pommel, dashed under the portcullis' spikes so fast that one of them grazed his helm. Out into the moonlight he clattered aware that Rosamund had lost her lance through not having lowered it in time. To a staccato rattle of hoofs the three riders dashed down that winding road which led to Sanseverino Mercato.

CHAPTER XVIII

Hunted

Although watch dogs in the straw-roofed village of Sanseverino Mercato rushed up to snarl and snap at the horses Sir Edmund nonetheless pulled up long enough to inquire the road to Venosa and allow Gerth opportunity to readjust his sister's stirrup leathers. Despite their maladjustment the girl had ridden admirably thanks to years devoted to hunting and hawking around Sussex. Panting softly, Edmund's long-limbed twin slewed about in her saddle and peered up at the castle now ablaze with lights. She then utilized the halt to reach up under her hauberk and tighten laces securing a linen band designed by herself to steady her breasts and so render the business of galloping a deal more tolerable.

"They follow already!" Gerth warned sharply. "I see torches at the gate." It was just as well Rosamund had lost her lance. Now she could with both hands manage this high-spirited palfrey.

When a drowsy tavern keeper pointed out the Venosa road Edmund indicated the other branch of a fork. "You are certain that is

not the Venosa road? It will go hard with you if you err. I ride on
Count Turgis' business."

"Oh, no, my lord. That road leads to Potenza, distant by a long
day's ride."

Having avoided inquiry concerning his true destination Edmund
led his companions out of the village at a sedate trot and only put
spur to Stormcloud once they were well down the road. The destrier,
outraged, flattened out in the ponderous, jarring gallop characteristic
of a heavily-built charger. Cool wind whistled by the coifs of all three
riders and pennons on lances carried looped over the two men's
shoulders streamed out straight in the half-light.

With good reason Edmund soon checked his charger's headlong
pace; a destrier being unable to carry his armored master over long
distances at high speed. Big-boned and heavy-set, such animals were
bred rather for size and weight in order that, at the end of a short
charge, they could, by bulk alone, bowl over lesser horses.

At the summit of a rise nearly a mile beyond Sanseverino Mercato
Edmund drew rein again and looked back, and was concerned to
realize that a pursuit could have been organized with such astonishing speed. Already an attenuated column of horsemen—he estimated
their number at thirty—were halfway down the road leading from
castle to village.

"Take care my lord," Gerth called out, "your destrier already
sweats apace. Shall we not discard our shields?"

"Why not?" Rosamund gasped while setting straight her helm
which, being much too large, kept canting to one side. "Against such
a number shields will be of no avail."

Edmund jerked a nod, so when the three galloped over an ancient
bridge, they slowed long enough to send their shields scaling down
into the dark water. To the former earl's relief his twin appeared to
be bearing up well under the unaccustomed weight of her hauberk
but to offset this encouragement he noted that Gerth's palfrey, because of the armiger's bulk and the unaccustomed weight of his mail,
was betraying signs of distress.

At a hard gallop the trio rode out over a causeway built centuries
ago to traverse a wide marsh in which glassy pools glimmered among
dense banks of reeds and cattails. It came as a shock that, before the
fugitives were clear of this causeway, half a dozen horsemen had
galloped onto its far end—not a half mile distant. An explanation for
this swift pursuit quickly offered itself. Among the riders from Sanseverino shone no gleam in the brightening dawn. The pursuers
therefore could be wearing no armor and must be depending upon
numbers to overcome the fugitives.

No longer able to endure this helm which kept slipping over her eyes Rosamund cast it deep into a thicket then pulled her coif free of features gone scarlet with exertion. At once her shortened hair flowed free.

A miserable anxiety gripped Edmund once he realized that Stormcloud with every passing moment was setting down his hoofs more heavily and shortening his stride. Perspiration was pouring in rivulets beneath his leather undercoat when he noted that his twin had commenced to sway in her saddle while gripping in desperation its high, nail-studded pommel. Gerth's palfrey, too, betrayed its increasing fatigue by dropping a full dozen lengths behind.

Aware that further simple flight must become futile the former earl studied the terrain ahead and with soldierly perception, noted that soon this road would become hidden behind a forested ridge.

"Spur hard!" he yelled over his shoulder. "Do not spare your mounts!"

Gerth's palfrey so responded that presently the young Saxon pounded up alongside his usually clear blue eyes bloodshot with effort.

"Gerth, is anyone ahead of us?"

"No, my lord."

"Good. Now whatever befalls, remember that we must keep together," Edmund panted to his sister. "Pray God this road takes to winding through yonder forest."

Aye. Pray God indeed! Terrible beyond imagination must be their fate should they be haled back, bound prisoners, before the dread lord of Sanseverino.

All at once Rosamund doubled over her pommel so completely winded that presently she lost a stirrup and commenced rolling awkwardly about her saddle. The girl's teeth glistened in an anguished grimace but her head swayed upwards and somehow she recaptured those loose-flying reins.

Hardly more than a quarter of a mile behind raced the pursuers, wearing steel caps but only leather jerkins for protection.

Once under the forest's high branches the age-old road veered abruptly around a rock solid enough to have defied even the perseverance of ancient Roman engineers, then swerved in a reversed curve to avoid a little waterfall. Thus all view from the road behind momentarily became eclipsed. Coldly perceptive, Edmund glimpsed a goat trail branching into the underbrush to their right and made for it.

"Slow down," he panted. "Try—leave no—marks as we quit highway."

Praying that the horses' iron shoes might not scrape moss from the stones the Anglo-Norman led into a dew-drenched alder thicket dense enough to offer complete concealment.

"Lower lance—fool!" he wheezed at Gerth. "Dismount—hold low horse's head. You, also, Rosamund."

That horses so thoroughly blown might whinny was unlikely yet he and his companions, by gripping their ears, forced their heads low. As he and Gerth had learned in boyhood, a horse must lift its head to whinny.

"Oh, dear Lord, allow yon dust to settle quickly," Gerth panted.

Save for the spasmodic lifting of their chests all three fugitives stood stock-still while the labored breathing of their horses sounded loud as wind in a pine grove.

Although Rosamund's iron-covered legs suddenly gave way she clung to her horse's ears and kept the creature's head depressed for now hoofs were rattling loud, louder on the road. Edmund bit his lip when the pursuers neared that spot where this goat trail crossed the ancient highway.

Although the former earl strained eyes to penetrate the alder screen he could make out nothing at all.

When perhaps twelve or fifteen horsemen had raced past the thicket two fresh problems arose. Were these riders the last of the pursuers? If so, how much longer would it take the men from Sanseverino to discover that the road was empty?

"Lead your mounts," muttered Edmund then carrying his lance at the horizontal, he led along this track deeper into the forest, wading through ankle-deep mud. Fortunately Stormcloud proved sufficiently blown to travel in silence and caused no noise beyond a squelching of hoofs and the scrape of branches over his massive back.

At a distance of two hundred yards from the highroad the big Anglo-Norman deemed it safe to remount. Once Count Turgis' followers found the highway deserted undoubtedly they would retrace their route searching a trail that branched off the highway.

Sweat bathed, the trio guided their mounts along a high ridge for a while then rode down into a silent, golden-green ravine. Here Edmund pulled up beside a brook then, as a good leader should, he bespoke pride and confidence in his companions.

"Allow your horses to drink, only five gulps, no more," he directed and swung down to the ground.

Noting Rosamund's near exhaustion the Anglo-Norman filled his helm with clear, cool spring water and raised it to his sister's dust-coated lips.

Rosamund drank thirstily then, to her brother's surprise, poured what water remained over her tousled red head.

"Better," she smiled faintly. "How can you men endure such a weight of mail and the heat of these smelly leather undercoats?"

From the valley below sounded the faint, discordant strains of that ancient Grecian instrument the bagpipe which long centuries ago Roman legionnaires had imported to Britain, along with baths, pheasants and peacocks.

"Tell me, Gerth," Edmund interrupted a vigorous massage of Stormcloud's weary legs. "Who gave you warning of Sir Hugues' intent?"

"An esquire, I think."

"Whose armiger was he?"

Gerth blinked, scratched his yellow pate. "Why, indeed, my lord, I cannot recall."

"Try Gerth, try. 'Tis of considerable import."

"For the moment I cannot, my lord," admitted the red-faced youth. "But he spoke truth."

"Aye. His warning was valid."

A light rain was falling when an hour later, the fugitives breasted a rise and beheld a road which, if Edmund's calculations were correct, should lead them to the town of Potenza and to the doubtful mercy of Duke Bohemund the Mighty.

CHAPTER XIX

Città Potenza

Silvery rain continued to drizzle gently but persistently from lead-hued clouds hanging low over a wide plain upon which, long ages ago, had been constructed the walled town of Potenza. Its towers and red-tiled roofs of every possible pitch loomed within a semicircle of low hills and straddled a pretty little river meandering away in a westerly course.

Reined in upon the summit of a wooded hill three drenched and mud-spattered riders paused to peer warily through the shifting downpour. The Lady Rosamund's lips had compressed themselves into a colorless slash so cruelly she was suffering from the pain of thighs and buttocks chafed raw by a day and a half's riding in the rain along a succession of cattle trails that paralleled the Roman road stretching between Salerno and Potenza.

Every muscle of the Anglo-Norman girl's long and slender body

ached and she felt miserably cold until an occasional trot could be
urged from the weary horses.

Despite concern over his twin's failing strength Edmund firmly
had rejected any notion of following that easy but dangerous highroad, so, on the preceding night, the fugitives had made bivouac in
the daub-and-wattle hut of a herder who had not tarried to receive
assurances of friendliness. Like a startled covey of quail the herdsman, his wife and children scattered and had vanished into the forest. That they had abandoned their food with such precipitation
argued bitter experience at the hands of men wearing shirts of iron.

The twins and their companion therefore had passed the night out
of the rain but miserable because this hut had no fireplace and
swarms of fleas, attracted by odors of damp and sweaty bodies,
promptly commenced to dine upon these fugitives who were so much
better fed than their usual hosts.

Now in anxious silence the hunted trio sat looking down upon the
red roofs of Potenza. Their horses stood wearily with low-held heads.

When the rain abated somewhat the young Saxon fetched a deep
sigh and observed, "My lord, is that not the Duke's encampment I
descry beyond this city?"

He was correct. Through the drizzle might be glimpsed many small
circular tents clustered about four large pavilions pitched in the usual
haphazard Norman fashion but the afternoon remained much too
misty to permit any identification of the banners dangling from
lances planted before various shelters. There could be no way of immediately recognizing the yellow-and-green gonfanon belonging to
Sir Toustain de Dives.

Absently, Edmund scraped a trickle of rain from his cheek then
pushed back the helm in order to ease its pressure. "Would to God
I could entertain hope that Duke Bohemund will receive me better
than I suspect."

Rosamund forced a pallid smile while wringing water from lank
and water-soaked red tresses. "Might it not be wise for Gerth and me
to enter the camp first and so seek out Sir Toustain?"

Such a course was not even to be considered, Edmund pointed
out. In the course of finding the former Constable's quarters her sex
almost certainly would be detected—with probably disastrous consequences. "No. We will venture into the Duke's encampment together
so let us on without further delay. Pray God this rain continues and
so drives all saving pickets under shelter."

Gerth nodded and shifted his short-handled *francisca* ready to
hand then, following the others, kicked his leaf-spattered palfrey onto
a path coursing with water.

Again the rain increased concealing behind a silvery slanting curtain not only Città Potenza but also Bohemund's camp. They soon entered a broad green meadow in which the Duke's horses and those of
his followers were grazing with tails turned towards wind and rain.

If ever Edmund had felt pride in his twin now was the moment
when he saw how valiantly she rallied and how straight she sat her
saddle although grimacing with pain. On passing through outlying
shelters of Bohemund's huge encampment Edmund realized that
only a very small contingent of the forces collected in this place
could have accompanied the Duke to Sanseverino.

To the former earl it was nothing surprising, indeed it was typical
of a Norman noble's loose discipline, that not once did a picket challenge the three riders although great numbers of men-of-arms and
serjeants sat gaming or dozing under dripping flies and marquees or
warming themselves about sputtering campfires.

Guarded inquiries at length guided the fugitives to that same
threadbare tent which, weeks ago, had sheltered them at Pesto and
on the night following their rescue from Agropoli. The encampment,
Rosamund noted dully, was pervaded by the pungent odors of dirty
canvas, wet wood smoke, horse droppings and human excrement
passed wherever man or beast had experienced the need for relief.

An esquire of Sir Toustain's proved the first to identify these riders dismounting so stiffly before his master's tent fly. The youth's eyes
grew great with astonishment when the tall former earl assisted a
very limping and slender armiger out of the downpour. Once he recognized the Lady Rosamund he dropped to one knee to kiss her
muddied hand.

"Your master is at hand?" Edmund's streaming and unshaven features were gray-red and the jut of his always bold cheekbones had
grown more pronounced through fatigue.

"No, my lord, but he is not far away. Shall I summon him?"

"Pray do so forthwith."

"Now by the Glory of God!" The old knight's remaining eye kindled when presently he splashed up to greet the three forlorn figures
waiting under his tent's fly. Beaming, he hurried straight over to
Rosamund. "'Tis wondrous fine, my lady, to behold you so soon
again." When he turned to Edmund, however, the gladness faded
from his mangled features. "And what do you here, my lord? With
matters as they stand, you are bold indeed to enter Duke Bohemund's
encampment."

"Then Duke Bohemund still is enraged over my failure to enter
his service?"

"Aye, he becomes wroth at the very mention of your name. Only last night when someone spoke of your refusal he hurled a goblet across the board." The veteran's hand closed over Edmund's arm. "Heed my advice and quit this camp at once. Hasten back to Sanseverino."

"But, Sir Toustain," Rosamund cried faintly. "That we cannot do."

"Indeed? What is amiss?" He broke off for Rosamund had commenced to sway and then, despite the support of Gerth Ordway's massive arm, her knees buckled and she would have collapsed had not her twin lunged to support her. Sir Toustain bellowed for his jackmen to heat wine and viands. Rosamund took but two uncertain steps before she fainted dead away onto the trampled muck. The former earl bent and in silence bore his sister inside and placed her upon a settle.

Plainly dumfounded, Sir Toustain drew a coverlet of wolfskins over the girl's supple, long-limbed figure and set about chafing her wrists. This much Gerth saw then tramped back out into the rain to gather up bridle reins that he might lead the three slowly steaming mounts over to a picket line.

"Had you not best remove my lady's hauberk and other gear?" suggested Toustain. "She is sodden to the very bone. I will guard the entrance while you do so."

Once the tent was empty Edmund contrived a rude screen of cloaks slung between lances driven into the earth, then behind it stripped off Rosamund's rusted hauberk, leather shirt, leggings and blood-marked breeches. Only then did he begin to appreciate what tortures his twin had endured so uncomplainingly. The skin of her inner thighs and seat had chafed raw and bleeding.

He made no effort to arouse the unconscious girl but clumsily mopped clean her face and arms before swathing her lovely form in a surcoat of clean white linen. Pale as a figure gracing some ancient marble sarcophagus Rosamund lay plunged in the sleep of utter exhaustion.

Only then did the former earl summon Sir Toustain and accept a cup of wine mulled so hot that it scorched his throat and sent blood surging through his chilled limbs.

From a jackman Edmund then accepted a bowl of stewed hare and eagerly dredged up the savory sauce with great chunks of bread.

Sir Toustain, tactful for once, banished all servitors from the tent ere seating himself on a saddle for lack of a stool. He listened to the Anglo-Norman's account of that misfortune which had befallen him in Castel Sanseverino.

"And this, my good friend," Edmund concluded while removing

his sodden surcoat, "is the whole tale which, upon my knightly oath, is true. What do you make of it?"

"I would never have deemed Sir Hugues so wanting in honor, for all that anyone could see that the Lady Rosamund's beauty was maddening him—as well as his younger brother."

"And what are we now to do?"

For several moments the one-eyed knight deliberated, gnawing at his lower lip and tugging perplexedly at long, gray mustaches. "Had you not been so intemperate in your refusal of Duke Bohemund's offer I would hazard that if he believed you he would shelter you from Count Turgis' wrath—especially since you slew young de Bernay in defense of a lady's honor." Sir Toustain cast an anxious glance at those faded watch cloaks slung before the settle. "However as matters stand——"

"Pray proceed." Hollow-eyed and long unshaven Edmund glanced up from the bowl gripped between mail-clad knees.

Sir Toustain shrugged beneath a mantle trimmed in worn red fox fur. "I can only say that I hold my lord Duke to be a farsighted and a just man when not ruled by sudden passions. He is held to be as faithful to his friends as he is merciless to those who offend him. You are scarce a friend of his, so you appear before Bohemund at your peril."

Edmund wiped his mouth on the back of his hand and got up. "Nevertheless I will chance speech with my lord Duke."

"Then you must wait until just after he has consumed his evening meal," earnestly advised the veteran. "Like most men with a full stomach, he is likely to feel less moved to wrath." He shook his head. "Alas, my friend, I doubt whether even at such a time you can prevail over the Duke's anger at you."

CHAPTER XX

Judgment

Towards sundown the rain clouds rolled away permitting a fiery sunset to reveal in sharp highlights and shadows the Duke of Otranto's dripping and bedraggled encampment. It also afforded a certain executioner good light by which to behead a pair of stubborn landholders who stupidly had refused to render homage to Bohemund or any overlord saving Duke Roger fitzTancred, now ruling in far-off Palermo. Once the headsman had discharged his duty the headless corpses, for the edification of all and sundry, were tossed into a wide mud puddle and their shaggy, still dripping heads were impaled upon spearpoints and displayed at the entrance to the red-haired Duke's pavilion.

Bohemund, thoroughly restless through the day's enforced inactivity, felt disposed to linger in the bright and relatively sweet smelling tent of Sybilla, Countess of Corfu. His massive bulk lay sprawled on its stomach diagonally across that beauty's silk-covered couch.

Restlessly the suzerain of Otranto, Apulia, Calabria and Campania ran fingers through his uncommonly short-trimmed shock of flaming hair and studied his current favorite's ever-graceful movements before a mirror of highly polished silver. Singing softly all the while, she was inspecting delicate, piquant and tawny features framed amid glossy blue-black tresses.

Sybilla Bryennius had reason to be vain, mused the Duke. What other woman in all Italy could boast such lovely violet-hued eyes, such full, satin-smooth and naturally scarlet lips or such tiny flat ears? Entirely captivating, too, was that little bluish mole beside her left eye. At the moment Sybilla deftly was coiling her plaited hair into spirals above each ear while permitting a bang to emphasize the gracious contours of a rather high forehead. Presently she secured her coiffure with small, ruby-headed golden pins and then concluded her toilette by binding a fillet of golden olive leaves above slim, provocatively-flaring black brows. Ever avid of attention she turned on her stool and, seeing him apparently wholly absorbed in cracking walnuts, banished her gay expression.

"Well, my lord? Can you not at least look upon the results of my efforts to please you?" she demanded. "Have I not lavished upon you my best arts to while away this miserable, endless day?"

Bohemund nodded. "I have found much pleasure in you, my little Grecian dove. If I seem distrait 'tis because I have been wondering"—he broke off and his color deepened when he beheld her diminutive and curvaceous figure advancing over a damp Turkish carpet —"whether I dare depart on this Journey of God leaving my beloved brother, Roger the Counter, behind?"

Sybilla, slim and infinitely provocative in a close fitting gown of crimson silk, seated herself before a chest, opened a small paint box and, employing the hind foot of a rabbit, commenced skillfully to tint her smooth, golden-brown cheeks.

"How many troops does my lord of Otranto deem necessary to leave at home as a reminder to his beloved half-brother that a Crusader's lands are exempt from attack?"

"I can spare seven, or perhaps eight hundred stout swords at the most," rumbled the Duke. "They should prove sufficient to keep him chary of crossing my boundaries."

The Countess' dark-lashed violet eyes widened. "Are so few truly sufficient?"

"Who knows? Roger is ever cautious. He prefers to win in parley what he cannot gain in battle."

A varlet scratched at a strip of gaily painted canvas hung to bar the entrance and announced the evening meal.

"Good. I could eat a bear hair, hide and claws." Roaring with laughter, Bohemund suddenly leaped from the couch in one of those amazingly swift movements of his which always disconcerted and sometimes annoyed the beauteous Sybilla and swept her off her feet to cradle her, kicking futilely in massive arms. He kissed her heartily, repeated despite her wails that he was sadly disarranging her clothing and coiffure. Cupping a hand over a small but superbly proportioned breast he grinned down at her.

"Do I now seem distrait—disinterested in your charms? I think I shall——"

"No! In Heaven's name take pity, you red-headed oaf. Do not ravage me now! I faint through hunger."

As he set her back on her feet, a frown returned to his brow. "Have your way for the present. Alack that I must remain late in council, but do not dare to fall asleep."

"Thank God for a little repose!" sighed Sybilla replacing a fallen hairpin. "I am bruised from head to foot through your bear-like caresses."

" 'Bear-like'? God's splendor! I crave pardon, I had no intention of hurting you, my lamb."

Laughing she gazed from beneath long and black lashes. "Can you never understand how very strong you are, you sweet Norman barbarian? Albeit, I do not complain in earnest." Her cleanly delineated lips slowly parted over glistening white teeth in a subtly alluring smile. "A little roughness now and then is not always displeasing to me."

"Well, poppet, let us to the festive board, else my lords will grow surly with waiting."

Employing a comb of Sybilla's Duke Bohemund ordered his disheveled hair, then combed his mustaches and short red beard. Next he donned a sleeveless tunic of green velvet trimmed in marten's fur and slipped into place a heavy golden chain supporting a religious medallion.

Already assembled about a table contrived of bare planks laid across hurdles stood a dozen-odd big, weather-beaten men in tunics belted tight over flat stomachs. They acknowledged the suzerain's presence by bowing slightly then, without further ado, settled down to eat.

The company, in which the Countess of Corfu was the sole representative of her sex, were cramming their mouths with gobbets slashed from haunches of wild boar when Sir Toustain appeared. Unobtrusively that grizzled veteran surveyed first the huge figure presiding so heartily at the table's head, then ran a speculative eye over the balance of the diners.

Which one of these was the traitor? That someone among Bohemund's entourage must be a Byzantine agent he had discovered not much earlier on this same evening. By chance the veteran had overheard a conversation being conducted in Greek among the shadows of a tent. Unfortunately one of the speakers had escaped while the other was being felled by Sir Toustain. A search of his dead body however had produced a document of considerable significance. Penned in Greek, it included not only a description concerning the Duke of Otranto's intended movements, but minute details of his forces such as no ordinary knight or serjeant could ever have come by. Who could be the traitor?

Bohemund had thrown back his leonine head to emit that snorting laugh so characteristic of him when he became aware of the one-eyed knight standing silently before the table.

"Well, valiant sir, and what brings you thus into our presence?"

Swiftly Sir Toustain decided to postpone the matter of that treacherous letter; there seemed small point in thus putting the spy on his guard.

"My lord, there has ridden into your camp a gentle man whom I hesitate to present to you. Nevertheless he is most desirous of entering your Grace's service."

The Duke of Otranto settled back in his armchair and using a dagger's point dislodged a bit of meat from between his teeth. "And who is this gentle man? Someone I have met?"

"Aye, my lord. 'Tis he who won the victory over Drogo of Cetraro."

"That same churl who was so forward at Sanseverino?"

"Aye, my lord."

Bohemund's brows merged and his nostrils flared as he bellowed, "By the Nails of the Rood! How dares so insolent a knave to seek my camp?"

· "Nevertheless, my lord Duke, Sir Edmund de Montgomerie humbly craves speech with you."

"Bid him be gone instantly! I will have none of him!"

Sir Toustain swallowed hard but persisted. "I crave pardon, most noble lord, but you, yourself, know this foreigner to be a most excellent champion. Can you find too many of his sort to serve you?"

Snarling under his breath Bohemund glared a long instant at the tough old warrior before him then growled, "Send the fellow in that he may suffer my contempt ere I have him scourged from my presence."

Bohemund fairly spouted curses until, at length, the Countess Sybilla reached over to stroke his hand and smile sidewise at him. "Pray do not rage on a full stomach, my lord. Recall what agonies you endured on the last occasion."

"Silence! By God, I'll show you all how I deal with——" He broke off when into an uncertain zone of light created by torches held by various servants advanced not one but a pair of tall figures in freshly oiled hauberks.

A startled undertone rippled through the pavilion when it was seen that the lesser of these two figures was that of a serenely lovely young woman.

In step the pair advanced towards him with heads held high and eyes steady.

Jaw outthrust, Bohemund arose and, placing both hands flat on the table, leaned far forward. Rosamund de Montgomerie he had beheld previously, of course, yet he found difficulty in associating this lithe Amazon with that stately young female who had curtsied so gracefully before him in Castel Sanseverino.

Sir Toustain held his breath while the twins halted before the dining board there to bow briefly, as became experienced courtiers. He noticed also how the Countess Sybilla's faintly oblique eyes subtly narrowed themselves as with convincing carelessness she appraised this red-haired giant with the wide jaw and high cheekbones. Um. Could this exotic lady possibly be finding a nascent interest in the former earl?

"Well, sirrah?" rasped Bohemund, his beard aggressively outthrust. "Well? And why have you sought me out? Me, whose service you felt too lofty to enter."

With difficulty Edmund restrained that soaring temper peculiar to most Normans.

"Circumstances have arisen, my lord Duke, which compel me to reconsider my decision concerning service under your banner."

"Do you indeed reconsider?" A rasping laugh escaped Bohemund and his powerful head swung to right and left. "Harken, my lords, and mark what a pretty turn of speech this foreigner possesses. Why, I vow 'tis almost worthy of some snot-nosed clerk!"

He shook a fist under Edmund's nose. To those who knew him

well the Duke of Otranto was about to enter one of those towering
rages which had brought death or disaster upon his enemies—and
too many friends. "By God, I will not have you for my service! Bohemund does not twice proffer his patronage!"

Veiled by a swirl of resinous smoke swirling down from the
torches Rosamund in her simple surcoat of green linen dropped onto
her knees, raised clear tourmaline eyes and hands joined in supplica-
tion. "Through my right as a damsel of gentle birth, I crave a boon
of you, my lord Duke."

"Aye. Such a right is yours, but wherefore should I pay heed?"
grunted the lord of Otranto and fingered the medallion about his
neck.

Sybilla, more radiantly lovely than ever, diverted her gaze from the
taller of the two suppliants, twisted sidewise her chair, and whispered into Bohemund's ear. Although he twice shook his huge head
he ended by nodding.

"The Countess of Corfu is pleased to urge that I heed your plea so
speak out, my lady, but be brief."

This tall young woman's large and luminous eyes peered steadily
upwards. "My lord Duke, I beg that you do not, in perhaps just wrath,
banish from your banner, a true and most valiant knight. Once my
brother renders homage and swears fealty he will, even to the death,
guard your person and cherish your cause."

Sir Toustain then spoke up, spreading gnarled hands in appeal.
"Once you have heard how well he acquitted himself in an evil matter which chanced after you departed from Castel Sanseverino I feel
confident you will find it in your generous heart to overlook Sir Edmund's ill-advised rebuff."

Bohemund dropped back into his chair, his attention no longer
upon the ruddy faced former earl but upon the war-like yet strongly
feminine figure kneeling before him. God's glory! Here was a rare
sort of female! Um. Accorded repose and garments befitting her station this stately cool-eyed young woman would rival the Countess of
Corfu in fascination.

On noting Bohemund's hand wander up again to caress his medallion, Sir Toustain relaxed. The gesture was characteristic of returning
good humor. Once more the Countess Sybilla, great eyes mischie-
vously alight, murmured something.

It was just as well, reflected Roussel de Ballieul's former henchman, that the lord of Otranto remained so preoccupied with this
stalwart mail-clad young female that he failed to notice a languorous curve shaping the Countess Sybilla's ripe red mouth and a more
rapid lifting of her notably rounded bosoms.

Gold-bordered blue mantle swaying Bohemund circled his dining board in order to assist Rosamund to stand.

"I grant your boon, most gallant demoiselle—on one condition." He considered the silent onlookers then grinned mirthlessly. "I will take your brother Sir Edmund into my service an he proves himself as able with the lance as with sword and mace."

"My thanks," Edmund broke in joyfully, the lance being a most favored weapon. "Against whom shall I try my skill?"

Bohemund, grimly smiling, turned to the Bishop of Ariano who, at the moment, was addressing himself in obvious enjoyment to a flagon of spiced Falernum. "I say, Girard, whom shall he meet? We must find him a worthy opponent."

"If this brash foreigner can worst Count Rainulf of the Principate, why then he will be worthy of your forgiveness, my son."

"Well said! And you, Cousin Rainulf? Do you care to settle this matter for me?"

All heads swung towards a short, powerfully built individual whose light brown hair framed a blunt, battle-scarred countenance.

Sir Toustain smothered a groan. Why the Devil should this muzzy Bishop have been prompted to nominate the most excellent jouster in Bohemund's service?

Count Rainulf's steel-gray eyes narrowed as that bandy-legged little man smiled thinly. "I thank you, my lord Bishop. Perhaps we shall both derive some small honor from the encounter." He turned towards his suzerain. "Did I not in your company, Bohemund, witness this gentle man's *combat à l'outrance?*"

"Tomorrow morning, then," rumbled the Duke. "I anticipate a certain amount of entertainment."

"Tomorrow morning?" Rosamund burst out. "Oh, no, my lord Duke, I implore you not so soon!"

"And why not?" Bohemund demanded in manifest surprise.

"My brother's destrier is sore fatigued, and so is he, though he will deny it."

"Aye, let the contest be delayed until the second day," murmured the Countess Sybilla. " 'Twill afford you a far better encounter."

Eyes fixed upon the Duke, Edmund drew himself up to his full six feet and two inches. "My lord, I will joust on the morrow, an it pleases you. A night's rest will fully restore both my charger and myself."

That this decision had created a favorable effect upon the lord of Otranto was evident. He grinned. "So be it. Get you gone, you stiff-necked foreigner, and pray to your patron saint whoever he may be, that tomorrow noon your destrier and accoutrements will not repose in my Cousin Rainulf's camp."

CHAPTER XXI

The Jousting

That reports concerning this tall Anglo-Norman knight's combat with Drogo already had been widely circulated became evident by the fact that every soul able to be present appeared at the jousting course—for all that this was not an intended mortal combat. Only blunted lances were to be employed.

In swarms burghers from Città Potenza accompanied by dumpy wives and shrill, wildly excited offspring, tramped out from town. Seldom did so notable an event leaven the drab tedium of existence.

Considerably more panoply and color were here in evidence than at the *combat à l'outrance* Gerth decided while smoothing Stormcloud's swelling crest. Gloomily the armiger noted, however, that his master's destrier was far from being in fine fettle. The stallion neither pawed the earth nor snapped playfully at the empty air, as was his wont at such moments. Also, his skin looked tight drawn over rump and withers. A vast majority of Duke Bohemund's leathery knights turned out wearing over their mail simple white surplices marked with a Crusader's scarlet Latin cross.

The jousting was to take place within a double line of stakes hastily driven into a stretch of turf nearly a hundred yards long and yet soggy from rain.

Chairs had been placed upon a low dais for the benefit of the ladies who were to witness this encounter. Because of Rosamund de Montgomerie's short-cropped hair and rumors which had begun to circulate concerning certain happenings in Castel Sanseverino, the motley and ill-smelling crowd stared upon this tall and striking beauty as if she had been some wondrous creature out of an unknown world.

Tensely Rosamund watched the two jousters swing up into their saddles and with the greatest of attention adjust the position of their shields. Edmund, having abandoned his shield during the flight, was about to employ a plain Norman buckler pressed upon him by Sir Toustain. Since the issue was to be determined through the use of lances neither champion carried sword or mace.

Edmund, settling into the now-familiar contours of his saddle, drew a deep breath before raising his gaze to the clear, azure-hued sky and so became reminded of Alixe de Bernay's limpid blue eyes.

"Dear my lady," was his unvoiced plea, "lend your champion

strength and grant him the victory that he may advance his cause and so bring you all the sooner to his side."

While surveying this long strip of turf Edmund weighed his chances of success and found them only fair. Although considerably restored after a long night's sleep he felt concern that his destrier neither fought his bit nor pawed the air. Small wonder that Storm-cloud should stand so quietly this morning. No warhorse could be expected to travel as far deprived of food, care or rest without tiring.

"Alixe! I fight for you—only you," he breathed as Gerth, his ruddy features a mask of suppressed anxiety, handed up the helm. Alas that this shield bore not even the rough effigy of a leopard. Curious, his sire, like his equally unlettered grandsire, had been superstitious in the belief that in battle the insigne of a silver leopard was for all de Montgomeries a most potent talisman.

With care he readjusted the guige, that strap which, passing over the right shoulder, supported his escutcheon independently of cross-grips securing it to his arm. Quietly he directed Gerth to lengthen his stirrup leathers. During his campaign against the Celts of Devon he had discovered that while short stirrups were more comfortable on a long ride, in battle lengthened leathers afforded a rider in-creased stability and enabled him more dexterously to avoid an on-rushing lance point.

Sir Toustain handed up the blunted tilting lance painted spirally in red and white. "You are ill-advised to risk combat so early but I have observed that Count Rainulf is given to settling and directing his lance somewhat earlier than do most jousters. Can you, at the last moment, slew your body to the right while keeping your own lance in line, you still may best him."

Edmund's dark blue eyes commenced to gleam to either side of his nasal. "My earnest thanks, Sir Toustain, and should I meet with misfortune, pray convey my eternal devotion to the Lady Alixe. Also, my friend, into your hands do I confide the safekeeping of my be-loved sister."

Surprisingly, while hefting this ten-foot-long shaft he recalled Rosamund's having twice murmured Cetraro's name in her sleep; a nightmare no doubt. Certainly she could have conceived not even the mildest attachment for the Lombard.

Once Duke Bohemund and his principal nobles had guided their palfreys into a space near the course's center encouragements were called to chunky little Count Rainulf. His destrier, rearing again and yet again, easily lifted clear of the ground grooms clinging to its bridle.

Gerth made a final and quite unnecessary adjustment to Stormcloud's poiterial, that broad, nail-studded breast strap designed to steady a saddle against the moment of shock and muttered, "May St. Olav steady you, my lord. God knows what will befall me an He does not."

Upon a signal from the red-haired Duke, a serjeant sounded a single, ear-piercing blast upon that oliphant which had so often screamed in victory over the Saracens of Sicily and against the Byzantines during the ever-memorable campaign of 1084.

Together with the Countess Sybilla, lovely as a pagan goddess in rich and liberally bejeweled garments, Rosamund sat upon the dais, white-faced and quite oblivious to pale brown crescents sketched beneath her eyes. Determinedly, old Roger de Montgomerie's daughter forced her lips into a smile of confidence although never before had she experienced such poignant apprehensions for her twin.

Once the jousters had collected their reins and were preparing to couch lances at either end of the course she cast a sidewise glance at the Countess Sybilla's cameo-sharp profile, noted that the Grecian girl's color was high and that she kept wetting her lips while exchanging sallies with Bohemund, gigantic at her side. The Countess Sybilla, Sir Toustain had averred, by descent was half-Greek and half-Byzantine.

Now that the champions had leveled lances, awaiting a second blast upon the oliphant, Sybilla's scarlet underlip became gripped between small and very white but somewhat irregular teeth.

A resounding yell arose when Bohemund leaned forward in his saddle and flourished a gauntlet. When the oliphant blared Edmund sighted his lance at the Count's plain, light-blue shield clearly seen in the brilliant sunlight, then his long-shanked spurs raked Stormcloud's barrel. Stung, the great destrier sprang almost from a standstill into a furious gallop down the level green course.

Alixe! The name reverberated in Edmund's mind while a succession of raw yellow posts dividing the course flashed by.

Sighting over the top of his shield the former earl received the impression of his opponent growing larger as if by magic, but concentrated his attention upon that blue shield above which his opponent's mailed shoulders shone a dull gray-brown. Now he could distinguish Count Rainulf's cold gray eyes glaring from either side of his nosepiece, so he settled behind his shield at the same time leaning far forward in the saddle with body braced against the lance butt.

Under the impact of Count Rainulf's lance his body was bent violently backwards and he became all-but unhorsed. At the same instant he felt his right shoulder jarred savagely as his lance dealt Count Rainulf's shield a glancing blow. Although his opponent's lance, well-aimed, had caused him to be driven far backward over the cantle the Anglo-Norman's unusually long and sinewy legs clamped themselves about the destrier's barrel permitting him, although badly shaken, to straighten up and gallop to the course's end.

In Edmund's ears sounded a reverberating tumult, a fierce clamor which beat like invisible fists upon his senses. All the same he *had* remained mounted despite Count Rainulf's skill and he himself had landed a terrific blow upon his opponent's shield. Did this tumult mean that he had been successful? Of course! He felt still more confident when he became aware that his lance was riven almost down to a metal guard protecting his fist.

Still a little dizzy from the shock, he reined in Stormcloud among hurriedly scattering spectators then turned. Lord God in Heaven! To his dismayed astonishment Count Rainulf remained astride his charger although he also was gripping a broken lance.

There remained nothing for Edmund de Montgomerie to do save to salute Bohemund with the splintered remains of his lance and trot back to his starting point.

Sir Toustain's one eye was glittering with anger. "Damn you for a headstrong fool! Why did you not veer as I said?"

"I forgot," Edmund admitted thickly, and to clear his head he shook it several times.

A fresh lance was being passed up when the oliphant sounded a warning note. As it brayed he braced himself and set off down the course. On this occasion Edmund fully intended at the last instant to shift to the right but, due to the severe jarring he had taken, his timing proved faulty and he bent too late.

He had the momentary impression of a lance head and a blue shield rushing towards him with the speed of a flung javelin then the sun seemed to explode before his eyes and he was flung to the ground with such violence that every bit of wind was driven from his lungs.

As he lay squirming in breathless agony he was too pained at once to realize that the incredible had happened. For the first time since he had become a belted knight, Edmund de Montgomerie had been unhorsed, defeated. In this awful moment had been lost all he had won from Drogo of Cetraro, so once more he and his twin were as penniless wanderers. Worst of all, his downfall had been witnessed by Duke Bohemund and the most puissant lords of Southern Italy.

In silence but with compressed lips and swimming eyes Rosamund placed her brother's hauberk across Stormcloud's saddle while Gerth, weeping unashamedly, slung sword, mace and shield to its cantle then, carrying the forfeited helm under one arm gathered up the gray's bridle reins. With tousled yellow head held high the Saxon trudged away from Sir Toustain's tent amid derisive hoots from idle varlets, grooms and jackmen. Too well he knew the route to that spot where Count Rainulf's green-and-red striped gonfanon fluttered bravely in the early June sunlight.

Fists clenched by her sides, Rosamund watched the armiger depart, then for a space her tourmaline-hued eyes considered the mockers in cold contempt before she stalked back into Sir Toustain's shabby tent. She discovered that grizzled individual using a wet cloth in efforts to staunch the slow flow of blood dripping from Edmund's nose and mouth.

"Had your destrier not been so weary you could have avoided Count Rainulf's second blow," the veteran was commenting. "I saw you attempt to rein aside, but his response was tardy."

"Blame not the horse," Edmund muttered and spat redly onto the muddy ground beside the settle. "He was a noble beast. The fault was wholly mine."

"Dear my Brother," Rosamund knelt by his side and pressed his blood-streaked and muddied hand to her cheek. "Even in defeat you were greater than many a victor."

He made an impatient gesture. "Many thanks, sweet Sister, yet the bitter fact remains that Edmund de Montgomerie has been unhorsed."

The girl's shortened red hair swayed to a sharp negative motion. "Not until you had shivered a lance and endured an onslaught from the finest chevalier in all of Duke Bohemund's array." She bent over and brushed his brow with her lips. "Take heart, Brother mine. We will rally, once more and yet succeed in restoring our name to greatness." She then draped a cool cloth across a forehead which throbbed as if all the imps of Hades were hammering it with red-hot sledge hammers.

Once Sir Toustain turned aside, ostensibly to polish the *umbo* of his shield, she continued to dwell on the future. "Nor are we truly as badly off as before. Do we not still possess two of the horses we rode out of Castel Sanseverino? Do not you have my hauberk and Gerth his? As well as maces, saddles and swords?"

The stricken knight managed a wan smile. "That hauberk of yours might have fitted me when I was a young bachelor but now I could not—— What's that?" He broke off listening to excited voices sounding outside the tent.

Sir Toustain leaped up and freed his sword. "By the Splendor of God, Sir Edmund," he rasped, "none shall drive you from my tent—not

even Bohemund's own self." After summoning his esquire, the former
Constable made ready to bar the entrance. Instead of hostile men-
of-arms, presently appeared a stalwart young knight garbed in
Crusader's white surcoat who addressed himself to Edmund and
spoke with calm courtesy.

"My lord from England," he began, "will you advance to this tent's
entrance?"

"He is not to be removed from my quarters?" queried Sir Toustain.

"Nay, Sir Knight, my business is to be conducted here," smiled
the visitor.

Edmund struggled erect but was forced to steady himself on a stick
thrust into his hand by an armiger. Lord! How painfully stiff his back
had become and how his bruised shoulders hurt when he attempted
to stand straight.

When the red-haired young giant appeared at the entrance he
halted to stare unbelieving upon his destrier standing, fully accoutred, before Sir Toustain's tent. Beside the great gray charger
waited a pair of pages bearing the hauberk, helm and weapons he so
recently had surrendered.

In a loud voice the young knight called out, "My lord, Count
Rainulf of the Principate would hold himself mean indeed were he
to accept the arms of a gentle man who, although knowing himself to
fight at a disadvantage, acquitted himself so honorably. My lord,
therefore, declines to accept the spoils of victory and begs that you
and your lady sister will deign to honor him at meat tonight in his
pavilion."

CHAPTER XXII

Bari, August 1096

In the lovely, azure-blue harbor of Bari in the County of
Apulia, a Venetian galley the long low lines of which suggested a
happy blending of speed and seaworthiness lay at anchor under protection of an ancient fort displaying Duke Bohemund's crimson banner. The *St. Leo*, although a merchantman, was armed. In these
parlous times none but an utter imbecile would have put to sea without sufficient fighting men to protect his vessel.

Out of Venice for Constantinople, the *St. Leo* already had crept
down the Italian east coast, and, after putting into Bari, would continue on around Cape Sallentinum to Taranto. From that busy port
she would, if all went well, traverse the Adriatic and so enter the

relatively secure waters of the sadly shrunken Byzantine Empire, still clinging tenaciously to memories of past grandeurs.

The day was still, humid, and swelteringly hot, so hot, in fact, that many fishermen had returned early from the sea to roller their double-ended boats up onto a cobbled landing slope and then drowse in the shade of often patched brown sails. Even the great white harbor gulls ceased their wheeling and settled upon the water.

From the battlements of Bohemund's stronghold on a height behind Bari, three tall Normans stood gazing thoughtfully down upon its glassy harbor, its guardian fort and the many coasters tied up to timeworn quays.

Bareheaded, Bohemund stood in the blazing sunlight perspiring so freely that his white tunic with its long red cross displayed dark stains on back and chest. He turned to him whose hair was as red as his own.

"Within three weeks' time, Sir Edmund, you should be entering those straits called the Hellespont by the Greeks. Next you will enter the Sea of Marmora and, God willing, a few days later you should tie up in the Golden Horn which I am told is the port of Constantinople." He spat over the parapet then frowned. "Years ago I dreamed of ruling over that rich and famous city but at the time God willed otherwise. All the same, mark you both," his voice swelled and his jaw jutted more than usual, "someday I shall fulfill my vow to sit upon the throne of Byzantium!"

Sir Toustain gazed absently upon the multitude of humble red-roofed dwellings straggling among clumps of cedars and pines down to the harbor. "My lord, be assured that we shall do our best to discharge our duties to your best interest and render an account of Alexis Comnene's true intent towards you and your array.

Edmund de Montgomerie's attention again had fixed itself upon that long, red-painted galley which, before sundown, was to bear himself, his sister, Sir Toustain and that lovely, languorous and enigmatic lady known as the Countess Sybilla to the greatest metropolis of Christendom.

Albeit reluctantly, he was coming to believe that these weeks spent refurbishing his faulty knowledge of foreign tongues had not been spent in vain, for all that it was unknightly to admit an ability to read or write.

"Had I but possessed the skill of writing," Sir Toustain once had stated, "even now I might be ruling a great principality upon the southern shores of the Euxine."

"How so?"

"A rascally interpreter—an interpreter mark you, is one who can both read and write a language whilst a linguister only speaks it—

instructed me to make my mark on a parchment which, instead of
securing to me a fief promised by Michael VII, instead bound me to
serve his Majesty during six long years—and for a very mean consideration. Ere I could discharge this service the Basileus, or Emperor as we of the West name such a potentate, was overthrown and
so my promised reward went whistling down the Bosphorus. Therefore, my friend, sharpen your pen as well as your sword lest you
too do not lose at the treaty table that which you have won by hard
fighting."

It was fortunate therefore that, a month earlier, Sir Toustain had
discovered an instructor, a corpulent, good-natured dealer in wines,
who, for the sake of some sound meals consented to drill the veteran
and his red-haired friend in Greek.

In the midday's heat Edmund fingered his long jaw pondering the
fate in store for him in Constantinople—wherever that city might lie.
He recalled a certain evening on which Bohemund had remarked,
"Perchance you conjecture, Sir Edmund, why I am dispatching two
emissaries to Constantinople? Well, 'tis so that one may remain to
serve me should the other meet with disaster.

"I hold it only honorable, Sir Knight, to warn you that Death forever hovers among the shadows of Byzantium. I must learn my old
enemy's intent, for all he swears on the Holy Sacrament willingly to
supply and to keep me free from attack once my array has crossed
the Sea of Hadrian."

The three lingered under the shade of umbrella pines gleaming
hot and fragrant in the sunshine. It was not strange that their
thoughts were running in much the same channels. Could Jerusalem
really be captured? If so, at what price? What would victory bring
to the Christians? Could the slippery, highly intelligent Byzantines
and their barbarous mercenaries be trusted in a pinch? And what of
the other princes leading this Crusade? Would they prove stupid?
Avaricious? Jealous?

Abruptly Edmund inquired, "—And how many men, my lord Duke,
think you to command on our march to Jerusalem?"

Bohemund uttered that snorting laugh of his then tugged at his
short red beard. "To be frank the last reports received from Sicily are
disappointing; at the moment I cannot expect to lead above ten
thousand well-armed men. Because of this I have dispatched envoys
to parley with various not-unfriendly nobles holding domains to the
north of my Duchy. Can they be persuaded to follow my standard
our numbers should be increased by a third."

Sir Toustain's lean slash of a mouth tightened. "Let us pray the
Virgin that no less than twenty thousand Cross Bearers depart under
your command, my lord." He shook his battered head. "Full many

will fall sick, lose heart, or perish in skirmishes on the road to Constantinople."

"Spoken like a wise old war dog," grunted Bohemund. "An I arrive before Byzantium with two-thirds of my original force I shall be surprised."

After a little Bohemund ordered the one-eyed veteran to inspect certain gifts designed as bribes for Byzantine officials. Once he had disappeared within the castle the Duke immediately gestured Edmund to follow him into a bare, stone floored apartment where they could be alone. Bohemund flung himself into an armchair.

"Now that you are my sworn liegeman and a companion in my bodyguard, Sir Edmund, heed with care the advice I am about to impart. Your life may well depend on it."

Big figure silhouetted against a narrow window through which beat cooling draughts, the Anglo-Norman folded arms and prepared to listen.

"Yes, my lord?"

"As you may or may not have learned, the Countess Sybilla is only half Italian and is descended on her father's side from the very noble and ancient *familia* Bryennius." The speaker glanced up with a sly grin. "My lovely friend from Corfu would have me believe that ever she keeps my interests foremost in her heart whilst I have indicated that, should all go well with me on this Crusade, she shall become my Duchess."

Bohemund spat resoundingly onto the flagstones. "Both of us are lying. Deeply I suspect her to be in the pay of Byzantium. Incidentally the Emperor is as crafty an opportunist as ever existed—to my sorrow I have learned that. Alas, I cannot yet prove this traffic betwixt the Countess and Alexis—that is for Sir Toustain and you."

He looked quite boyish as he winked. "I no more would make that fascinating, but politically unimportant lady my Duchess than I would turn Moslem. So we are quits." He sobered, treated Edmund to an intent inspection. "I presume you have become aware that it was not *wholly* through accident that I have persuaded your beauteous sister to accompany the Countess Sybilla as lady-in-waiting?"

"Indeed, my lord Duke, I had not thought on the matter."

Amazement entered Bohemund's manner and he surveyed his big retainer with a penetrating regard. "Then you should! An you hope to survive in this mission you must be suspicious, ever suspicious, of every deed or word coming to your attention. You are not dull-witted, Sir Knight, so spur your wits and do not remain a typical Norman clod who cares for naught save combat! You will win small rewards in that direction."

The lord of Otranto's manner changed. "Tell me, am I muddled or does the Lady Rosamund flush at every mention of Cetraro? Why does she hate him so well? Or, perchance, has she conceived some small attachment for that troublesome Lombard?"

The Anglo-Norman colored down to the round, embroidered collar of his tunic. "I am not aware of any interest she has in him, my lord. How could my sister become enamored of the man who impugned her honor and who came so near to slaying me?" A tinge of scarlet crept out along Edmund's high cheekbones as he said, "I shall remember your words, my lord Duke. No. Such a thing could not be."

"Possibly not," Bohemund admitted. "Well, returning to matters of moment, my treasurer will bestow upon you a purse which you are free to spend as you list about Byzantium. I warrant," he grinned in an evil, esoteric way, "—you will find ready use for these monies if even a half of what is said concerning the females there prove true.

"Alas, that this purse cannot be heavier but, as you have noticed, too many of my fiefs are both barren and sparsely inhabited. And then there is all this outfitting to be paid for, so I am poor, Sir Edmund, poor, poor!"

The seated figure's head went back and his deadly little blue eyes glared into space. "That is why I mean to win a kingdom from the Infidels *and I shall!* Never doubt that one instant. I shall conquer, just as you and many another poor knight will seize rich lands and towns for himself." He fell silent and the cries of archers shooting at a clout in the courtyard drifted indoors.

Mood again changing, Bohemund got to his feet and strode over to clap the former earl on his shoulder. "For all our disagreements, Sir Knight, I think so well of you that aboard the galley you will discover a gift. 'Tis a sleeveless shirt of light but very fine and strong mail. I warn you to wear it whenever you fare abroad. And another thing, above all beware of poison! Should you become suspicious then plead a queasy stomach or insist, as a delicate honor, on an exchange of cups with your host. Never sleep unless an armiger or some other trusted servant remains awake and at your side."

"For the shirt of mail I thank you from the bottom of my heart and I shall heed your advice to the letter, my lord Duke."

"See that you do," came the grim admonition. "Now a word concerning Sir Toustain. I greatly esteem his services because of his great knowledge of the Byzantines, their language, politics and manner of warfare. Yet for all his bluff, rough-and-ready manner he is both subtle and ambitious. Never will I trust entirely a man who has served under Roussel de Ballieul nor one who once was friendly with my enemy, Alexis Comnene."

"Then Sir Toustain has served the Byzantines?"

"To be sure, after his master de Ballieul was poisoned. So watch him therefore on my account."

Again the Duke tugged at his curly red beard and chuckled. "'Tis well that most princes take Bohemund for a valorous but slow-witted and honor-bound Norman, like that rock-headed paladin named Roland of Roncesvalles. Bah! How could a commander be so careless as to permit himself and his followers to be cut off and massacred? Yet endlessly the minstrels sing this Roland's praises because the poor fool died bravely. Bah! He should have been given a dog's burial."

Suddenly grave, the Duke placed hands upon the former earl's shoulders. "Do you but serve me faithfully, Sir Edmund, then your rewards shall pass all expectation. As my liegeman you shall rule rich cities and a domain greater by far than that which you say you have lost in England."

For a minute, perhaps, the two, singularly similar, save in the matter of age, looked steadily at one another, then Bohemund said, "One final caution. Beware of Byzantine women even more than their men; but make no mistake concerning the latter. These East Romans, as they call themselves, are clever in war and very brave when they choose despite their curled and oiled hair, silken garments and luxurious way of life—of which you will taste more than a little. Go. Obtain for me sure proof of Sybilla's treachery. It should be easy an you play upon her fondness towards you."

"Fondness—for me? Surely, my lord Duke, you jest."

The other cut him short. "Nonsense. Sybilla pines for your embraces as a bitch in heat yearns to be covered by some strong hound. Do you desire her?"

"Nay, my lord, not in the least," Edmund replied instantly.

"And why? Is she not as succulent a morsel as ever warmed a warrior's couch?"

"She is lovely beyond comparison, my lord," Edmund thought it wise to say. "Yet, in Sanseverino Castle there awaits my return a most tender and pure demoiselle—the Lady Alixe de Bernay." His heart lifted. "With her I exchanged vows which nothing in this world will tempt me to betray."

Bohemund burst out laughing. "Boast not too soon, valiant sir, you have experienced only the clumsy arts of our crude and artless Frankish females. In that great and glittering city for which you depart ere long you will encounter women, patrician and otherwise, who possess arts so voluptuous that they may beguile an honest but simple gentle man from his allegiance. I would even wager on it!"

BOOK II: *Byzantium*

CHAPTER I

The City of Constantine

Already almost eighteen hundred years in existence, the city founded by Byzas of Megara upon the Thracian Bosphorus sprawled in breath-taking majesty up a long, pear-shaped peninsula thrusting out into the confluence of the Bosphorus and the Propontis —called by some the Sea of Marmora. Even the most sophisticated of voyagers could only gape at the sixteen miles of yellow-gray stone walls which, punctuated at less than bow-shot intervals, girdled Constantinople and on tier upon tier of villas and palaces climbing from the water's edge.

At the tip of the Golden Horn as this peninsula was named, stood the Imperial palaces, huge public buildings, the Hippodrome, all dominated by the soaring dome of Sancta Sophia, that monument to the pride of Justinian I and to the genius of his architects.

Situated thus at the axis of the known World's trade routes, Byzantium, far more than her Imperial predecessor, Rome, might be truly termed "the Hub of the Universe."

Destined to survive as a Christian capital for another half millennium, the City of Constantine existed as an island of culture in dire peril of becoming submerged under successive barbarian invasions for the empire ruled by Alexis Comnene in 1096 had shrunk to a pitiful remnant of those far-flung domains which had acknowledged Constantine, Theodosius II, Justinian I and Leo III as their Christ-loving Supreme Autocrator, Augustus and Basileus.

During a month in Byzantium Sir Edmund de Montgomerie had come to understand something of the Empire's parlous condition. Why, in Asia, just across the Bosphorus, Turkish raiders at the moment had penetrated to within thirty miles of the city's walls and actually had entered the suburbs of Chrysopolis.

From Count Maurice Skleros, a grizzled squinting veteran who in

1071 had fought in the catastrophic battle of Manzikert in Central
Anatolia, he heard about the death struggle which then had raged
between the Emperor Romanus Diogenes and Alp Arslan, leader of
the Seljuk hordes.

After Manzikert the Empire's richest themes and fairest recruiting grounds had become lost and, ever since, the Seljuk Turks on
ugly but fleet and hardy ponies mercilessly had ravaged Western
Asia Minor not halting until they had captured Jerusalem and the
great walled city of Antioch. Then they had halted because of en-
countering lands held by Saracens only—fellow followers of Mohammed.

Successive hordes of Turks led by Alp Arslan and his heirs, Yagi
Siyan and Kilidj Arslan, surnamed the Red Lion, had blighted the
Emperor's richest farm lands, had felled fruit and olive orchards and
had leveled to the ground not only villages but also sizable cities.

The Seljuks thus created what suited them best, a wilderness of
grass suitable for a nomadic existence and subsistence of vast herds
of war ponies.

Repeatedly Count Maurice declared that a horseman might ride
for days across the once-rich Anatolian plateau and never encounter
a human habitation saving the malodorous goatskin tents of some
Turkish encampment.

Edmund, although continuing to marvel over this ever-confusing
and incredible city, by now had learned not to gape, open-mouthed,
like some Saxon churl at a crossroads fair. Further, he was beginning
to identify various components of that never-ending stream of humanity which circulated through the capital's narrow and generally
filthy streets.

Thanks to Sir Toustain he had learned to recognize certain of those
mercenaries who guarded the city and, fully armed, strutted its
streets in outlandish garb, swaggering as though they were the pro-
prietors rather than the hirelings of the State.

Among these barbarian defenders of Byzantium were the Sclavonians. Ugly beyond belief, they were distinguishable by sloping
skulls, pug noses, slanting eyes and shocks of greasy black hair. Even
more numerous about the city were the Turcopoles. Bow-legged and
restless as cats, for the most part they were renegade Turks from
tribes hostile to the rule of Kilidj Arslan. Such barbarians seldom
were to be seen afoot but generally riding blunt-headed ponies and
lashing at the crowd with plaited quirts of rawhide. There were also
other savages in the pay of Alexis Comnene; Kumanians, Bulgars,
Betchenaks and Patzinaks.

Edmund made particular efforts readily to identify all these bar-

barous races for, as Sir Toustain grimly pointed out, someday soon
his life might well depend upon it.

Shouldering their way along the boulevards and supremely contemptuous of these shaggy fellow soldiers were troopers from the
Schools of the Imperial Guard. These, Edmund noted with interest,
were hulking fair-haired Saxons, ex-Vikings or Varangians. These
last, he was told, were a Norse people who, during the course of
several generations, had migrated from the Gulf of Finland through
Rus-Land and down to the Black Sea.

Most interesting of all to the former earl were numbers of hard-
bitten Frankish free lances, who, rather desperately seeking employment, haunted the courts of the War Ministry. They were truculent,
ignorant and avaricious but according to Sir Toustain these men in
shirts of iron scales were second to none in battle and loyal when
regularly paid.

In small and dingy markets, semi-fragrant with pungent odor of
spice, rugs, fabrics, jewelry and perfumes of the Near East lay exposed beside amber, furs and linens from Western Europe. Chaffer-
ing was conducted in at least half a hundred languages and dialects,
most of them totally incomprehensible even to the one-eyed former
Constable. Greek, fortunately, was the language most commonly
spoken and was the only one understood by Sir Edmund. Of course,
now and then he caught snatches of conversation in Norman-French,
Italian, or in the Saxon speech.

Always the red-haired former earl rubbed his eyes on surveying
those incredible double walls which, four and a half miles in extent,
protected Byzantium on its landward side. He still blushed over his
simple notion that Castel Sanseverino constituted the acme of military engineering.

Even now he wondered whether he might not awaken some morning to learn that the wonders he had beheld hereabouts were but
figments of an extraordinarily vivid vision. How he gaped awe-
stricken, upon the colossal statue of Constantine the Great, who in
A.D. 324 had moved the Empire's capital from Rome to the City of
Byzas. Even more breath-taking was the Hippodrome, that vast
monolith of masonry which could seat upwards of fifty thousand
people, more souls than existed in all Sussex. In fact he had wondered as he stood gazing upon those tiers after tiers of benches climbing skywards whether he had partaken of some drug. Inspection of
the capital's huge government buildings, countless churches and
splendid palaces stirred his simple mind to incredulity and ambition.

On his way with Sir Toustain for yet another visit to Count
Maurice Skleros' villa in the Augusteon quarter, the two Normans

penetrated a bazaar largely occupied by lean, hook-nosed merchants whose bright black eyes seemed never to be at rest.

"—And of what nation are these people?" Edmund inquired on noting their dark complexion and invariably small hands and feet.

"These quick and noisy merchants," Sir Toustain explained, "are Arabs or Saracens, Infidels. In fine, they are worshipers of Mahound."

"*Infidels!* What are these blaspheming dogs doing here as free men?" Edmund's fingers closed over his sword's grip.

"Leave be, lest you find yourself flayed alive," snapped the one-eyed knight. "It has always been the law that merchants of any race or belief shall be free to trade within this city's walls, so long as they keep the Emperor's peace."

Edmund's amazement became intensified when into this bazaar clattered a detachment of light cavalry, brown-faced, thin-limbed warriors who trotted arrogantly along under swaying lances topped by tufts of red-dyed horsehair. They wore curious curved swords and carried several daggers jammed under wide leather belts. To a man, these fierce-looking barbarians were protected by round shields and conical helmets of gray steel intricately inlaid with gold. Each of these helms, Edmund perceived was supported by a twist of white linen bound tight about the wearer's head. Further they occupied high peaked, sheepskin-covered saddles and used stirrups so short that their upper thighs paralleled the ground.

"Look well, friend Edmund," came the veteran's advice. "These are Turcopoles and blood-brothers to the Turks we soon will face in battle. Observe how lightly they go armed and how quick and nervous are their horses."

On recalling Brother Ordericus' preaching Edmund scowled while the detachment clattered up. Upon noticing the two Franks towering above the crowd a Turcopole called out what must have been an insulting observation which Sir Toustain returned with such fluency that the barbarians scowled and then laughed heartily.

Sir Toustain's route led presently through a series of noisome alleys in which Hagarenes, Copts and Jews in dirty *shubas* and yellow *kaftans* tugged at the Crusaders' white surcoats, whining pleas and offering bands of embroidery, cunningly carved ivories or boxes of camphor and sweet-smelling sandalwood. So dense grew this screeching pack of vendors that soon the two Normans were forced to swing sheathed swords in order to create a passage.

Everywhere wailed beggars, all hideous beyond description and so many of them blind or lacking one limb that Edmund remarked upon it.

Toustain explained. "'Tis due to the sentence of the some judge.

Maiming is the penalty here for even petty crimes but blinding is generally inflicted only upon suspected traitors, deserters or spies."

Clad in rags fluttering in foul festoons the mendicants whined for a brass tartaron and the stench of their sore-spotted bodies became all-but unbearable. Several times the wayfarers passed a figure lying huddled and motionless in an overflowing gutter.

"What ails them?" demanded the Anglo-Norman. "Is this some trick?"

"No. These poor devils have died of sickness or, more likely, of hunger. They will lie there till the street cleaners appear tomorrow."

The sight of a group of wolfish, half-naked children playfully gouging out a dead man's eyes with sharpened sticks so nauseated Edmund that he turned aside and became involved with a file of shaggy baggage camels being driven along by ebony skinned Nubians. Wise pedestrians quickly drew aside fearing the bite of these malodorous and proverbially ill-tempered beasts.

It came as sheer delight at last to penetrate the Augusteon quarter in which the ceaseless pandemonium of the markets and bazaars sounded like distant surf. The tops of graceful cedars, bare-branched sycamores, locust and Judas trees now showed above high white walls protecting various residences and swayed under a cold breeze beating in off the Sea of Marmora. Soon the wind grew so penetrating and raw that both knights belted their white surcoats tighter about them.

The villa of that politically powerful patrician, Count Maurice Skleros, Edmund had discovered to be neither large nor pretentious, yet it was most advantageously situated on a small rise overlooking the Sea of Marmora's sapphire blueness.

At the moment a long, swift-looking guard galley was to be seen threshing out to sea, undoubtedly on guard against Saracen sea raiders. Rhythmically, her eighteen-foot oars raised diamantine spurts of spray as she passed an inward-bound Imperial dromon. Every detail of this big trireme became clearly visible, even a dragon-shaped brass effigy on her prow. Through it, Sir Toustain explained, could be squirted a terrible secret compound known as Greek fire—a combustible liquid which could not be extinguished by water.

In reply to Sir Toustain's knock a small door, let into a larger nail-studded gate, swung open and there appeared a yellow-faced, slant-eyed guard whose cheekbones flared outwards and upwards in pronounced ridges.

"A Patzinak," Toustain muttered, then throwing cloak over shoulder, the veteran managed his sword over a high sill and stepped inside.

They found Count Maurice Skleros and his wife, a sloe-eyed Armenian, who, fifteen years earlier, must have been extraordinarily pretty, seated in a small walled garden and occupied with tossing bread to a flock of white pigeons strutting about their feet.

Although the two Frankish visitors had become thoroughly familiar with this villa Edmund still could not cease marveling over the quiet beauty of this little court the center of which was graced by a circular pool now dotted by frost-killed water lilies.

Count Maurice arose somewhat stiffly thanks to a Turkish arrowhead still lodged in his left hip. After most courteously making welcome his callers he clapped that servants might fetch out glasses of honey flavored with rose or violet leaves and mixed with water.

The day, for early winter, was so crisp that the Byzantine had pulled a fur-edged mantle closer over a supratunic of bright green edged with gold. Count Maurice's neatly pointed beard was flecked with gray but the dark eyes set in a face of classic Greek construction were lively and young-looking. After a few moments the Countess arose, smiled on the callers then beckoned waiting women, lingering discreetly in the background, and departed.

Although limping a little, Count Maurice conducted a brisk circuit of the court in order carefully to inspect each clump of shrubbery, for all that most of them had shed their leaves.

"Ah, Maurice, you've not altered," smiled Sir Toustain. "You were ever suspicious—and careful."

"And that, friend Toustain, is why I still live when so many others have departed to knock on Heaven's Gates," remarked the Byzantine. "Well, and have you yet received word from your lord? Everywhere in the Sacred Palace one hears conjecture on Duke Bohemund's progress."

"Not yet," Toustain grunted. "I begin to fear his couriers may have been intercepted. You know full well the Emperor holds small love for the man who so nearly dethroned him eleven years ago."

The patrician's black head inclined. "That may well be so. Tell me, are you comfortable with the Countess Sybilla's cousin, Eudocia?"

"Comfortable, and most agreeably entertained, one might say."

The one-eyed Norman grinned, directed a sidewise glance at Edmund, who reddened and pretended to survey the evolutions of flute pigeons wheeling above and creating soft music by means of tiny silver tubes attached to their wings.

"For a fact, the Lady Sybilla is proving greedy for my friend's attention and humors his slightest wish."

Count Maurice turned carefully painted features towards his tall, red-haired guest.

"And how fares your sister, Sir Edmund?" he inquired most courteously. "I trust the Lady Rosamund finds our winter climate not too harsh?"

"Not after England, my lord. In fact, we do not even yet understand the use of so many comforts which, to us, are amazing beyond belief. I think that we shall soon seek simpler quarters of our own among the Venetian merchants who dwell in Pera across the Golden Horn."

The Byzantine's manner became less casual but he inquired easily, "Indeed? Then you are becoming uneasy in the Bardas Palace?"

"Hardly uneasy," Edmund said all at once conscious of the iron mesh shirt beneath his tunic. "It is only that wherever we go my sister and I are followed. Even now, I venture there is some spy lingering before your gate."

Momentarily the Byzantine's thick mouth tightened then Count Maurice observed, "In Constantinople one becomes accustomed to being spied and eavesdropped upon from sunrise to sunrise. In your case this is especially so since those of Alexis Comnene's party know you are a liegeman of Duke Bohemund the Mighty."

"What! How is that known? Sir Toustain and I have given out only that we are free lance knights in search of a paymaster."

An amused laugh escaped the plump figure in the green fur-trimmed cloak and Sir Toustain's scarred visage fell into a pitying grin.

"A dozen informers talked with the master and crew of your vessel ere she was well tied up. They learned when you sailed, from whence, and everything that you and my one-eyed friend did whenever your ship touched a port. Really, Sir Edmund, you cannot for an instant imagine that the whole Court does not know just why you are here or that you live as guests of the Princess Eudocia together with the celebrated"—he lingered on the word and half smiled —"Countess Sybilla of Corfu?"

Edmund's white Crusader's surcoat gleamed and the scarlet cross on his chest flamed as he arose blinking bewilderedly. "Then no one credits that Sir Toustain and I are but masterless knights in search of employment?"

Count Maurice's pointed beard quivered to laughter so loud that a pair of smoke-gray angora cats took alarm and scurried off into the shrubbery. "No one. My old fellow campaigner here entertains no such illusions."

"Of course not," the former Constable of Sanseverino admitted. "It is an accepted rule in Romania for visitors to offer some harmless explanation for their presence." He accepted a silver goblet of wine from a tray fetched out from the villa by a towering Numidian slave. "Tell me, Maurice, do you still retain your great and abiding love for the Emperor?"

"That damned blunt Frankish tongue of yours will get you in trouble yet," snapped the Byzantine. "Can you never be subtle about such dangerous matters?"

"I'm afraid not. Well, are you still at odds?"

"The former Emperor Nicephorus is a cousin on my mother's side. We were brought up as brothers. Can I be expected to forget that he now exists as a blinded, shaven-headed monk confined in a monastery on Prinkipo Island?"

Edmund's bright blue eyes widened at the deadly passion evident in the Byzantine's manner.

"All the world recognizes Alexis Comnene for an usurper who revolted against the man who elevated and trusted him."

Mildly Sir Toustain added, "But are there not those who will swear that, by doing so, Alexis preserved this Empire from certain destruction?"

Count Maurice tugged irritatedly at his short beard and perfumed oil from it came off onto his painted fingernails.

"That is possible. Nicephorus was weak and vacillating. Nevertheless, the diadem is not rightfully Alexis' and I would——" He broke off, adding hastily, "Forget my last remark, Sir Edmund, I beg of you! I have no yearning to grasp the purple. Indeed not. It is dangerous to have the blood of the Botaniates family in one's veins; so much so that Gordian Botaniates, a cousin, recently deemed it wise to order his eldest son secretly castrated lest the lad be blinded or murdered by the Comnenes."

From the city beyond the high white wall, sounded a blaring of trumpets and the dull booming of many drums. Toustain glanced up questioningly. "This is not the hour for the changing of the guard. What means this?"

"Oh, 'tis a vain and pompous Frankish lord who names himself Hugh the Great, of Vermandois, and claims brotherhood to the King of Frankland who has arrived and is being conducted in state to the Palace of the Lion."

"How does this Frankish prince speak?" Edmund inquired cautiously.

"As a prideful windbag, it would seem. *Par Dex!* You should have read the letter he forwarded to our Christ-loving Emperor."

Count Maurice fell to chuckling, fingered a gold and enameled brooch at his throat. "I can even now recall a part of what he caused his clerks to set down. 'Know you, O Caesar, that I am setting forth and that I am a lord above all kings therefore do thou prepare to greet me in a manner befitting my high estate.'

"This Hugh of Vermandois is receiving undue attention at the Sacred Palace not because of his silly pretentions but because he is the first of the Cross Bearers to arrive," Count Maurice explained. "Other arrays we know to be passing through Greece. Duke Godfrey of Bouillon with his Germans and Lorrainers yesterday left Thessalonica and a few days' march in his rear is Robert, called the Duke of Normandy. Another Robert, Count of Flanders, should also arrive here before the Feast of the Nativity." The Byzantine's steely gray eyes shifted to Edmund's ruddy countenance. "And when do Duke Bohemund's levées expect to sight the dome of Sancta Sophia and camp before our walls?"

Sir Toustain spoke before his companion could make up his mind what to say. "Much depends, old friend, upon the arrival of certain ships hired from those ever tricky Venetians who are allied with the Emperor, you know."

"I know," said Count Maurice grimly. "And what progress eastwards is being made by Count Raymond of Toulouse, sometimes called de St. Gilles, and his great band of Provençals? The Grand Logothete has heard that these lag far behind the rest. Is this so?"

Toustain shrugged lean and wiry shoulders. "The Emperor is better informed than are we."

"Let us hope he does not fall by the wayside for his is the greatest army of all."

The Anglo-Norman sat his curule chair, long face intent and trying desperately to comprehend an underlying thought within this conversation. Why was everything so subtle, so complicated here in Byzantium? No one ever seemed to be forthright and speak his mind openly and without guile. "May I inquire why?"

The Byzantine arose, crossed to a marble bench and from it plucked up a scarlet woolen mantle edged with soft gray fur of some sort. In a gesture which appeared mechanical he again surveyed his little courtyard before he turned to his visitors and murmured, "You should inform Duke Bohemund thus: He must hasten with all his might and so reach this city *before* the other Frankish armies! It is the Emperor's intention to keep the Crusading hosts apart so far as is possible and ferry into Asia each array as quickly as it appears. He quakes at the thought of Frankish armies uniting and laying siege to his capital."

A bitter smile curved Count Maurice's full lips. "Not that these Western princes will fail of a warm welcome. The first comers especially will be showered with gifts costly beyond imagination.

Therefore let Bohemund the Mighty make haste since he is a poor man and hard-pressed to support his levées."

Amazement again filled Edmund. What did these smooth talking Greeks not know about their Frankish allies?

"It is Alexis Comnene's intent that your ironclad warriors unite *only* beyond his city of Chrysopolis in Asia and there prepare to march against the hordes of Kilidj Arslan, called the Red Lion of Islam."

Sir Toustain spat on the leaf littered marble pavement. "So the Cross Bearers are to fight to recover the Empire's lost themes in Asia Minor?"

"Exactly. They are expected to exhaust and diminish themselves in fighting Alexis' battles; it should prove easy for him to bend your remnants to his will."

"But we have come to free the Holy Sepulchre and drive the Infidels out of Jerusalem!" Edmund burst out.

"Beyond a doubt." A diamond set into a band securing the Byzantine's thick black hair flashed to a quick nod. "It is Bohemund who must see that you Franks remain steadfast on their course and refuse to play cat's-paw for our Emperor." His laughter sounded metallic. "Among all you slow-witted Franks only the Duke of Otranto can match guile with guile and deception with deception."

CHAPTER II

Gideon of Tarsus

The lovely little palace of the Despoina Eudocia Bardas, a former royal residence dating from the reign of Michael VI, was most fortunately situated upon a hillock facing the Golden Horn and surrounded by splendid new residences. To Rosamund de Montgomerie and her brother its vaulted corridors at first had seemed endless. Now, in mid-November, they frequently felt chilly despite numbers of handsome bronze braziers glowing day and night in every apartment. The palace, however, remained a wonder of beauty and luxurious comfort hitherto undreamt of. Whenever Rosamund recalled the bare, rush-strewn stone floors, the icy sleeping cubicles and those glassless arrow slits which passed for windows in Arundel Castle she shivered. Surely the Bardas Palace must in reality be a segment fallen from Paradise! Probably it was the cleanliness, the sweet, fresh odors prevailing especially within the Gynecaeum or

Women's Quarters, which no male might enter—that most impressed the Anglo-Norman girl—and its baths! At first Robert de Montgomerie's tall, red-haired daughter obdurately had refused to join other ladies of the household in ablutions conducted in the *therma,* a most amazing chamber walled in black and yellow marble. It contained a number of shallow pools or plunge baths the bronze taps of which could produce clear water ranging in temperature from scalding hot to icy cold. Here the Countess Sybilla, her cousin, the Despoina Eudocia and their companions were given to lingering in magnificent indolence a good part of the day lovely, but shamelessly naked. Best of all they loved to extend their sleek and shapely bodies upon padded marble benches there to be massaged by the cunning hands of strange neuter creatures called eunuchs—luckless males deprived of their virility.

The Anglo-Norman girl gasped when Sybilla, finally out of patience, had ripped off garments still fresh from only a week's wear and literally had pushed her into a warm bath. She had screamed out loud, had knocked flat two of the black, sexless creatures and had fought like a red-haired wildcat until the laughter of the Despoina and her ladies had made further protest seem both futile and absurd.

Even now she would not admit how thoroughly she had come to enjoy and finally to anticipate the caress of warm and fragrant waters and the stimulating glow of her dead-white skin under pressure from some black attendant whose hands were quite as impersonal as those of a small child. The contrast in her reactions to this subtle care and to the awkward ministrations of smelly serving wenches back in England, was astounding.

Just how many servants, from the burly Sclavonian barbarians guarding the palace, to seemingly innumerable slave scullions, sweepers, masseurs and grooms were included in the Despoina's household? Certainly the Bardas servitors could not number less than two hundred. The Despoina Eudocia, a petite and lively old lady of forty, was a widow and had practically no male surviving relatives, the Bardas clan unfortunately having supported the late Emperor Andronicus of unhappy memory.

From the beginning Rosamund had sensed herself to be the object of considerable covert interest about the palace and those who called there. Everyone spoke of her proudly erect posture, muscular build, smooth and marble-white skin. Moreover she towered a generous head higher than the tallest of these nervous, soft-bodied Byzantine ladies.

The fact that she, a gentle woman, not only could ride a horse but also draw a bow and fly a hawk, filled these languorous beauties more with wonderment than envy. She could prepare a plain repast with her own hands and was strong enough to strike flat an impudent servant with a single blow of her fist. Her lustrous red-gold hair, growing long again, also seemed to fascinate the ladies of the household, most of whom were brunette although a surprising percentage were blonde in varying degrees.

Bitterly the Earl of Arundel's daughter came to lament that her knowledge of Greek was rudimentary, limited to a few phrases acquired in Bari and aboard the ill-fated *San Giorgio*. But nowadays she was improving rapidly, thanks to a good memory and an ear for accents. Ever since her arrival in Alexis' capital, life had seemed like an extraordinarily vivid dream, at once delightful but confusing. Desperately she sought to discover some basis of orientation since she remained hopelessly bewildered by her surroundings unless her brother, Sir Toustain or Gerth of the dog-like devotion were present.

Often she found herself glancing from one to the other of these familiar faces in order to conjure up remembered vistas and predictable reactions. How steadying it was to realize that Gerth, too, could recall the ramparts of Arundel Castle with rooks circling and cawing around them and just how the clear brown River Arun wound among those green and billowing bends she had known since infancy.

From a balcony of the Gynecaeum she looked down upon gardens lovely even at this season of the year, because of the statues and fountains in them. Somewhere a water clock sounded the hour because three silver balls had become released by a cunning mechanism to fall upon a brass gong. Surely Edmund must soon return? She felt a mounting alarm over the increased time he now spent outside the palace walls. Much could happen to Edmund, confused, ignorant and all-but cowed as he was by the complexity of life in this metropolis of over a million polyglot souls. As she sat sewing up a rip in her best house mantle she wondered over the tenacity with which these Byzantines, Greek in race, philosophy and language, clung to trappings peculiar to the long-vanished Western Roman Empire. Hardly anyone employed Latin any more, except in official communications. Inscriptions on important public monuments, too, invariably were expressed in that tongue.

Even more bewildering to the Anglo-Norman and to all Franks, for that matter, was the thinly veiled hatred and distrust these Greek Orthodox Christians held for the Church of Rome; indeed, sometimes it appeared that the Byzantines preferred pagan beliefs.

From where Rosamund sat gazing across that long and fairly narrow inlet known as the Golden Horn she could view literally hundreds of vessels lying at anchor or tied up to an endless series of always busy wharves.

By now she had learned to distinguish between different types of craft—Byzantine dromons, naviculae and olerons; Venetian, Genoese or Pisan galleys and galleons. Then there were the pleasure caïques of the rich, brown-sailed fishermen and rangy feluccas, up from Cyprus or Rhodes. While most sea-going craft lacked a cabin house or other superstructure Italian ships generally mounted castles of fighting platforms over bow and stern. These defenses were crenelated to protect archers and javelin throwers exactly like the walls of a fortress.

Invariably, Western ships appeared high and clumsy, steered as they were by a huge, double-bladed oar secured to their right-hand side; they could sail into the wind hardly at all. When tied up, a ship invariably presented her left side to the shore, hence a vessel's sides had become known as the "steerboard" and "portboard," so Sir Toustain had explained.

"Will you ever tire of looking out over the port, my sweet Barbarian friend?"

Rosamund started and dropped her sewing so silently had Sybilla, Countess of Corfu, entered the balcony. Today her dark loveliness was emphasized by an over-gown of heavy yellow silk secured by gold and enamel bodkins and a girdle of wondrously knotted scarlet silk. That blue-black mole near her left eye never had seemed more fetching nor her voluptuous mouth more alluring.

The Anglo-Norman girl vented an embarrassed laugh and got up. "I was just recalling that once I deemed Bari to be a great city! I still cannot accustom myself to these Eastern wonders."

"Your noble brother," softly observed Sybilla while seating herself upon a broad coping of purple-veined white marble, "appears to be adjusting himself to our ways with somewhat greater celerity."

"Small wonder," Rosamund burst out. "Is he not free to wander about the City as he pleases whilst we poor women can only occasionally fare forth under guard in a litter and then only to visit selected streets in approved quarters."

Sybilla gravely shook her glossy head. "That is so because it must be. Would you see yourself pounced upon and dragged off to a stinking brothel in the Street of Women? Nay, Rosamund. Because of the flood of desperate and moneyless refugees from themes lost to the Turks our City teems with lawlessness. The City guards can only pretend to keep order even with the half-hearted help of the Heteria —the Imperial Guard."

"I suppose you Greek women should be careful, but I can defend myself." Rosamund stood up slowly flexing long arms then abruptly reseated herself and queried, "Tell me, has aught been heard of Lord Bohemund's intentions and whereabouts?"

The Countess' intricately coifed blue-black hair glistened as she turned sharply to look back into the palace where some minor altercation had broken out among the Despoina's orange robed eunuchs. "No, but by tomorrow we shall."

Rosamund's clear bright blue eyes widened in surprise. "How do you know that?"

"Don't trouble your straightforward mind over that. Suffice it that a galley from Brindisi just now has entered the Dardanelles."

"But, in the dear Jesus' name, how can you know this? By witchcraft?"

A tinkling little laugh escaped the other. "No, my sweet simple. Have you never noticed, on bright days, a light winking on yonder hilltop across the Bosphorus?"

"Long ago I noticed such lights on several hills," Rosamund admitted, once again feeling infinitely childish and ignorant. "I had thought the sun to be striking the shield of a marching soldier."

Mechanically, Sybilla straightened an emerald and topaz bracelet. "That blinking has purpose. It is our sun telegraph which when the weather is right in the space of minutes can transmit messages over hundreds of leagues. Thus our Emperor quickly learns how matters fare in his most distant themes."

A flight of raucous voiced jackdaws beating their way to rookeries in the remains of some ancient palace destroyed during the Nike riots cast a series of shadows over sere lawns below the balcony.

"So," Rosamund observed thoughtfully, "your Emperor will learn at once just when and where our Suzerain will make his landing?"

Sybilla glanced in sudden but covert suspicion at this tall, red-haired girl who appeared so completely disingenuous. "To be sure; but in these dark days of winter the heliograph becomes less and less useful."

In the distance arose a sound of cheering then the screaming of many trumpets. Hollowly their notes reverberated among massive buildings above the Bardas Palace.

"Tell me the reason for this tumult." Rosamund folded up her sewing, tucked it into a raffia pouch. "You know everything that takes place."

"To say that I know even a little of what transpires is wild flattery, but I do chance to know that a Frankish prince named Hugh, who claims brotherhood with the King of the Franks, has arrived before the gates and is about to be received at Court by the Emperor. Tonight at the Hippodrome there will be a mock battle and fireworks discharged to impress this arrogant, though simple, barbarian. Two days later my cousin the Despoina will entertain him here. It has all been arranged. Have you ever seen a real Frank, I mean one hailing from the center of that province which in Roman times was called Gaul?"

"I have never beheld those peoples called Lorrainers, Flemings, Germans or Provençals."

Sybilla's delicate nose wrinkled itself in a delightful little expression of dismay. "*Par Dex!* You are to be congratulated. All these Frankish warriors are uncouth, ignorant and just as vicious as hungry bears."

The bitterness of this petite and elegant Byzantine girl was striking. "However, I shall do my best to welcome these Franks and to entertain them."

"Shall you sing? You have so lovely a voice that I almost wept the time you sang for us in Bari."

"Oh, no. As the daughter of a noble house I may not sing or dance before strangers."

As they turned away from the balcony and the smoky haze gathering over the Golden Horn, Sybilla, in an impulsive gesture caught Rosamund's hand. "Tell me, sweet friend, what are your brother's impressions of life in this city and what does he make of us?" She checked herself. "The Byzantines, I mean?"

On quitting Count Maurice's villa Sir Toustain suggested, "It might create a favorable impression were we to attend the candle-lighting service in Sancta Sophia."

Sir Edmund started. "But is that not a church of the schismatic and heretical Greeks?"

"True, but 'tis all the more important that we be seen there and perhaps we will find opportunity to view Alexis Comnene, Equal of the Apostles and Christ-loving Basileus of Byzantium."

En route to the cathedral the two Normans entered a crowded square in which stood a tall and weatherbeaten Ionic pillar. Still lovely it undoubtedly was the last remainder of a pagan temple. The passage of a half-troop of glittering cataphracts—the Empire's superb heavy cavalry—momentarily checked their progress.

Looking about, Edmund was astonished to notice, perched upon weed choked pieces of fallen masonry, throngs of obviously expectant citizens.

In his immediate vicinity stood numbers of long bearded black-robed monks of the Greek rite, mingling with beggars, mercenary soldiers off duty and even a few well-dressed patricians wearing white, scarlet-edged robes.

Edmund soon became aware that most of these onlookers were peering upward and, following their gaze, perceived that on the capital of this single column crouched a white-haired and rag-clad figure. Obviously the man up there must have occupied his perch for months, if not years, so streaked and stained with dark brown splashes was the column's beautifully fluted shaft.

Darkly outlined against the bronze-blue evening sky this creature suddenly got to his feet and raised arms thin as hop poles to form a cross; thereupon comparative stillness descended upon the square. All about, people were falling onto their knees, clasping hands, and gazing eagerly up at the wildly flowing locks and ragged beard of him who stood glowering down.

"Silence all of you!" shouted a tall young fellow wearing the silvered breastplate of an Imperial guard. "That most holy man, Gideon of Tarsus, is about to make prophecy."

Edmund had retired into a doorway but his mantle of vivid blue must have attracted the stylite "saint's" attention for he pointed at the Anglo-Norman and screamed down something in an incomprehensible language.

"Stand forth, you barbarian blockheads!" someone hissed in Greek. "The saint has noted you."

"And well he might!" giggled a very young and boldly-painted girl as she advanced, thin hips a-sway, in a pitiful effort to appear seductive. "By the Panagia! Where else can one hope to behold a Frank with hair so coppery, with eyes so sea-blue or loins so fitted for a tumble on the couch of Venus?"

There was something so droll about this pale child and the expert way in which she aped the invitations of a practiced harlot that Edmund burst out laughing. Thereupon the girl pressed closer and parted her faded yellow gown to expose tiny, immature breasts. "Yours, all yours, my lord, and for only a byzant."

"A byzant?" railed a bushy-bearded bystander. "Christos! You can roll Chloë for a brass tartaron!"

"He lies! I never couple for less than a silver denarius!" The street girl, great-eyed and with greasy yellow hair falling in untidy strands about scrawny shoulders appeared desperately eager. She clung to Edmund's sleeve and peered up into his long, red-brown features. "Try me, my lord! Try me! My arts can make men out of boys and boys out of men."

"Silence! Accursed spawn of Jezebel!" From atop the pillar the anchorite's voice rang out. "Silence! Thou swaggering Frank who, by wearing the livery of Our Lord, thereby sullies it!"

Edmund flushed, stared up at that indescribably unkempt figure some sixty feet above him and so noticed dangling from the platform a wooden pail by which the anchorite might draw up food donated by the superstitious.

"A pox on yonder mangy rascal!" growled Edmund. "When he calls me unfit to wear a Crusaders' Cross he lies in his maw."

"In God's name be still!" implored Toustain aware that baleful, if not threatening glances were being directed at his companion. "Such stylite monks have great power. The mob fears them like the horns of the Devil."

The harlot raised her face and yelled something in an outlandish tongue at the scarecrow then, with the speed of a hunted vixen seeking her den, she darted off through the congregation. Just before she squeezed between two fallen moss-covered segments of masonry and disappeared Choë paused long enough to blow a kiss at that red-haired Frank. Alarmed by the crowd's growing hostility Edmund drew his sword and with Toustain at his side retreated further into the doorway.

"Peace, my children, let the harlot flee to her doom," cried the anchorite. He then dropped onto hands and knees the better to peer downwards. "Thou with the red hair, stand forth and have no fear. Gideon of Tarsus would gaze upon thy countenance and perchance read thy destiny."

Obediently the crowd fell back enough to leave the two Normans in a cleared area in which they stood with feet braced apart and swords held ready.

Now that the anchorite spoke Greek neither Crusader found difficulty in following a shouted prayer. When he had done and the crowd was commencing to rise to their feet Gideon of Tarsus leveled a bony forefinger at the former earl.

"Look upon me, unhappy fugitive from Angle Land and take heed," he called down. "This I foretell for you: in the land of Israel thou shalt find a sepulchre!"

The crowd hooted at Edmund's awkward Greek when he called back, "True, but does not every man sometime find his grave?"

The dainty pattering of donkey hoofs passing down a side street sounded loud in this square hemmed in by tall, lichen-stained buildings of great antiquity.

"I said 'a sepulchre' thou Norman dolt—not a grave," cried Gideon of Tarsus and his sparse gray beard wagged like that of a venerable buck goat. "Now harken well to my words!"

A soft moan circulated the heterogeneous crowd and many crossed themselves in expectation of another of those prophecies for which this anchorite especially was celebrated.

Gideon of Tarsus straightened suddenly and raised both arms high above his shaggy head.

> "The Lion and the Eagle, the Leopard need not fear,
>   But the Nightingale and the Boar bring his undoing near."

The stylite monk's prophecy ended in a curious whining cry then he seated himself, cross-legged, upon his pedestal and drew a tattered cloak over his head, quite ignoring the upturned faces below.

> "The Lion and the Eagle, the Leopard need not fear,
>   But the Nightingale and the Boar bring his undoing near."

The words burned themselves into Edmund's memory.

"Come," Toustain urged. "Else we shall be tardy for the candle lighting."

By now the curious and superstitious had risen brushing mud and filth from their knees and, putting away rosaries, resumed their various ways.

The two Normans had commenced to ascend that eminence upon which loomed the breath-taking majesty of Sancta Sophia when Edmund felt a tug at his surcoat and, glancing downwards, was amazed to recognize the street child named Chloë.

"If it please you, most noble knight," she whispered, "I have not eaten since dawn and I—I—do very much crave your embraces. Truly I——"

"Begone, mangy alley-cat!" Sir Toustain dealt the girl a cuff which knocked her flat onto the muddied cobbles, dirty limbs a-sprawl. She lay still, blinking dazedly and looking so utterly forlorn Edmund sought his wallet then into the soiled little creature's palm pressed a silver denarius he could ill afford to part with.

Uncomprehending, she stared up into his bronzed features. "A—a denarius? Ah, noble lord, I lied. I have no cubicle. We must seek the arches of the Hippodrome."

"Nay. Purchase yourself clean garments, food and mayhap a bath. God knows you stand in dire need of them."

While they joined in a flood of humanity streaming towards Justinian I's famous edifice, Toustain uttered a disgusted snort. "Curse you for a soft heart. That child-harlot dogs us."

This was true, but once Edmund turned, the girl Chloë darted out of sight behind a passing wagon. She still was lingering outside

Sancta Sophia when the two knights emerged from the incense-tinctured atmosphere of that vast and soul-stirring cathedral.

CHAPTER III

The Courier

At a respectful distance from handsome bronze doors giving into the Bardas Palace slouched a leather-featured individual clad in seafarer's garments. Once Sir Toustain and his companion had passed him he lengthened his stride and in an undertone urged, "Pray keep on past the portal, my lords. I bear tidings for you."

Edmund would have halted to challenge the speaker but Toustain muttered, "Keep on till we turn yonder corner."

Presently they followed this bandy-legged stranger's salt-stained black cloak into a short cul-de-sac among the handsomely decorated dwellings of the lesser nobility. There he halted and faced about.

"Which of you is Sir Edmund de Montgomerie?"

"I. Who and what are you?"

"Sir Ugo of Palermo. I travel in the service of Duke Bohemund," he announced in hoarse undertones. "Show me a certain ring once bestowed upon you."

Upon identifying the ornament to his satisfaction, Sir Ugo led the way into a snug little wineshop which, at this hour, proved deserted. Nevertheless he in the seafaring garb looked searchingly about and maintained his wary manner even after he had seated himself back to the wall.

"How came you here?"

"By vessel from Bari."

Suspiciously, Sir Toustain's single eye fixed itself upon the messenger. "How can that be? There has been no ship from the East arrived in the Golden Horn in many days."

A bleak smile twisted on the stranger's features. "That may well be true but last night when the Venetian galley I sailed in touched for water at Gallipolis, I made my way ashore and bribed the master of an Imperial dispatch galley to fetch me here." He chuckled, nodded to himself. "At least two days must pass before Alexis Comnene's agents will search the Venetian."

Edmund fingered his chin. "And how do my lord's preparations proceed? His vassal knights and liegemen appeared promptly?"

A low curse escaped Sir Ugo and his gaze shifted as he hunched far over the table's scarred top. "There were dangerously many laggards. When I left levées still were straggling in and from many a company nothing at all had been heard."

"What then?" Edmund prompted. "Is Duke Bohemund's crossing of the Adriatic to be postponed?"

Cautiously, the courier peered about, then inclined his battered head. "By a month at the very least."

"A month!" grunted Toustain rubbing the lid lying flat over the socket of his lost eye.

"That is most unfortunate."

"How so?" tensely demanded Toustain.

"Other Western Princes will arrive in Constantinople long in advance of Duke Bohemund."

"And so?" Edmund leaned forward to catch the courier's whispered reply.

"This leaves the Byzantine Emperor free to dispatch large bodies of troops for action in Thessaly!"

The three lowered their voices because a small girl came running in to capture a woolly little puppy. She looked brightly about then scuttled out of sight behind a bead curtain leading into the kitchen.

"You mean that Alexis Comnene plots to fall upon our lord?" Edmund queried.

"They are old enemies," Toustain reminded, "and the Emperor fears Duke Bohemund like the plague."

Sir Ugo shrugged. "I do not say this is so. Only my lord thinks it would be wiser that the Emperor does not learn his intended route across the mountains of Greece."

"A most sensible precaution," Toustain commented.

"And when does our array depart from Bari?" Edmund wanted to know.

Sir Ugo took a long pull of excellent Chian wine that set his hairy Adam's apple rhythmically to working. He smacked his lips, then fumbled beneath a coarse brown woolen tunic. He was wearing no Crusader's surcoat, not even a steel skullcap. On his head was a mariner's leather cap equipped with earlaps which might be tied under the chin in the event of hard weather. What he produced was a tight scroll of parchment inscribed in neatly-executed Latin characters.

Eyes narrowed in the dim light, Edmund shifted on his stool and, without too much facility, read the message.

"Well?" sharply inquired the one-eyed veteran. "What does my lord say?"

Edmund drew breath to commence a translation but fell silent and caught up his wine cup because a detachment of guards, off-duty from some palace situated higher on the slope came tramping along with arms linked as they bawled a ribald song.

Edmund started, as if a wasp had stung him. *Par Dex!* These fellows were *singing in Anglo-Saxon!* From the tavern's entrance he watched the passage of several tall mercenaries, all men in their later middle-age. Although too old to go campaigning they nonetheless remained stout axemen quite capable of interior guard duty. If only Gerth were present! Alas, that cheery young armiger had crossed to the Asiatic shore in search of pasturage for Stormcloud; in the City of Constantine neither space for exercise nor proper forage was to be found.

"What barbarian speech is that?" demanded Sir Ugo over his wine cup.

"My mother's," snapped Edmund and could have bitten his tongue. After all, he held himself to be a Norman.

"After William the Bastard's conquest of England," explained Sir Toustain, "there appeared in Constantinople numbers of landless Saxon nobles forced to seek employment as mercenaries. Today great numbers of their sons serve in the Empire's forces.

"—And now, Sir Edmund, what is our lord's intended route?"

Narrowly Edmund scanned the yellow strip of parchment. "'Tis said here that Duke Bohemund, after landing at Durazzo, will depart inland as quickly as possible. He intends to march his array up the Apsas River's valley. And where is such a river to be found?" The Anglo-Norman raised inquisitive red brows.

Sir Ugo spoke promptly. "I know the Apsas well since during Duke Roger the Weasel's war against Alexis, I led a column up it. 'Tis ever a poor and a rugged country, but it becomes perilous once one enters the Grammos mountains. A few men well posted in the passes there could exterminate a multitude."

Edmund glanced upwards, surprised. "Oh, then you have read this letter?"

"No, my lord. It is only that the Duke required me to memorize its contents lest I should be forced to destroy the parchment." He closed his eyes, recited: "From the town of Antipatria the Duke's levées will enter the mountains betwixt Mount Boius and Mount Tymphe. It is a very narrow and difficult pass he has selected yet it remains the shortest route to Elimea, Tyressa, Alorus and later to the great Byzantine city of Thessalonica."

The one-eyed knight then several times rehearsed the list of place names and did it so earnestly that both his companions noticed it. Sir Ugo shrugged, shouted for another jug of wine.

"What tidings do you bear of the other Frankish armies?" Edmund presently demanded, himself memorizing the Duke of Otranto's new route.

"The Saints alone know," Sir Ugo grunted, snapping a stick of bread between powerful, tar-stained hands, "but it is certain that a duke who names himself Godfrey of Bouillon and a Count of Paris, together with a great host are marching somewhere within the borders of Romania. These princes, therefore, should be the first to arrive here." He yawned, stretched prodigiously. "Tomorrow I must learn what intelligences you have amassed for our lord that speedily I may take ship back to Bari. Where can I find lodgings?"

"At the Inn of Kosmos in the Genoese enclave across the Golden Horn," Sir Toustain suggested. "The food there is passable and," he grinned, "the serving wenches are said to be clean, cheap and agreeable."

"I thank you. Where shall we meet on the morrow?"

"There is a tavern on the waterfront near the Imperial arsenal known as the 'Net and Trident,'" Toustain replied. "That place would be as good as any."

Edmund arose, offered his hand. "Sir Ugo, I fear I must leave. Already I am over-late at the palace."

"Depart by all means," drawled Sir Toustain. "To anger the Countess Sybilla through tardiness would be unforgivable."

While he was breasting the hill toward lights gleaming within the palace, Gideon of Tarsus' words recurred. What in Perdition could the stylite monk have meant by that mumbo-jumbo concerning beasts and birds? The only understandable reference was to a boar. Drogo of Cetraro. But who did he mean by "the Nightingale"?

The former Earl of Arundel, aware of a chill wind nipping at legs encased in linen *bracae*, drew his cloak tighter. Drogo of Cetraro! It was long since he had given thought of his former foe. Odd, how clearly he could visualize even now the Lombard's brutally handsome face encrimsoned by effort as he had whirled up his mace.

"A plague on my slow wits!" Edmund grunted. "Why did I not question Sir Ugo concerning the levée of Sanseverino?"

Alixe! He slowed his gait when a pair of cloaked and armored Sclavonian sentries on guard at the gate loomed near. He wished, momentarily, to dwell upon the perfection of Alixe de Bernay's cool loveliness.

On nearing the Bardas Palace Edmund became aware of a soft whispering sound as of bare feet hurrying behind him. He spun about and was in time to glimpse the figure of a girl darting behind a clump of oleanders. *Par Dex!* It was Chloë. Why in the world should the wretched child still haunt him? Although several times he called her name he received no reply, so, with fur-trimmed mantle a-sway and long sword slatting at his hip the Anglo-Norman strode up to the palace entrance.

CHAPTER IV

Diplomatic Banquet

In the Despoina Eudocia's great marble-walled banquet hall unusual activity was to be noted. Under the tongue lashing of a Grecian major-domo house slaves scurried about decorating a long, U-shaped table. In deference to Frankish guests, benches and chairs had been grouped. Tonight there would be in evidence no *triclinia* upon which guests reclined sidewise in the fashion of the ancient Romans.

Sir Edmund encountered the Countess Sybilla at the top of a broad flight of steps. Radiantly lovely in a gown of filmy amethyst-hued silk she hurried towards him. How could she endure such a minimum of protection against the winter's bitter draughts? Even now they were causing braziers to flare and window hangings lazily to flutter.

"You are tardy returned, my lord," Sybilla reproached, advancing upon tiny, thick-soled sandals of gilt leather. In a seemingly negligent manner she adjusted a silk gauze scarf the better to reveal an amethyst and gold necklace glittering upon the white and symmetrical perfection of a daringly-revealed bosom. "What has detained you?"

Edmund flushed, hesitated. "Sir Toustain and I lingered to take wine at Count Maurice's villa."

Only the faintest reaction to this was a tautening of Sybilla's delicately patrician features. The little mole beside her eye had been effectively darkened and a faint bluish tint applied to her huge, violet-hued eyes.

"How pleasant. And what did you learn from Maurice Skleros? How far distant marches the host of Duke Godfrey de Bouillon, for instance?"

Again a sensation of helplessness, of bewilderment seized Edmund. How had she so swiftly learned of his visit with Toustain to the Skleros villa? To dwell in this weary, teeming old city was like playing the victim in an endless game of blind man's buff.

"We spoke of other matters," said he.

Sybilla smiled slowly. "Of what, then?"

"Oh, politics among the Infidels. It seems that of late the followers of Mahound have become divided and live in enmity and fear of one another much as do our dukes, counts and barons."

"Ah, yes. Since the death of the Great Sultan Malik Shah in 1092 his heirs, Kilidj Arslan and Kerbogha, have been at daggers drawn, while both hate and despise the Emirs of Aleppo and Mosul as well as the Sultans of Egypt." Sybilla bit her lip in impatience, moved so close that an aura of subtle perfume enveloped him.

"All this has long been known. Now tell me," she continued softly, "why you preferred talking to a tiresome old man whose loyalty is suspect, to taking cakes and wine with me?"

"I had meant to," he admitted. "It was simply that Sir Toustain and I overstayed our intent with Count Maurice and then prayed at vespers in the Great Cathedral."

Shepherding him into a small side room she slipped her hand into his. "Oh, Edmund! Edmund! Take warning. This Count Maurice of the famous Skleros family is the secret and mortal enemy of the Comnenes. To be seen too often in his company," her powdered shoulders rose in a little shrug, "would be to prejudice the Sacred Palace against you and through you, my lord Bohemund, whom the Emperor already hates and mistrusts."

Better attuned now to the nuances of life in the City of Constantine he sensed rather than saw an intense scrutiny on her part. Those carefully shadowed violet-hued eyes peered steadily into his face as if seeking to detect some item of knowledge being withheld.

Hum-m. Was she recalling her long liaison with the Mighty Southern Norman or what lay back of this searching look?

"You will be careful, oh most gentle knight, on my account?"

Before he was well aware of it, Sybilla had slipped cool, slender hands behind his neck to draw down his copper-hued head and so bestow a lingering kiss, the art and fervor of which he had never previously experienced. Before he could begin to emerge from a delicious daze, the Countess Sybilla's amethyst gown had drifted out of sight down that long, basalt-floored corridor which bisected the Bardas Palace.

This was to constitute the first in a series of surprises destined for the former Earl of Arundel during an evening which ever would remain memorable.

Still aglow he hummed, off-key as usual, and changed *bracae* and undertunic, for thanks to a generous sum found in Bohemund's purse he had been able to assemble a modest wardrobe. He took special delight in a new supra-tunic he would wear tonight for the first time. It was fashioned of some lustrous green material that shimmered in

the sun. Trimming the ends of its sleeves, its hem and bordering a
Y-shaped yoke which was passed over his head was cunningly executed embroidery in silver thread. What a pity he needs must draw
his Crusaders' surcoat over so splendid a garment. Still, because such
a surcoat lay open from shoulder to hem on its sides and was only
belted in, the company should be afforded ample opportunity of ad-
miring his new tunic, as well as crimson-gartered *bracae* of snowy
linen imported from the land of the heathen Bulgars.

To his belt the Anglo-Norman slung a handsome but serviceable
poignard and balancing it on its opposite side a small enameled box
containing a powder claimed by Sir Toustain to be an antidote for
most poisons. Beneath his tunic he smoothed the reassuring weight
of that fine, steel-mesh shirt which had been the Duke of Otranto's
parting gift. He now was prepared to enjoy a Byzantine banquet as
much as he might.

In a narrow street below his huge flame-tinted bedchamber, Edmund recognized a trampling of horses and the sound of harsh voices
speaking in French and in Italian. Obviously, Hugh the Great, flamboyant brother of the King of France and his cortège had arrived
so Edmund ran a coarse, sandalwood comb through coppery hair
now dangling almost shoulder-length and sped down the corridor to
meet his twin. They had made it a rule always to appear together on
any occasion when the sexes mingled.

Never had Rosamund de Montgomerie appeared lovelier, more
statuesque, than in this gown of canary yellow girdled in emerald
green silk cord. Somehow the Despoina's tiring women had wrought
miracles with the English girl's hair, grown fairly long again, but
still far short of those hip-length braids she had sacrificed that night
in Castle Sanseverino. She wore it parted down the middle secured
by a diadem of silver filigree which seemed to float upon a smother
of many small curls.

Edmund chucked his twin under the chin and grinned proudly.
"Before God, dear sister, you make these Eastern females appear
like peahens before a royal peregrine."

Affectionately, she patted his long red-brown cheek. "And you,
my Twin, will find every wench in the place cooing over you—in
addition to the Lady Sybilla." Her wide mouth formed a mischievous
half-smile.

At the foot of a wide staircase of black marble and beside a sunken
pool filled with bright little fish, sounded a babble of voices mingled
with the patter of servants running to attend new arrivals.

Several sharp frosts having occurred, relatively few flowers were
in evidence but varicolored candles by the hundred flared and

danced effectively to illuminate the designs of magnificent tapestries and hangings. Any one of them Rosamund reflected would have sent a Frankish lady to swooning in envy.

The guests numbered twenty in all and included, aside from the Franks, such famous Byzantine generals as Manuel Butumites, the Grand Primicerius Taticius, and two other weatherbeaten *strategoi* of the Imperial Armies. All four Byzantines wore dress corselets of solid silver wonderfully wrought and gilded, cloaks of Tyrian purple, buskins of gilded leather and the classic military kilt of long-vanished Western Roman legions.

For the most part these Easterners were dark featured, but had gray or blue eyes and the slow, steady regard of men habituated to surveying wide distances. Fluent in French, Romanese and Italian, Manuel Butumites gravely presented the Franks to the Despoina, a glittering diminutive figure in cream colored silk. Her zone was clasped in gold and studded with all manner of precious stones, as were a succession of bracelets climbing almost up to her elbows. A band of brilliant purple-red running about her sleeves indicated her connection with a former Imperial House.

Alas, the Bardas clan was no longer in power—a fact emphasized by the absence of any male Bardas with the exception of a superannuated grandfather. Obviously the poisoned cup, the headsman's axe and blinding irons had been busy, and not too long ago.

Seated upon a dais and assisted by the Grand Primicerius, the Despoina in musical Latin greeted these hulking, fur-clad strangers who reeked of leather and horses and introduced into her palace an aura of cold air and of immense vitality.

These Frankish barbarians Eudocia knew came from lands of which she had heard little save that the ground there was covered by snow during five months of the year and that their domains once had formed provinces of the Western Roman Empire.

She could even recall the names of a few—Armorica, Belgica, Aquitania, Helvetia, and Narbonensis. As a typical Byzantine patrician, the hostess despised these big men's ignorance, hot tempers and, worst of all, their senseless worship of physical prowess for its own sake.

Through experience with certain Francopoles—leaders of West European mercenaries—she was aware that these magnificent, animal-like barbarians called themselves "gentle men" but preferred nothing better than to get swinishly drunk, to smash things and then to slay one another over some trivial point of honor.

How abysmal was their lack of education of any sort. Why, hardly a Frank could read, or write, let alone understand anything concerning history or geography. Philosophy, they deemed to be some kind of outlandish religion.

Not one of these Franks, swaggering about in ankle-length mantles of bear, fox or wolfskin, could have suspected the Despoina's thoughts. Painted lips forming a gracious smile, she extended a pallid, perfectly-manicured hand to be kissed by the hard, bristle-rimmed mouths of the Cross Bearers who stared in open and childlike wonder upon the splendors of even this minor palace.

Inevitably, Sir Edmund's skill as an interpreter was called for so, reluctantly, he deserted Rosamund's side and stalked forward, towering above all of the Byzantines and most of the Franks. When his white surcoat blended with those of the French Crusaders a murmur arose among the handful of perfumed, splendidly appareled ladies in attendance.

Suddenly some Frank called out so loudly that the King of France's brawny, but vapid-faced brother glanced about. As an echo to that cry sounded Rosamund's sibilant gasp then Edmund stared unbelievingly upon that same massive figure he once had beheld bearing down upon him with death in his eyes. Drogo of Cetraro was pushing through a knot of Frankish nobles, features alight.

"Lady Rosamund! By the Holy Rood, 'tis the Lady Rosamund!"

She gasped and convulsively pressed fingertips to her mouth while Sybilla looked on, quite expressionless.

To Edmund de Montgomerie's astonishment, the Lombard swung over to him roaring, "'Fore God, here is my worthy conqueror of Sanseverino! Greetings!" There seemed nothing in the least uneasy or covert in his bearing.

Vastly puzzled, Edmund accepted the other's outstretched hand, said quietly, "Sir Drogo, I bid you welcome to Constantinople."

A thousand confused conjectures rushed about Edmund's brain. In the face of so hearty a greeting from a defeated antagonist, could it be possible that he really *had* dispatched that trouble-making armiger at Sanseverino? Perhaps for the hundredth time he ran back over the events of that one unforgettable evening. Why had Sir Hugues appeared armed in Rosamund's room? That point had clung like a burr to the mane of a horse. Curious too that the armiger should not have identified himself. He stared fixedly at Drogo's brutally handsome countenance, vainly seeking some betraying flicker of expression that might resolve these doubts.

"When I learned you had sworn to ride with Duke Bohemund," laughed the scarred, but boldly personable seigneur of Cetraro, "I would also have done so but I am ever impatient so I marched with a host already on the move. My gonfanon therefore follows that of Hugh of Vermandois."

Even as he spoke Drogo's clear, dark blue eyes probed that brilliant background created by the glittering costumes of Byzantine nobles, the jewelry and vivid gowns of their ladies until they came to rest upon Rosamund's tall figure.

Drogo's teeth gleamed white in the depths of his short forked jet beard. "I am delighted, my lord, to perceive that the ever-lovely and gracious Lady Rosamund has accompanied you to the wars. I trust," he added in a lowered voice, "that you will do me the honor of presenting me to your sister once more. I wish to attempt amends for my previous lack of courtesy."

Edmund hesitated, not knowing what to think. Had the Boar indeed changed his ways? Was he really innocent in that matter of Hugues de Bernay? The Lombard's next words decided him.

"Further, valiant sir, I bear tidings from Sanseverino—tidings two months old, to be sure, but still something that you may not yet have learned."

Edmund drew Drogo aside at the first opportunity, urged in taut tones, "How fares the Lady Alixe?"

Before Drogo might have replied, the *strategos* Butumites came tramping over. Although an Armenian by birth that crafty campaigner must have found the blood of many an ancient Roman patrician in his veins for he was neither swarthy nor did he display the fleshy lips and large, hooked nose so characteristic of that war-like and often ruthless people. His eyes were of a hard gray-blue and his bronze profile suggested that of some minor Western Emperor, a military leader of the type which had been briefly elevated to the Purple on the shields of the legions he commanded.

"Her Highness, the Despoina, requests, my lord, that you condescend to act as linguist between her and his Royal Highness of France."

There was no choice save to comply so Edmund approached the green velvet covered dais and the two strangely contrasting figures seated upon it. Hugh of Vermandois' hair was long, fine and yellow as any gold byzant in the Imperial Treasury. His was a long, straight nose, two small pale blue eyes set close, a broad chin and a petulant, too-red mouth the expression of which at once suggested sensuality, arrogance without nobility and cruelty without restraint.

While translating the subtle and convincing flattery addressed by the Despoina Eudocia to her guests and the ponderous and often coarse pleasantries of Vermandois, Edmund from the corner of his eye, noticed Baron Drogo inexorably making his way to Rosamund's side. He witnessed also the Lombard's profound bow and the cold little smile with which his twin acknowledged it. Then Count Baldwin of Hainault mounted the dais to join in the conversation. A chunky, immensely powerful appearing nobleman who lacked the half of an ear and most of his left cheek spoke heavily-accented French in a voice so guttural it proved difficult to catch even half of what he said. Shortly after his arrival the Bardas major-domo to a flourish of trumpets announced that the banquet was about to be served. Viols, harps and gitterns commenced softly to play when curtains of azure and gold damask were drawn back and the French knights gaped in honest wonderment upon the splendor of this red-marble walled banquet hall illumined as it was by hundreds of candles.

Not until a majority of the guests had staggered out into the courtyard and commenced bellowing at the tops of their voices for their mounts was Edmund able to escape from his place between the Countess Sybilla and the Grand Primicerius, Taticius, a Cappadocian commanding the Imperial siege trains.

Two matters had conspired to render the repast a wretched occasion. First, Cetraro, beetle-browed and as brusque as ever, had scarcely glanced at either of the pretty Byzantine ladies seated beside him at the great U-shaped table. He only stared hungrily at Lady Rosamund de Montgomerie, several places removed.

This might not unduly have bothered the former earl if his sister on several occasions had not acknowledged Drogo's stare with an enigmatic half-smile. Also disconcerting was Sybilla's refusal to disclose how she had learned about the arrival of Sir Ugo, Duke Bohemund's courier. To his persistent queries she merely gazed mockingly up from under heavily fringed eyelids. Later she had whispered, "I must see you as quickly as these drunken boors, er—I mean these over-stimulated gentle men, have taken their leave."

When at last it became possible to escape the banquet hall and only Baldwin of Hainault and a few other nobles, too drunk to mount a horse, had been bedded in the Bardas Palace, Edmund, his head a trifle light from too many draughts of a tawny Lesbian wine, wavered down the great central corridor peering owlishly into a succession of libraries, small dining apartments, music rooms and such, until in one of these he came upon Rosamund. The girl was seated upon a divan face buried in hands. She was weeping violently. Almost all the way across the dim, lamp-lit chamber Baron Drogo stood with feet braced apart and hands clenched behind him. He seemed to be staring fixedly into a brazier. A quick and sobering glance confirmed that not the least violence could have been offered to his sister, so Edmund's hand fell away from the poignard he had half-drawn. At the sound of footsteps, Drogo turned, a bitter smile on his scarred visage.

"It has been my sad task, Sir Edmund, to impart to this lady the tidings I spoke of concerning Sanseverino. Alas, that my news is so unpleasant, since I fain would earn the friendship of you both."

Edmund drew a deep breath and surcoat a-flutter entered the music room. "Before we speak of friendship, Sir Knight, will you answer me one question?"

Rosamund raised brimming eyes, burst out, "He already has done so. He swears on his knightly word that he knows naught concerning the sending of that armiger."

"Is this indeed so?" Edmund's voice grated like a galley's ram over a rock.

Solemnly the huge dark-haired figure raised his right hand. "I swear it. I know nothing as to how that vile deed was brought about."

"But did you not leave an armiger behind to care for a sick destrier?"

"Aye. But the lad was a simple fellow and honest as clear sunlight." The large, dark blue eyes shifted momentarily to Rosamund. "You must seek elsewhere for the culprit."

"Where, for instance?"

"I make this not as a hint, but as an observation, plain and simple. You witnessed how often Sir Hugues' younger brother fawned upon your lady sister? You knew also that Sir Robert hated his elder brother?"

The implication was so logical yet so unexpected as to leave Edmund briefly bereft of speech. On thinking back it seemed that Gerth had not been entirely convinced concerning that shadowy messenger's identity. The Anglo-Norman advanced with hands outstretched.

"Forgive my suspicions, Drogo of Cetraro. I should have known that so worthy a champion as yourself would prove incapable of such perfidy."

Once they struck hands Drogo did not loosen his grip. "Nay. Do not turn aside. Whilst I grasp your hands in friendship please to hear me out."

A fresh burst of weeping sounded from Rosamund's direction. "The wound you dealt Sir Hugues did not prove fatal."

"That is excellent, but how fares Sir Hugues? Will he recover?"

"Aye, but only in part. He has lost the use of speech and his sword arm dangles useless by his side. Further, his mind wanders into such strange fantasies that often his varlets must restrain him by force."

"God forgive me!" muttered Edmund. "For it was my arm that dealt him hurts so grievous."

"You have yet to learn the worst," sobbed Rosamund. "Come, dear my brother, and sit beside me whilst you hear."

" 'Worst'? What worse could there be?"

"Sir Drogo brings ill tidings concerning your beloved."

A series of icy ripples seemed to stiffen Edmund's shoulder-blades. "She—Alixe is dead?"

"Nay. She has entered a convent and is preparing to renounce the world."

Successive, invisible blows beat at Edmund's consciousness. He went scarlet, stood staring blankly at the powerful figure confronting him. "How did you learn this?"

"From no lesser person than the Bishop of Benevento I learned that the Lady Alixe de Bernay entered the convent of St. Ursula at Benevento nigh two months ago." Drogo placed an arm about Edmund's rigid shoulders. "Curse the luck that I should be the bearer of such cruel tidings."

He then crossed the music chamber to make a profound bow before Rosamund. She now sat bolt upright tears streaming unchecked down her cheeks. "I trust Lady Rosamund that you will receive me on a happier occasion."

Dully Rosamund replied, "Should I care to see you once more, Sir Knight, you will receive word."

Had Edmund de Montgomerie not been plunged in profound misery he undoubtedly would have noticed that a sudden flush stained the Baron's features. Certainly he was ill-accustomed to so casual a response from a mere female, no matter how beauteous.

CHAPTER V

The Library

Activity within the Bardas Palace so completely had ceased that the barked command of a serjeant of the guard posting a relief below distinctly could be heard. Edmund de Montgomerie heard him slumped in a deep armchair, chin on chest staring with unseeing eyes into a brazier's glow.

Alixe in a convent! Alixe occupying a bare and narrow cell. Alixe a postulant in a heavy white habit. Alixe shut off from the wonder, warmth and joy of life on earth.

Why had Alixe de Bernay taken so fateful a step? *Why?* As clearly as if the words had just been spoken, her cry: "I shall trust in you, my own true love, as you trust in me. I call upon God to witness that, so long as ever I shall live, I will become wife to no man saving Edmund de Montgomerie."

His fingers clenched themselves over the lion-headed arms of the chair. Alixe had vowed to become the bride of no man other than himself. *No man?* Maddening it was abruptly to realize that although she would marry no *man*, yet she remained free to become the bride of Christ!

Again he recalled that evening on the battlements of Sanseverino. So very clearly he could visualize her lovely features seen by starlight and the rich, warm pressure of her lips. No, there could be no reproaches over her having violated their troth, but the vision of Alixe, immured forever behind a nunnery's chill walls, prompted his every fiber to revolt.

What to do? *What to do?* Seek a ship to Italy and regain Sanseverino ere Alixe could bend her head to be shorn of those pale gold locks he had so loved to caress and thus become forever wedded to the greatest Lord of all? Savagely Edmund sucked in his breath, and glowered at the floor.

Could he in honor turn back? No. His oath as a Cross Bearer remained to be fulfilled. Moreover the Lady Alixe never would return to the world in order to wed a forsworn knight whose soul was doomed to eternal torments. And yet—and yet, his whole being cried out for Alixe's fragile beauty, for the ineffable sweetness of her presence.

" 'Tis of no avail," he muttered, unseeing of a small brown mouse which had appeared to warm itself beneath the brazier. "No. To return is—is not to be thought on. My liege lord's enemies are many and these Byzantines as deceitful as summer squalls upon the Arun River."

The former Earl of Arundel's ruddy head inclined still further and his eyes were closing when he noted the mouse's abrupt flight. Twisting sidewise he arose and had his poignard ready just as a hand came lightly to rest upon his shoulder. This was no assassin, only a small and lithe figure in flowing amethyst-hued robes.

"Put away your steel, my lord." Sybilla's features, always classic in their beauty, seemed softer than he had ever beheld them. Perhaps this was because they had been cleansed of that tinting which, of custom, magnified her charms and diminished her few defects.

"What an unwary Frank you remain. Long since I could have stabbed you, had I wished." Mockingly, she tapped a slender stiletto dangling from her girdle of yellow silk. "Really, Sir Edmund, will you ever learn not to drowse with an open door at your back?"

He shrugged. "Perhaps it would have been better had you dispatched me."

The young woman's expression became transitive. "For many minutes now I have stood not a yard behind your chair observing the depth of your grief and my heart cried out for you. What ill news have you learned?" She knelt beside him. "Have no fear, Edmund, but confide in me. I am wonderfully discreet—when I choose," she added with a flicker of a smile.

"'Tis a private woe, naught that you could understand," he protested and sat up flexing limbs grown stiff through prolonged immobility.

"Be not so sure. I—well, during my eight-and-twenty years, I have observed and perhaps have learned much. For instance, I would swear that at this moment you stand in dire need of consolation. Come with me into Eudocia's private library. A good fire is kindled there. Perhaps it will assuage your grief to tell me something of your troubles?" Delicately, her hand closed over his and a necklace of Venetian glass sparkled about the slender pillar of her throat emphasizing the dark luster of her hair. "I would comfort you, mayhap advise you, dear Edmund. Shall we take a cup of wine and then retire? The banquet was over-long. What a dull and tedious evening! Why are Franks incapable of conversation on subjects other than war, wenches and the hunt?"

Numbly, as in a dream, Edmund de Montgomerie followed the Byzantine girl's small supple figure down the hall and through tall bronze doors depicting scenes from the mythology of the ancient Greeks. Two great armchairs comfortably upholstered in Chinese silk stood sketching sable shadows before flames projecting lively patterns upon the walls tinted a warm Pompeian red. This chamber's ceiling shone blue as any summer sky. On a stool before the hearth stood a wonderfully fragile pitcher of Venetian glass and goblets finer than a meadow-mist, together with small raisin cakes, fruits and cheeses.

Briefly the flames effectively revealed the pulse quickening outlines of Sybilla's figure when, gracefully, she removed wine warming before the hearth and filled two tall glasses. Steaming, they gave off a pungent scent of cloves and cinnamon. Ignoring Edmund's refusal she thrust a goblet into his hand then sank into the chair opposite. Deftly the flames high-lighted her tawny cheeks, firm little chin and upturned nose.

After they had sat many moments in silence gazing at the flames,

Sybilla inquired gently, "Do you care, Edmund, to tell me, who secretly has kept your interest foremost in my heart, what intelligence causes you to glower so despairingly upon the world?"

Although he had resolved never again to make mention of Alixe de Bernay, by the time the Byzantine had refilled his goblet, his restraint was carried away by tides of emotion. He heard himself pouring out his anguish.

Sybilla listened, eyes fixed upon the fire and only smiled encouragingly when he paused. From time to time she arose to offer cheese and biscuits. Without a word she replenished again, and yet again his goblet. He perceived that her gown was diaphanous without seeming to be so—and that this lovely clever little creature really understood the depths of his despair.

While floundering in a pleasant, yet confusing tide of sensation he decided that his companion's brief comments seemed calculated to present a new and workable philosophy for him. In short the Countess Sybilla, all at once surpassingly and indescribably desirable, was convincing him that life was indeed short and that time was fleeting. What did it accomplish to mourn a lost love? In her low and softly vibrant tone she reminded him that about Byzantium many fair, noble and wealthy damsels were to be discovered, and without much effort on the part of a paladin as famous as himself.

When his head swayed in negation Sybilla added hurriedly, "None of these, of course, could approach the perfection of your lost Alixe, but I know several who would give much indeed to become chatelaine of that great domain you surely will wrest from the Infidels. Remember, Edmund, that you are much alive and that it boots nothing to mope over the cold and dead past."

"Perhaps," he grunted, relaxing in the great armchair. After a little, as he sat sipping the Lesbian wine and studying his companion's slender fire-lit figure so diminutive in her great chair he became aware of a pleasing sense of relaxation.

"Today we heard," he informed her, "that Kilidj Arslan, the great Turkish sultan, not only has summoned his vassals from the length and breadth of his realm but has sent his brother as an emissary to the Saracens in the south, urging that they join with him to exterminate us once we penetrate a certain flat land beyond the mountains. I do not know what this province is called but you Byzantines have a name for it."

"Can you mean the theme of Cappadocia or of Kosmodion or of Opsikon?"

His mind groped to grasp the correct name but failed. "No matter, but 'tis said the Infidels will swarm like the locusts that plagued you here last summer and that their numbers will be as the sands of the seaside."

"And if this is so—as surely it is—what then?" Sybilla slid onto the front of the chair and bent forward eyes intent and apparently unaware that the front of her gown had swung loose betraying the tender contours of her bosoms.

Unhappily, Edmund rumpled his coppery red locks. "The greater their numbers, the greater the honor to be won by valiant knights. No matter how many, they cannot withstand the charges of Frankish chivalry. We shall regain the Holy Sepulchre."

The Countess of Corfu leaned forward, her great violet eyes holding his relentlessly. "Of course. How can you Cross Bearers fail? Have they not for a leader that sage veteran of many wars, Duke Bohemund the Mighty?"

"True, true," he mumbled. "From what I hear and see—take that vain fop of Vermandois for example—no army of Christendom will be better led than ours."

"Always provided that the Duke arrives *before* the other Western princes can fill our Emperor with fear and envy against him," Sybilla suggested while smoothly refilling his wine cup. "That would be very easy to accomplish by simply reminding the Emperor that Bohemund and Robert Guiscard, his father, failed by very little of capturing this city. Will he arrive early? And will he advance on Constantinople by the speediest route?"

A flame of instinctive caution flared in the Anglo-Norman's brain but flickered and became extinguished among heady fumes seeming to swirl out of the goblet.

Sybilla laughed soothingly, arose to pause momentarily before the flames long enough to reveal the intimate perfections of her body.

A loose motion of one hand dismissed the queries. "I can't tell you."

"But you know, Edmund, my precious, surely you must. Or don't you? Possibly my lord of Otranto lacks sufficient trust in you?"

"Not so. He trus' me greatly." He was finding it increasingly difficult to enunciate clearly.

"Then say no more, I beg of you. Keep his faith unblemished," she murmured, then hovering over his chair she enveloped him in an aura of fragrance. "Your tunic is so thick and your surcoat so heavy no wonder you sweat like a peasant bridegroom! Permit me to loosen your collar and belt."

He hardly realized that Sybilla had settled lightly upon his knees and with one hand was undoing the silver and steel brooch securing the throat of his tunic.

She emitted a mock cry of dismay and shook her head so that delightfully fragrant locks brushed his forehead and chin. "Surely the Despoina Eudocia would take it amiss, Edmund, were she to learn that you had worn a shirt of steel mesh to her banquet. It was so warm in there you must have become fearfully uncomfortable."

"Yes," he sighed shrugging off surcoat and supra-tunic. "Such a shirt grows plagued heavy after a while."

The sensation of cool fingers laid upon his forehead, stroking, ever so gently, his hair, became agreeably stimulating.

"How odd that your locks and those of my lord of Otranto should be of so nearly the same hue. But why not? You are both mighty warriors."

He gazed up into the luminous outline of features held scant inches away, sensed the yielding warmth and pressure of her slight body strike through his undertunic as they lingered in the great chair and peered at the dancing flames. How wondrously soft was Sybilla and how light. Her head came to rest just beneath his chin while her fingers enlaced themselves with his.

"You can have no notion of how long and stubbornly I argued with Duke Bohemund concerning his course once he crossed the Sea of Hadrian and put foot once more in Greece." Her voice dropped still further until she seemed to purr. "Would you believe it? He refused my most earnest advice and insists on leading his array across Macedonia by way of—let me see—yes, Ochrida and Dodona." She stirred, nestled close upon his broad and muscular chest. "And did you know that his army really will embark not from Bari as he gave out but out of Brindisi?"

His hand wavered out towards the goblet, captured it. While the wind stirred long linen curtains concealing the library's wooden window shutters he swallowed a long and warming draught and then became pleasantly conscious that her cheek now was pressing his, then of an arm creeping to encircle his neck, of breasts bruising themselves against him.

"You are wrong, fair lady," he informed owlishly. "My lord Duke plan' such a route but long ago abandon'——"

The snapping of a log within the fireplace checked him. In the pool of firelight glowing amid the shadow-ruled library, Sybilla held her breath, then her hands busied themselves with his belt buckle, unfastened it.

"Come," she invited smiling up into his eyes, "rid yourself of this penitential iron shirt." The Countess of Corfu proved deft and, a very few moments later, the fine iron links clinked onto the floor beside his belt, poignard and the amulet of antidotes. He sat with chest bare save for an undertunic of white linen. She reseated herself in his lap, fell to fingering his ear lobe and then to nibbling it gently.

"But you must be wrong, my love," she resumed, "that *is* the route Lord Bohemund intends to follow. I am sure of it."

"No," he insisted thickly, "he will not follow in the path of France, Flanders and Bouillon. The Cross Bearers will have raided the country, scatterin' or imprisonin' the inhabitants, for all they're fellow Christians." Edmund licked lips suddenly gone stiff and dry. "I tell you he will land at Durazzo."

"And then?" her voice sounded drowsy, disinterested.

"The line of march follows Apsas River to place call' Antipatria, I think. Then the levées will descend some river—don't know its name. Anyway, it runs between Mount Boius and Mount Tymphe on the road to Elimea, then through Tyressa, Alorus from there to Thessalonica. You see? He—great leader, great prince. Ver' brave an' famous——"

"Oh, I am glad. So very glad! Even though my love for him has died. You—*you!*"

He crushed her with such cruel ardor that she cried out but then amid a roseate haze he watched her suddenly slip free of her amethyst covering and rejoin him silver-hued in the great armchair. Then in an agony of rapture everything became as nothing.

Perspiring, still breathless, Sybilla arose and resumed her garments. Causing a thin-whispering sound the stiletto slipped from its sheath. Swaying a little Sybilla leveled her slim streak of steel in line with his heart.

"Drunken oaf of a Frank!" she panted. "No recollection of this for you!"

Her supple figure gathered, straightened to apply its full power behind the knife. She actually had commenced her thrust—none would know, none would care in this vast and cynical community— but then the knife's point swerved.

"Oh, Edmund, Edmund! Wherefore?—Wherefore, should I be condemned to adore you—you, the stupid spawn of a barbarian wilderness?"

CHAPTER VI

Intelligences to the Maritime Palace

Long before either the Despoina or her besotted Frankish guests had roused, the Countess of Corfu called for a litter and an

escort of household guards. Leaving at the Bardas Palace no inkling
of her destination she was borne away, jaded and heavy-eyed, at an
hour when shopkeepers scratched and yawned while unshuttering
their places of business and gaunt street cleaners labored to collect
trash and refuse.

"To the Maritime Palace and without fanfare," Sybilla instructed
the *moirarch* of mercenaries. Relaxed upon her litter's cushions Sybilla listened to the staccato cracking of whips clearing a passage
through a press of farmers and hucksters on their way to Constantinople's teeming market places.

A sense of satisfaction filled her once the litter curtains commenced to sway regularly to the pace of stalwart Nubian porters selected for their uniform height and stride.

Surely Mary the Alan, Alexis Comnene's adored favorite concu-
bine could not have sallied forth this early in the day? Mary, whom
Alexis had usurped along with the diadem from that feckless poet,
Nicephorus III, was possessed of beauty reported to equal that of
Helen of Troas and to surpass in loveliness an ivory effigy of Venus
which once had graced the Pantheon in Imperial Rome.

More important, it was said of Mary the Alan that not only was
she tolerated by the Empress Irene, but also she was admired and
favored by the Emperor's precocious and erudite daughter Anna. At
the age of fourteen she was writing an account not only of her father's reign but also of the coming of the Frankish Cross Bearers.

At the gates to the Maritime Palace, white and shimmering in this
early morning sunlight, the Countess of Corfu was greeted and her
litter immediately admitted. Under a portico she alighted and, amid
a swirl of somber draperies, disappeared within.

An hour later, the *strategos* Manuel Butumites appeared in the palace court, mounted his horse and together with a detail of lancers
went clattering away towards the Sacred Abode—otherwise the Lion
Palace. A tight smile graced the Armenian's weathered features.
Certainly, Alexis Comnene, Christ-loving Emperor of the Romans
should prove well pleased with the news he was bringing.

"My lord! My lord! The sun is high and there is much to be done
today." Gerth's broad and windburned face was looming above Edmund de Montgomerie. The latter stifled a groan. Never before had
he been tormented by so severe a headache, not even after taking a
heavy mace blow on his helm. He was shocked and surprised to find
that he could recall practically nothing of what had been said or
done after having sought the library. Of a certainty he and Sybilla

must have conversed at length over more than a few cups of wine. Sweet Jesus! What a fiendish pain now throbbed within his skull!

"You discovered a suitable stable for Stormcloud?"

"Yes, my lord," Gerth grinned, bringing forward a cloth and a brass basin of icy water, "but I do not know whether it is wise to leave your destrier in Chrysoplis."

"And why not?" grunted Edmund raising a dripping face from the bowl.

"Not only are the Infidels marauding more boldly than ever along the south bank of the Bosphorus but yonder in Asia roam many masterless men, desperate cutthroats and the other armed rabble which, last summer, escaped the Red Lion's massacre of Peter the Hermit's and Walter the Penniless' followers." He laid out a fresh tunic, a pot of shaving unguent then fell to stropping a shaving knife on the callused heel of his hand.

"My lord," Gerth began uncertainly, "I know not what to make of it."

"Make of what?"

"When I returned to the city a young girl accosted me without the gate."

"'Tis small wonder. You're a lusty rogue," Edmund said, preoccupied with attempts to recall events of the night before. He summoned a wan smile and started to rise but settled back on his couch with a grimace. "Well, what of this wench?"

"It was not I she spoke of, but you, my lord."

Edmund yawned. "Me? What is her state?"

"Common, very common, my lord. For all her tender years she is painted and she dresses like a whore."

"So? What said she?"

"Most piteously she begged for honest employment in this palace. She swears she can sew and embroider more cunningly than most."

An Homeric yawn escaped Edmund. "'Tis a rare day when a whore seeks honest work." It was good to find excuse for not mulling over certain dreadful doubts commencing to simmer at the back of his mind. "What is she like?"

Gerth Ordway rumpled his coarse yellow hair and smirked. "She'd be a pretty piece, my lord, were one to scrub her clean."

"Are you so eager to undertake such a task?"

"St. Olav, no!" burst out the young Saxon and, catching up a brass-studded leather baldric, inspected its buckle with unnecessary care.

"But you would that I bespeak her to the Despoina's major-domo?"

Gerth lowered his gaze. "She is very young, my lord, and most forlorn. I know nothing of her tale," he added in response to Edmund's raised eyebrow.

"Methinks you had better address her petition to the Lady Rosamund, she could bespeak her case better than I." Again he yawned, then pulled on his undertunic. "After all, 'tis a Christian duty to raise the downfallen and if this wench is sincere in the matter of honest employment perchance my sister might employ her as a body servant, provided, of course, the girl has no sickness upon her."

Now that the floor had ceased to shift beneath his feet Edmund bound about his loins a fresh linen breeching and knotted the strings over his right thigh. "I will break my fast with eggs, milk and a morsel of meat."

The Saxon's bright blue eyes rounded themselves. "Is that all, my lord?"

"Yes. Now get you gone to the stable, order me a mount and prepare to attend me. I will ride out of the city northwards in search of a suitable campsite among the suburbs for my lord's array."

"Then my lord Duke is soon to arrive?" Gerth's broad features lit and he caught up a mace from an arms rack beside the horse supporting Edmund's hauberk and swung it in vicious circles. "I burn to ride against the worshipers of Satan. Has my lord heard what the Turks did yesterday before a watchtower a little east of Chrysopolis? They raided the vicinity then, before its walls, they planted a hundred lances and impaled a Christian child upon each. They left an equal number of men blinded and deprived of virile parts and as many more females ravished and helpless because the Turks had cut the great tendon of their legs."

"God send these outrages soon will cease."

Once Gerth had departed on his duties Edmund sought a windswept balcony that afforded a view of the port and, in hopes of clearing his head, stood there enduring the buffeting of a cold wind. For once he found no interest in the comings and goings of slender passenger caïques, of blunt, black sailed fishing craft, or of feluccas from Cyprus, Rhodes, Crete and other islands still owing allegiance to Byzantium.

Certain it was, he mused, that for the first time he must have become drunk to forgetfulness. Why? *Why?* Often he had consumed much more and had been none the worse. Could it have been because of his grief, this despair over the news of Alixe that he had lost mastery of himself? A nauseating revulsion flooded his being. Alixe! No. He must banish all thoughts concerning her were he to retain his reason and fulfill his oath. He simply must not allow himself reminiscences of Sanseverino.

His chausses' soles tapping heavily he tramped the length of the balcony, hands clenched behind him. What might he have said during those still watches of the preceding night? Try as he would he could recall nothing at all save the nearness of Sybilla's enchantingly lovely features, the beguiling softness of her body and nimble fingers busying themselves with the tie cords of his tunic and shirt of mail, which garments he had discovered beside his couch. How had they, or himself, for that matter, gained his sleeping chamber? He could summon no recollection at all.

Were not Alixe de Bernay irretrievably removed from his ken his agonies of remorse would have been even more severe. As it was he intended immediately to make confession in a lovely gem of a chapel adorned by the finest of mosaics in honor of St. Michael. Here, for the convenience of the Despoina's Frankish guests, a Latin priest had been invited to administer those comforts and disciplines peculiar to the Church of Rome.

Yes. It was necessary to unburden himself that he might again don his white surcoat and its flaming cross without qualms of conscience. As soon as possible he and Rosamund must find quarters among the Venetians over in Pera across the Golden Horn.

Just how much of Bohemund's order of march might he have confided during his drunkenness? Fiercely his knuckles pressed his temples but, try as the Anglo-Norman would, he could not recall anything.

A sound of slippered feet advancing along the corridor's mosaic floor roused him ere Rosamund appeared, fresh and reposed as if candles had not guttered in their sconces ere the Bardas Palace had quieted the night before. One glance at his drawn and haggard countenance brought Rosamund hurrying to his side. In silence she gazed into her twin's features, obviously seeking reactions to the news from Sanseverino. Presently she forced a small, metallic laugh.

"I have received two curious requests. First, the Despoina's major-domo fetched in a message," her eyes wavered aside and she brushed into place a stray reddish lock, "from Drogo of Cetraro inviting me to attend the candle-lighting service of St. Saviour in the Khora—'tis that big church between the old and the new walls—and then to attend a reception at the Subastocrator's palace."

"Subast—what in God's name is that?" Edmund snapped. "These idiotic Greek titles longer than a day without bread, are ridiculous. I yearn to hear simple Norman or Saxon talk once more."

His twin shrugged. "I know no more what a subastocrator is than you; only that he is a very high official in this great, smelly city, who ranks just below the Emperor and the Caesar."

"Shall you accept?"

Rosamund dropped her eyes to gold embroidered slippers of wonderfully delicate scarlet leather. A few odd months ago she would never have dreamt such could exist. "No, I do not think so, dear my brother. The Baron of Cetraro does not find favor with me."

With a forefinger he tilted her face upwards then looked steadily into her eyes. "Sweet Sister, keep your fibs for someone who knows you less well. You *do* favor that mighty champion." He said this without the least touch of braggadocio, quite forgetting that he himself had worsted the Lombard.

Rosamund's chin went a little higher and the rose hue of her cheeks deepened. "Nonsense! I will admit the fellow's very boldness does intrigue me, but that is all. I fear him. Drogo is too impatient, too harsh and too wedded to his own will. Furthermore has he not twice been a widower?"

"Other men have lost their wives," he laughed, then grew serious. "Beware how you tantalize such a man. He is no cub bear to be led around by a collar."

"Nevertheless," Rosamund said evenly, "I shall decline his invitation. Besides, I plan this evening to pray at a little Latin chapel just completed by some Pisan merchants. I should like to bestow upon it an altar cloth and burn some candles in prayer that Sir Hugues grows better of his afflictions."

In the act of turning away the Anglo-Norman checked himself. "And what was that other matter you mentioned?"

"You sent Gerth to bespeak my favor for some wench."

"I did nothing of the sort!" he snapped. "I only said he might address you. She is a child-like trull I was fool enough to favor with a small coin yesterday afternoon."

Mockery shone in Rosamund's lively blue eyes. "In exchange for what?"

"Nothing. I have only seen the creature twice; once when the anchorite was speaking his gibberish, and again last evening when she dogged me here."

"No doubt you would like to behold her for a third time?" teased the tall red-haired young woman. "The Despoina Eudocia's majordomo has permitted her to enter the palace."

A few moments later a slack-bellied Cyprian eunuch, bald as any boulder and oily of expression, appeared and salaamed in the Oriental fashion with hands held horizontal beside his head. "The street girl is here, my lady."

At a signal from Rosamund the servant withdrew, yellow robe rippling, then through the door was pushed the girl Chloë, a little less unkempt than before but still wearing her street-stained blue gown. Her grimy toes curled themselves away from the chill of the marble floor, but, surprisingly, she displayed none of the timidity Edmund had expected. Her eyes, he noted for the first time, were of the same color as a rich brown ale. They flickered about, taking in the rich hangings, the handsomely hammered bronze utensils at a fire-place. Next he noted that Chloë must have made a pathetic effort to cleanse herself. Her hands and face shone in cleanly contrast to whit-ish-gray dirt coating her arms and neck.

"Well?" Edmund demanded, not unkindly. "And what would you with my lady sister?"

"Oh, my lord!" The little harlot flung herself down and embraced his knees. "Do not let them drive me onto the street again. I swear to you, I will prove an honest and faithful servant to my lady. Believe me I know what is expected."

To his surprise her Greek was pure and spoken with a clear in-flection. On hands and knees she crawled over to Rosamund, then prostrated herself, touching the floor with her forehead.

"Get up!" Rosamund directed quickly. "In England we prostrate ourselves before none except God and the Virgin."

But the girl's small figure remained prone, with long yellow-brown hair streaming in disordered torrents over the mosaics.

"Who are you?" Rosamund bent and hauled the suppliant erect. "Why do you say you know how a maidservant should act?"

"Because once I had a slave girl of my own," the sorry figure informed. "Nay, I speak truth, my lady. I am Chloë Chrosoe. My father was a prosperous silk merchant of Nicea until the accursed Turks captured our city and slew all my family saving only me.

"In my thirteenth year my master sold me in concubinage to an old Saracen. I will not weary my lord and lady with an account of what chanced with me until I could hide in a baggage hamper and escape to this city—and even a worse life under the arches of the Hippodrome." Face buried in hands she commenced softly to weep.

"But why," Sir Edmund demanded curiously, "have you dared to follow me?"

"Because, noble s-sir, since I c-can remember, you have been the f-first man to look upon me with pity rather than lust or contempt." She raised a pointed, sharply chiseled face, peering up into the ruddy expanse of his features.

"You are willing forever to abandon your—your profession?" que-ried the Anglo-Norman girl, towering over the little Byzantine.

"Before the Holy Panagia, my lady, I have sought to do nothing else ever since I came here, but a weak and friendless girl it was impossible if I were to keep alive."

Before he quite realized it, Edmund had stopped, gripped her pitifully thin wrists and peered intently into the child's faintly oblique eyes. "Would you swear upon a holy relic," he said in his awkward Greek, "that all you have told us is no less than the truth?"

"Oh, my lord! Only grant me opportunity——" She sank onto her knees and again clung to his legs at the same time pressing her face against his thigh with such ardor that color surged into Edmund's features.

Rosamund commenced to laugh. "What say you? Shall I retain this Chloë for a tiring maid?"

"Why, yes, an it pleases you."

Neither of the tall Westerns would soon forget the transfiguration of that pinched, colorless and heart-shaped visage.

"In your hour of Judgment, dear my lady," Chloë quavered and tears coursed down her cheeks, "the Recording Angel will recall this charity. I shall try, oh so hard, to please my Lady Rosamund." She hesitated. "And you, Sir Edmund."

CHAPTER VII

Street Brawl

Sir Edmund de Montgomerie and his esquire were in no great hurry returning from hearing Mass in the Latin Chapel of St. Leo, a place of worship tolerated for the convenience of highly valued Western merchants and the Emperor's Venetian allies.

So many independent knights and their turbulent followers had appeared in Constantinople during the past few days that St. Leo's had been overcrowded. These warriors, so they said, had come to enlist in one of the Frankish armies, reportedly six in number, now converging upon Alexis Comnene's capital. A vast host, the army of Duke Godfrey de Bouillon said to number 80,000 swords, already lay encamped not two days' march from the city.

Gerth Ordway further ascertained from fellow Saxons serving in the *Heteria,* or Imperial Guard, that Duke Godfrey's levées en route through Macedonia had fought several skirmishes with Alexis Comnene's Turcopoles, but that the army of lower Lorraine on the whole had been restrained from looting the countryside through which it had passed. Also it was reported that Byzantine officers, for the most part, had received the Cross Bearers with real though wary generosity.

"And how fares your protégée?" Sir Edmund demanded as they strode along with mantles flapping under the coldest wind the winter yet had produced. It amused him to watch Gerth flush to the roots of his yellow mane.

"The wench Chloë is not my protégée, as my lord well knows, but one hears that she seems eager to learn our language, that she anticipates my Lady Rosamund's every wish and takes only a very little food from her table."

"Now that she has been cleansed and dressed in decent raiment would you say this Chloë is pretty?" Edmund's blue eyes gleamed.

"Indeed yes, my lord," the Saxon burst out while elbowing aside a passing donkey. "Her skin shines with the purity and pallor of— of that stone from which the great screen in the Despoina's reception hall is fashioned."

"You mean alabaster?"

"Yes, my lord, and her hair is soft as thistle down," the youth rattled on, heavy axe a-swing to his stride. "I am instructing her in the Saxon tongue—because my lady prefers to use that language in her chamber."

"How kind of you," Edmund grinned then, glancing down the street, noted the flash of a Crusader's surcoat a moment before Sir Toustain appeared cleaving the street crowds like the beak of a war galley. A single glance at his expression warned that something must have gone very much amiss; the veteran's single eye was glowing like a hot coal.

"Dismiss your armiger," he snapped in an undertone; "and come with me to my lodging."

Sir Toustain de Dives slammed and bolted the door to his small, ill-lit chamber then turned, his battered features dark with rage.

"What has gone amiss? Are there ill tidings from our Suzerain?"

"*Certes!* The Lord of Otranto has been betrayed by the babbling tongue of one in whom he placed the greatest of trust."

Edmund started up hand on sword. "Let me seek him out and slay this treacherous dog."

"That you cannot do," growled the veteran, "unless you would commit the mortal sin of *felo-de-se.*"

"Kill *myself?*" Frigid currents seemed to descend Edmund's neck and envelop his ribs. "*I* betray my liege lord? Are you gone mad?"

"No," came the veteran's harsh accents out of the gloom. "But two persons heard Sir Ugo, my lord's courier, describe the new route to

be followed by the levées of Otranto and *I* have kept a closed lock
on my lips."

That night in the library! As the appalling realization came home,
Edmund sank heavily onto a three-legged wooden stool. "God forgive me! In my drunken state——"

"Then you do not deny your guilt?" Sir Toustain's voice sounded
as insistent and penetrating as the notes of some oliphant. "How
came you to betray my lord's secrets?"

From the depths of a profound misery, Edmund related what must
have chanced in that firelit library of the Bardas Palace. He jumped
up, glaring wildly about.

"There is but one thing to do."

"And that is?"

"Dispatch a courier to warn our Prince that, under no circumstances, must he follow the road he spoke of."

" 'Tis easier said than done. God knows where Duke Bohemund
can be found. Oh, Edmund! Edmund! How could you be so slack-
witted as to tumble into that Greek witch's toils?"

Heavily, Edmund reseated himself. "I cannot understand save
that this news of Alixe rendered me distraught. Perceiving this, Sybilla seized her advantage." Characteristically, the Anglo-Norman
wasted no time in further repinings. "Know you of a messenger who
might hope to reach Bari?"

"Yes. Yesterday I encountered one Wolfgang of Amalfi, an old
companion-in-arms. He is crafty and skilled in languages and might,
with good fortune, reach Duke Bohemund ere misfortune overtakes
him."

"Should I not go myself?"

Sir Toustain shook his iron-gray head. "Will you never learn the
ways of Romania? If, for many a day, you set foot outside this city's
walls you will perish. Nay. Do not gape. Your least move is known
and mine as well. We live on borrowed time."

"How came you to hear of this, my error?"

"Count Maurice employs as good informers as any politician in
Constantinople. They informed him that the Countess Sybilla was
seen to call at the Maritime Palace very early in the morning; also
that Manuel Butumites shortly departed in great haste to the Lion
Palace.

"Yesterday, so they report, secret orders were dispatched to the
Byzantine Catapans at Durazzo and Thessalonica, through which
Bohemund must pass."

Slowly Sir Toustain's fist beat upon the table. "Neither of us can hope to win through. We must gamble upon the luck and wit of my friend."

Wolfgang of Amalfi received instructions, most of the contents of Edmund de Montgomerie's slim purse and the promise of far greater rewards were he successful in his attempt.

It came therefore as a crushing blow that the next morning Wolfgang of Amalfi should stagger into the Tavern of the Golden Swan, pierced by half a dozen dagger thrusts, and gasp his last before Sir Toustain could hear his story.

When, heartsick and burningly conscious of his responsibility, Edmund learned the news he summoned Gerth and bestowed upon him that shirt of steel mesh Bohemund had given him.

"Give out among the servants that you soon depart to Chrysopolis to attend my destrier," he instructed in the privacy of his bed chamber. "Then, when the Saxons among the Bardas guards go off duty tonight, you must mingle with them and await an opportunity to slip away. Be wary, be bold if you must, and never once forget that upon you depends the honor of Montgomerie. May our Lord Jesus Christ watch over and ever guide your course."

Two evenings after Gerth's departure Edmund, despite warnings from the former Constable of Sanseverino, persisted in visiting an armorer's forge there to supervise the working of a new helm—one with an adjustable nasal like those of the Turcopoles. He had discovered that only when so occupied could he find surcease from his gnawing anxiety over the fate of Gerth Ordway. The only reassuring fact was that the Saxon armiger had not turned back, nor had Count Maurice Skleros' informers heard of any yellow-headed barbarian youth being found dead.

Tomorrow he intended, with Sir Toustain, Count Maurice and an escort to view the Frankish host which, during these last days before Christmas had been occupying the suburb of Pera across the Golden Horn. It was reported that, at sunset, the twinkling of steel among the Westerners' weatherbeaten tents suggested sparks blown from some Titan's forge. From a tower of the city's battered and slimy seawall Sir Edmund had found it wondrously inspiring to behold across the waters of The Horn, such veritable forests of spears and lances, all displaying Cross Bearers' white pennons.

A splendid idea this, of riding out with Count Maurice who, in his office as Great Domestic, must negotiate with the Frankish leaders for the procurement of food and forage.

Edmund guided his steed into a narrow cobbled street which was neither mean nor yet pleasing. As, slowly, he rode among the deep-

ening shadows past the dwellings of better class merchants his
thoughts reverted to Rosamund. How moody his twin had become
during these last few days. Had she, perhaps subconsciously, contracted his own sense of shame, concern and miserable uncertainty
over Gerth's mission? Why had she, with feminine perversity, de-
clined a second and more insistent invitation from Drogo of Cetraro?

"On a third occasion," she had smiled, serenely stitching a new
leather backing to his coif, "perhaps I shall accede to this headlong
Lombard's wishes."

"You had best humor him, dear my Sister, an he approaches you
once more," he had advised. "This headlong fellow well deserves his
cognomen of 'Wild Boar.'"

Boar? Again he recalled the stylite saint's warning. What was it
he had said? "The Lion and the Eagle the Leopard need not fear.
But the Nightingale and the Boar bring his undoing near." Could
Gideon of Tarsus really foresee the future? Nonsense! Sheer nonsense. And yet he had mentioned a boar, who certainly had come
close to proving his undoing under the walls of Sanseverino.

He was passing the mouth of a short cul-de-sac when out of it came
confused sounds, the hurried trampling of feet, panted curses and
the distinctive shivering noise caused by steel rasping against steel.
Spurring into the cul-de-sac the former Earl of Arundel glimpsed a
tall young fellow garbed in the white, scarlet edged robes of a Byzantine patrician hard beset by six or eight hulking mercenaries. Bellowing drunkenly, they swung with clubs and daggers at him whose
slender sword licked out with amazing speed.

"A rescue!" gasped the young Byzantine backing slowly into a doorway.

Edmund hesitated not an instant but jerked out his sword, charged
into the cul-de-sac and was upon a long-haired fellow in a blue and
yellow cloak almost before he realized it—but not quite. Half the
assailants whirled to engage him with surprising readiness. Edmund's blade hissed down and he received an impression of a freshet
of bright scarlet bursting from a Norseman's neck where it joined
his shoulder. At the same moment, however, a mercenary leaped up
behind him and literally tore him out of the little palfrey's saddle.
Somehow Edmund regained his feet, aimed a cut at his nearest enemy and found time to lunge at a third of these howling figures in
the winged helmets and blue capes before he felt a searing pain in
his right side. Then a club came crashing down upon the steel skull
cap he wore beneath a peaked hat of blue-dyed leather.

Shuddering like a stunned ox, the Anglo-Norman sank to his knees,
then toppled over, senseless, upon the cul-de-sac's slimy pavement.

CHAPTER VIII

In the Street of the Winged Bull

Aware of strident street cries and the crack of whips beating a passage through teeming traffic for her horse litter, Rosamund de Montgomerie braced long limbs against hard, brocade-covered cushions and angrily wished that it was not so unheard-of for a well-born female to ride horseback abroad in Byzantium.

Opposite her Chloë's diminutive body bunched itself as, fighting the litter's jolting, she clung, highly pleased, to a leather handloop.

The last few days had wrought a remarkable transformation in the former street girl's appearance. Even in this short time Chloë Chrosoe's emaciated figure had commenced to fill out and a hint of color showed in her pointed features. Her hair when washed for the fifth time proved to be of a rich and lovely shade of yellow brown.

Such conversation as passed between mistress and maid necessarily was conducted in simple Greek and occasional phrases in Anglo-Saxon, of which already the girl was acquiring a considerable vocabulary—thanks no doubt to Gerth and the Despoina's Saxon house guards.

For the past three days Rosamund had fought a slowly mounting uneasiness over her twin's prolonged absences from the Bardas Palace, for all he merely had ridden to assist in securing supplies for Godfrey de Bouillon's iron-clad followers.

Like a steel tipped river the Lorrainers, hard-faced barons, rapacious serjeants and men-of-arms had appeared on the old Roman roads from the north, their spearpoints sparkling like wind-whipped water under a bright sun. These Cross Bearers spoke varying languages, most of them guttural, ugly to the ear and quite incomprehensible to a Norman. Proud and quick of temper, they burned with a fanatical desire to assault the hated Infidels without delay. Many of these doughty seigneurs evidently had entertained no idea of the distances to be traveled for they had fetched along hawks and hunting dogs, as well as wives and children. These last had grown thin and sickly during their long and arduous southward progress.

Penniless Cross Bearers and those of low degree by all accounts had suffered severely and had traced Duke Godfrey's line of march with a small army of skeletons. These had been serfs, villeins and free farmers who had quit their plows to catch up axe, scythe or bill and kiss wives farewell. Hopefully had they trudged off to win

salvation in a holy war which, undoubtedly, would end in time for
the next Spring's planting.

"My lady has been fortunate," Chloë smiled, "so quickly to discover
an iron shirt of a size suitable for my lord Edmund."

"'Tis fine and light, to be sure," Rosamund admitted over a brisk
clatter of hoofs and the shrill curses of Syrian camel drivers disputing the right-of-way, "but it would never turn a Frankish arrow or
sword."

"Still it should serve well enough against Seljuki arrows and scimitars, which I am told are much lighter than Frankish weapons. My
lady could, of course, seek further," Chloë added quickly. "Perhaps
another and a heavier shirt of mail could be discovered?"

"So that I might bestow this one upon Sir Edmund's armiger when
he returns. Is that it?" Among shifting shadows caused by the litter's
swaying leather curtains sounded Rosamund's deep laugh.

"Oh, no! No! Such was not my thought," Chloë protested. "It is
only that there are so many sharp knives and evil men abroad in
this modern Gomorrah. When does my lady think Gerth Ordway may
return?"

"The saints alone can tell. You *are* daft over that yellow-pated
lout, are you not?"

"I pray every night in the palace chapel that good St. Basil will protect him and speed him back to—his lord."

By peering through the gilded curtains Rosamund ascertained that
her litter and escort were turning into the Street of the Winged Bull
—a thoroughfare so narrow that the houses along it seemed to touch
eaves overhead and exclude most of the light.

The Despoina's outriders, four in number, were cursing and slashing lustily at the crowd with their whips but even so the litter inexorably slowed to a walk.

Irritated by the approach of a file of shaggy and evil-smelling
camels the litter horses commenced to fidget and snort then, abruptly, the litter halted. Feet trampled, men shouted and women
shrieked. The gaily caparisoned horses had been seized by the bridle
and were being forced back on their haunches causing their burden
dangerously to pitch and cant. Uttering squeaks of terror Chloë
clung to the handholds but Rosamund's strong voice rang out in a
volley of outraged Norman oaths.

Now the *wheep!* of steel being drawn from scabbards was added
to the rising tumult.

On peering through the curtains Rosamund was aghast to perceive
the entire little street to be swarming with armed men wearing
pointed steel caps. For the most part these were Vikings but, in-

credibly, a few appeared to be Normans! Quickly she noticed that not only her outriders but also their assailants seemed to be making only a show of conflict, for all that they were clashing swords and yelling at the top of their lungs.

"Fight, you cowardly dogs! Fight!" shouted Sir Roger de Montgomerie's red-haired daughter. "I could do better myself!"

All at once the curtains were wrenched violently apart and a yellow-maned Northman reached in to wrap an arm about her waist. Although she struck out and scratched like a trapped wildcat Rosamund was hauled from the swaying litter towards a low doorway handsomely decorated in the Byzantine style.

"*Au secours!*" she shrilled until a sweaty hand clamped down over her mouth. When she bit so hard the salt-sweet taste of blood welled into her mouth someone then dealt her such a stinging clout on the cheek that her head swam and she could struggle no longer.

As from a great distance, the Lady Rosamund heard a Norman voice growl, "Fetch along the serving wench and if the slut screams, stab her." A door studded with rusty nails swung open then crashed shut while the emptied litter lurched on down the Street of the Winged Bull.

Hours later a meal, evidently Frankish cooked, of stewed beef garnished with leeks, carrots and garlic together with a pitcher of wine were placed upon a table in that dark room where Rosamund de Montgomerie yet raged in futile rebellion.

A sturdy, sallow-faced female in Eastern robes then appeared and in silence offered a salver upon which reposed a delicate golden diadem. The candle light drew flashes from several tear-shaped pearls and a heavy incrustation of amethysts, rubies and emeralds.

Rosamund, because she was very hungry, ceased railing at these ox-stupid servitors and, watched by Chloë round-eyed with fear, commenced to stuff her mouth in the Norman fashion.

As her jaws worked on beef which, after the highly seasoned fare in the Bardas Palace seemed wonderfully tough and tasteless, she gazed about. This apartment she perceived to be stone-walled but its severity had been disguised by a number of mouldy-smelling hangings which appeared to be of considerable antiquity.

Try as she would, she still could not grasp what was afoot. Why should her litter have been diverted into the Street of the Winged Bull? Whose residence was this? For what purpose had she thus been abducted? A chill descended when she recalled Sybilla's talk about the not-infrequent disappearance of comely girls and young women.

Again the confusion, the endless complexity of life in Constantinople baffled and discouraged her. Had the Despoina, for some un-

fathomable purpose, arranged this abduction? Certainly her servants
had not put up any sort of a resistance.

Irritably, she pushed aside her plate whereupon Chloë bore it to a
corner where she squatted and like a famished little animal hurriedly conveyed remnants of the stew to her mouth with the help
of a curious three-pronged instrument much resembling a miniature
eeling spear.

A peremptory knocking caused Rosamund to jump up and turn so
violently that her gown of jade green cotton and her amber-colored
street mantle swirled about her. At the door appeared two broadly
grinning Norman men-of-arms bearing torches, then entered a well-
dressed individual wearing a heavy golden chain about his neck. In
Italian-Norman he said as he executed a profound but awkward bow,
"Be pleased to accompany me, gracious lady."

"That I will not! I am here against my will." Like the peal of a
silver trumpet Rosamund's voice went winging down a dark col-
umned passage visible behind the door.

"Then, my lady, no matter how regretfully," the Italian announced,
"these men must be forced to bear you to your destination."

An imperative gesture from Rosamund checked the two underlings. "Lead," she directed icily, "but keep your filthy paws from me."

To boast so small and unimposing a street entrance this structure
through which she was being conducted, appeared to be surprisingly
commodious. It seemed, however, not to have been inhabited in considerable time. No signs of family life were anywhere in evidence
while the air smelt damp and an odor of rats and mice everywhere
was strong. As, haughtily, she paced along she suspected that this
might be one of those properties which, long ago, had been seques-
tered from some rival of the then ruling Imperial House.

At length the little cortege halted before a bronze double door
green with verdigris but wonderfully worked and ornamented by
squares of porphyry. When this portal was opened an odor of burnt
candle grease mingled with that of stale incense beat out into the
corridor. Rosamund took four steps into this dim chamber with low,
vaulted ceilings and then halted abruptly.

Standing squarely in the center of the floor with powerful legs
straddled and wearing the scarlet Cross of a Crusader bright upon
his snowy surcoat, Drogo of Cetraro was waiting. A few jewels
flashed upon his fingers and from a chain about his neck when he
hurried forward and would have kissed her hand had she not jerked
it away.

"Welcome," he said, "to the House of the Winged Bull, which, although not my own, still is mine until I have no further use of it."

The chamber was vaulted, supported by four massive and ornately carved pillars that must have been very ancient indeed. Here and there tall candles glowed more brilliantly and less smokily than the wooden flambeaux to which they both were accustomed.

Ranged statue-still behind the Baron of Cetraro and sharply outlined against the gloom, stood four Viking mercenaries. They towered almost as tall as did the former Earl of Arundel. Their long scarlet cloaks and silvered helmets glowed in the candle light as if fashioned from molten metal, but metal hawks' wings sprouting from beside these Norsemen's steel caps shone less brightly.

Rosamund stood rigidly straight, eyes level and chin outthrust. An initial surge of relief at beholding the Lombard's familiar face drowned swiftly in a sense of outrage.

Teeth shining Drogo took a forward step. "And why did you not honor me by donning the diadem I sent you?"

"I would not touch the gift of one so utterly despicable, arrogant and so completely lost to honor."

Drogo's expression hardened, erased his smile and replaced it with cruel lines. "For your own good, lay no more hard terms upon me. I will not tolerate such from man or woman. Now harken and harken well. I only had you fetched here because it pleased your silly whim to ignore my most humble, polite and ardent pleas." He tried to smile again. "In truth never before has Drogo of Cetraro so abased himself before a female."

Rosamund, quite unabashed, continued to look him squarely in his eyes. "This time my brother will not spare you."

Drogo emitted a rasping laugh. "You forget that, mindful of his Crusader's oath he may not, without prejudice to his immortal soul, attack me. Nor would he find cause—provided you act with common intelligence."

So outraged was Rosamund that her hands commenced gently to tremble as like a fiery current her sire's headstrong blood raced through her.

"Only a perjured craven would have reasoned out matters thus!"

By a great effort the lord of Cetraro restrained himself. His feet, in pointed scarlet shoes, moved towards her.

"Rosamund de Montgomerie," he cried in thick accents, "I do now sue for your hand in honorable marriage, so greatly do I love and respect you. You shall be chatelaine over five goodly estates in Italy, each richer than Sanseverino. When this war is done I swear that you shall reign as Princess over a realm so broad that it cannot in two days be traversed on horseback."

"Get you gone!" Her head jerked backwards. "You cannot bend me like some whimpering peasant maid."

To her astonishment he burst out laughing and an excited gleam lit his large, dark-blue eyes. "Now before Christ and all His Apostles, you please me more and more, Rosamund de Montgomerie." Suddenly he wheeled and called an order over his shoulder which sent his four retainers to lumbering across this dim, low-ceilinged chamber. A pair of Vikings sought one door, two another. They waited, expectant and grinning behind long and drooping blond mustaches.

"Wulf!" One of the Norsemen wrenched open the door before him.

A dazzling burst of radiance broke forth. Amazed and bewildered, Rosamund could by the light of many candles see a small and fragrant smelling apartment dominated by a huge couch, canopied and covered with flame-hued silk, and a table upon which glittered a number of rich ornaments. A trio of blind musicians uncertainly fingered their instruments beyond a table loaded with all manner of delicacies.

"Look!" commanded Drogo with a violent gesture. "In that room we bed tonight."

"You will slay me first!" the Anglo-Norman girl appeared not in the least frightened; only coldly defiant.

"Sigurd!" Another door was pulled open and a radiance not so brilliant as the first dissipated the gloom.

"From where you stand you cannot see." His hand shot out and closed over her wrist. She aimed a blow at his head with all the strength of her supple young body behind it, but his other hand intercepted it.

"What good is a kitten without claws? Now, dear my lady, pray peer into this other room."

Although Rosamund set her weight against him so much he had to haul her over the stone floor he brought her before the door of a chapel. Silver lamps suspended from the ceiling were giving off cloudlets of perfumed smoke and glittering ikons encrusted with jewels and framed in gold stood upon an altar. Before a crucifix of extraordinary beauty waited a priest of the Latin Church, and a pair of acolytes. Slowly these last commenced briefly to swing their censers.

"Now make your choice, my lady," Drogo invited. "Shall we now exchange marriage vows before Father Gregory or," he grinned, "shall I carry you directly into the other chamber?"

Incredulous, Rosamund gazed into the chapel. Could all these scenes and events be actual, or visions from a dream? Were those live people within? They stood so motionless that the priest's gray hair shimmered not at all in the golden effulgence.

"I warn you, Drogo of Cetraro, I will have none of you!"

"Ah, but you will!" said he in a suddenly subdued voice. "You, I must and will have, and within this hour. Surely, Rosamund, you must have known that my heart, such as it is, has been yours ever since that day I first beheld you upon that tower at Castel Sanseverino. Look at me." His hands gripped her shoulders, forced her to face him. "Look at me!" he repeated. "Dare you to swear, before God, that you *really* hate me, that you have never experienced more than a passing fondness for me?"

There was that about him, something in his eyes so dominant that a measure of rigidity departed from Rosamund's body.

"No—I—I cannot in truth swear to such things."

"Well?" he queried softly. "Shall we enter the chapel before we seek the sleeping chamber?"

"God help me!" Rosamund burst out, her lovely features crumpling, "I cannot help myself. Perhaps 'tis witchcraft but I *will* have you to be my lord and husband, headstrong, cruel and willful though you are. No!" Placing both hands against his chest she fended him off as she blazed, "You must listen to the promise I now make: mishandle, humiliate or betray me but a single time and I will slay you."

"I would have you under no other terms." He stooped, kissed her hand and then offered an arm. As the priest commenced to chant he led Rosamund de Montgomerie into the chapel.

CHAPTER IX

Count Leo

The winter of 1096–97 proved to be uncommonly severe, especially for the ever-augmenting host of Cross Bearers. Forbidden access to the City of Constantine save in groups of six or eight and then only for the purpose of worshiping in one of the hundreds of churches, Duke Godfrey's ragged followers were transported to the Asiatic shore after a small pitched battle fought with some Betchenak mercenaries before one of the city's gates.

A few important counts and barons had been quartered in some ancient barracks but the great majority suffered in thin tents while their followers, numbed by cold, contrived rough huts or burrowed into steep hillsides behind Chrysopolis.

To make matters more difficult a plague of locusts the preceding Autumn had devastated the countryside therefore food and forage of all sorts were in short supply and, had not Imperial galleys fetched corn in from the Euxine Sea, many more Franks would have starved to death.

That there should be clashes between Frankish hotheads and their barbarian allies was inevitable, but, even more frequently, did Western barons assail one another despite the Crusader's oath. Another cause of dissension was the fact that Alexis Comnene cunningly exacted an oath of fealty to himself from each Crusading leader as quickly as he arrived. Only a few stoutly resisted the Emperor's lavish gifts, blandishments and veiled threats.

Following the example of courageous but vain and shallow Hugh of Vermandois these simple gentle men guilelessly knelt and placed clasped hands between the Christ-loving Emperor's jeweled palms.

One by one, Godfrey de Bouillon, Robert of Flanders, Baldwin and Eustace of Boulogne solemnly promised to restore to the rule of Romania any captured province or city which *once had belonged to the Empire!* So ignorant were these unlettered princes that not until much later did they learn, to their incredulous astonishment, that the Byzantine Empire once had stretched as far west as the Straits of Gibraltar and had embraced all Italy and the entire North African littoral as well as Egypt and the Holy Land!

Nevertheless a thousand problems and uncertainties assailed the Wearer of the Purple, ever patient, ever friendly-appearing. Lights burned late in the white marble halls of the vast Augusteon Palace. The Grand Logothete, or Minister of War, the Emperor's brother—dignified by the title of Subastocrator—and the Caesar, who served as tribune for the entire Empire, sat in council, tugged their beards and gnawed their lips while awaiting the arrival of dispatches from Manuel Butumites in Thrace whither that able and politic general had been dispatched ostensibly to welcome, and then to guide, Duke Bohemund of Otranto's rapacious Southern Normans towards their destination.

It was as well, they smiled, that nearly all of the Frankish arrivals now lay encamped amid sifting snow on the Asiatic shore where they could bicker and pillage to their heart's content without jeopardy to the Imperial capital. Meanwhile Constantinople's arsenals were working night and day to equip a Byzantine army which, in the Spring, was to join in the Crusade.

Already Imperial recruiting officers were penetrating the bare hills of Greece and Macedonia and emissaries, equipped with heavy chests of gold, were negotiating with certain savage fur-clad khans, independent Seljuk chieftains and Betchenak minor sultans prowling the Black Sea's northern coasts. Therefore ugly, stunted-looking Betchenak, Patzinak, Sclavonian and Seljuk barbarians appeared by the thousand to swell the ranks of Christendom. There were no Christians among them, only moon-worshiping pagans or Moslems. The only things these men held in common were bravery, a more than bestial cruelty and an insatiable thirst for loot.

News of these events penetrated only gradually to that sumptuous bedchamber in which Sir Edmund de Montgomerie lay recovering from a deep wound in his back—one which Bohemund's mail shirt easily could have prevented.

One evening he felt sufficiently restored, thanks to the ministrations of various Greek physicians, to sit up and consume a real meal. Only then did Count Leo Bardas make his appearance. He was undoubtedly the handsomest older man the Anglo-Norman had ever beheld. Clad in gorgeous scarlet robes stiff with gold brocade, the Byzantine advanced and to Edmund's complete astonishment, bent his noble head in order to kiss the patient's hand with fervor.

Said the old patrician in heavily-accented Norman-French, "I have waited, most valiant Knight, until your strength should have become somewhat recruited so that my expressions of gratitude should not weary you."

At the Anglo-Norman's startled expression he smiled, then quietly seated himself before a brazier and extended blue gaitered legs towards its heat.

"Do you know who I am?"

"Are you not my host, he who was *Klissarch* of the Anatolic Theme? Was it not you who thrice has routed Saracen armies of invasion?"

Still smiling, the older man stroked a short and pointed silvery beard. "That may be so, Sir Knight. Ah, me. In those days the Empire had a real army not miserable European starvelings but sturdy fighting men from the Asian themes of Cappodocia, Armenia and Anatolia. Who told you of my unimportant campaigning? My niece Sybilla, no doubt?"

Edmund's red head inclined and hair which again hung down his shoulders gleamed in the candle light.

The veteran leaned forward at the couch side elbows on knees. "Has she told you why I hold myself profoundly in your debt?"

The former Earl of Arundel shrugged. "She said only that I saved some relative of yours from death at the hands of drunken Varangians."

"A relative indeed!" Count Leo snorted. "He whom your valour preserved is merely my one and only son, Titus." He added gravely,

"Titus Bardas, alas, all that is left to perpetuate my line. Can you now understand why I shall ever remain profoundly in your debt?"

"And where is your noble son? I would greet him."

"Alas, he is no longer in Byzantium. He lingered a full week but you were so slow in regaining your wits that he has sailed on recruiting duty to the lands beyond our Chersonic Theme."

Wine was fetched and the oddly-assorted pair commenced to converse as they were to talk on many a chill evening. Apparently the veteran found much pleasure in seeking his guest's chamber there to discuss famous and victorious campaigns fought against the Infidels before the Emperor Romanus Diogenes' catastrophic defeat at the hands of Sultan Alp Arslan.

He caused to be brought in copies of Leo the Isaurian's *Tactica* and *Artis Militaris,* written by an emperor called Maurice almost an even five hundred years earlier.

"The work of Leo," Count Leo explained seriously, "in truth was largely based upon that of Maurice since he made no fundamental changes in our Army's organization or tactics but only adapted them to modern conditions."

Into Edmund's ready ears he poured all manner of wisdom concerning the waging of war not only against the Turks and Saracens but also against the Franks.

On one particularly fine January evening the wounded man straightened a light fur blanket covering his knees but still could not suppress a grimace of pain. That slash, he told himself, certainly must have severed several minor muscles.

"Which do you deem your most difficult enemies? The Franks?"

"No. The Saracens, by far," came the prompt reply, "although your Franks, individually, are not to be withstood. There is not a Roman"—it was curious that the Byzantines invariably referred to themselves as such—"no matter how brave and well armed, who can stand against one of your armored knights astride a well-trained great horse."

Count Leo burst into a contemptuous laugh. "By the Panagia! You Franks are brave, but military imbeciles! Nay, do not flush with rage, Sir Edmund, for this, alas, is so. The best fashion to fight the Franks we know is to pretend flight until their lumbering destriers, which must support big men like yourself, become exhausted. Once a Frank is afoot and armed but with his sword or mace, why 'tis child's play to shoot him down with arrows or to so exhaust him under our hot sun that he will fall fainting under his suit of mail."

"But 'tis shameful to fly!" Edmund burst out. "Our code of chivalry judges flight akin to cowardice."

"So 'tis doubtless wise to ignore a general's commands to deal mighty blows against long odds and perhaps lose the battle?"

"How else can a knight win fame and honor?"

"Then the winning of personal renown is to be preferred to a battle won?" Count Leo was tolerance personified.

"We think so."

"Exactly. That is why Alexis Comnene's much smaller army drove your Duke Bohemund out of Greece. Oh, Edmund, Edmund. Harken and be not wroth. If your Crusade is to succeed you Franks must learn discipline and tactics else your bones will bleach upon the hills and plains of Syria. Raw courage is not enough. And as for your gallant chivalric nonsense—faugh!—forget it. Neither the Turks nor ourselves value valor which does not advance a victory."

Somehow the wounded man fought down instinctive outrage to inquire thickly, "And what course should our princes follow?"

"They must organize their forces into battalions, exact obedience and plan their campaign far, far in advance. Also they must try to foresee what supplies will be needed when, and where. At present your armies are but unequally armed mobs. Like the barbarians of the steppes they obey none but their clan chieftains. Is there a corps of engineers among them? Nay. Are their followers divided into *turmae*, each with its own colors and trumpet signal? No. Have they any *scriboni* who follow the fighting, succor the wounded and so preserve many a good soldier to fight another day? Worst of all, you Franks follow no strategy thought out in advance whereby a mighty enemy can be compelled to surrender without fighting for want of food or water. All you Westerners dream about is trading mighty blows with some enemy foolish enough to stand fast until you can cut him down."

Count Leo signaled a slave to scatter more charcoal upon a brazier for the night was growing raw and a cutting wind had commenced to sigh through the cypresses below the windows.

The elder man suddenly leaned forward, freckle-mottled hands locked before him. A twinkle shone at the back of his penetrating gray eyes. "You amaze me, Sir Edmund, indeed you do. Most Franks would have tried to slap my face and have challenged me to mortal combat. You, however, only listen."

"In Italy, my lord Count, I learned the bitter taste of defeat," Edmund said slowly. "I would savor it no more. Pray inform me, how should the Infidel be fought?"

"That depends upon what Infidel."

The older man put down his wine cup, settled back and steepled fingers before his nose. "When you mention Infidels, never forget this:

they fall into two principal categories. First, there are the Seljuks, peoples whom you call 'Turks.' Their hordes, and they number as the sands of the desert they spring from, primarily are horse-archers.

"Fortunately they are almost as wild and undisciplined as you Franks. What they lack is armor like yours and real weight in their weapons and horses. The chief advantages they enjoy are limitless numbers and their hardiness and the maneuverability of their troops. Each man among these savages goes to war with no less than four horses, all small but enduring. During the course of a prolonged battle a Seljuk warrior changes mounts several times. He lives off his horses, too."

"The Turks *eat* horses?" Edmund was aghast. Here was an abomination far worse than the slaying and torturing of pilgrims.

"Eat their horses? Nay, they love their mounts. But when hard pressed they will drain off some of their blood and mix it with a coarse meal to provide a repulsive yet nourishing diet. But to continue, to deal successfully with these nomads one must reverse one's tactics in fighting Franks. In battling Franks one must simulate retreat until their array is broken up and then shoot down their paladins piecemeal. With the Turks you must pursue them until some natural obstacle forces them to stand and fight; they are then no match for our cataphracts."

"So? And what chanced at the Battle of Manzikert?" Sir Edmund gibed, still smarting over the Byzantine's appraisal of the chivalric code.

Count Leo's rather pale features reddened. "That battle only was lost through the base treachery of Andronicus Ducas and the desertion of our Turcopoles the day before."

"—And what of the Saracens?"

"As I have said these are the most dangerous enemies of all. Instead of bows they rely upon lances, are armored and, being our most ancient foes, have copied far too many of our tactics, but even now in a pitched battle they cannot stand against us. Their arrows are lighter, their mail thinner and their horses somewhat smaller, yet I hope you never will have to stand the charge of their lancers who are the finest cavalry in all Asia and Africa. Always you should remember this." He broke off. "Have you progressed in your studies of the Emperor Leo's *Tactica?*"

With a shamefaced grin Edmund confessed, "I deemed my understanding of Latin to be fair, my lord Count, yet I make hard going of this *Tactica*. Alas, many of the writer's military terms are very strange."

"Nevertheless, persevere, Sir Edmund, and study well this work, particularly certain chapters dealing on war against the Saracens. Through God's mercy such knowledge next Spring may save many of your kind from captivity or death."

"—Or dishonor," Edmund could not help adding.

"Honor? Honor is like a coin, esteemed by some for one reason by some for another." The Byzantine savored a sip of wine then absently loosed lion-headed brooches securing his military cloak. "Credit this if you will. A good general amongst us had rather win a battle without killing an enemy than to lose a single man of his command. Nay, do not look so bewildered. War is not merely an opportunity for the winning of personal glory, neither is it merely an excuse to hack and hew away the lives of as many fellow humans as possible." Count Leo Bardas arose, nodded in a friendly fashion. "Think on that, Sir Edmund, and I will hope to see you on the morrow bringing news which I trust you will find pleasant whilst I discharge in part, my debt of gratitude."

Once Count Leo's tread had faded in the corridor, the former Earl of Arundel drew a deep breath. What had the old general meant by his parting, "discharge in part my debt of gratitude"? He would query Sybilla who, alternating with Rosamund and her beetle-browed husband, had taken thrice a week to visiting the patient in Count Leo's villa.

After poking the brazier to a brighter glow Edmund thumbed idly through the *Tactica*, but ended by staring fixedly at a lovely mosaic depicting a lion hunt which covered two whole walls of his chamber. In all England one would not find anything even faintly comparable save, perchance, on the floor of a Roman ruin.

How astounding, he mused, that Drogo of Cetraro should in so short a time have come to understand his lovely but fiercely independent sister. By St. Michael! The Lombard had judged well when tact must give way to boldness. And he had won. Rosamund exhibited no trace of resentment towards her massive husband but spoke of, and regarded him with deep, if well-restrained affection.

Could this fierce Lombard's previous wives, perchance, really have died of natural causes? It seemed possible since very few females attained the age of forty. Usually child bearing carried them off should they manage to survive those many plagues and pestilences sent by God to scourge Humanity into humility.

To his surprise he had achieved something like an affection for this brusque and overbearing brother-in-law so tireless in his efforts to facilitate transfer of newly arrived Crusaders across the Bosphorus. Drogo, however, proved to be taciturn and gave out little or nothing concerning the movements of the various Frankish arrays. He saw to it also that Rosamund should be granted small opportunity of conversing privately with her twin, so he learned nothing concerning Duke Bohemund's fate.

After a few visits he concluded that his sister was happy enough, for the present at least, and was finding satisfaction in administering her gloomy old mansion in the Street of the Winged Bull as efficiently as she once had kept Arundel Castle. Once or twice, though, he noticed small bruises and discolorations on her arms, but since she made no reference to them he concluded that these might be the result of too ardent love-making. Was it not always a subject for coarse humor whenever a bride appeared with a blackened eye or livid finger marks showing on her?

So it was from the Countess Sybilla that he obtained the bulk of his news about happenings outside Count Leo's villa. When, one night she had sung for him, he suddenly taxed her with betrayal of Bohemund's new line of march and she had appeared at once astonished and outraged and had hotly denied any knowledge of how news of Duke Bohemund's changed route had reached the Lion Palace.

"Why blame yourself and not your former friend Toustain?" she had insisted. "Since boyhood he has been a landless knight, a mercenary owing loyalty only to the best paymaster."

"He is still my friend."

Sybilla's red lip had curled. "Has he visited your sickbed even once?"

"No. I have pondered that."

"You need no longer. Remember that I loathe that ugly, one-eyed sour pickle!"

Later Drogo had vouchsafed that the veteran, very quietly indeed, had quit Constantinople in the direction of Narona.

"'Tis no wonder he has fled," Sybilla had commented. "This Sir Toustain was known to be an intimate of that scheming half-traitor Count Maurice Skleros. Unless this Maurice is more careful he will find himself in some dungeon on Prinkipo Island. He is a most dangerous man and gladly would stir up trouble between our Christloving Emperor and Duke Bohemund the Mighty."

Long hours Edmund debated this possibility, examining it this way and that, and concluded by being sure only that his slow Norman wits could never aspire to keep pace with the deviousness of the Oriental mind.

A eunuch clad in dull red robes and bearing an ebony staff topped with gold, struck the floor thrice outside Edmund's door. "The Countess Sybilla Bryennius, my lord."

Without awaiting invitation Sybilla swept in, slightly slanting violet eyes bright with excitement. She must have come directly from some important function since her dark hair was elaborately trained and more than the usual quantities of jewels glowed on her neck, arms and wrists.

Ignoring the prostrated eunuch the Byzantine girl embraced Edmund with a passion which, of late, was becoming increasingly unrestrained.

"Duke Bohemund has landed!" she announced joyously. "An hour ago a courier from Thrace reached the Ministry of War." She signed to the servant to withdraw and close the door. In a lowered tone she added, " 'Tis said the Emperor is greatly agitated and has not ceased to pace the floor since this intelligence arrived."

"Where did my lord land?"

"He returned to his original route," Sybilla's brilliant lips whispered into his ear, "and landed the most of his forces at Narona and even now his array marches northwards towards Teval." She was fairly aquiver with excitement. "Such a surprise to all in the Lion Palace. The Court had felt sure he would land where the rest had crossed the Sea of Hadrian."

Still limping a little Edmund took a turn down the chamber. "Then he will not use that pass betwixt Mounts Boius and Tymphe?"

"No. His levées march swiftly to a pass north of it." Were there any trace of disappointment in Sybilla's manner Edmund could not detect it as once more she reached far up to twine fingers behind the muscular pillar of his neck.

"Oh, this is the finest of news. Then my—Toustain's careless talk has wrought no harm, after all. Gerth must have won through."

As an immense burden slipping from his shoulders was this realization and he laughed joyously for the first time in weeks.

Tonight Sybilla was wearing some particularly sense-titillating perfume and had been more indiscreet than usual in the application of cosmetics no doubt because of the function she had deserted. Her gown certainly was no model of conservatism being very low cut and of semi-transparent blue silk embroidered with minute golden stars, comets and other astral bodies.

"Oh Edmund, you look so wonderfully improved tonight," she declared presently. "For the first time I see color in your face again." She sank onto a fur rug beside his couch and gently toyed with his copper-hued hair cut short only that morning and trimmed into a bang across his forehead, a Frankish fashion introduced by foppish Count Stephen of Blois.

"Can it be that I detect certain traces of affection in your manner?" she murmured.

"There would be more traces," he assured her with deliberation, "if only I could be certain of what I said that night in the Despoina's library."

"Have I not sworn a hundred times that I neither asked, nor did you say a word concerning Duke Bohemund's intended route?"

He passed the back of a hand over his forehead. "You have and— and I believe you now, sweet lady."

A smothered cry escaped the Byzantine and she pressed herself so hard against him he could feel the maddening softness of her breast against his thigh.

"Oh, Edmund! Edmund! Can you not see how greatly, how truly I have come to love you?" Her words rang as low notes struck upon a harp. "This love I have for you is as profound as the sea and as enduring."

For the first time in many weeks his blood stirred, quickened by her peculiarly subtle and feminine aura.

"But—but—" he stammered, "you—Duke Bohemund, were you not—?"

Sybilla sighed, settled her head onto his lap and talked as if addressing a small and lovely statue of the pagan demi-goddess Psyche. He felt her figure tauten. "I became my lord Bohemund's concubine openly and without shame for the reason that he promised, on his honor, to make me his Duchess once he had wrested Amalfi from his brother. This promise he broke because on taking the Cross he could not fight his brother."

Tears commenced to slide slowly down her cheeks. "This, I swear, Edmund, my beloved, that saving him and my husband who was killed in battle against the Patzinaks before I scarce knew him, there has been no other man in my bed. Believe me! You *must* believe me!"

His hand touched briefly a golden pin securing her hair then his fingers cupped themselves beneath her chin. "This is indeed the truth?"

"By the Panagia, I swear it!" she cried, piteously avid for belief. "May our Lord Jesus strike me dead if I lie!"

Yielding gladly to his lifting pressure Sybilla flung herself upon him, crushed her mouth upon his, then kissed his yet sunken eyes and hollowed cheeks until they warmed and filled. At length she broke away, breathless and somewhat disheveled.

"Forgive me, Edmund. Indeed I had not meant thus to tax your strength. You must recover swiftly and commence collecting your band."

"My band?"

"Did not my uncle speak—?" She checked herself.

"No. Of what are you talking? What band?"

"Tonight my noble uncle Count Leo will convey his intention of presenting you with sufficient gold to recruit a band or company to follow your gonfanon against the Seljuks."

"To follow my banner? The insigne of the Silver Leopard?"

"Yes, and I pray that you shall survive to lead these men to the redemption of Jerusalem."

Sir Edmund de Montgomerie became seized by a sense of exultation but then his elation faded.

"But I cannot accept so princely a gift for having done only that which any knight would attempt—to rescue a fellow gentle man from deadly peril."

A small inscrutable smile from Sybilla. "Nonsense. Or would you see that swaggering ruffian, your brother-in-law, excel you in chivalric deeds? Here in Constantinople Baron Drogo of Cetraro has assembled near a hundred well-trained and well-armed warriors of all degrees." Lightly as a moth settling she traced the line of his heavy reddish brows with her fingertips. "Surely it is not fitting that the former Earl of Arundel should depart against the Infidel without a following of some sort?"

"But—but, I have sworn fealty to Bohemund."

Sybilla settled sidewise on the couch, vented an exasperated sigh. "Are you so bereft of wit as to fancy that Bohemund will welcome you back into his service? You whom he must deem a traitor? Of course not. Therefore is it not wiser to enlist this band you will raise under the banner of some doughty fighter such as Count Baldwin of Boulogne?"

"There is much in what you say," he agreed but wondered in passing why she had said "*you* whom he must deem a traitor." "Yet—and yet, I cannot in honor quit my lord's service until he absolves me of my oath."

"He will," Sybilla predicted so quickly as to give Edmund a second pause, "for my sake, an I ask it. So much at least that lusty scoundrel owes me."

CHAPTER X

The Recruitment

By the middle of March when Judas trees, apricots and almonds had commenced to blossom amid stepped gardens climbing the hills of Constantinople and wild flowers glowed upon the steep, olive-gray heights of the Asiatic shore, Sir Edmund de Montgomerie's strength had returned so far that he now could remain half a day astride a palfrey and, in moderation, resume his warlike exercises.

Not yet did he deem himself ready to mount and manage Storm-cloud. The destrier had grown disgracefully sleek, fat and vicious amid the lush pastures beyond Chrysopolis. Neither could the former earl swing his heavy Norman sword for more than half an hour at a stretch or his mace twice as long. However, flesh had returned to his bones and only a wide purplish scar above his right hip remained to mark the point at which his life so nearly had drained away.

The better to conduct his enterprise the Anglo-Norman established quarters in an abandoned barracks situated outside the city walls in the Galata sector. Here, masterless men-of-arms, knights and unemployed mercenaries of all kinds could find ready access to him. The barracks was an old, semi-ruin dating back to the reign of Theodosius II, draughty and damp and impossible to heat but in it gradually were sworn, or enlisted, the thirty-five hard-faced veterans who, someday, would fight under Sir Edmund de Montgomerie's blue and silver gonfanon.

Having absorbed considerable wisdom concerning the art of war in the East from Count Leo and a tedious study of the *Tactica* and the *Artis Militaris* he was deliberate in his selections.

To find the men he wanted was proving more difficult than he had anticipated. He still had to discard certain precepts drilled into him since he first had flourished a bachelor's wooden sword. To his astonishment a good many masterless gentle men appeared, all denying the possession of lands or pledged allegiance.

Many, Edmund recognized as downright deserters or disgruntled knights who had ridden out of the West after Duke Godfrey, Robert of Normandy or some other crusading prince. These he turned aside courteously but firmly.

There also came to the old barracks certain hard-bitten knights who had fought for the Empire of Alexis Comnene and great numbers of barbarian ex-mercenaries, skilled warriors all. They tramped in by the score once it became bruited about the City that a certain Norman giant stood ready to disburse a generous wage.

These last arrived on foot generally hungry but truculent and well-armed. During the course of a fortnight Edmund interviewed hundreds of applicants but he delayed definite acceptances until he was able to sift out the unreliables and include veterans qualified to complete a well-balanced unit.

While aware that he would be unable to depart entirely from accepted Frankish practices in the field he devoted long hours in attempting to blend Byzantine military skill with the tremendous energy and raw physical courage of the Frank.

One early April afternoon in the year 1097 he lingered late at his recruiting quarters for all that he still lived and took most of his meals in Count Leo's villa and, after dipping his quill into a leaden ink bottle, scrawled a name which completed the roster of his band.

While rubbing his eyes, the Anglo-Norman considered the results of his recruitment. Of belted knights only five had satisfied his requirements as to physical fitness, military knowledge and, he hoped, integrity. Therefore under the Silver Leopard would ride two French-Normans, as many Italian-Normans and a silent and immensely powerful gentle man called Sir Aethelm. His father, said this Saxon, had been that Thegne who had carried King Harold's Banner of the Fighting Man at Senlac and by consequence had fled England shortly after the Conquest.

The French knights he had listed as William Bras-de-Fer and Gaston of Beaune. Both of them claimed to know something of siege-craft, acquired while in service of Venice. The two Italian-Normans, Reynard of Benevento and Arnulfo of Brindisi had seen hard fighting under Count Amaury of Bari, he who had fought and soundly beaten the Byzantines more than once.

Briefly the Anglo-Norman then reflected upon the nature of these veteran free lances, who perhaps a little too readily had pledged fealty and unswerving obedience.

How fine it was to be among armed men once more, to hold command and hear the familiar squeal of an angry stallion from the ancient barracks' yard. A warm breeze titillated his nostrils with odors from a stewpot a-boil in his men-of-arms' quarters.

For serjeants the former earl had enlisted a trio of leather-faced Anatolian Byzantines, all former cataphracts of the Imperial Guard. Lean of body, tough as tripe and superb horsemen, they should make admirable scouts.

His other serjeants included five Italian-Normans, a Norseman and one Toraug, a smooth-skinned Christianized Turk. This wiry and gray-eyed individual claimed to be a real, and not a "meat-pot," convert through having been born the son of a Seljuk captain raised in the Christian faith.

This hawk-nosed Toraug's familiarity not only with Seljuk tactics but with the geography of the Empire's lost themes, Edmund foresaw should be well worth the seven gold byzants paid into the renegade's callused palm. His Norse serjeant was a stocky, red-haired ruffian naming himself Rurik who, reputedly, had been the most formidable axeman ever to have served in the Emperor's Varangian Guard.

Apprized of enormous distances to be traveled, of scant supplies and the non-existence of heavy horses, Edmund had avoided selecting extra large applicants for his twenty men-of-arms. One half of these were Vikings, the other steady, biddable Anglo-Saxons of a generation which never had known England. Curiously, these expatriates one and all cherished a fierce loyalty to that misty, far-off island.

All serjeants had been required to arm themselves for the campaign with a shield, a lance and either an axe or a sword. Further they must ride in chain mail reaching down to their knees.

On Count Leo's advice the men-of-arms, expert archers all, he had ordered to equip themselves with bows longer and more powerful than any employed by the Infidels and in addition they were to carry throwing axes as well as long-hafted, double-bitted battle axes for use when an issue must be resolved in hand-to-hand combat.

Sir Edmund's chiefest concern was to find proper mounts for early-arriving Crusader contingents had swept the countryside clean and so had forced the price of decent horseflesh so high that many desperate and impoverished Cross Bearers had ambushed dealers driving herds towards Byzantium and had murdered them.

Since it was understood that each hireling must find his own equipment, the Band of the Silver Leopard congregated only for a morning meal and at sundown, they then barricaded their quarters in the mossy and rat-haunted old barracks to defend themselves against nocturnal assaults by packs of outlaws, deserters, cutthroats and other castoffs from the forces of de Bouillon, Normandy and France, as well as from that wretched rabble once led by Peter the Hermit.

God alone knew, cried terrified dwellers in the suburbs what would befall when Duke Bohemund's rapacious and quarrelsome Italian-Normans finally put in an appearance. These, Byzantines of all stations feared even more that mighty host being led southward by Count Raymond of Toulouse. His array, the greatest of all, was rumored to number one hundred thousand souls; chiefly Gascons, Provençals and Catalonians. They were reputed to be among the most accomplished pillagers in all Christendom.

From the Band's quarters atop Galata Hill the cooking fires of Franks already encamped along the Asiatic shore suggested fiery lakes of varying size. Every ferry or landing was patrolled by the Emperor's savage Sclavonian and Turkish mercenaries ready to drive back small Crusader parties which, after sundown, forever were attempting to recross the Strait.

Some of these skulkers were faint-hearts seeking to follow the homeward road, but a majority were men grown dissatisfied with the meager and monotonous rations furnished by the Imperial War Office.

To Sir Edmund's ears again came familiar sounds. The scrape of a knife against a pot's rim and the snuffle and stamp of chargers picketed in an easily defended courtyard and the guttural curses of his serjeants intent over a game of knuckle-bones. The stake for which they played might be a scrawny fowl, a stolen lamb and a kid or two for, like all mercenaries, they long since had drunk or whored away their last tartaron.

Sir William Bras-de-Fer evidently was drinking with Sir Reynard and bawling out verse on verse of a ribald ballad as they traced onto battered shields the rough outline of an animal purporting to represent a white leopard. Similar insignia, all in widely varying attitudes already had made their appearance upon shields carried by less important members of the Band.

By the time his little company moved to take the field, Edmund planned that from his lance point should flutter a magnificent square gonfanon embroidered by Sybilla's skilled hands.

A white device on a blue field such as his, the Anglo-Norman knew was readily to be recognized by a poor light or amid the whirling dust of battle.

From the court below arose the bickering of starvelings retained by his knights as rough and ready body servants to replace armigers which they could in nowise afford—mingled with the shrill voices of females who inevitably had appeared to cook, sew and otherwise gratify the needs of the men.

Easily a hundred souls now must be sheltering in this part of the old barracks, Edmund mused. He straightened upon a stool to gaze at a new moon hanging slim and pristine above the smoke and lights of the Crusader encampments across the Bosphorus. A slim new moon, Toraug had informed him, represented to followers of Mohammed what the Cross meant to Christians. Now the emblem of

Islam glowed above the Cross Bearers' camp. Was this not an evil omen? Edmund sighed and, mounting his palfrey, rode down to the row-ferry which would bear him across the Golden Horn and back to Count Leo's villa.

He was anticipating sight of Sybilla's version of a silver leopard. What an unfathomable female! Gay and sparkling one day, moody and silent the next.

That evening while they sat at dinner with Count Leo and the Despoina Eudocia, she looked searchingly at Edmund. "There was deep consternation in the Lion Palace this morning."

"Why?" drawled the Despoina. "Is Mary the Alan with child by a Negro?"

"No. It seems that Duke Bohemund is proving far wilier than most Normans."

Count Leo's iron-gray brows mounted a trifle. "And why do you say that?"

"It now appears that the Duke of Otranto embarked his men—the *Strategos* Butumites estimates them at thrice ten thousand men by the way—not from one port, but from three: Otranto, Brindisi and Bari! These three divisions then landed at separate points in Thrace, marched through the mountains and assembled at Seres. So, if our Divine Emperor indeed had planned ill for his old enemy in the mountains, two parts of Bohemund's array must have won through."

The Despoina Eudocia laughed and used a little trident to convey a morsel of pheasant's breast to her painted lips. "Tell me, Leo, does the Emperor really wish to destroy the son of Robert Guiscard?"

To Edmund's astonishment Count Leo shook his head. "Definitely not for 'tis these Italian-Normans that Alexis Comnene counts upon to deal the Infidels the heaviest blows of all."

"Why so?"

"Because for years they have fought Saracens in Sicily and so understand their mode of warfare. What the Emperor really fears is sudden treachery on the part of Bohemund."

The older man shifted his gaze to the Anglo-Norman, sitting tall and again sun-bronzed across the table. "I presume you are aware, Sir Edmund, that during the siege of Castoria Duke Bohemund swore a mighty oath that someday Constantinople would be his and that he would occupy the throne of the Caesars?"

"No, my lord, I had not heard so."

"*Par Dex!*" grunted the old general. "How can you Franks remain ill-informed on so many weighty matters?"

"Be that as it may," murmured Sybilla, "you scarce can blame our Christ-loving Emperor for entertaining certain misgivings."

"But our Emperor no longer mistrusts Bohemund," quietly observed the Despoina.

"—And for an excellent reason which should amuse you, Sir Edmund." Sybilla smiled, her collar of pearls glistening as, leisurely, she sipped from a goblet frail as if manufactured from river mists. "It is reported that our Sacred Emperor, having at last won the trust of Duke Godfrey, has extracted from him a solemn promise that should Bohemund break the peace and attempt to seize this city, then Godfrey's host, which must still number thrice that of the Duke of Otranto, *will join with the Imperial troops in exterminating the lord Bohemund and all his following!*"

Silence prevailed while servants fetched in a salmon boiled in wine and platters of delicious little red snappers and langoustes.

"Pray tell me, dear Cousin," the Despoina turned to Count Leo, "has Duke Godfrey said anything about assisting Bohemund should the Emperor decide to attack the Southern Normans at an auspicious moment?"

The host's finely-lined classic features flushed above his tunic's gold embroidered collar so brightly that Edmund noticed and remembered. "Why no. Such a piece of treachery is not to be even imagined!"

Sybilla's violet eyes sparkled and a derisive laugh escaped her. "Is it not? Since when has our beloved Emperor become so righteous?"

The quick glances exchanged by Count Leo and the Despoina did more to arouse Edmund's fears than if they had spoken out.

Later, when the ladies withdrew to seek litters back to the Bardas Palace, Count Leo and his big, red-haired guest remained at table drinking, slowly savoring their wine. He treated the younger man to a searching regard.

"Are your coffers—er—empty as yet, my son?"

Unaccountably, the Count of late had fallen into the custom of thus addressing his guest.

A wry smile tightened Edmund's lips. "Not yet, but soon. The price of everything useful has risen beyond imagination."

"Then tomorrow I will order to your credit some five hundred byzants," the older man said. Like waves candle light rippled over his supra-tunic of sea-blue silk and lingered among the small jewels upon his fingers. "I shall add another five hundred should you require wedding garments suitable to your estate and that of my niece."

"Wedding garments!" Edmund stiffened, stared at his host. "I fail to comprehend."

Leo Bardas winked. "Ah, you young lovers. How you love to pretend——"

"But, my lord, I—I—I cannot——"

"Of course not. Your purse is flat so let this be a wartime marriage."

Edmund, his slow wits in a turmoil, could only stammer, "In truth, my lord, I do know nothing of any wedding. The Countess Sybilla and I have not spoken on such matters."

"If this is so, do you not think that you should?" The old Byzantine demanded, suddenly grim. "Has not my niece visited your sick room at almost every hour of the day—and night?"

The glittering figure's voice softened. "Here in Constantinople we are lenient about such—er, meetings, having long since discovered that the more a couple learn concerning one another before an exchange of marriage vows, the greater is their chance for happiness."

Rings on Count Leo's hands flashed as he arose and spoke with dignity. "It is my desire that you two should marry. Nay, nay do not interrupt. My niece already has told me of your lost love. A tragic happenstance indeed, that your vows of fidelity to this undoubtedly lovely barbarian should have become nullified through her decision. Therefore you are enabled, in all honor, to espouse my niece who, by the bye, holds many a fair property on our Isle of Corfu." The veteran sighed, clapped Edmund on the shoulder. "How fortunate that she is so mad with love for you that she has arranged—— No matter, anyone with eyes in their head can see what is in her mind."

Edmund floundered, tongue-tied and miserably torn. "But, my lord, whilst I hold the Lady Sybilla in the highest of respect and affection, I—I—I do not love her."

A steely gleam entered the older man's eyes. "I think," said he, in crisp accents, "that you would commit a very great error were you ever to allow my niece to suspect this. She is proud, and loves you with a deep and an abiding passion. Somehow I feel convinced that should Sybilla not become your wife—no one else will."

Long after the city had grown as quiet as it ever did Edmund remained before the *prie-dieu* in his room. Long and earnestly he racked his soul but despite all efforts his mind continued to conjure up a vision of Alixe as he had beheld her in her nightrobe with pale hair flying loose. How would she look in a nun's gray habit?

So intense was his misery he was forced to bite back a moan. Delicate as any ivory carving the image raised her hand as in benediction then dissolved amid a shaft of moonlight beating across the marble floor. A benediction? Had she not, in this vision, absolved him of his promise that Alixe de Bernay alone should become his bride? While a single candle guttered and the cold of the floor ate into his knees he continued to pray for guidance.

He next sought to examine his feeling for Sybilla of Corfu. That she was as truly enamored of him as was possible in so sophisticated and so ardent a nature could not be doubted. Certainly she had bestowed herself and her fortune most generously upon him.

Surpassingly lovely of face and figure, Sybilla further was brilliant in many directions and descended from the best blood of this ancient Empire. She could sing as sweetly as one of God's own angels yet remained capable of accurately interpreting the most complicated political situations of the day. Also she administered her properties, it was said, with justice, firmness and efficiency.

Against all this remained the fact that this lovely creature had lived openly as Bohemund's concubine; it was no palliation that, basely, he had perjured himself on the matter of marriage. Sybilla, it must be admitted was calculating, imperious and cruel at times, but no more so than any other Byzantine of her rank.

Odd, how a sense of guilt concerning that night in the library still gnawed, rat-like, at his peace of mind. Um. Since he had had unsanctified carnal knowledge of her was he not in honor bound to obliterate their sin by espousing her?

Gradually it became borne in upon him that such a marraige might not be intolerable after all. He never felt so stimulated yet so content with his lot as in Sybilla's presence. Count Leo's niece was tactful and tolerant of his deliberate Norman reasoning and what she considered his quaint Western concepts of duty and honor.

It lacked little of dawn and cocks were crowing for a third time when stiffly he arose, and sought a window there to stand gazing down upon fruit trees freshly-budded in Count Leo's gardens. Perhaps after he had conquered a domain in the Holy Land, he would found with Sybilla a dynasty which might brighten History with great and honorable deeds?

CHAPTER XI

The Duke of Otranto II

In a small, walled garden behind the Baron Drogo's damp, half-furnished residence in the Street of the Winged Bull, the Lady Rosamund uttered a glad cry and fiercely hugged her brother.

Only the serving maid Chloë, now sleek of figure and surprisingly attractive as to voice and manner, was in attendance this warm and

sunshiny afternoon. She had been occupied in stitching a new white
surcoat for the lord of Cetraro.

"The Despoina this morning sent a footman with the glorious tidings," Rosamund cried. "Oh, I am so very, very happy. For weeks
now I have prayed to St. Michael that you might forget poor Alixe."
She brightened, kissed him again. "I wondered how long it would
be before you saw what everyone else has known a long while—
that Sybilla is mad for the love of you."

"Do you really think so?"

"Yes, and, dear brother, you are most fortunate. She is a most suitable and advantageous match. Think of the wealth and power she
commands."

He frowned a trifle then grinned uncertainly. "Um. 'Tis something
like the marriage you contracted, is it not?"

Rosamund's red head swung aside and her bright nether lip disappeared between her teeth. "Thus far I have not for one moment
regretted yielding to his—persuasion," she admitted softly. "True, my
lord on occasion drinks too deep then grows violent but at such times
I am not gentle either."

Chloë smiled. Indeed, a week ago the Lady Rosamund had not
been in the least gentle about laying open her tumultuous lord's scalp
with a well-swung candlestick. Surprisingly, he had taken no offense;
indeed, he had thought the better of his spouse for her act.

"Such excitement has been aroused in Court circles," Rosamund
resumed. "The Despoina declares you are the first Cross-wearing
Frank to marry into the Greek aristocracy. Yours, I suspect, will
prove to be a most splendid nuptial Mass." Abruptly she checked
her chatter. "In which church are you to be married? The Greek or
the Latin?"

Edmund laughed, led his tall sister to a sun-warmed bench. "First
we will wed in our little Genoese chapel and later in the Cathedral
of St. Irene." He made a wry face. "God in Heaven! Do you know
'tis rumored that their Empress will attend the Greek service, together with many senators, dukes, counts, and several *strategoi* of
the Imperial Army?"

Chloë, all ears, hovered dutifully at the far end of the little garden, pretending to fill a pot at a spout of water issuing from a graceful bronze dolphin.

When at last a pause occurred in the conversation she edged forward, eyes wide and pointed features tense. "I crave your pardon,
my lord, but—but have you heard aught from your armiger?"

"Not so far, little one, but, come sundown, I may. Today I ride
out to greet Duke Bohemund."

"You're not!" Rosamund burst out, suddenly sobered. "You dare not."

"But I do. I shall lead the Band of the Silver Leopard into my liege lord's camp."

"Do not do so, I implore you! Word has reached Drogo that Bohemund of Otranto is very wroth with you. In God's name, Edmund, take service under some other than Bohemund's banner."

His jaw assumed a stubborn angle. "That I shall never do until he releases me from my oath of fealty."

"But he may seize, torture and slay you," came Rosamund's anguished cry.

"Nevertheless in honor I cannot do aught than present myself and offer my Band—also I must warn him concerning certain plots."

"Warn him?" It was Edmund's impulse to disclose the understanding arrived at betwixt Duke Godfrey and the Emperor, but, after these several months in Alexis' capital, he was learning at last to guard his tongue. Suppose his twin were to speak to Drogo? Who knew what might chance?

He beckoned Chloë and pinched her buttocks in friendly fashion. "Be there a piece of honest Norman bread and cheese about this place, go fetch it."

The girl nodded, gave him a searching glance then darted away, light as a frightened fawn. Once she had disappeared Edmund demanded seriously, "In all truth, sweet Sister, how fare you with your husband?"

"Well enough," Rosamund's lashes fell, became outlined upon her cheeks. "At times I hate him, but more often I love him with a terrible passion. It affrights me. Tomorrow he and his men depart to join Hugh of Vermandois beyond Chrysopolis."

"And shall you accompany him against the Infidels?"

To his surprise Rosamund blushed and shook her head. "It is his express command that I do not."

"But many Frankish ladies are riding forth with their lords. I thought that Drogo of all people, would demand your companionship."

She looked him squarely in the eyes, said simply, "I am with his child."

"Capital! 'Twill be a lusty brat I'm sure."

"Drogo will not have me campaign for fear of losing this infant who will become his heir. For some reason, neither of his other dames produced a child which survived beyond a few weeks, therefore I must remain here, penned for all the world like some damned brood mare." Tears welled into those blue-green eyes which so suggested tourmalines. "I know I could ride for many weeks without jeopardy but Drogo will not have it so. And you," with the back of her hand she brushed aside tears commencing to parallel her straight, faintly uptilted nose. "Will your wife accompany you?"

"She is so insistent upon it I begin to wonder why," Edmund replied uneasily. "She says several of her cousins are to campaign with a Byzantine force which is to support us and can be made of vast assistance to the Frankish host."

"That probably is true," Rosamund caught up her sewing. "Come and let me show you the gown I prepare against your wedding day. Is it not just a week distant?"

He nodded, stalked after her into the big, hollowly resounding mansion.

Sir Edmund de Montgomerie swung up on his destrier, then, through Bras-de-Fer, ordered his followers to form a column of twos. Narrowly the gigantic Anglo-Norman inspected each of these thirty-five warriors riding under the gonfanon of the Silver Leopard. Although they seemed better than passably well-turned-out he noticed here a stirrup leather worn dangerously thin, there a poorly patched hauberk or flecks of rust on a shield or helm. All the horses' coats and even those of the pack mules, shone however and all the animals appeared sleek without being fat.

As *lieu-tenant*, or "place-keeper" in case he should become disabled, he had selected he of the flattened nose and restless gaze, Sir William Bras-de-Fer and after him, dark and severely silent Sir Reynard of Benevento. He would have liked to name Sir Aethelm as his second in command but the Saxon was much too slow-witted and quarrelsome to qualify.

In an unequal and irregularly spaced column Sir Edmund's Band rode out of those ruinous barracks in Galata which had sheltered some of them for going on six weeks and turned their horses' heads towards that sodden plain upon which Duke Bohemund's levées were bivouacked.

Situated a full league outside the walls of Byzantium the Italian-Normans' camping place proved dreary in the extreme. Previous expeditions had denuded the countryside of every bush and tree and the ground had not only been grazed flat but had been fouled with noisome excrement. Clearly visible were the remains of burrows dug by the men of Hugh of Vermandois, Eustace of Bologne and the rest.

As Edmund, long body yielding gently to Stormcloud's slow trot, led his little company into the outskirts of Bohemund's bivouac he noted that relatively few camp-followers cluttered the Southern Norman encampment. Among other items of interest was the fact that the proportion of foot soldiers to mounted ones certainly was far less than in earlier Crusader arrays; also their Duke's baggage train was short and light. This last was not surprising. All Constantinople had heard that Bohemund the Mighty was by far the most impecunious of all the crusading princes, which fact had caused Byzantine *catapans* along the route considerable concern. Through sheer necessity these ancient enemies would swiftly have taken to pillage and rapine had they not been promptly supplied from the Imperial storehouses. Of course not one Frankish host boasted even an elemental service of supply, a siege train or a hospital detachment of any sort. Once the assault on Islam commenced every man would be expected to find food for himself and for his mount, if he were lucky enough to ride. Wars in the West always had been fought on that understanding.

Observed from a low rise, the tents and shelters of the Italian-Norman encampment straggled in disorderly ripples, sizes and colors away from that weatherbeaten pavilion above which fluttered Bohemund's crimson banner.

To Edmund de Montgomerie's experienced eyes a démarche from the camp apparently was about to take place. Crowds of serjeants, men-of-arms and common foot soldiers were deserting their cook fires to congregate along a highway leading northwards from Constantinople's Golden Gate, the westernmost and most powerful of the City's portals on the landward side.

Since the Band of the Silver Leopard was riding west along a cross-roads Edmund, when he gained the intersection, pulled in his destrier then ordered his followers, amid a yellow dust haze, to form a double rank facing the highway. They sat under blue-and-white pennons curling from their lance tips and cursing the heat and dust and watching the progress of a detachment of cavaliers riding out of Bohemund's camp.

From an incessant blaring of oliphants it seemed evident that some very puissant barons must be setting out for the City. Sitting easily in his high-peaked saddle with the new gonfanon fluttering bravely above him, Edmund de Montgomerie's heart lifted when he recognized Bohemund's plain crimson flag advance along this road amid a flashing of mail and the sparkle of pointed helms.

Presently the Band discerned perhaps a dozen big horsemen wearing Crusader's surcoats cantering along, with varicolored gonfanons flashing in the warm spring sunlight.

The former earl's wide mouth tightened with the realization that, in a few moments now, he and Bohemund the Mighty would meet

face-to-face for the first time in over half a year. Come what might
he must lose no time in apprizing his liege lord of that nefarious
understanding entered into by the Emperor Alexis and Godfrey de
Bouillon. Blood commenced to roar in his ears as he recalled
Sybilla's and Rosamund's almost tearful pleas that he avoid this meeting.

Growing uneasy despite himself Edmund glanced over his shoulder and was pleased to note that his five hard-faced knights, ten
serjeants and twenty men-of-arms were sitting straight and steady
in their saddles for once without spitting, grinning or scratching
themselves. The crude white leopards painted on their burnished
kite-shaped shields lent them an unusual note of uniformity.

Now that the brief but brilliant cavalcade started up a short slope
leading to that point where waited the Band of the Silver Leopard
they one and all steadied their mounts and peered curiously at
Bohemund the Mighty's massive figure.

Edmund's throat contracted when he saw the Duke's brilliant blue
eyes probing this orderly double rank of horsemen and sweat commenced to trickle down his cheeks beneath his coif. Of a certainty
the next few instants would determine his fate.

When the cavalcade clattered up to a point some yards distant
Edmund suddenly spurred Stormcloud, set him to rearing and paw-
ing the air and at the same time saluted by lowering his lance to the
horizontal.

Bohemund must have recognized him instantly for his right hand
shot up causing his whole escort to rein in amid a swirl of dust.

"My lord! My lord Bohemund!" In quivering apprehension Sir Edmund rode forward.

Ominously Bohemund's jaw line hardened and his eyes shone like
swordpoints to either side of his helmet's nasal.

"Hah! 'Tis the English rascal at last! How dare you approach me?"

"Because I would warn you, my lord, of certain dangers within the
City. I would present to you the services of this Band; every man
is a proved and excellent campaigner who can deal many a lusty
blow against the Infidel!"

While easily restraining his destrier, an immense golden bay stallion, Bohemund ran an expert eye over the Band. He grunted. "They
have a tough, rascally look about them."

Unexpectedly he grinned and held out his fist. "Sir Edmund, you
are tardy in reporting yourself but you have ably discharged that
errand upon which I sent you. My thanks," he winked elaborately.

Had a mace come crashing down upon Edmund's casque he could

not have been more dazed. What was it Bohemund had said? "For having *so ably discharged* the errand upon which I sent you."

The Anglo-Norman blinked in such patent confusion that Bohemund burst into snorts of laughter, and clapped his thigh.

"'Fore God you were cleverer than I expected about passing on that false information concerning my march-route. I understand that my dear friend Alexis swallowed it whole, coming as it did. So we found never a Byzantine *turma* among the mountains of Thrace." The Duke's broad red-brown features further relaxed. "Surely you have sharpened your wits while dealing with these slippery Greeks."

Edmund hesitated, debating the wisdom of altering Bohemund's astonishingly friendly manner. "My lord, can you tell me aught of my armiger Gerth Ordway or of my stout friend Sir Toustain?" Bohemund merely laughed and spurred ahead.

Still too thunderstruck to speak or to search for the reasoning behind Duke Bohemund's approval Edmund again saluted with his lance. His liege lord gathered his reins, snapped, "Dismiss your company and follow me into the City."

Enthusiastic cheers and yells for Bohemund the Mighty arose on all sides as the Duke controlled his magnificent stallion to a slow trot and resumed his progress towards those lofty yellow-gray double walls and bastions defending Constantinople.

On falling in with the escort, Edmund recognized several among the principal lords riding at Bohemund's heels, Girard, Bishop of Ariano, as red-faced, loud voiced and plump as ever wearing a gold cross on his bosom and a hauberk under his clerical robes. A mace swung at his well-filled belt.

The Anglo-Norman received a nod of recognition from tough, softspoken Rainulf of the Principate, he whose knightly generosity Edmund would never forget. Also riding under a red and green banderole, Rainulf's hideously scarred brother Richard, and yellow headed Count Tancred fitzTancred, beetle-browed and arrogant. There were other younger barons present whose hard, brown faces recalled the preceding summer. These clapped him on the back, made ribald inquiries concerning Eastern vices rumored to be rampant in Byzantium, but not without a certain respect. Many of them evidently recalled a certain bitter *combat à l'outrance* fought upon a green meadow below Castel Sanseverino.

Alas, neither Gerth Ordway nor Sir Toustain de Dives was present.

The audience hall of the Lion Palace was long and shadowed, its ceiling supported by many slender marble columns of a wondrous beauty and its walls decorated by magnificent gold, red and black mosaics. At its far end Alexis Comnene, chosen of God and Christ-loving Emperor of the Romans, occupied a golden throne upon a scarlet carpeted dais awaiting his dreaded guest.

Alexis was short of stature but broad in the shoulder and of commanding bearing. His large and liquid dark brown eyes peered steadily from a deeply tanned face and from above a short and curling brown beard which glistened with an application of perfumed unguents.

Upon the Emperor's luxuriant brown locks had been set the Imperial diadem aflame with magnificent jewels and, to either side of his head, its lappets of precious stones dangled flashing down to the jaw line. Alexis' costume for the occasion was a mantle of Imperial purple clasped at his shoulders by brooches adorned with enormous pearls. Beneath this covering glittered a heavily embroidered knee-length tunic of cloth-of-gold. His broad feet were shod in scarlet and gold buskins which in no detail differed from those worn a thousand years earlier by Augustus Caesar, Tiberius, Caligula and Nero.

About the dais' base was gathered a bevy of Senators, *Strategoi*, high Government officials and several long-bearded patriarchs of the Greek Church. These wore bulbous golden crowns glittering with more wealth than any Norman might hope to behold during all his lifetime in Europe.

Ranged in a statue-still semi-circle about the base of the platform stood a rank of Scandinavian axemen from the famous Varangian Guard. On their yellow heads these giants wore winged bronze helmets while from their massive shoulders swung scarlet cloaks edged in gold embroidery.

Lining the aisles and walls in silvered breastplates and helmets were men from the Heteria, or Imperial bodyguard. All were Byzantine nobles, proud, handsome and completely unashamed of paint tinting their cheeks and lips.

From his throne Alexis Comnene had a clear view through the long, marble-floored audience chamber of a sunlit doorway giving access to the palace's courtyard. Near it stood lesser dignitaries, civil and military, and several red-robed eunuch secretaries who bearing portable desks slung to their shoulders stood prepared to transcribe all that might be said.

Now sounded the clatter of many steel shod hoofs, then loud, rough voices commenced to echo through the cool silence indoors. Mechanically, Alexis raised hands to set straight his diadem as the Commander of the Imperial Guard, splendid in a breastplate of gilded silver, and bearing a blue-crested helmet on his left arm, came tramping up the aisle. Arriving before the dais he handed the helmet to an aide and prostrated himself at his master's feet three times touching the floor with his forehead.

"Speak." Alexis' voice sounded gentle yet not weak.

"A certain Bohemund, who names himself Duke of Otranto, craves an audience with your Sacred Imperial Majesty."

"Arise, most worthy *Strategos,* make him welcome and bid him enter without fear."

There was a stir in the audience chamber's still, incense-tinctured atmosphere. Hardly a soul present was unaware of the bitter enmity existing between these two strong rulers.

To a ringing of mailed feet and the jingle of spur chains the entrance was darkened by a number of big figures in white, red-crossed surcoats. Foremost and biggest of all, strode the red-haired son of Robert Guiscard.

Bareheaded, straight and powerful as his own sword, Bohemund advanced toward the throne with an emerald green war cloak rippling from his shoulders. Pride, confidence and dignity were in his every aspect as the big Norman came to a halt with his nephew, Tancred, and the Bishop of Ariano a step behind. In their rear the other barons crowded forward and an odor of horses and sweaty leather commenced to spread throughout the chamber.

Edmund, in the rear of Bohemund's escort, experienced an overpowering sense of awe. To think that this splendid chamber with its silver hanging lamps, huge tapestries and richly carved pillars already had stood for half a millennium! Although accustomed to the opulent costumes of Byzantine nobles the former earl became nearly blinded by the splendor of the background here created by them.

Spellbound, he watched Bohemund, green cloak billowing, ascend the dais as, on signal, two interpreters stepped forward, for all that Alexis Comnene was an experienced linguist, while Duke Bohemund possessed more than a smattering of Greek.

Of what passed between these two imposing figures Sir Edmund could hear nothing although the conversation lasted a good while.

After considerable time Bohemund abruptly knelt stiff-kneed, joined palms as if in prayer and then placed them between the bejeweled brown hands of the Emperor. Immediately angry outcries burst from Bohemund's thunderstruck barons and Tancred, in a fuming rage whirled toward them. "I protest! I call you to witness that, before God Almighty, I refuse to render homage to this Greek, for all that my uncle has!"

Girard, Bishop of Ariano was the first to quiet Bohemund's tempestuous light-haired young nephew and the commotion quickly was stilled. Among the Greek courtiers eyes shifted and lips moved hur-

riedly but what they were saying Sir Edmund de Montgomerie had
no notion.

CHAPTER XII

A Scroll of Vellum

With the wedding hour but three days removed, a veritable
flood of rich and varied gifts, many of them curious or wondrously
beautiful, commenced to arrive at Count Leo Bardas' villa where,
recently, the Countess of Corfu had decided to domicile herself. Received was a plethora of tableware, a palanquin adorned with fittings
of solid gold, magnificent Venetian glassware, tapestries, jeweled
ikons, and yards upon yards of precious silks and brocades from
Ispahan.

A wealthy aunt bestowed not only a gorgeous pleasure caïque but
six powerful slaves to row it about the Golden Horn or on the
Bosphorus. The Despoina Eudocia's gift was a handsome villa on
one of the many wooded islands visible from the heights of Constantinople.

In the servants' quarters appeared slave-domestics presented for
use in the new household and dumbly resigned to this change in
owners. There came presents, too, for the Countess' Frankish hus-
band-to-be such as warhorses, magnificent jeweled breastplates, light
but tough helmets, and curved swords of the finest Damascus temper.

Overjoyed by Duke Bohemund's inexplicable attitude, Sir Edmund
had entered into a happy state of mind. He derived especial pleasure
in joining Sybilla to inspect their gifts. His cup of happiness over-
flowed the day a troop of Frankish men-of-arms appeared bearing
handsome presents not only from Duke Bohemund but from Richard
of the Principate, the Bishop of Ariano and others of the Duke's
military family. Most welcome of all was a handsome saddle from
Sir Toustain who, it appeared, had been delayed by his duty of
rounding up Italian-Norman stragglers and recruiting masterless
men along the line of march to replace those who had died, had
fallen ill or had been slain during the march across Greece.

"Are they not sublime?" Sybilla, black rimmed violet eyes flashing,
opened an ivory box to display a string of large and lustrous pearls
interspaced by golden beads. After replacing Sir Toustain's gift on
its rack Edmund drew close his radiant fiancée, and, after kissing
her, secured the necklace in place. These indeed were heady moments; never had the Anglo-Norman dreamed that such wealth

peacefully could become his, since in Byzantium, as well as in Frankish realms, whatever a female possessed she held only through her husband.

"If only we were not to depart Byzantium so very soon," Sybilla sighed, then glanced upwards slender brows knitted. "Edmund, my beloved, I am convinced a word from Count Leo to the Emperor would persuade your Duke to grant you leave to tarry."

Decisively he shook copper-hued locks. "No, my dear, this I cannot honorably permit. My Band must be among the first of my lord's array to cross into Asia and smite the Infidels."

"Then I shall follow close on your heels; an easy matter, since my uncle is to command a *turma* of horse in our expeditionary force; fine well-disciplined cataphracts all armored from head to toe."

"And who is to command these Imperial forces?"

Sybilla looked up in patent astonishment. "Surely my darling simpleton, you *must* have heard that Manuel Butumites is to be *Strategos*-in-Chief?" Then she laughed. "Why is it you Franks never learn these things without long delays? Yes, this morning the Emperor signed Butumites' orders in the sacred red ink."

"Be patient," he smiled stroking her glossy blue-black curls. "Some day I shall become as wily and well-informed as the best of you Byzantines."

"Don't say 'you Byzantines' because, through our marriage, you will become one—in the eyes of the Empire, at least. The royal blood of the Paleologues flows through my veins."

He sobered a little, gazed down into her exquisite features. "Do you really intend to come campaigning?"

Quite seriously Sybilla nodded. "Are not a great many Frankish ladies preparing to do so?"

"But, but you were not reared as they, in cold and draughty castles and nourished on rough food nor can you ride a horse."

"I can learn," she announced decisively, "and I am far stronger than you imagine and will be quite safe in Count Leo's camp."

Edmund's reactions remained mixed. It fitted no part of his intent to suffer distraction from his steadfast purpose of mightily smiting the Turks until he perished or Jerusalem the Golden became cleansed of Infidel pollution.

Soft sounds made by hurrying slippered feet anticipated the appearance of a steward. He bowed low before the couple, shaven head glistening in the candle light.

"My lord, a Frankish warrior who claims to be your body servant awaits in the antechamber."

"Body servant?"

"Yes, my lord. This barbarian has a round face and hair the color of wheat straw. He gave me his name, but alas, I cannot pronounce it."

"Was it Gerth Ordway?" Edmund demanded sharply.

The servant's jowls swayed to a quick nod. "That is the fellow's name, my lord."

"'Tis your armiger!" Sybilla cried pressing herself against him. "Now, surely you are rejoiced. I know well the love this Saxon youth bears for you, and your fondness for him." Smiling sweetly, she caught a filmy mantle of saffron-hued silk. "You have much to discuss that can be no concern of mine so I shall retire to inspect the progress of my nuptial dress."

Hardly had Sybilla sauntered away than Gerth appeared, dropped on one knee and eagerly kissed his master's outstretched hand. He sprang up when Edmund clapped him on the shoulder. His armiger, the former Earl of Arundel decided, had matured perceptibly during his absence. He seemed less awkward and had grown short blond mustaches. Some of the youthful smoothness had departed from his cheeks and his bright blue eyes appeared more thoughtful, as he cried, "I am infinitely rejoiced, my lord, to find you so hale of appearance. I had heard that last winter you suffered a grievous wound."

"I am as good as ever. Now give me all the news." He wondered at a sudden solemnity which abruptly obliterated the armiger's joyous expression.

"What is it, Gerth? What troubles you?"

"I bear tidings, my lord," he explained uncertainly. "I do not know whether you will be gladdened or saddened by them."

"Out with it! Let me decide."

"My master, this was handed me by Sir Robert of Sanseverino."

"Robert of Sanseverino!" Edmund's heart leaped like an arrow-struck charger.

"Aye, my lord." Gerth's thick fingers fumbled at the front of his tunic, produced a small, sweat-marked scroll of vellum bound with blue silk thread.

"Yes, my lord. Sir Robert commands the levée from Sanseverino in lieu of his elder brother who is, alas, often quite mad."

"And does he—?"

"—No, my lord. Sir Robert swears he bears you no ill will, no more does poor Sir Hugues."

"The old Count Turgis?"

"He is dead these many months."

A curious internal trembling seized Edmund, as in strained accents he inquired, "—And what of the Lady Alixe?"

Gerth dropped his gaze. "My lord, the missive you hold in your hand comes from her. It was penned by the monk who now serves as Chaplain of Sanseverino."

Scarlet mantle asway, Edmund strode over to a candelabrum and with quivering fingers broke the scroll's tie-string.

The parchment crackled softly then starkly black but ill-formed Latin characters revealed themselves. Edmund very quickly perceived that this scribe's spelling was poor and his syntax deplorable. Aware of a furious inner turmoil he read:

My Most beloved lord and Champion: A merchant traveling westward from the realm of the Romans has fetched intelligence of your safe arrival in Byzantium, for which I have offered many Masses of thanksgiving. I would have you know, my beloved, that shortly after your departure a dire pestilence struck the domain of Verona. Because I was mourning your absence past endurance I did accede to pleas from the Abbess of St. Genevieve's that, for a space, I should assist her nuns in comforting a passing band of Cross Bearers sore stricken low by this plague. I had been in this nunnery but for a space of a sennit than I myself, took the sickness and for many weeks lay at no great distance from the Gates of Paradise, wherefore it has become bruited about the countryside that I had become a postulant and would become the bride not of you, Cherished of my Heart, but of our Sweet Lord Jesus.

Once my strength became somewhat restored I returned to Sanseverino where my Sire had sickened of his wound. Soon afterwards that valiant knight departed to his Heavenly reward.

Oh, Edmund, Best Beloved, how often do I not pass entire nights on my knees in prayer that our Lord in His mercy, has preserved you from the dangers which must beset you in that great city and about the wickedness of which we hear almost daily.

Know that Hugues, my elder brother is much restored in strength but is given to falling in foaming fits. Poor Hugues! At times he becomes so violent that four strong villeins must be summoned to restrain his ravings.

In a few days now our levées of Cross Bearers will appear to follow the gonfanon of my brother, Robert. He is delighted to have inherited the command.

Edmund's throat contracted and the candles beside him seemed to sway as if the earth were shaking under one of those terrible convulsions which more than once in these parts had laid great cities low.

I pray that you return to command the second levée of Sanseverino, composed of those who could not, or would not, ready themselves in time to depart with Robert. It will depart for the wars next Spring.

I know that steadfast in the pursuance of your oath you have kept yourself pure, strong and determined to free Jerusalem. I beg of you, however, not to be rash and to remember always that to me you will ever be the bravest Knight who ever drew sword in the Holy Cause. I yearn to receive word from you, Edmund my beloved, and pray that you will honor the vows we exchanged. Believe always that I cherish you beyond any created mortal.

There was no signature beyond a crude cross and splashes which might have been caused by dripping water.

Anxiously surveyed all the while by his armiger, Edmund de Montgomerie stood for many moments stock-still in the great shadowy chamber surrounded by heaps of wedding gifts. "Alixe is *not* lost! Alixe awaits you." Voices, strident as the screaming of some great storm, were howling in his ears. "Alixe! *Alixe!* ALIXE may still be yours!"

"My lord," Gerth spoke from amid the gloom, "is it indeed true that you intend to wed this Grecian lady? Lord Bohemund's camp talks of little else."

"No," replied the tall, red-haired figure in quivering accents. "It is so no longer."

The former Earl of Arundel roused from his confusion and beckoned his burly esquire closer that he might whisper what he had to say. By now he had learned that somehow, every word spoken in this villa as in other Byzantine dwellings, was overheard and noted, and knew that, within a very few moments, Sybilla and Count Leo would have been apprized that information of a critical nature had been delivered by Gerth.

He directed in a low voice, "Pretend to adjust this buckle for me."

Bright blue eyes wide, Gerth hurried forward.

"Now harken well. The moment you leave here go seek out Sir William Bras-de-Fer who commands my Band during my absence."

"Your Band, my lord?"

"Yes. 'Tis called the Band of the Silver Leopard and lies quartered in an abandoned barracks in the Galata quarter of this city. Sir William is to rally our people, together with bat horses and such provisions as he may most readily come by. Bid him lead my Band to the landing below Galata where the boats are accustomed to ferry troops over into Asia."

The Saxon tugged doubtfully at his new and silky mustaches.

"Yes, my lord, but can I pass the City gates at this hour?"

"I care not how you reach Galata, Gerth Ordway, but my company must be alerted before dawn. I will meet them at the ferry place." He raised his voice. "Present my humble thanks and loyal duty to my lord Bohemund. Inform him that greatly I thank him for his wedding gift, that I soon ride to lift my gonfanon behind his. Now, get you gone and hasten."

For many minutes Edmund de Montgomerie lingered uneasily among the wedding gifts but of them he saw nothing, only a vision of Alixe de Bernay as he last had beheld her. At length he squared his shoulders as if preparing for combat and sought the private apartments of Count Leo Bardas.

"Well, Nephew, and how does today's loot tally up? A fine total when last I looked at it." In readying himself for bed the patrician had donned a knee-length garment very similar to the simple white chiton of the ancient Greeks. Upon signal the veteran's two black body servants prostrated themselves, then retired.

Once they had departed, Count Leo's manner changed abruptly. "Who was the servant of yours who sought you out, and what had he to say that you should appear before me gone pale as yonder statue?"

The Byzantine's hard gray eyes by the candle light bored steadily at him. "Has aught gone wrong with Duke Bohemund? Has conflict broken out betwixt his troops and the Emperor's?"

Edmund's dark red head shook slowly as abruptly he became aware of the weight of that chain mail shirt Rosamund had bestowed upon him and was glad of it.

"No, my lord Count." He spoke in a loud, clear voice that the inevitable eavesdropper might hear. "It is that the Lady Alixe de Bernay to whom I pledged my troth in Italy has *not* taken Holy Orders. She is, in point of fact, at this moment awaiting my return to the Castle of Sanseverino."

Without once removing those penetrating gray eyes from his caller, Count Leo arose and drew near. "How very sad for this unfortunate lady that you are about to wed another. No one is to blame save the stars in their courses."

Hangings rustled and Sybilla swept into the room, sable hair flowing free and dressed for slumber in loose white robes. Cleansed of the usual cosmetics her face by the golden lamplight appeared softer, younger and more sensitive. Her great eyes were gleaming and her breathing was so quick that the material stirred rapidly upon breasts which, quite unbound, jutted boldly outwards and upwards.

"You heard that your former love has *not* become a nun?" she demanded breathlessly.

"Aye." In anguish Edmund pressed fingertips to his temples then let his hands fall sharply to his side. "Incidentally, the Lady Alixe is not my 'former love,' Lady Sybilla, but my one and only love. She had no intention whatever of retiring from the world but a false rumor to that effect became bruited about."

The Greek girl's eyes became simply enormous as, folding arms over her breast, she stared tragically, unbelievingly at him in the scarlet mantle standing so tall before her.

"That was unkindly put," Count Leo's deep voice observed. "I trust your future wife will overlook your Frankish rudeness."

In his desperation Edmund flung wide both hands. "I beg of you, my lord Count, to try to comprehend how deeply I grieve that this mischance should have befallen your niece and me. You well know that on neither part did bad faith play a part in our betrothal. It is only," said he simply, "that, in honor, I cannot violate my plighted troth to one who is pure and sweet beyond comprehension."

"Ass! Idiot! Stupid Frank!" The words exploded from Sybilla's lips. "Think you I, Sybilla Bryennius, am content to be flung aside in favor of some whey-faced barbarian wench who doubtless reeks of onions and stale sweat? Would you desert a Paleologue before all Christendom?"

A deep breath expanded Edmund's broad chest and color poured into his face and neck but he spoke evenly, patiently. "Pray recall, that long ago, I informed you concerning my betrothal to the Lady Alixe, and later I related that, in all honesty, I believed her to have relieved me of my oath."

"That may very well be so." Grinning like a winter wolf Count Leo strode over to a pitcher standing on a side table and decanted two goblets of wine. "However, you must be reasonable, Nephew. In the morning you surely will perceive how impossible it is to abandon my niece who loves you with all her heart and soul. Nor would you disgrace me, who have ever been your stout friend and benefactor."

"I cannot marry your niece," Edmund declared in choked undertones.

"But you will!" blazed Sybilla and her lips writhed into an anguished grimace. "You shall not humiliate me! Attempt to betray me and you will not live long."

"Come, come, Niece! Let us not indulge in unnecessary dramatics." Count Leo, the soul of unruffled hospitality, offered a brimming goblet. "Sir Edmund will not be so tactless or shortsighted as to insult so fair a lady."

"My lord Count, I most readily acknowledge your noble kindness and surpassing generosity, yet, as a Christian knight, I shall not break my oath to Alixe de Bernay."

Emitting a low cry Sybilla treated the Anglo-Norman to a tigerish look, turned and darted out of the chamber. Edmund would have followed her but the old Byzantine caught him by the shoulder.

"Let be! She will value your constancy all the more when you meet before the altar."

Edmund raised his hand in military salute. "I crave your pardon for having thus disturbed your slumbers, my lord Count. Now I must depart."

"Of course. Go with God," Count Leo smiled. "I will inspect this Band of yours on the morrow."

But this he could not do, because, shortly after sunrise, the Band of the Silver Leopard was ferried, cursing excitedly, over the swift and darkly blue Bosphorus and at length clattered into the camp of Bohemund of Otranto.

BOOK III: *Jerusalem*

CHAPTER I

In Nomine Deus

Like a tide sluggishly spreading over a marsh the Crusader arrays streamed southeastward, eddied among high, pine-covered hills which loomed ever steeper. The further this host penetrated Asia Minor the more difficult became their progress for among the foothills they encountered hardwood forests so dense that leaders among the Cross Bearers ordered forward parties of axemen to hew a road. Along this would struggle disorderly streams of fighting men, starry-eyed pilgrims, priests, camp followers and scavengers who, during the night, would seek to murder weak or sickly stragglers.

The distance to be traveled in a single day never was set. Each levée, company or band simply struggled after its leader's standard as best it might along any route fancied by him until it arrived at a campsite. The more important levées moved the slowest, hampered as they were by ox-drawn baggage wagons, women and priests mounted on mules, and swarms of barefooted jackmen. The duty of these humble folk was to raise tents, cut wood and fetch water for their masters and their chargers.

Thanks to war-wise Richard of the Principate's goodwill the Band was commanded to ride well in advance of this bewildered and disorganized multitude so, on a pleasant afternoon in June, the Companions sat their horses atop a high hill with a light breeze curling Sir Edmund's gonfanon and the Band's blue-and-white lance pennons.

In the valley below hairy, half-naked axemen were felling trees, their broad blades twinkling and flashing. Experienced campaigners among Edmund's following dismounted, drove lance butts into rocky ground and set about easing cinches and smoothing saddle cloths for none dare risk a sore-backed mount in this silently hostile country. Gerth, his round face peeling and burnt brick-red by the merciless sun, busied himself by dislodging a pebble from under Stormcloud's shoe.

The Companions heaved grateful sighs because the pitiless Asiatic sun was sinking. All day it had made cauldrons of helms and caused ring-mail and scaled hauberks to burn like so many shirts of Nessus. Long since the heat had caused the Band's horses to abandon playful ways and travel soberly along.

Edmund opened his hauberk at the throat then pulled off an unornamented casque and mopped his brow all the while running blue eyes over the surrounding terrain. When he noted blisters forming on Sir Arnulfo's and Sir Aethelm's scarred noses he was glad of his adjustable nasal copied from a Saracen helm.

On the whole the Companions successfully had weathered this two-day march through mountains rising southeast of Chrysopolis. A serjeant's horse, though, had gone lame so its rider had been forced to mount one of a half-dozen led horses brought along to meet such a contingency.

All at once Toraug, the Christianized Turkish serjeant, uttered a low whistle and his hand, small and very brown by contrast to his Crusader's surcoat, swung sharply to indicate the summit of a thinly wooded mountain across the valley.

As the Italian-Norman knight, Sir Reynard, shaded his eyes the Band glimpsed the white glimmer and sparkle of steel on that distant mountainside. Excitement set Edmund's arteries to hammering while he watched a seemingly endless column of white-clad horsemen commence to traverse the mountaintop. He then became aware of a curious tingling sensation in his fingertips such as he had not experienced since his first skirmish as an armiger before Seagirt in Cornwall.

Presently the foremost of those distant riders reined in and swiftly the thin line collected into a great white patch suggestive of snow on a rocky hilltop.

"Hah!" burst out Gerth. "'Tis the dog-delivered Infidels at last!"

Yonder, undoubtedly, must be riding a reconaissance force detached from the main horde of Kilidj Arslan, the Red Lion, Lord of Nicea and a host of other cities.

"'Tis the Turks indeed, my lord," Toraug agreed quietly, "and not the Emperor's Turcopoles, as at first I had imagined. See their green standard? No mercenary troops would ride under such. We shall likely view more such scouting parties ere the sun disappears."

The convert's prediction swiftly became fulfilled. More and more Turkish horsemen were to be seen cautiously riding along trails high among these rocky, yellow-gray foothills. But always they appeared at such a distance that no details of their appearance or equipment might be discerned. Indeed in this wild and unfamiliar terrain sudden death might lurk ambushed in any bush-screened gorge or wooded slope.

The former Earl of Arundel cast a final searching look about, then beckoned Gerth to lead forward that sturdy chestnut palfrey Edmund rode unless fighting became imminent. Only then would he swing up onto Stormcloud.

"Mount the men," he instructed Bras-de-Fer, whereupon that big-limbed individual bawled an order which set the Companions to gathering their reins. These, on Toraug's advice, had been reinforced by chain from the bit halfway up a horse's neck lest a Turkish blade shear the leather and in the heat of battle deprive its rider of control.

Leather creaked and stirrup irons jangled while the Companions swung up into their saddles, slung shields and plucked lances from the ground all the while squirming shoulders under their hauberks' hot weight.

Sir Edmund's hands, callused once more, closed happily on the well oiled, braided leather of his reins, then gilded spurs gleamed briefly as he thrust mail-covered feet deep into the stirrups. Settling back in the saddle he allowed his lance to cant far back from a shoulder loop in order to avoid low branches and led his followers downwards to protect a throng of big, bearded woodsmen.

They proved to be Lorrainers from Godfrey de Bouillon's forces and spoke a curious harsh tongue called German. The axemen stared in dull disinterest upon this column of brown-faced and white clad riders who bore the likeness of some strange animal painted in white upon their shields.

Dawn of the day following revealed the Crusader vanguard emerging from the mountain passes to spread far out over a rolling grassy plain. For the most part the Franks, however, followed a time-worn road which ran parallel to a great lake the shores of which were choked with masses of weed and rushes.

At their first opportunity mounted men rode girth-deep into warm, brownish water, allowed horses to drink their fill, while, bending in the saddle, they scooped water into helms in order to slake their own thirst.

Jackmen, villeins and ordinary foot soldiers flung themselves flat in the cool waters, drinking as they wallowed. It had been a long, trying march down from the mountains. At noon Cross Bearers by the tens of thousands commenced to skirt the great lake, plodding eastwards towards Nicea. Like a lazy river their shapeless columns eddied about natural obstacles only to reunite beyond them.

The Band had jogged into a little vale between two hills when Sir Aethelm, riding a few spear casts in advance of the company, uttered a resounding oath for, among weeds and underbrush, lay human bones, many draped with fragments of rag. The pitiful remains lay scattered as snowdrops about a forest floor but often small mounds of bones marked the spot where some of Walter the Penniless' rabble had collected to go down fighting. A few crucifixes were visible half buried to attest the fact that here had perished the bulk of Peter the Hermit's leaderless followers.

"Five times a thousand men must have perished here," estimated Sir Gaston of Beaune wiping sweat from his forehead. This seemed more than likely if one were to judge by the broken sword blades, shreds of chain mail and the quantities of shattered arrows and spears littering this long, yellow-green vale.

"By the Glory of God, these Moslem hounds shall pay for this a thousandfold." Sir Arnulfo licked sun-cracked lips.

Slowly, painfully, the van of the Crusading army appeared and, horror-stricken, passed through the Vale of Death to make camp upon the plain beyond. Their Captains planned a great circle in which a gap was left to admit the army of Count Raymond of Toulouse. His Provençals had reached Constantinople only a few days before the Frankish invasion of Asia Minor had commenced.

After spreading far out over the plain the Christian host set about pitching camp even while their fellows still toiled down from the mountains. Pack animals were driven in for unloading, jackmen strung picket lines for the horses and planted poles and rigging ropes on which to erect their masters' tents and pavilions. Other servants unyoked oxen or slaughtered driven sheep and goats for the evening meal. Esquires were dispatched to fill jars of water for the benefit of ladies, invalids and priests. By the thousand cooking fires sent smoke spiraling into the evening sunlight.

The Band rode in from the right flank, cheered by visions of hot stew kettles, horns of wine and an opportunity to put aside heavy coifs and hauberks the leather linings of which dripped with sweat.

The Band, on Edmund's signal, had reined in when a horseman raced towards them all the while yelling something and pointing over his shoulder.

Directly opposite that gap in the Crusaders' circle left for the benefit of Raymond's tardy levées stretched a low ridge crested with dark green bushes. Over this was streaming an avalanche of white-robed horsemen. Yelping like hounds in pursuit of a stag, they brandished weapons on high and lashed their ponies into a headlong gallop.

Quickly, but not quickly enough to suit either Edmund de Montgomerie or William Bras-de-Fer, the Companions rallied to the blue and silver gonfanon. In desperate haste the humbler Companions tugged on gauntlets and readied swords and axes while the six knights swiftly rebridled their great horses which, sensing impending combat, squealed, laid back their ears and snapped at the empty air. All about the Band Normans, Flemings, Lombards and Lorrainers hurriedly resumed their mail. Priests lifted crosses on high and raised hymns of encouragement while circulating among the swarms of surprised Christians.

Gradually that dull rumble caused by Turkish hoofs increased to a loud drumming, then swelled to an awesome billow of sound. Various barons, counts and the leaders of independent companies ordered oliphants sounded then, shouting war cries, they spurred forward, lances couched.

A stretch of knee-high hay grass separating the two forces narrowed with incredible speed as further Turks swarmed over the ridge crest. In ragged waves the Cross Bearers bent over their pommels and streaked to meet them with pennons snapping and swords a-glitter.

Edmund, peering through Stormcloud's flying mane singled out a group of dark faced riders in wide-sleeved and striped *khalats* galloping ahead of the main Turkish force. He realized that none of these men bore lances but only round shields, swords or bows and arrows.

"Allah! Il-Allah, Allah il-Allah!" howled these men in the silver mail and spike-pointed helmets bound about by strips of linen. Standards fashioned of green dyed horsehair and topped by slim golden crescents, swayed above them.

"St. Michael for Montgomerie!" Edmund's deep voice rang out over the thundering hoofs. "St. Michael!" chorused the Companions as they fanned into a wedge-shaped formation with the former Earl of Arundel riding at its tip and his knights and serjeants at his left and right. Men-of-arms constituted the depth of the arrowhead. When flying robes and a black-bearded face materialized just beyond Sir Edmund's blue-gray lance point he shifted his shaft in line with this outlandish rider's midriff and set his shoulder in anticipation of the shock.

Although this Turk wore a light steel shirt the stout Frankish lance penetrated his chest as easily as a sharp knife would a slab of butter. The destrier's momentum then spun the transfixed Infidel out of his red leather saddle and carried Edmund into the heart of a knot of

screaming Seljuks. An arrow hissed by his ear and he half-heard a
Norman scream followed by a crashing fall.

More Turks were jarring against him but as he cleared his lance
point he heard Sir Gaston shout, *"Dieu et St. Dénis!"* Already the
French-Norman had jerked out his long sword and, towering above
a whirling press of Asiatics, was laying about him with a ferocious
eagerness. Under his blade sank a succession of Turks some lacking
arms or split to the chin.

As quickly as they had come the bulk of Infidels melted away,
racing headlong back up the slope. Here and there, however, Seljuk
contingents lingered—to their cost—for this was no ill-led rabble such
as they had massacred not far from this spot almost a year earlier.

"Sound the rally on my oliphant!" Panting, Edmund reined in
when it became obvious that none of the Band's horses could over-
take the Turkish ponies, which, unencumbered by heavy riders or
weight of mail proved as fleet of foot as so many frightened deer.

Gerth clapped the oliphant, a semicircular brass horn, to his lips
and sounded the Band's rallying call: three long blasts, two short and
then another long one. Grinning Sir Reynard rode up wiping blood
and brains from his mace's head upon his saddle cloth.

"A well-fought battle, my lord," he grinned exposing yellowish,
gapped teeth.

"Battle, my butt!" grunted Sir Aethelm. " 'Twas only a skirmish."

"Montgomerie! Rally to the standard!" Gerth shouted himself
purple-faced but the serjeants and men-of-arms were too busy plundering those scarlet-splashed bodies dotting the slope.

Dismounted, the Companions were leading their horses by the
bridle while hewing heads from fallen Turks, jerking off bracelets
and cutting free golden earrings or gathering up such scimitars, helmets and daggers as took their fancy.

"Sound my oliphant again!" Edmund roared in a fury. "By God,
the last two in will feel a surcingle across their shoulders."

One by one the Companions rode up. Most of them, grinning in
triumph, carried a Turk's head impaled and dripping upon lance-
point. They paid no heed at all to dull red streams descending their
lance shafts to spatter their fists. All of them were leading one or
more captured horses loaded with plunder.

"Sir William! Mark those last two rogues." A Saxon and a Norman
were the last two to ride up, shouting in childish delight and waving
a cluster of Turkish heads by their beards.

"Harold! Rurik!" There was that in Edmund's voice which caused
the stragglers to gape and hurriedly drop their gory trophies.

"Bras-de-Fer see that these disobedient dogs receive twice ten stripes. *Par Dex!* When my oliphant sounds recall you will rally on the run."

Had not war-wise Emperor Maurice written in his *Artis Militaris* that full many a battle had been lost through plundering before an enemy had been finally routed? Why, even now, clouds of enemy horsemen still could be seen maneuvering in the distance.

Sir Reynard of Benevento nodded. "Our Band will survive much longer, my lord, provided you enforce this rule. I should have returned more swiftly."

The Italian-Norman, apparently contrite, slipped a pair of massive ruby-studded gold bracelets into his leader's food pouch. Edmund accepted them without comment; such should prove useful in the purchase of supplies.

De Bouillon's foot soldiers, outdistanced by the cavalry, fanned out over the battlefield and, shouting *"Dieu lo vult!"* commenced savagely to hack their fallen enemies into shapeless lumps of flesh while high in the heavens appeared flocks of heavy-winged vultures.

CHAPTER II

Imperial Headquarters

The skirmish had cost the Band a Viking serjeant who had received a Seljuk arrow full in his left eye. The poor fellow took all night a-dying and mumbled strange Scandinavian words while coughing up quantities of blood. The only other casualties were a brace of chargers which shrieked horribly when Sir Gaston of Beaune cut arrows from their quivering flesh but the French-Norman, a most knowledgeable horse master, declared that these would be ready for use within a few days.

The Turks attacked again later in the evening, this time assaulting a sector held by Duke Godfrey's stolid Rhinelanders. The Franks mounted up, half-armed, but used spurs and swords to such good effect that, for a second time, the green horsehair standards of Islam melted far back among the hills.

This encounter proved to be a real battle, forced, as it was, by a Turkish army en route to reinforce the Red Lion's garrison at Nicea. That night triumphant *Te Deums* were sung in every quarter of the Christian encampment which now was said to include all of two hundred thousand souls.

Sir Edmund, on attending a council in the pavilion of Count Tancred, ascertained that this last Turkish column, on finding its way barred into Nicea, had retreated from whence it came, leaving behind hundreds of dead and many prisoners.

Next day the Frankish tide crept onwards over undulating yellow-green hills always keeping the great, weed-filled lake to their left. Upon its waters could be seen maneuvering numbers of small sail-boats, most of them undoubtedly Turkish. Not a few however showed Byzantine colors and crosses.

Alexis Comnene, the Council was informed by a glittering Byzantine staff officer, had decided to take the field in person and had set up an Imperial Headquarters at a town called Civitote. All around it this veteran campaigner's magnificently trained and equipped troops lay in orderly encampment, *drunge* by *drunge,* *turma* by *turma, mesne* by *mesne,* with the Imperial Guard in the center. Following their Emperor's example nobles, *strategoi* and *comites* had left behind luxury but not intrigue.

Bohemund was with Alexis, apparently beguiled by his former enemy's gold and flattery, growled Tancred, shaking straw-colored hair loose over his shoulders.

On the morrow steel-tipped waves of Franks lapped around the tall, yellow-gray walls of Nicea. This city the besiegers soon learned was defended by double walls reinforced by no less than two hundred and forty-six towers of varying heights built never more than a bow-shot apart.

The Turkish defenders sallied forth and were decisively beaten by swarms of wild-eyed, psalm chanting zealots, but once Nicea's gates crashed shut the men of the West could accomplish nothing since they possessed no siege train. Alexis had one though, complete with rams, sows, ballistae, onagers and other terribly powerful military engines.

When for the third time the Crusaders saw their scaling ladders broken and their men blinded or scalded to death by streams of burning pitch and sulphur Duke Godfrey de Bouillon, nominal leader of the Crusading forces, summoned a council at which it was decided to request not only the loan of the Byzantine Emperor's siege engines, but the advice of Taticius the Armenian, a military engineer of vast renown.

Count Tancred stared hard at Sir Edmund de Montgomerie standing tall and sun-bronzed before him.

"Because of your seeming ability in the field, my lord, you and your Band have been chosen to bear our appeal to the Emperor's camp. Prepare to depart within the hour."

A sinking sensation gripped Edmund. For him to enter the Imperial camp would be tantamount to thrusting his head into a lion's mouth. Count Leo was there, commanding a *drunge* of Moslem mercenaries and no doubt stung by humiliation and burning with rage over a certain Anglo-Norman's apparent ingratitude.

"I have selected you for two further reasons," Tancred continued. "I am told you not only speak and write Latin but also Greek. While in the Emperor's camp I would have you use your ears. The other reason is that your Band seems strangely well-controlled and so should win through against roving troops of Infidel cavalry and, worse still, those accursed Christian marauders who plague our rear."

There was nothing for it but to nod.

Richard of the Principate held up a bandaged hand. "Before you depart, Sir Edmund, you must, by rote, learn a message and deliver it to Duke Bohemund. Tell him we insist that he quit this shameful dallying with the Byzantine Emperor and immediately assume his rightful place at the head of his liege lords."

"Else," rumbled the Bishop of Ariano fingering the grip of his battered mace, "we will follow no longer his red banner but the yellow one of Lord Tancred."

It would scarcely prove pleasant to witness Bohemund the Mighty's reactions to such an ultimatum, mused Edmund as, at the head of his Band, he retraced their route around the lake.

To trace the eastward advance of the Frankish hosts would have been possible for a blind man. They had drawn across plains, foothills and mountains, a blighted, sordid swath of destruction. Only splintered and charred stumps of trees remained along their course. No bushes and hardly a tuft of grass had been left standing by the thousands of horses, oxen, sheep and goats which had passed this way only a few days previously.

At a comfortable and energy-saving dog-trot the Band of the Silver Leopard left the great encampment and rode through the scattered bivouacs of straggling and completely unfamiliar Crusading forces. Continually they encountered bewildered detachments, large and small, dust-covered, hollow-eyed and hungry which, for some reason, had failed to keep up and so stood a good chance of being massacred by swift-striking Seljuks.

Occasionally these haggard groups preserved some semblance of a formation but mostly they slunk dispiritedly along under the rusty bills, pikes and axes they had carried all the way from Central Europe. Everywhere were visible the calcined bones of beasts slaughtered to feed the Christians. Frequently the big riders in soiled white surcoats rode past bloated and naked corpses a-swarm with maggots and covered only by clouds of blowflies. Piteous pleas for food and help sounded on occasion from such patches of shrubbery as still existed but the Band paid them no heed. There were too many of them so the mailed riders, spurs a-jingle, trotted on.

By the roadside lay a woman, naked, dead, and beside her the tiny, blackened corpse of a newborn infant.

Gerth, happy to be among fellow Saxons, viewed the debris left by the passing host with clear and dispassionate blue eyes.

"By St. Olav!" he laughed. "Are not you rejoiced to follow a lord who can see beyond the end of his lance?"

"True," snarled a blond giant, "but the Devil take him all the same. He needn't have caused my back to smoke the other night just for a little extra pillage."

Gerth chuckled, pointed to the fellow's bulging haversack. "And was it not worth a few stripes to fill yon sack so well with brooches, rings and necklaces?"

The Saxon grinned, uttered a reluctant grunting laugh. "I have suffered worse and for less. And you? You fared as well?"

"That I did not. What with having to sound that accursed oliphant and minding my lord's led horses." The armiger dropped his eyes and said nothing of the wallet slung to his belt. In it reposed a necklace of strange green stones which glowed like verdant fire, and a Turkish gorget upon which pearls glistened as the sheen of snow new-fallen upon frozen ground.

After slapping a fly from Stormcloud's neck as he trotted riderless alongside, Gerth ran an eye back over the brief column, noticed that the two wounded horses were limping along quite easily, unburdened as they were by either packs or riders. Hum, already those scarred and battered faces rising and falling rhythmically beneath the fluttering pennons looked darker than they had a scant week earlier.

The armiger's gaze then sought Sir Edmund riding at the head of the Band with Bras-de-Fer on his right and Sir Aethelm at his left.

After the Band had trotted twenty minutes and had walked for forty, the entire company dismounted and on the insistence of Sir Gaston, the veteran horse master, eased saddle girth then, on foot, led their beasts for a quarter of an hour along the rutted, befouled track.

The succession of abandoned encampments they passed seemed without end. Already vultures had picked clean the bones of fallen horses and cattle. Crudely contrived crosses here and there marked that spot where some poor wight who might have tramped all the way from Denmark, lay awaiting the call of Gabriel's horn.

Among the shrubbery on slopes overshadowing the route furtive movements were to be noted and on occasion figures materialized only to melt back among dusty cedars. Such half-seen forms were not those of Moslems but unmistakably Franks. These, remarked Rurik, Serjeant of the Norsemen, most likely were supporters of a power- ful, not unhumorous, outlaw known as "King" Tafur. His horde of followers were murderers, weepers, fit-throwers, actors, cutpurses, jugglers and whores spewed up from the gutters of Paris, Lyons and many another French city.

Voicing the most pious of declarations, these ribalds had followed Peter the Hermit on his disastrous and abortive Crusade—but not so devotedly as to get themselves massacred with their over-eager fel- lows.

The Norseman blew his nose between his fingers. "Woe betide any honest pilgrim lacking arms and companions who encounters these ribalds. They get short shrift."

Near the brief column's head Sir Arnulfo of Brindisi to avoid a cramp eased a foot out of its stirrup. "A plague on Count Tancred. Ordered away from the siege like this there will be small honor won by us—and no spoil."

"'Tis outrageous," gloomily agreed Bras-de-Fer. "I had scarce bloodied my sword in that bicker the other day ere it was over.

"These Turks," he observed while the rutted road unwound before them, "appeared better armed, mounted and more richly dressed than those we met under the banner of the Sieur de Mauron back in '85. These Spawn of Satan seemed bigger and not so ugly. I wonder why?" The Norman's nose, long ago flattened by some vicious blow, attempted to wrinkle itself. "God above. You should meet a Turk fresh out of Asia. He is ugly as sin, filthy, and since he never bathes, the stink of him can be smelt at half a league's distance."

Observed young Sir Reynard of Benevento, long-limbed body yielding gracefully to his charger's trot, "I am most curious to behold the Emperor's encampment. By my faith! 'Tis laid out like a city, so they say. Alas that I have never fought against these Greeks, nor do I understand their mode of warfare."

"When they choose to give battle they are magnificent soldiers," Sir Arnulfo of Brindisi informed. Lean as any bittern, the Italian- Norman owned a great beak of a nose which furthered the illusion. While in the field his gaze never was still but shifted perpetually first to one side and then to the other. "But these Byzantines lack the least love of daring, for its own sake. Sweet as are the uses of chivalry, yet these Easterners understand them not. For them, as our lord Edmund has explained, there is no glory to hew down a dozen men in a single battle. They find no joy in the shock of a well-swung sword biting into a helmet, or the single sweep of a mace emptying a saddle."

"But surely, Sir Knight, they must be mean of spirit to feel so."

"Mean or not, they have for centuries beaten Bulgars, Turks, Sclavonians, Betchenaks—even us Franks as at Castoria."

In midafternoon the Band arrived at that place where their route no longer followed that used by the Crusaders so trees grew beside the roadside, flowers bloomed, brooks rippled clear and birds sang. No longer did the stench of excrement and manure pollute the air.

The Band was riding between the base of a steep hill and the lake, now rippling to their right, when suddenly a trumpet brayed in the forest ahead. In an instant the Companions gathered rein and closed up into the same broad arrowhead formation they had employed during the first skirmish.

Blue and white pennons fluttered from the Crusaders' downswung lances and they steadied their mounts until straggling pack animals could be secured in the base of their steel-tipped wedge. Then at a slow walk the Band continued on its way until out from the woods appeared a column of *cataphractoi*, the heavy-armed lancers of the Empire. The banderoles curling from their lance heads were yellow and green as were their surcoats and rings on their heavy circular shields.

To a man these burly cavalrymen wore steel caps surmounted by a short, stiff crest of feathers, in the case of this *mesne* they were of a brilliant green and yellow. Mail shirts reached to these riders' hips while their extremities were sheathed in iron shoes or gauntlets. The Byzantine horses looked larger than the Turks' but smaller than the Frankish destriers, and were protected across chest and forehead by frontlets and poitrails of plate iron.

The Band could see as these presumed allies came cantering across a little field that they were armed with broadswords and daggers in addition to short horsemen's bows and quivers. Again the uniformity of their arms and equipment impressed these big Westerners accustomed to the heterogeneous weapons, arms and apparel of feudal levées.

Swiftly it became evident that these horsemen entertained no hostile intent for they pulled up ten spear casts away and stood up in their stirrups brandishing lances in friendly fashion.

When an officer wearing a dull gray surcoat over a silvered breastplate spurred forward calling out in Greek that he must speak with the Franks' leader Edmund raised his lance, slung his shield and trotted forward wishing that his surcoat and scarlet Crusader's cross had not become so dimmed by dust and sweat.

The *moirarch* in command, a nervous, olive-skinned young man with profile as sharp as that on a cameo raised his arm before him in the ancient Roman salute and politely inquired the nature of this *bandum's* business.

On ascertaining that the red-haired Frank bore a message for the Emperor's own ear he immediately dispatched two gallopers that they might warn other outposts of his coming. "His Sacred Clemency is most anxious that there shall be no clashes between brother Christians," he added seriously.

The Band of the Silver Leopard penetrated the fringes of the Byzantine Army's camp just as a purple-red dusk commenced to settle over the great lake and dark blue shadows appeared among surrounding hills and mountains.

Edmund and his knights found little difficulty in recognizing various types of Imperial soldiery, *scutati* or heavily armed infantrymen wearing crested helmets, short mail shirts and oblong shields. The chief weapon of these muscular Isaurians was a long-handled battle-axe equipped with a crescent shaped blade on one side and a spike on the other.

They also carried bows, much longer and more powerful than those of the *cataphractoi*. Occupied with interior guard duty were *psiloi* who carried two or three throwing javelins, lighter axes than the heavy infantry and round shields slung between their shoulders.

It was the camp itself, however, which filled the Franks with astonishment if not awe. Here was no sprawling, helter-skelter expanse of tents and horse lines. In effect this encampment reproduced a *castrum* or fortified camp of the ancient Roman legions. Just as Sir Edmund had seen them depicted in the Emperor Maurice's book, yonder was the required ditch and the palisade with guard towers at corners and gate. Everywhere lights shone among tents regularly spaced. Horse lines of equal length had been established along company streets. At the head of each stood a commander's tent displaying a distinctive standard and guarded by a squad of motionless sentries.

Trumpet calls of various pitch assigned to various units their evening tasks. Here, common soldiers, instead of crowding and fighting about a cauldron filled with scorched and stinking stew lined up each with his wooden bowl to be served bread and meat prepared by cooks who had no other duty.

At the gate a Slavonic Officer of the Guard saluted smartly and undertook to lead these tall Franks to an area reserved for the accommodation of visitors. Here stood stacks of firewood, tents, a pile of forage and a picket line for horses braced upon the sturdy stakes.

Once his band had dismounted and had set about caring for their mounts, Edmund beckoned Bras-de-Fer and, being aware of an inviolable rule among Byzantine Commanders in the field, requested immediate audience with Alexis.

The Emperor's pavilion of purple and gold occupied the exact center of the *tuldum* and before it waved the Holy Labarum. This was not the original Labarum which Constantine the Great was believed to have received from the hands of the Archangel—that hallowed standard unfortunately had been lost twenty-seven years earlier following Romanus Diogenes' crushing defeat at Manzikert. The copy, however, looked imposing enough for above it an ornament of solid gold—a "P" was superimposed upon an "X"—blazed with jewels and the banner itself was of cloth-of-gold hanging from a crossarm. Rubies formed the Cross upon its center.

About it, motionless as statues, stood a detail of the gigantic Varangian Guards, winged helmets glowing softly in the twilight. Shoulder-to-shoulder, more of the Heteria completely surrounded Alexis Comnene's pavilion. Not a cat could have passed between them. Just before entering the Imperial pavilion Bras-de-Fer's fingers closed on Edmund's elbow.

"Look!" he hissed. "See yonder?"

Starkly outlined against the twilight were such strange and mighty outlines as the Anglo-Norman never had seen in actuality. There, under heavy guard, stood the siege train, engines which must be brought forward if the walls of Nicea were to be penetrated.

Deep rugs, soft as a bed, lined the Imperial antechamber. Inside loitered such high-ranking officers as *strategoi, catapans* and *klissurarchs* in field armor that not in the least resembled the lavishly silvered and gilded accoutrements worn about the Sacred Palace in Constantinople. Neither was any trace of ceremonial paint visible on any Byzantine's face.

To Edmund's amazement he had hardly removed his casque and run fingers through sweat-dampened locks than the *Moirarch* of the Guard approached, bade him enter the inner enclosure. A moment later he and Sir William came to halt before a long table illumined by golden candelabra supporting dozens of tapers.

Alexis Comnene sat behind it wearing a gold edged purple cloak over a corselet of gilded steel. Otherwise he was bareheaded and wore no bracelets or neck chains. Only a few rings showed on his broad, hairy and powerful hands. To one side of the seated Emperor was standing Manuel Butumites and on the other Count Leo Bardas, his classic features fixed in an expressionless mask.

CHAPTER III

Private Conversation

Alexis Comnene, Emperor of the Romans, little resembled that short, bandy-legged and jewel-laden figure Edmund de Montgomerie recalled seeing on the throne of the Caesars. Today no trace of cosmetics showed on his broad, essentially peasant's features and his glossy brown beard had been clipped close while the sun and the wind had restored to his cheeks that healthy red-bronze hue they must have worn while, campaigning as an ambitious and ever-successful young *strategos,* he had plotted to seize the Purple. One could understand why barbarian chieftains so often fell into error concerning Byzantine fighting ability.

Here, under canvas, Alexis' voice sounded succinct and strong, no longer low and almost musically modulated. He had, he crisply informed the big Anglo-Norman, foreseen Count Tancred's need for their siege train. He would be glad to assist fellow Christians so valiant and ardent in their war against the Unbelievers. Yes. He had heard all about the repulse of the Turkish cavalry. On the morrow the *Strategos* Taticius would commence to ferry his great engines across the lake so that, as promptly as possible, Roman *ballistae* might start showering iron darts at the enemy's battlements, while catapults and *petrariae* hurled tons of rock into the Infidel stronghold.

Edmund listened in respectful silence, hands crossed on the brass, lead weighted pommel of his long Norman sword but at the same time he was supremely conscious of Count Leo's searching gaze. Uneasily the former Earl of Arundel wondered just what that grizzled veteran's thoughts might be now that the Band of the Silver Leopard lay completely at the mercy of him who had made possible its formation.

He pondered just what outraged demands for vengeance Sybilla might have poured into her uncle's ear ere he had quitted his comfortable villa above the Golden Horn. The Byzantine patrician, however, remained impassive, only interpolated occasional suggestions as to the siege train's movements.

"Pray inform your valiant lord," said Alexis Comnene, "that my army will attack Nicea along its water wall once vessels which we are hauling overland can cut off those supplies which the Infidels now receive by water."

Par Dex! How casually this famous man mentioned the hauling of great boats God alone knew how far!

The Emperor extended his hand so, as became a man owing fealty to Duke Bohemund, Edmund knelt and kissed a huge ruby glowing on Alexis' middle finger.

Count Leo gave no sign of former intimate relations even when Edmund de Montgomerie strode from the tent with dusty mantle rippling about gilded spurs.

From the *moirarch* he ascertained that Duke Bohemund of Otranto occupied a yellow dyed pavilion situated to the right of the Emperor's so, with Bras-de-Fer, he betook himself thither.

To his joy, presently appeared the single eye and battered features of Sir Toustain de Dives, who rushed forward to fling cable-like arms about him.

"Ah, my lord! My lord! 'Tis wondrous fine again to press your hand. Much of great import has chanced since we parted so unluckily at that Tavern of the Golden Swan."

At his first opportunity the veteran drew Edmund aside, described in tiresome detail Bohemund's march across Thrace and fierce petty fights waged with the Emperor's barbarian mercenaries.

"To be sure, old friend, I have heard about that from both sides. Tell me——"

Sir Toustain hesitated, his single eye bright and inquisitive. "You have heard the latest intelligence from Sanseverino?"

A warm surge of joy welled up in Edmund's being. "Not since Gerth Ordway rejoined me. Is—is there word from the Lady Alixe?"

"Nothing direct. I have learned that she is well and assists as best she may the raising of a second levée from the domain. If all goes well it should sail to reinforce Duke Bohemund sometime next winter—or perhaps in the Spring."

Cautiously Edmund considered his old friend. "And just why does my lord Duke tarry here while knights of the Cross daily smite the Infidel and achieve eternal glory thereby?"

Sir Toustain bent over, pretended to adjust a spur chain. "Be not deceived. If the Emperor Alexis is wily, our lord of Otranto is his peer. Full well does Bohemund perceive that Nicea is but a way-station on the road towards the Holy Land." The one-eyed knight's voice dropped to a whisper. "You should know that Nicea never will be permitted to fall before the blind fury of Godfrey, Tancred and Raymond of Toulouse."

"What? Dare you dream that the Turks of Nicea can withstand an onslaught by the mightiest princes of Christendom?"

A low, derisive laugh escaped the veteran. "Did I say that the city will not fall before a Christian army?"

"What do you mean?" Edmund stared, cudgeled his weary brain in search of the other's meaning.

"You will see, my lord earl. You will see—if you live long enough."

"If—?"

"You were daft so foolishly to offend Byzantine pride. Soon or late you will be made to pay for that affront to the House of Bardas. I know these Greek bastards all too well."

The contrast between that smelly shelter occupied by Count Tancred, with its muddy earthen floor and threadbare hangings and the clean confines of this cool pavilion, was striking.

Duke Bohemund, when Edmund tramped in, was lolling on a plain ebony armchair. At the moment the son of Robert Guiscard wore no armor beyond a mail shirt without which no man of ordinary intelligence would dream of going. Between freckled hands he poised a goblet of gilded silver and for several moments considered his tall young liegeman over its rim.

"Tell me," said he at last, "just why in the Name of our Sweet Jesus dared you so affront not only the famous *Strategos* Count Leo and my former—er—playmate Sybilla, but the Emperor and the whole aristocracy of Byzantium?"

"My lord Duke I—alas, I fear I could never explain to your understanding."

"Tell me, you owe me that. After all I have suffered much embarrassment on your account."

Visions of Alixe's delicate beauty shimmered before Edmund as, briefly, earnestly, he described the matter of Alixe and the nunnery and what else had chanced at Sanseverino. Bohemund listened to it all, fingers laced under his short red beard, then growled, "You're a great fool but 'tis not too late to forget your moon-eyed maid. One does well to forget such unfortunate and improvident attachments. I have, often enough. Sybilla, for example. I could do better by marrying instead the French King's daughter—a bastard child to be sure but a richly endowed and very winsome one. Come man, come! Surely Sybilla of Corfu, her family and connections can better advance you towards the winning of that principality you yearn for than this—this country wench from Sanseverino?"

The Anglo-Norman stiffened beneath his yellowed surcoat. "My lord, I love the Lady Alixe with all my being—and none other."

The Duke's small and dark blue eyes narrowed a trifle. "And what if I order you to wed the Countess?"

"In all honor I would refuse, my lord. When I placed my hands between your palms I swore fealty—but of the arm and spirit—not of the heart."

Bohemund grunted, heaved his vast figure to its feet. "True enough," he admitted. "And yet—and yet, I would you were clearer-sighted. By relieving this mistrust you have caused betwixt Greek and Frank you could earn my eternal gratitude."

"I would, my lord, that I might oblige you, but," Edmund's long unshaven jaw tightened, "in honor, I cannot follow your suggestion."

To it all Sir Toustain listened, his one gray eye flickering from one to the other of these two dominant figures. An esquire hurried in, dropped onto one knee and, with head bent, waited permission to speak.

"My lord, an officer from the Byzantine Count Leo's staff waits without. The *Strategos* begs that you feast with him tonight. A tender young doe has been taken by his foragers and prepared for your delectation. The *Strategos* also especially requests that that famous and valorous knight, Sir Edmund de Montgomerie likewise honor him at table."

To the messenger's astonishment, Bohemund broke into peals of snorting laughter. "'Fore God, I do accept—and so does my red-haired vassal. Pray inform the *Strategos* that we appear within the hour."

Sir Edmund became bereft of speech. God in His high Heaven! What was afoot? Why was he being forced into the company of that fine old patrician who had so generously befriended him? Could Count Leo Bardas ever be expected to comprehend that ingratitude had played no part in the cancellation of the wedding?

There was no help for it save to obey Bohemund's implied command, but the former Earl of Arundel resolved to be most cautious about what he ate and drank. He would help himself only from a platter passed to everyone and then select morsels from its far side; also he would instruct Gerth to fill his cup direct from a common supply.

Subconsciously Edmund wriggled shoulders under that fine steel shirt which had become almost a part of him.

Bohemund cast his stalwart vassal a penetrating glance then caught up a handful of walnuts and commenced to crush them between powerful hands covered with coarse red hairs.

"Since you have elected to keep your troth with Alixe of Sanseverino, you should know that Sir Toustain returns on the morrow to command a second levée being raised by that County. I hereby grant him permission to travel by dispatch galley and to bear an epistle for the lady of your choice."

"I thank you, Sire! Never will this kindness be forgotten by me." He understood better now why so many tough and valiant barons held the Duke of Otranto in such high esteem. Edmund hurried to an opening in the hangings and disappeared behind them.

"A fine, gallant idiot who cannot see beyond the end of his nose!" Bohemund growled at Toustain de Dives. "All the same, Sir Knight, you will bear his missive to that pretty little fool in Sanseverino. I well remember her. Send in my scribe."

Sir Toustain disappeared and presently a tonsured monk with quill, ink horn and parchment readied, hurried in on sandaled feet.

"To my worthy nephew, Count Tancred of Apulia," growled the massive figure at the council table. "Say that the Emperor's siege train, commanded by the Grand Primicerius Taticius, will appear before Nicea within the space of two days. Write also, that I, valuing the prowess of Sir Edmund de Montgomerie, do desire that he be afforded *continual opportunity*," Bohemund emphasized the words, "to prove his valor against the Infidel. The more hazardous the exploit, the greater the honor that will become his.

"Say also that I have the best of reasons for tarrying at the Emperor's side and that I will rejoin my nephew and our army within a fortnight." His voice grew harsh. "Woe betide any who harbor in the least disloyal thoughts towards me or my cause."

Despite a body aching with fatigue from lack of sleep Edmund borrowed writing materials and, in awkward Latin script, penned a brief message reaffirming his constancy. He had, he declared, the honor of remaining the Lady Alixe's champion against all comers. Her image constantly was in his mind and strengthening his arm and purpose against the Infidels of whom he had already slain a few during a skirmish. The campaign had opened auspiciously so, without doubt, Jerusalem would be taken with a few weeks. He remained her devoted lord-to-be.

Sir Edmund knuckled hot and burning eyes then bound a scarlet cord about the scroll and himself delivered it into Sir Toustain's hands. For the first time that gaunt individual talked resentfully over being, for a second time, sent back to Italy and away from the winning of glory and loot. Only lavish gifts from those treasures Alexis Comnene had heaped upon his former enemy mollified the veteran's ire.

The former earl followed Duke Bohemund into Count Leo's pavilion and found it surprisingly simple for a *strategos*. His fatigued perceptions were jolted into activity when he perceived Sybilla standing beside Count Leo. The Countess of Corfu appeared more

radiantly beautiful than ever in a silken gown of white and green
gathered tightly beneath her breast only to fall, outlining in subtle
fidelity her hips and loins. The zone of emerald damask emphasizing
the Countess' delicately rounded abdomen was adorned by rubies
which flashed midway between her hips like coals in a stirred watch
fire.

To Sir Edmund's growing astonishment Count Leo Bardas strode
forward and with hands extended bade him welcome as if no mischance had occurred. Courteously the patrician then made inquiry
into the Band of the Silver Leopard's welfare and its exploits thus far.
No less gracious, natural and entirely winning was Sybilla's manner.
Only her eyes clung hungrily to those bronzed and wind-reddened
features she had known so intimately.

From the Duke and his handful of Franks issued the strong odor
of horses, perspiration and garlic to mingle with the fragrant scent
of burning sandalwood pervading Count Leo's quarters.

As naturally as if they had been conversing in the Despoina's palace, Sybilla begged news of Baron Drogo and his bride and appeared
genuinely disappointed when Edmund denied having caught even
a glimpse of his dark-browed brother-in-law.

Duke Bohemund, of course, occupied the seat of honor at the
handsome old Byzantine's right while darkly beauteous Sybilla ful-
filling the role of hostess, placed the former Earl of Arundel by her
side.

Although a trifle contrite concerning his suppositions, Edmund
nonetheless kept a wary eye on such salvers as were passed by or-
derlies and rejoiced that Gerth, who stood heavy-eyed with fatigue,
alone was handling his horn drinking cup.

Count Leo's "simple repast" dragged on through several courses.
Certainly commanders in Imperial forces still dined well in the field,
but, of course, the capital lay behind but two short days' ride.

Wine continued to appear. While Bras-de-Fer gulped down enormous quantities yet seemed quite unaffected Sir Gaston commenced
to grow noisy and Sir Aethelm sank ever deeper into his habitual
morose taciturnity.

As skillfully as ever Sybilla plied charm and conversational dexter-
ity in extracting anecdotes concerning the March of the Cross Bearers
and conduct of the skirmishes before Nicea. At length various gentle
men of the Band produced captured bracelets, earrings and brooches
as well as jeweled daggers and sword belts.

Again and again Edmund's cup became refilled but only by
Gerth's hand, so presently he was surprised to find himself describing his Band's discipline and how he had caused to be punished

those tardy in answering his rally call. Despite himself, he became aware of Sybilla's perfume, reminiscent of so many delightful evenings in the city of Constantine.

Count Leo's azure supra-tunic gleamed in the light of several candelabra when he turned from the lord of Otranto to address his other red-haired guest.

"—And have you, Sir Edmund, put into practice certain of the Emperor Maurice's precepts?"

"My lord Count, since our march began, I have put to good use many of his, and your, wise instructions."

The old patrician asked something more but the question became lost amid Bohemund's roaring laughter.

That the gentle men Companions were becoming inebriated was inescapable. The exertions of the march, of the skirmish and of their long ride around the lake had affected even their rugged constitutions.

Gradually voices sounded blurred in Edmund's ears save for the Countess of Corfu's clear and dulcet accents. What irony that she and her former lover must have been forced to occupy the same encampment for some time! Coolness was evident between them, thought Edmund, on recalling first impressions of the pair in that pavilion near Città Potenza. Tonight she and Bohemund had exchanged no burning glances only a few formal phrases demanded by courtesy, and the lord of Otranto had cast his former mistress never a smile.

Gently the ground beneath Edmund's feet commenced to rock while he wondered whether this repast ever would end. He became aware of Sybilla's goblet raised in his direction, half eclipsing those still provocative golden white features.

"A toast to your continued success, my love."

"'My love'?" His imagination wrestled with the appellation. "I am not her love—any more, nor is she mine." Owlishly he repeated the assurance to himself despite an overpowering sleepiness descending upon him. Soon only an occasional word penetrated his fading consciousness, not that he felt ill, only relaxed and vastly pleased with life. After all, Sybilla seemed no longer angry, and someday Alixe de Bernay would be his. Despite the firmest of resolutions he fell sound asleep.

Only his schooling as a page, then as an armiger, enabled the former Earl of Arundel at the first light impact upon his shoulder to rouse, dagger in hand, so abruptly that a startled gasp reached his ears. Wildly he gazed about. The amber radiance of a single lamp illumined only unfamiliar surroundings.

"Silence! In God's mercy, silence!" Sitting upon a couch bed he managed to focus his eyes and found Sybilla bending above him. She was clad in a white gown so diaphanous as to suggest mist drifting over a forest pool.

Gently her hand restrained his dagger wrist and he felt himself borne back onto the couch, dizzy and half smothered by a swirl of perfumed draperies.

"Ah, my darling, beloved of my soul and body. I knew you must return." She spoke in Greek. Then Sybilla lay beside him with body trembling, her hair a soft, maddening screen.

"I had thought we Romans were cruel by nature, yet you Franks have far more cunning in the arts of torture. Oh, Edmund, Edmund!" Her lips brushed his ear. "What miseries have I not endured these past weeks? Ah-h, how my flesh has craved to press against yours. How my ears have strained to hear you making love in your graceless Greek—and loving you all the more because of it."

He drew a deep breath, blinked and recaptured a measure of intelligence. "Why are you here? In what place am I?"

"A guest tent of my uncle's, Beloved. When you fell asleep I ordered you brought here."

Parted lips descended avidly to smother his. Somewhere the guard challenged and a picketed charger whinnied, evoking a torrent of curses from its grooms.

"Sybilla!" he choked. "Why—do you——"

She placed fingers over his mouth, and again pressed herself against him. The mesh shirt no longer was there.

Sybilla suddenly stood up and from her zone of crimson silk produced a tiny vial of greenish-white chalcedony. "You ask why I am here?" By the half-light her eyes became simply enormous. "It is to save your life!"

" 'Save—life'?"

"Oh, you great, doltish Frank!" she cried in a trembling voice. "Think you my uncle has forgotten or forgiven your affront to our family? Of course not. During the course of that meal a poison was administered, one which is not quick to act but will reduce you day by day, week by week into a gaunt, senseless and simpering living cadaver."

"You—had me poisoned?"

"No, not I, but my uncle." Once more fragrant fingers brushed his cheek. "Never would I willingly harm so much as a single hair of your beloved head. And here, here, I have a proven antidote."

When he lunged for the chalcedony vial she sprang away, quick as a squirrel and paused in the center of the tent, close braided hair emphasizing the extraordinary pallor of her features. Again she reached into her zone and held up a small richly enameled box which barely covered the palm of her hand. "Edmund de Montgomerie, here is a splinter from the True Cross." She cried, "Swear upon this that you will take me to wife. Then you shall have the antidote."

He stared at her as if she were some fey creation conjured up by a necromancer's spell.

"Will you swear?"

A hundred blurred images slurred before his eyes. "No. I cannot."

"Then you will die; die in agonies undreamt of outside the dungeons of Prinkipo Island."

"Sooner that than——"

A soft wail escaped her. "But you must take me! I worship you, my heart, as an ancient pagan girl adored Apollo." Her tawny features contracted. "Do you imagine that I will stand weakly by while you wed another? Never. Not after I came so near to losing you through that street brawl I arranged."

"*You arranged that fight?*"

Her small, dark head inclined. "How else would I have found opportunity to be near you for so long and so intimately? Oh, I did not intend you should have suffered so grave a wound. I had that stupid lout of a barbarian scourged to death for his carelessness."

Edmund simply gaped. "But your uncle?"

"It pleased him to please me by taking you in. Of course he became very fond indeed of you as time went on."

"But his son?"

"He has no son," said she evenly. "The youth you 'rescued' was an actor from the theatre. All this I did for love of you, so swear you will keep me by you always; even as a concubine I shall be content." She seemed to float towards the couch, offering the enameled reliquary. "Swear to keep me always near you."

A rolling, softly roaring sound as of snows loosed by a Spring thaw from some high peak sounded in his ears. With visions of Alixe spinning crazily before his eyes he knew that, quite without intending to do so, he struck the reliquary from her hand then rushed out blindly into the starlight.

CHAPTER IV

River Sangarius

Nicea fell not to Frankish valor but through the exercise of typically Byzantine guile and Sir Edmund came to realize the meaning of those cryptic words spoken by Bohemund in the Emperor's camp. It became known to the Frankish princes later on that Alexis, through his *Strategos,* Manuel Butumites, secretly had entered into negotiations with the Turkish commander in Nicea. That harassed officer was more than ready to treat because the Red Lion's family chanced to be in his care.

A further inducement for the Moslem to conclude an understanding with Alexis was the unrestrained and headlong valor of the Franks. These, chanting hymns, with fierce abandon had attempted to scale ramparts from which they were beaten back with ever-increasing difficulty. Further, the Turkish commander was informed of an understanding extant between Duke Godfrey de Bouillon, titular commander in chief of the Franks, and the Emperor that the city should go to him who first planted his banner upon Nicea's battlements.

Byzantine engineers hauled overland to the great lake a number of small boats while, from garrisons in Europe, the Emperor temporarily called into the campaign heavy contingents of Patzinaks, Betchenaks and every available Turkish mercenary. Upon arrival these barbarous warriors were embarked and sent sailing over the lake towards Nicea.

Before its water wall they made a brave demonstration by waving banners, sounding horns, drums and cymbals. On the day after their arrival these Turkish renegades pretended to attack their own kin and conducted a noisy simulated attack on the water walls where the Westerners could not see what really transpired. Exhibiting a masterful sense of showmanship the Byzantine hirelings pretended to be beaten off—much to the Crusaders' satisfaction, because on the next morning they intended to mount a grand assault against walls seriously weakened by those *petrariae* and the fire of onagers and *ballistae* on loan from the Byzantine Army.

While a pre-dawn fog yet obscured the great lake's reedy waters the Asiatic mercenaries re-embarked, rowed across the lake and at sunrise were admitted to Nicea after staging a convincing tumult and sounding many trumpets. Swiftly the Infidel garrison, Kilidj Arslan's family and Moslem civilians who wished to flee were ferried across to the north shore of the lake. Once there many of the garrison, disgusted by the Red Lion's failure to relieve Nicea, promptly entered the Imperial Service.

When the men in gray iron helms and white surcoats advanced upon Nicea's crumbling walls that morning they beheld, to their angry amazement, Alexis Comnene's banners flying from the city's principal towers! Had the Crusading princes for an instant suspected that Nicea had not honestly been carried by assault upon the water wall then most certainly a second siege would have commenced.

As it was, the Emperor promised, and indeed paid, the Frankish leaders a great sum in compensation for their disappointment. Butumites was created Duke of Nicea and the city, quite unravaged, was returned to the rule of Byzantium while, grumbling and growling, the deluded Westerners started on again, this time marching in a westerly direction along roughly parallel roads.

Only a detachment of turbaned Turcopoles, quivers and bowcases rattling, preceded the Band of the Silver Leopard across a bridge over the Sangarius River constructed by some long-dead Roman governor. It being early Summer the stream had not yet commenced to dry up so great flocks of waterfowl arose from surrounding fens and circled into the cloudless Asiatic sky as in a compact column Sir Edmund de Montgomerie's liegemen joyfully followed him into Anatolia.

Duke Bohemund was riding in high good humor for once he crossed this bridge there was reason for self-congratulation.

Thanks to his prolonged stay at Alexis' headquarters not only had he gained the opportunity of viewing this campaign in perspective but also he had been enabled to judge the character of his fellow leaders. Best of all, he not only had earned Alexis' good will but had obtained much-needed funds with which to pay his array in addition to the promise of supplies at regular intervals.

To Robert Guiscard's huge red-headed son it seemed incomprehensible that not another Western prince was devoting even passing attention to how his troops were to be fed, watered and otherwise supplied. True enough, it was only to be expected that, during a long campaign like the one in view, hundreds if not thousands of the weaker sort inevitably must perish through exhaustion, hunger or disease. Already the Cross Bearers' route was clearly marked by whitening bones and shallow graves.

Yes, the Duke of Otranto felt like a newly ransomed prisoner once he had crossed the Sangarius and so emerged from Alexis' immediate jurisdiction. Somewhere ahead lay his goal—that rich principality for which he had yearned for so many years. A similar eagerness was written large across the faces of such principal lieutenants as Richard of the Principate and his fiery tempered nephew, Tancred.

Well ahead by now must be riding his advance guard under that amazing Anglo-Norman who could be trusted not to allow himself to be trapped in a Moslem ambuscade.

What a curious mixture of wisdom and simplicity was this Edmund de Montgomerie. Probably he was the most powerful swordsman in all the Italian-Norman levées and only on occasion had displayed an insensate eagerness to do battle under any conditions.

The Duke wiped a coating of dust from his lips, grinned when he visualized the other Crusader columns toiling along in careless and complete disorder. These were the men of stern old Raymond of Toulouse, flamboyant Hugh of Vermandois, courteous and valiant Duke Godfrey de Bouillon and elegant and romantic Stephen of Blois. His own column was much smaller and included only his own forces and those of hard-bitten French-Normans who followed the sluggish, and usually besotted, Duke of Normandy, "Robert Cut-Hose" as he was known among his followers. William the Conqueror's eldest son, as Bohemund long since had learned, could be counted on not to dispute decisions, make rash moves or even to advance ideas of his own. This selection of a marching companion had been astute. Godfrey, Raymond and Vermandois were forever snarling and snapping at each other, hotly disputing the seniority of command.

All the same a distressing proportion of non-combatants had become included in this column. There were too many foot-sore pilgrims wild-eyed with religious fervor, half armed and wholly lawless ribalds who plagued the camp marshals. Then there were quantities of women; fewer, now, were those of gentle birth but there remained a good many riding horse litters or mules.

Of course the presence of innumerable monks, priests, hermits and other religious figures was to be expected and they did much good among the weak and faint-hearted. In brown, black or white habits they trudged along bent under gilded long shafted crucifixes and bearing also a variety of religious banners and holy relics calculated to inspire the fighting men.

Accompanied by his staff Bohemund commenced to canter along, paralleling his array as it trudged southwards under a shifting pall of reddish dust above which only pennons and lance points were visible from a distance.

To his ears came the bawling complaints of the thirsty oxen and the incessant screech of ponderous wooden wheels slowly turning on ungreased axles.

To Bohemund's relief hills in the vicinity showed fewer and less lofty and therefore offered less concealment for the Red Lion's swift riding squadrons. As he continued to trot along on a tall, heavy-footed charger—no ordinary palfrey could long have supported his great weight—flankers came galloping up bearing the news that fresh horse droppings and recent campfires had been discovered among the hills ahead and in such quantity that obviously a considerable force of Seljuk Turks must be lurking nearby.

"Remain wary," the Duke told them. "But these Infidels will not attack until many more of them come up."

Again and again detachments of Cross Bearers riding out on the flanks of the main body and seeking whenever possible to avoid the choking dust clouds recognized Bohemund's crimson banner and raised deep-throated yells of enthusiasm. The other Christian leaders were envious to see how fiercely loyal these Normans were to their celebrated Duke.

Whenever they recognized his massive figure riding by women waved bright scarfs and priests raised hands in benediction, calling down blessings upon this, their sagacious and battle-tried prince.

Far ahead of the Norman column the Band of the Silver Leopard traveled at an easy but space eating jog.

Well out on the Band's either flank rode skirmishers, veteran serjeants on unusually swift mounts. They should detect any threat in plenty of time. The balance of the Band rode as comfortably as possible, close by Sir Edmund's blue and silver gonfanon. All now were grown bronze-faced through sunburn and lean of limb and feature. Every unessential weapon or item of equipment long since had been left by the roadside and now a blackened cookpot was strapped to only one saddle in five, and a single tent weighted the Band's pack mules.

The Companions' eyes ached from a steady glare reflected by the sun-baked ground and they had taken to slinging helms to their pommels and removing torturingly hot coifs and replacing them with cloths wound about their heads in a manner taught by Toraug the renegade Turkish serjeant. When they obeyed his instructions these bound linens would not come undone and when water was plentiful it proved a great relief to soak the fabric.

The kite-shaped Norman shields with their clumsy white devices now were slung to the pack animals which previously had carried tents. Some knights even had taken to removing their kilts of iron rings, so fiercely did these radiate the desiccating heat.

Edmund, to his chagrin, was feeling a bit lightheaded because, to set an example, he had for hours refrained from sucking at a small waterskin riding his horse's withers.

He wondered whether the sun actually could grow any hotter then, to divert his mind he thought back to an evening in the camp of Alexis Comnene and found he could recall ever so clearly the bitter and deadly hunger in Sybilla's expression as he had rushed from her presence. Later he had lain, spent through retching up various antidotes hurriedly procured by Toraug's friend, a *hakim* wise in the arts of medicine. These precautions, it turned out, had been all in vain, for, just as the sun had commenced gilding the tent cloth a *moirarch* of cataphracts appeared before that couch upon which Edmund lay gasping, pale and sweat-bathed. In silence the Byzantine had saluted, thrust a small scroll into Gerth's hands, then saluted again and stalked out, yellow-edged blue cloak rippling to his stride.

Beloved [the message had read], Last night in the agony of my humiliation I told you a shameful lie. You were administered no poison. I lied because I wished further to test your constancy towards that unwashed female back in Sanseverino. Do not delude yourself that I have ceased to plan for I *will* have you for a husband or a lover! By the Panagia, I swear this!

Fearsome were the curses he recalled having called down upon Sybilla when he perceived the depths of her trickery and determination.

He glanced skywards and stifled a sigh. Long hours still must pass ere the sun would lower sufficiently to alleviate this blasting heat.

Sir Gaston of Beaune pursed lips upwards and blew a heavy beading of sweat from jutting brown brows then reined in a horse upon which white stains, left by sweat drying on its flanks and foreshoulders, showed like irregular fish scales. "Yonder serjeant must have noticed something to spur his beast like that," he mused.

"Many Infidels ride in the next valley, my lord," called the rider.

Edmund flinched as, hurriedly, he pulled on his overheated helm. "How many?"

"Too many to count, my lord," puffed the serjeant, "but Turks swarm there like locusts during a plague."

Briefly Edmund cursed the big fellow's inability to count. "Locusts" in a plague might mean a thousand or ten thousand, for that matter. Promptly he detailed a serjeant to ride back and report to Duke Bohemund.

By consequence Bohemund ordered his van to halt on a wide plain surrounded on three sides by low hills. On the fourth it stretched off to the horizon like a sea of brown grass and on this, to indicate a campsite, the Duke of Otranto's banner was planted by Richard of the Principate, and Robert of Normandy's by a doughty knight called Pain Peverel.

As various detachments rode up, they fanned out over the brown earth, each knight seeking for his company the best available location. Most of them pitched tents along the borders of a wide marsh at the edge of which they could cool themselves and water their dreadfully weary horses.

For over three hours the combined Norman forces, French and Italian, continued to flood the plain—on foot, a-horseback or in creaking oxcarts. At once jackmen and other villeins set about pitching tents for their lords and ladies. Here and there cooking fires blinked into existence, but there were not many; only a little fuel was available, the sun-dried droppings of cattle long since herded away by the Infidels.

CHAPTER V

Dorylaeum I

To lithe and restless Toraug and brown bearded Theophanes, the Byzantine serjeant, both of whom had campaigned many times against the Seljuks, it was little short of insane that this great multitude should settle down for the night protected only by outposts stationed in the most hit-or-miss fashion.

"Ah, these proud, deluded fools!" growled Sir Aethelm busily cleaning his saddle's bearing areas. "They boast that any one of them can slay a dozen Turks but they'll more likely wake with their throats cut and their hides scorching in Purgatory."

Encamped on the southeastern periphery of that great bivouac which might well include sixty thousand souls, the Band slept soundly. In that sector, at least, the Companions and men from an unusually alert Norman contingent commanded by Sir Ralph de Mauron, a former mercenary, were maintaining ceaseless vigilance.

Towards midnight a ground fog gathered over a little river which fed the marsh and gradually enveloped the sleeping Frankish host.

"My lord, if those sons of Shaitan plan to strike tomorrow it will be towards dawn," Toraug softly predicted, his pointed black beard silvery with moisture.

"And so say Sir William and Sir Aethelm. I ride to seek my lord
Bohemund." Edmund arose somewhat stiffly since only his mantle
and a thin blanket had separated his body from the earth. While the
tops of lofty hills rising to the northeast commenced to display faint
grayish highlights he roused Gerth and together they threaded their
way through haphazard clumps of sleeping beasts and humans.
Deep snores sounded from the dark on all sides and hardly anyone
roused up, so wearied were the Cross Bearers from their long march
of the day before. Somewhere a sick child was whining and a few
dogs barked.

The light had increased somewhat when a familiar standard,
dangling from a lance head revealed itself before Edmund and his
armiger. It was the red and yellow banner of Sanseverino.

A row of figures scrambled to its feet snatching at weapons, yelling
challenges at these two strange horsemen. Then, through a half-light,
Edmund with a start, recognized the broad shoulders of young Sir
Robert de Bernay and the familiar, evil countenance of Sir Volmar
of Agropoli. He only reined aside crying, "God wills it!" and spurred
ever deeper into the tangled mass of humanity.

Flambeaux still flared palely and mail glinted before Duke Bohemund's tall pavilion. Apparently someone else had become uneasy
over the slack watch being kept and was preparing to ride out of the
encampment. The restless one proved to be Count Tancred whose
yellow maned head glowed like molten gold in the torchlight as he
swung up onto a destrier and slung his shield into position.

"I tell you, Count Richard, the valleys to either side of us must
swarm with enemies. Just now I pressed my ear to the earth and it
seemed as though there was thunder underground."

"What of it?" yawned a beetle-browed knight. "Do not God and
His Angels fight on our side? The good Bishop of Ariano so preached
last night. Besides, our swords are heavier and longer than those of
the devil-worshipers and our arms stouter by far."

"Let the Turks ride where they please," growled Pain Peverel, the
Standard Bearer of Normandy. "Once the battle is joined their masses
can never withstand our charge. They never have and never will."

Mercifully, no attack was delivered while dawn brightened into
day and revealed the gently rolling hills about the plain devoid of
anything more dangerous than terrified gazelles and gray jackals,
slinking off among the rocks.

In the distance bagpipes commenced to skirl and drone and then
horns blew and oliphants sounded from several directions. More and
more breathless outposts came galloping in. Everywhere, it seemed,
dense formations of Turkish horse archers were being sighted. At this

the knights of the Cross cried out joyfully that the hour of judgment was at hand and a confident clamor swelled throughout the Norman camp.

Without waiting even to break their fast warriors of all degrees readied their arms, then many sought out priests in order to confess their sins and so ride into battle with a clear conscience. Still others turned aside to kneel before their planted swords silently praying that they might bear themselves worthily once the conflict began.

Brother Ordericus, thinner than before, and ever saintly of bearing, appeared among the Band ready to confess all who cared to receive Absolution. None of the Saxons or Vikings availed themselves nor did Toraug or Theophanes; all in some degree adhered to the Greek Rite.

Once the white bearded old man had hurried on Sir Edmund ordered an inspection of horses and equipment then sent his bat animals into the main camp. Everywhere bronzed liegemen were collecting about the gonfanon of their immediate lord and would straggle after him once that gentle man made for the bravely fluttering standard of his overlord.

The confusion grew incredible as, amid whirling clouds of dust, various companies kept cutting across the path of others and became entangled with them, often never to get sorted out again. So eager were the Cross Bearers to do battle with the followers of Mahound, that they neglected to fill their waterskins and instead dried their throats through bawling out rally cries.

Gerth Ordway, helm in place and adjusting the wrist thong of his great ax, felt thankful that the Band would ride ahead of this tangled mob. Looking over his shoulder he could discern women, invalids and children beginning to climb upon baggage wagons and piles of equipment the better to peer over the mist-veiled plain. Louder sounded the fervent chanting of priests, the eager war cries of the Cross Bearers and an insensate clamor from jackmen and other servants assigned, as usual, to protect the encampment.

Sir Edmund and his armiger found the Band sitting quietly beside their horses and tearing at cold meat. That capable lieutenant, Bras-de-Fer, had seen no use in mounting up so early, thus wearying beasts which might be called upon to exert every stride in their power before this day might end.

Below the gonfanon which flaunted the Silver Leopard serjeants and men-of-arms donned pointed helms and took position in the Band's now-familiar broad arrow formation. They still led their horses that the great beasts might browse until the last moment and slake their thirst upon dew-wetted grass.

To the tramp of several thousand iron hoofs, the jingle of bridle chains, the creaking of leather and a sharp clatter of equipment, the Norman host fanned out over the sere and yellow grass in a great and irregular half-moon. Since there was no wind, pennons and gonfanons dangled limp along sturdy lance shafts growing shiny through handling.

Chewing lustily all the while Saxons and Vikings in the band followed Gerth's example by running thumbs along the half-moon edges of their spike-backed axes. Then they hefted their *franciscae*, smaller throwing axes dangling ready from the pommel.

To the former Earl of Arundel's relief Stormcloud held his head high but wasted no energy in futile caracoles and curvettings. The destrier several times gathered his great body under the ponderous high-peaked saddle but ended by only arching his neck. All at once his ears went back, flat against his poll.

"Turks are near. My stallion, too, can smell them," Toraug commented then shifted his round shield forward on its sling when, at a strident note on Sir Edmund's oliphant, the Band moved out at a very slow walk.

Layers of mist mingled with dust shimmered briefly in the first rays of sunlight then commenced to lift. A glittering, colorful mob of knights in Crusaders' red-crossed surcoats hurried to close in on the patrols riding in their van. In the center of the Norman line the huge figure of Bohemund and his personal banner easily were recognizable. Behind the mounted men toiled a dense crowd of archers, pikemen and axe wielders, all on foot.

For the first time it really came home to Edmund how many knights and esquires had become totally dismounted during the past few days or bestrode such ignoble beasts as baggage mules and asses. At least two-thirds of the Christian array must have been toiling afoot along the hard dry ground, still chanting hymns or shouting defiance against the invisible enemy.

Urged by various marshals and constables, the horsemen gradually moved out ahead of the footmen, until the Crusader array still more suggested an enormous half-moon fringed along its curved edge by cavalry, its center packed with dense and hopelessly disorganized masses of infantry.

Theophanes, the Byzantine serjeant, groaned loudly when the Band, riding slowly towards the extreme left of the Christian host, became able clearly to perceive the Christian dispositions.

"Where is that second line of horsemen which should follow the infantry? As surely as God reigns in Heaven those accursed Turks will ride around us, so fall upon our rear and pillage the camp since there is nothing to hinder them."

Sir Aethelm having adjusted the thong of his lance cast a sidewise glance, saw Sir Edmund settle his helm over his coif and wince when he lowered its nasal over a raw and peeling nose. How tremendous the red-haired commander looked on that great destrier. His pointed casque towered easily half a head higher than any of the knights about him who with sunburned faces red and intent, were slinging shields to the long leather guiges which held them in place. Mechanically the knights grouped back to make certain that their maces dangled over the off-side of their cantles. Their swords on the near side now were steadied beneath the left knee, ready for instant use.

Once Bohemund's main battle had come up with the van the Band found space between de Mauron's tough Norman company and, of all things, the levée from Sanseverino! Sir Robert must have recognized Edmund's towering form for he made his charger rear then waved his lance; whether in salutation or in threat there could be no telling. What he shouted was lost amid the indescribable tumult.

The slowly advancing waves of iron-clad horsemen presently pulled up, puzzled by an inexplicable phenomenon. In the distance was sounding a rumbling noise suggestive of distant thunder. Gradually the sound swelled and swelled until the air quivered, horses trembled and men stared at one another in perplexed dismay. Soon it seemed that a fearful thunderstorm must be raging just beyond a long, low semicircle of hills.

Sir Aethelm, grinning, turned in his saddle and spoke to Gerth. "Now, Housecarle, you can say you have heard the famous kettledrums of the dog-delivered Infidels."

The armiger's blue eyes had never seemed so great as he quavered, "That is not the roaring of devils?"

"No. The Turks stretch hides over the mouths of those cook pots which always they carry into battle slung beside them. Before launching a charge they strike the leather with their fist or a dagger handle to cause a fearsome sound which greatly discomfits an inexperienced enemy."

The rest of the Saxon knight's speech became lost amid an avalanche of sound assaulting the Christians' ears, as from all sides raced into sight seemingly endless waves of horsemen. Dark-faced, carrying round shields and wearing silvered, pointed helmets, they stood high in their stirrups to brandish standards of green dyed horsehair topped by golden crescents. Some waved scimitars or yataghans, but the vast majority thundered along with bows drawn and arrows on strings.

"Close up! Close up!" shouted Sir Edmund, whereupon, Gerth, Bras-de-Fer and Aethelm and the other knights reined knee-to-knee, shoulders hunched well forward, while the serjeants extended the wedge to either side and men-of-arms formed a second rank.

Never before, Edmund realized, had he beheld horses so fleet and agile as those whose hoofs came drumming across half a mile of almost level brown turf separating them from that waiting line of lances and waving pennons.

The Turkish saddle-covers were of every imaginable hue and brilliant with silver or gold embroidery. The poitrails protecting their horses' chests glittered like a sunlit sea. Most of the riders' wildly flying robes were white but others wore garments of crimson, green or blue, sometimes striped, sometimes not.

Somewhere cymbals commenced to clang and crash adding their shivering clangor to that heart-chilling uproar created by the kettledrums. Thereupon Duke Bohemund's oliphant screamed and every other war horn in the Christian host brayed defiance. As Gerth sounded the Band's oliphant a shiver coursed down Edmund's spine and a great uplifted feeling of exaltation seized him. Yonder rode the accursed, spawn of hell, defilers of Christ's tomb and the torturers of His followers!

"St. Michael for Montgomerie!" he yelled then struck spurs to his destrier. Outraged the great animal reared then bounded a full length ahead of the Band.

In a ragged line the enemy were closing in fast, yelping like hounds in full cry and shrieking appeals to Allah. "Ul-ul Allahu Akbar!" screamed the Turks. "La-El-il Allah!"

The whole Christian front line then lowered lances and moved out, first at a trot then at a canter, and finally at a pounding gallop that set manes to tossing, pennons and surcoats to streaming. Edmund felt the wind tear by his face, settled lower in the high-peaked saddle. Now! Surely on this plain was about to be fought one of the greatest battles in all history? Upon raw Norman valor might hinge the fate of the entire Crusade, for the main Frankish force was toiling along—no one knew how far behind. Fresh waves of brown faced horsemen kept surging down the slopes until the entire plain swarmed with them. Magically that strip of green-brown earth separating the foremost Turks diminished.

"Companions! Cover your faces," screamed Toraug ducking head behind shield. It was well that he did so. At that instant the Turkish horsemen abruptly reined to their right and, raising short bows, loosed a storm of arrows. The hot sunlight glistened upon the swift white flicker of rushing, whistling shafts. Like iron hail their points

clattered against shields, helms and hauberks or with dreadful ease
sank feather-deep into exposed flesh. The Norman horses, largely unprotected, suffered terribly and went down screaming, lashing out
wildly and tumbling their riders onto the dust.

At this point, Bras-de-Fer, Toraug and the others who had met the
Seljuks before, expected the enemy to circle and race away beyond
reach of those gleaming lances and ponderous chargers, but on this
occasion their own numbers made such an evolution impossible. Unable to get away, the Moslems drew their swords and the two armies
crashed into each other, full tilt.

In an instant screeching Turks appeared on all sides.

Edmund drove his lance straight through the midriff of a towering,
red-bearded Turk wearing silvered mail and lifted him bodily out
of his saddle. With difficulty the Anglo-Norman cleared his point and
had time to strike down another enemy before the press of squealing,
shoving horses rendered its further use impossible.

Stormcloud's training now proved its worth. The great stallion
reared up on his hind legs and lashed out with heavy hoofs, smashing
flat the smaller Turkish horses.

No longer was there space for either archery or lance play and
the crush became so great that warhorses could no longer rear and
had to content themselves by savaging anything which came within
reach.

"St. Michael! Montgomerie!" Sir Edmund heard Companions panting, amid the press and whirling dust clouds. His long Norman
sword, wielded by a mighty arm, commenced its terrible play. Easily
its broad, blue-gray blade sheared through light Turkish mail. From
one howling Infidel he slashed the sword arm but so great was the
press that the Turk could not fall off his steed and was pushed away,
spouting blood all over his white robes.

A hook on some Moslem's axe lodged in the Anglo-Norman's surcoat
and all-but pulled him backwards out of the saddle but the fabric
gave way and, in a fury the former earl nearly beheaded his assailant. Stabbing lance and sword points, horse heads, all staring eyes
and flaring scarlet nostrils ringed him, but so terribly effective was
the sweep of his weapon that he hewed a path over to where Gerth's
axe and Bras-de-Fer's mace were wreaking similar havoc.

Fresh waves of Moslem riders kept charging into the melee but
the Normans stood fast and, amid choking, blinding billows of dust
men fought with the fury of zealots and the valor of paladins.

The serjeant Rurik, worried because an arrow had lodged in his
horse's shoulder, gripped his *francisca*, and raising the old Viking
war cry of "Yutch-hey-saa-saa!" hurled it flashing at a freshly arrived

standard bearer. A gasping shout arose from the Band's axemen when taken full in the face he tumbled over backwards bearing with him his green standard.

For an hour the battle line swayed first in one direction and then in the other. The ground became so encumbered by fallen men and animals that such horses as remained on their feet, found increasing trouble in maintaining a footing.

Gerth noted a dismounted and badly wounded knight laying heavily about him so charged and made such good use of his long-handled axe that three stalwart Moslems were felled ere they became aware of his presence.

On raged the combat with the Normans stubbornly, stupidly refusing to give ground towards their camp for all that they had been fighting without letup since sunrise and were becoming seriously diminished in numbers. Only a breed of iron could have swung such heavy weapons so long and so hard.

Still the Red Lion flung into battle squadron after squadron of frenzied tribesmen burning to hurl themselves upon these Westerners. Secure in the belief that Paradise would be theirs and that soft-bodied and sloe-eyed houris of unbelievable beauty awaited them in shady dells beside perfumed brooks, the Turks fought like demons incarnate.

There could be no telling in one part of that desperate field of Dorylaeum what was happening elsewhere until, unbelievably, the Turks commenced to fall back. Frankish knights riding nearly exhausted destriers, foolishly attempted to give chase, only to find themselves surrounded in detail and again fighting for their lives. Many a brave Norman was leveled with the dust in this fashion.

The Turkish withdrawal recommenced but this time they fled so rapidly that pursuit by the blood splashed iron men was a sheer impossibility, so they halted on the field and many sank to the ground, panting, sweat-blinded, and hideously tortured by thirst.

Dully, Gerth Ordway watched one of the Band's Norsemen grip an arrow which had transfixed his forearm, jerk it free to hurl it onto the ground and then stamp on it in a childish rage.

The young Saxon's breath still was coming in great, searing gasps when suddenly he wondered what fate had befallen his master. Where was Sir Edmund? His horse limped heavily as he rode it over piles of groaning or silent figures and all the while kettledrums and cymbals sounded in the near distance. It was appalling to note how many tall bodies and once-white surcoats lay among slain destriers and fallen Infidels.

He came at length upon the former Earl of Arundel attempting to rig a sling about Sir Gaston's arm. It had been shattered above the elbow when his charger had fallen, bristling with arrows. The French-Norman's swarthy face shone bright with sweat and had assumed a sickly greenish-bronze hue.

After a hurried count Gerth estimated that at least a third of the Band must lie among those tumbled heaps of slain while a half of those who remained now erect must fight on foot.

Sir Edmund was about to lead his survivors over to form a line with the levée of Sanseverino—Sir Robert de Bernay still was up and striding about dismounted and blood streaked as any butcher—when a dreadful outcry arose from the Norman rear. Toraug, stanching an arrow graze across his jaw uttered bitter curses as he saw his prediction being fulfilled. For from the Cross Bearers' camp dense pillars of smoke were rising together with terrible screams, yells and shrieks.

From a rise on which they paused, the weary Companions could watch white-robed riders racing about among the tents, mercilessly cutting down jackmen, priests, women, and other non-combatants. One Seljuk squadron was herding away the pack animals. Others were shooting arrows deep into the sides of terrified draft bullocks. Gradually everywhere in the terror-stricken encampment galloped the Red Lion's followers. Many raiders were dismounting the better to slay kneeling women, children and priests with the bloodthirsty efficiency of weasels ravaging a rabbit warren.

The Turks however soon mounted hurriedly and fled leaving behind fresh evidence of those abominable cruelties for which they were renowned.

"Water! For the love of our Sweet Jesus, give me to drink," croaked Harold, the Saxon serjeant. He half-sat, half-lay upon the ground hopelessly pressing a sodden rag to his side at a point where some Moslem scimitar had discovered a weak spot in his mail. But there was no water. The sun was nearing its zenith and its fiery rays lashed the battlefield with a pitiless intensity.

A galloper came riding heavily over from a knot of barons gathered under Duke Bohemund's standard. "Rally to the crimson banner! We must shorten our line," he called.

Sir Robert of Sanseverino heard and, after signaling with a bloody mace, led his levée after the gonfanon of the Silver Leopard in a lateral movement to close in upon Duke Bohemund's cruelly punished main battle.

Dismounted men ran along clinging to the stirrups of those more fortunate, pled for water and begged the riders not to move so fast, but the latter had no choice. Already fresh waves of Turks could be seen collecting on three sides, their kettledrums creating a hell of sound.

"In God's name!" shouted a tall French-Norman. "Where are Godfrey de Bouillon, Vermandois and the rest?"

"Who knows?" rang out Tancred's bitter laughter. "Probably he and those damned Provençal guzzlers have halted for meat and a drink. A drink! Oh God, a drink!"

CHAPTER VI

Dorylaeum II

The unbelievable had occurred. A charge of mailed Frankish chivalry had been stopped and battered to a standstill and now, equally incredible, Bohemund of Otranto was ordering his Normans to fall back upon their camp. A few chivalric hotheads refused to retreat and died a little later buried under the Moslem onslaught. Among them perished the vainglorious Count of Paris and nearly thirty of his picked knights, most of them shot through the face by arrows for only occasionally could the light arrows used by the Turks succeed in penetrating a Frankish hauberk. It was the light-armed footmen and the horses which suffered the worst losses inflicted by the Red Lion's horse archers.

Gasping, limping and half-strangled, choking with thirst the Christians came upon terrible sights. Amid collapsed or sagging tents and piles of burning equipment lay the bodies of the unarmed, the weak, the sick and the cowardly. The bodies of several priests lay crucified upon the earth, emasculated, disemboweled and otherwise mangled. The tender bodies of women had been impaled through their secret parts by Turkish lances. When they saw these things outrage sent strength welling back into Norman arms.

The faces of Duke Bohemund, Count Tancred and stout Richard of the Principate grew taut with mingled grief and rage when knight after knight, and serjeant after sergeant came stumbling into camp on foot, swaying with fatigue and bent under the weight of their saddles and weapons as they had been able to bring away. Everywhere voices now called out to learn the whereabouts of Duke Godfrey de Bouillon and the bulk of the Christian army.

Such women as had survived the massacre proved to be of good courage; all the while offering prayers for victory they bound up wounds, poured water into sun-cracked lips and produced morsels of food for men suffering from their ill-advised impetuosity in attacking the Turks.

Monks and priests bearing crucifixes and monstrances circulated among the dusty, hollow-eyed warriors or knelt to administer the Sacraments to those unfortunates who, in depressing numbers, were being brought in only to gasp their last.

Theophanes, the Byzantine serjeant, uttered a disgusted grunt. "And how many of these trained warriors will not perish through want of even simple care? Why do you stubborn Franks refuse to raise bands of *scriboni?* Our *strategoi* pay such men well for the recovery of every wounded soldier."

"God knows." Edmund, still shaking from the morning's exertions, poured water from a goatskin over his head and inside a hauberk which seemed to have doubled in weight during the past hour.

A solemn chanting of monks swelled in the stiflingly hot atmosphere.

> "*Lignum crucis, signum ducis,*
> *Sequitur exercitus, quod non cessit,*
> *Sed praecessit, in vi Sancti Spiritus.*"

A strange renewal of spirit seized the weary Cross Bearers when once more were raised gonfanons and religious banners and the oliphants brayed their call to the standards. Alas! Where five armed men had gathered in the morning only three now marched in the wake of their leader. Many famous knights now plodded along on foot or astride one of the few surviving bat animals.

Many, too exhausted to move, had to be left behind. Not a few of these extended themselves on the burning ground with arms outstretched to form the sign of the Cross and silently awaited a blow from some Turkish sword that would put an end to their lives.

Jackmen and villeins, inspired by the exhortations from clergy however swelled the thin column arming themselves from the fallen as they advanced. They snatched up a shield here, a helm or a sword there and pulled on hauberks that were usually too large or too small.

Unbelieving of their eyes the Red Sultan's men gaped at these beaten, heat tormented scarecrows who issued from out of their camp singing hymns and shouting, "*Dieu lo vult!*" to straggle forward in long irregular columns and deploy among the bodies of the fallen.

A pitying smile came to the sunburnt face of Sir Aethelm, himself dismounted and striding along armed only with shield, dagger and his huge, double-bitted axe. He was leading the dismounted survivors of the Band. Although limping badly, Gerth's horse had stopped bleeding and was able to shuffle on through the dust clouds. Already the great destriers had accomplished more than could reasonably have been expected of them.

Again the rolling thunder of kettledrums reverberated among the foothills and there arose a gale of shrill, yelping warcries from Infidel squadrons spurring to the attack. In desperate haste, Duke Bohemund's principal barons, marshals and constables beat their levées into a double rank in which dismounted knights and men-of-arms leveled their lances like hoplites in a Macedonian phalanx. At intervals gaps were left through which the mounted chivalry moved at a slow trot.

Again sounded the shattering, plangent noise created by mounted forces crashing straight into each other.

On came successive waves of Turks screaming and brandishing scimitars or shooting clouds of arrows which did fearful execution. Once again, however, the very weight of those behind the foremost Moslems forced them into hand-to-hand combat with these tall, hollow-eyed men whose sword arms never seemed to tire and which worked havoc among the Red Lion's lighter-armed followers.

Dark, yelling faces came crowding in on all sides, then some Infidel's hook jerked Edmund de Montgomerie out of his saddle and he surely would have perished had not Gerth's axe come sweeping down to behead a Turk crouching to sever his lord's throat.

Head ringing and with the whole world become a fantastic spinning tumult, Edmund struggled to his feet and looked about for Stormcloud. That great beast had charged off, rearing, striking and biting, a veritable equine demon of destruction.

Slash, cut and thrust. Thrust, slash and cut minute after minute at a solid wall of white-clad, brown faced warriors. At long last Edmund's sword arm grew heavy and its muscles burned like red-hot irons. Now he could only whisper, "St. Michael! Montgomerie!" as he fought on and on.

Presently he dropped his shield—the sword had grown too heavy to be swung in one hand so, bracing feet wide apart, he gripped his weapon in both hands and created such a windmill of glittering steel that the Infidels shrank away in amazement.

Elsewhere on this Field of Dorylaeum the warriors of Islam were experiencing much the same sensation of amazed disbelief as earlier had gripped the Normans on discovering that the headlong charge of mailed knights on destriers actually could be withstood. For nearly three hundred years now, Seljuk horse archers had crushed all opposition and at Manzikert had humbled the pride of the supposedly invincible Byzantine Army. Allah the Almighty! Here stood an array which, though decimated in number would neither retreat nor yield. They must be *djinns*, evil spirits, these tireless iron men whose swords still drank so thirstily of Moslem blood. Before sinking to the ground a single Frankish paladin might dispatch to Paradise ten or more of the Faithful.

Bras-de-Fer drawing his breath in great whooping gasps hacked his way to Edmund's side, then Sir Aethelm and Sir Arnulfo and finally Gerth Ordway. Of Sir Reynard or of Sir Gaston of Beaune there was no sign nor of that Viking giant named Rurik. Doubtless they lay buried under piles of Moslem corpses.

Like waves beating at a half-tide reef, Sultan Yagi Siyan's horsemen raged about the gonfanon of the Silver Leopard to which Gerth had clung.

All over the plain little knots of Normans, although dismounted and assailed from all sides, fought back-to-back, stubbornly defending chosen positions amid rings of dead and dying of both sides. Their thirst had become so intolerable that swollen tongues protruded from between their teeth and their eyes became glazed. Lesser men would long since have surrendered, but they fought on until, in midafternoon, a sudden wavering became noticeable among the Infidel horsemen but they did not turn in flight, and only reined off to their left under the tossing green standards. They flourished curved swords, stood up in their stirrups and shrilled defiance before they wheeled about to face the main Frankish forces, at long last toiling out upon the Field of Dorylaeum. By the thousand a dark mass of Cross Bearers from Lorraine, Flanders, Gascony, Catalonia and France appeared from the north, weapons sparkling and banners flying.

The Red Lion's hordes, although reinforced by fresh supports turned away from the undaunted Normans who could only stand panting and watch them go, their ponderous weapons lowered and their surcoats showing rose-red instead of white.

The Seljuks' hoofs rattled off past mounds of moaning wounded, past tumbled bodies in white robes, past armored hands extended stiffly towards the brazen sky.

To support him erect Edmund de Montgomerie drove his sword point into the earth just beyond the lolling tongue of a dead horse. He panted as never before, sucking hot air into laboring lungs. Well, the Band had stood firm, had never recoiled during hours of successive assault. His remaining serjeants and men-of-arms sank onto the ground and sat with heads bowed, fighting for breath.

The Saxon and Viking companions better acclimated than the rest through long service among the Byzantines, were the first to recover.

They stood up uncertainly and gazed about, then shuffled off to capture Turkish horses which riderless were wandering about. Others, tethered because of reins held in the death grip of fallen masters, were easy to come up with.

The Turks, deeming their original adversaries impotent, had disdained to leave a rear guard in order to fling their whole might upon Godfrey de Bouillon's weary Crusaders, who, by forced marches, had at last come up.

"Get to your feet, Companions!" croaked Edmund. "Find remounts, we must mount and swiftly!"

These famished and exhausted men tapped a reserve of energy and, after six hours of continuous combat, somehow found strength to mount captured horses. How small these shaggy and short-coupled Turkish mounts appeared beneath heavy Frankish saddles! Yet they proved far stronger than they appeared.

All about the Band the Norman array somehow struggled to its feet. Drawing on stamina never since equaled they lurched into a new and very short line.

More and more Franks became mounted and made ready to advance once Pain Peverel shook aloft the red and black banner of Normandy and Richard of the Principate waved Duke Bohemund's standard.

Turks, watching from a nearby ridge witnessed this incredible rebirth of Frankish power and quailed. Mere mortals could never have thus recovered! Surely these must be the children of Shaitan and endowed with more than human strength?

Now the combined forces of Vermandois, Flanders and Duke Godfrey's steady Flemings lowered lances and with hate in their hearts charged the Moslem hordes.

Because Kilidj Arslan's generals never for a moment had imagined that those forces they had been battering all day could come on again they were unprepared when these incredible Normans fell upon their rear thus imprisoning them between two Christian armies. Then were the Sons of the Prophet defeated and slaughtered by the tens of thousands. Valiantly they fought and called upon Allah but died all the same.

Gerth Ordway never had dreamed that the day might come when he might weaken, but he could no longer raise "Penda's Avenger" above his shoulder. Neither had Bras-de-Fer, bleeding from a heavy wound in his side imagined that that arm from whence he took his name could falter, yet before the robed horsemen streaming away in panic-stricken flight he had found the end of his strength.

There followed a ghastly interval towards sundown during which captive Turks were forced to kneel to be beheaded by a sweep of axe or sword or, if some conqueror was too fatigued, to have his throat cut. Far and wide the Red Lion's followers sprayed their blood over the hot, trampled ground.

It was Theophanes, the Byzantine, who pointed out that the Companions must be indeed a tough lot for when there were no more Turks visible among those rounded, rock-topped hills above the Plain of Dorylaeum, no less than twelve survivors responded to Gerth's sounding of Sir Edmund's oliphant. They limped towards the familiar gonfanon, blood-spattered, and on wavering legs, but nevertheless carrying haversacks bulging with the choicest of loot.

Italian-Norman serjeants reported having last seen Sir Arnulfo astride his fallen horse and hard beset. Edmund forced his aching body into obedience, summoned Gerth Ordway, Toraug and with Sir Aethelm searched among the sad debris of battle amid deepening twilight.

The sickish-sweet stench of blood and the reek of scattered entrails were attracting great flocks of carrion birds. Planing down, these loathsome creatures commenced first to peck at bodies scattered along the fringes of the plain for everywhere Normans were prowling the field.

The base-born, practical as ever, first despoiled the dead of arms and mail such as they could never, in ten lifetimes have hoped to own on their liege lord's domain. Then they robbed fallen Seljuk officers.

From every direction sounded plaintive cries from the wounded and dying but no one paid them much heed except a scattering of monks and priests who, swaying with fatigue, patiently shrived one stricken Cross Bearer after another.

A wounded enemy of course was dispatched as quickly as he was discovered, no matter how desperate his shrill pleas or offers of ransom. Unfortunate it was for many an impoverished esquire and landless knight that he could not understand such offers. Many might have become enriched beyond their wildest hopes by those whose heads they hewed off amid hysterical laughter.

The thought that a seigneur must be faithful to his liegemen was, perhaps the only force which kept Edmund on his feet as slowly he traversed the battlefield. Broken lances, shattered shields and swords, bloodstained garments and empty helms littered the earth between dead men and fallen horses all bristling with arrows.

Sir Arnulfo of Brindisi they discovered very much alive and

propped up against the carcass of a splendidly caparisoned Turkish
stallion. Grinning, weakly he waved a steel clad hand.

"By actual count, my lord, this day I have slain twenty-and-two
Infidels and I pray God will spare me to slay as many more but He
won't if somebody doesn't tie up this leg of mine." A Turkish scimitar
had slashed his left calf almost to the bone.

"*Au secours! Pour l'amour de Dieu. Au secours!*" Faintly and from
many directions was arising the same cry the former earl had raised,
ages ago it seemed, in Castel Agropoli. Resolutely he stayed his
body's swaying. Never before and he hoped never again, had Roger
de Montgomerie's son felt so weak, so completely exhausted.

Dark visaged Sir Arnulfo he ordered to be slung on the near side
of a palfrey in a sling cunningly contrived by Theophanes; for coun-
terweight they used Sigurd the Viking serjeant—unconscious from
some heavy blow on the head.

"*Au secours! Au secours!*" The cry sounded in the evening sky faint
as that of some storm tossed kestrel. On leaden legs, Edmund scrambled over a ghastly windrow of fallen Franks and Moslems from
which arms and legs protruded at awkward angles. Blood flowing
out from this fly-clouded pile and in the withered grasses had formed
a dreadful, shiny pool several yards across.

"*Au secours!*" From a lance shaft, a torn gonfanon was fluttering
feebly.

Big blond-headed Sir Aethelm pointed it the while wincing from a
wound he would not allow to stiffen. Presently Edmund recognized
the gonfanon's device as that of a black boar's head upon a red field
so, aided by Gerth and other unwounded retainers, he tugged at
stiffening mailed bodies and hauled aside fallen or dying horses until they uncovered Baron Drogo of Cetraro, semi-conscious and se-
curely pinned by the left leg beneath a gray destrier.

Edmund pulled off his brother-in-law's coif and recognized those
vitally handsome features he had beheld, encrimsoned with hate,
on that blue-green meadow below Sanseverino. Undoubtedly the
Lombard's limb was broken and in addition he had taken a gash in
his right wrist which still wept slow red drops. Being lightheaded,
he kept on moaning, "*Au secours! Au secours!*"

The stricken knight lay with unseeing eyes half open, his breathing
sounded shallow and his strong white teeth glinted rosy in the sunset.
Drogo indeed must have fought a lone and desperate battle, since
no other Frankish corpses or wounded lay within ten spears' lengths
but his great fist still was closed over a sword broken at half its
length.

Some knights of Vermandois's array came riding up and one

Roger of Barneville, a very great captain with a huge crimson beak of a nose and a jutting chin dismounted.

"I am come," he announced in harsh Gascon-French, "to find the body of a most valiant champion, the King of France's brother."

"You are well come," Edmund said heavily, "for Sir Drogo here still breathes. Under the Virgin's mercy he may survive to smite the Idolaters another day."

Vast and infinitely varied was the loot discovered in Kilidj Arslan's camp; jeweled weapons, silvered mail shirts, gold and silver mounted saddles, hundreds of fine horses and camels, wondrously soft carpets, silken robes, boxes of spice and many strange golden instruments the use of which could only be guessed at.

Meanwhile the defeated Sultan's followers were scattering far and wide bearing such fearful tidings of Frankish prowess that fresh Seljuk armies riding towards Dorylaeum deemed it sagacious to turn about and seek their homes upon those broad plains lying beyond the mountains around Nicea.

CHAPTER VII

Victory Bells

During an entire day the many-toned bells of Constantinople's myriad religious buildings had clanged briskly, more joyously than they had in a generation. A strange vitality animated crowds which, attired in their brilliant best, attended victory masses in Sancta Sophia, at St. Saviour in the Khora and in a host of other great churches. Later, exultant mobs waving palm branches surged along the city's broader avenues and finally sought the Hippodrome there to yell their throats hoarse over a specially arranged program of chariot races.

They had reason to rejoice. First had come the glorious news of the recovery of Nicea and of rich lands surrounding the city, lands which, alas, had been desolated by Turkish power, but which could be restored to fruitfulness within a few years.

Then the sun telegraph—the heliograph—had winked and blinked a description of that overwhelming triumph of Christian armies on the Plain of Dorylaeum. These tidings, however, had been so cleverly worded by the Emperor himself, it appeared that the victory had been largely won by the valor of Byzantine arms.

Through streets sweltering under a summer sun, moved long processions of monks and nuns holding crucifixes on high and chanting

"Christe eleison! Kyrie eleison!" Upon orders from Alexis Comnene, Imperial coffers disgorged largess to be fought over by the populace.

In her great, gloomy mansion in the Street of the Winged Bull the Baroness of Cetraro summoned a Latin chaplain and caused him to sing several masses of thanksgiving then to offer endless prayers for the safety of husband and brother. To her dwelling were invited such Frankish knights as chanced to be passing through the city on their way to join the forces fighting to the southward, and a scattering of Western ladies left behind by their lords. It troubled the tall and stately Rosamund not at all that nowadays her waist was beginning to thicken and that her breasts strained against cloth which previously had been comfortably loose.

Through various channels she learned news less gratifying. Byzantine garrisons, withdrawn from the Empire's European themes kept passing through the city on their way eastwards—*not southwards!* Apparently, the remains of Kilidj Arslan's horde was to be harried out of Anatolia and not a single unit she could learn about was destined to reinforce the little more than token force Alexis had dispatched to support the Cross Bearers.

Beyond a doubt, Alexis Comnene must be preoccupied in reconquering provinces lost by his predecessors and secretly cared very little whether the Franks redeemed the Holy Sepulchre or not.

She sat at dinner attended by Chloë, now a graceful young girl of pleasant face and lissome figure. In glowing candlelight the Lady Rosamund again was attempting to master the use of that three-pronged eating implement so favored by the Byzantines, in place of fingers, for the conveyance of food to the mouth. Not for some time had the red-haired Baroness of Cetraro stuffed her mouth as full as possible in the Frankish fashion, then spit small bones onto the floor beside her chair.

Tonight she dined upon a particularly luscious dish of kid meat seethed in milk, thigh of roasted bustard, lotus fruit and walnuts. Her major-domo a liquid-eyed Greek eunuch, silently appeared, bowed from the waist and remained bent until she bade him stand up and speak.

"A Frankish knight waits in the anteroom, my lady. He says he is of your noble brother's Band. He lost a hand at Dorylaeum."

"Stupid dolt! Why have you not shown the gentle man into the *atrium?*" Rosamund jumped up, sent her three-pronged eating instrument clattering onto the marble floor and with long, easy strides sought the antechamber.

Awaiting her among smoky shadows wrought by a flambeau stood a gaunt, wide-shouldered figure who supported his shortened left arm in a stained and filthy sling.

Gravely, the visitor bowed. "I am Sir Gaston of Beaune, lately Companion of your noble brother's Band."

"Be welcome, Sir Knight, thrice welcome," Rosamund smiled. She clapped her hands, and ordered wine to be fetched. Undoubtedly Sir Gaston had come to her house directly from the road to Antioch, since dust still coated his tunic and pointed shoes of soft leather. Dark sweat marks also showed about his neck and under the arms of his tunic.

"Come. You must refresh yourself." Something in this leathery apparition's manner checked her. "What is it? Has mischance befallen Sir Edmund?"

"Nay, my lady, for all he fought like Roland at Roncesvalles."

"Then—then 'tis my lord husband who is dead?"

"Not dead, my lady, but he suffered heavy wounds at Dorylaeum. The week before I started northwards Sir Drogo knew not where he was, but continually he cried out my lady's name."

"Praise God in His high Heaven! What other news have you?"

"The spoils of the Red Lion were past belief," Sir Gaston stated then gulped thirstily from a goblet thrust into his hand. His voice strengthened, reverberated against the dim and vaulted ceiling. "Never have Western eyes beheld such riches! Jewels, gold, thousands of fine horses and bat animals, brocaded garments, chests of sweet and pungent spices and such heaps of fine weapons that the poorest villein among us today carries a gold-mounted dagger. Our bat animals are weighted down with such plunder as would purchase several fine fiefs in France or Italy."

"Then my brother escaped injury?"

"Not only that but Bohemund and his army talk of little save his valiant stand—and that made by Baron Drogo," he added with one eye on the wine jug. "'Tis told that a charge led by Cetraro started the Infidels in their flight from the field, much as our Band and Sir Edmund's valor detained the Turks until the Lorrainers and Provençals could order their array."

In the gloomy, musty dining hall where curiously carved birds and beasts glared down from various capitals they sat late at table. Chloë hovered in the background until she found courage to inquire concerning the armiger called Gerth Ordway. Was he safe? Unhurt?

"He suffered a slight wound which has since healed. We of the Band will be long in forgetting his axe-play," Sir Gaston mumbled while gnawing meat from a mutton bone. "The Saxon youth's fury has been well noted throughout all Duke Bohemund's array."

For Rosamund it was pleasurable to watch the color come streaming into Chloë's piquant, heart-shaped face; her eyes fairly shone.
Once the board had been cleared, Rosamund led the way out into
a small garden in which bulbuls sang drowsily and a cool breeze
off the Bosphorus dispelled the day's heat. Under a graceful umbrella pine they sat, the knight resting his wounded arm upon a
pillow. Gaston of Beaune, warmed by many cups of wine, talked on
and on, relating the consequences of Dorylaeum.

There had been great sport for several days, that of avenging tortured Christians by beheading Infidel prisoners with a single sweep
of an axe or sword. By the hundreds the blaspheming Turks were
stripped to the waist then, with hands bound behind, had been
forced to kneel. A blade would flash then their heads would go rolling, bounding away with eyes still live and lips forming the name of
Allah the Compassionate.

Too long the dead remained unburied, Sir Gaston reported so the
Plain of Dorylaeum had become a vast charnal house giving off an
insufferable stench. The badly wounded had perished—as was only
to be expected—Sir Gaston had attributed his own recovery only to
the prompt application of a red-hot axe blade against the stump of
his arm. The glowing metal had seared severed arteries and so had
halted the loss of blood in time.

Apparently it had not occurred to this bronzed veteran that it was
remarkable that, less than a week later, he should have been strong
enough to mount an easy-gaited mule and ride back to the City of
Constantine.

His present mission he explained to the ladies was to recruit re-
placements for the seventeen Companions who at the moment undoubtedly were enjoying the delights of Paradise—as had been
promised to those who fell on the road to Jerusalem.

He also mentioned a strange pestilence which struck the Christian
host just as it resumed its slow progress over the barren plains towards the mountains of Armenia and the famous towns of Philadel-
phia, Caesarea, and Heraclea. Beyond these, it was reported, lay
the fabulous cities of Aleppo and Antioch, the streets of which were
paved with silver. Jerusalem? Well, nobody seemed to know just how
distant the Holy City really lay. Sir Gaston privately was under the
impression that Jerusalem could not lie more than a week's easy
march beyond Antioch, which, in turn, lay but a scant hundred
miles from the Golden Horn, or so it was bruited about the armies.

Narrowly, Rosamund queried her guest as to the nature of her husband's wound and learned that a Turkish spear had been driven,
with the full force of the lancer and his mount behind it, into Baron

Drogo's side. His hauberk's stout steel rings had not parted but could not prevent a serious bruise. Blood vessels certainly must have severed within his body for, cursing weakly, the Lord of Cetraro had kept on coughing up dark brown clots. Moreover, a terrific blow deflected by his casque had left his mind clouded. For a fact, many Cross Bearers, who had sustained heavy blows on their helms still wandered about the camps like sleep walkers; they had stared straight before them and muttered incoherently.

"Are many ladies left to the host?"

"Only a few, my lady. Such gentle creatures have not been able to endure the sun's blasting heat, the bad water and scarce food."

"How do those poor wights exist from day to day?" Queried the red-haired daughter of Roger de Montgomerie.

"They sleep rolled in blankets upon the bare ground beside their lords—or protectors." He sniggered. "No privacy is theirs, nor have they means of restoring spoiled garments or replacing those thieved by the Ribalds, who are proving such intolerable pests."

"Then what do they do for clothes?" Chloë's voice inquired from the shadows.

"Why, 'tis robes captured from the Infidel, they wear. And greatly do they admire their lightness and fine texture."

The Christian migration—it amounted to that—since there was no set plan of campaign—Sir Gaston estimated to have become diminished by twice ten thousand souls. These, added to losses suffered around Nicea, meant that already a fourth part of the Crusading armies had died, been captured, or had lost heart and had turned back. On the road to Byzantium he had encountered many cowards of all degrees.

Rosamund straightened on her seat. "Forgive me, Sir Gaston, I have been thoughtless and selfish in the extreme. You must be wearied unto death and your arm a burning torture."

No. He felt well, lied Sir Gaston, and manufactured a feeble jest. He claimed to retain the sensation that his hand had not been lopped off and that he could still direct the movements of its fingers.

Rosamund stood up. "From the bottom of my heart I thank you for this courtesy. Alas that I must now retire."

"Retire?"

"There is much to be done before morning."

"Before morning?" The French-Norman stifled a groan while arising.

In the starlight Rosamund of Cetraro had never appeared more regal. "Aye. Tomorrow I shall seek out some band departing on the Crusade and with them I shall ride south."

He gaped at her. "But my lady, have you not heard me describe the sad fate of our Frankish ladies? How miserably they perish?"

"Only one thing do I know. The sire of the babe I bear within me lies stricken and helpless," stated Rosamund evenly. "My duty and pleasure is to be by his side."

The Baroness of Cetraro did not add that she burned to escape the subtle decadence, the never-ending suspicions and intrigues of Constantinople. How fervently she yearned again to breathe clear, unperfumed air and once more to feel a horse moving between her thighs. It would be sheer delight again to overhear rough banter and the clatter of accoutrements being cleaned. Such camp noises, she had come to appreciate, were sweeter to her ears than the music of violas and nakers.

Next morning, Sir Gaston sought his lord's sister and described a party of Catalans. Delayed through shipwreck, they planned on the following day to depart to reinforce the army led by Count Raymond of Toulouse. Their leader was prepared—for a generous consideration of course—to escort the Baroness Cetraro southwards.

CHAPTER VIII

The Chronicler

The Chronicler was among those knights following Duke Robert of Normandy who, though a drunken sluggard, could fight bravely enough when the occasion demanded. The name he gave was that of Charles de Coffre-Fort but also he let it be known that this was only a *nom-de-guerre*. Sir Charles evidently was desperately poor and had departed for the Crusade from some tiny fief in Eastern Normandy. He was endowed, however, with a penetrating observation of character, military understanding and a facility with his pen unequaled save among such religious scribes as Fulcher of Chartres and Bishop Adhemar of Puis.

Sir Edmund first encountered this gaunt, bittern-nosed and witty individual during a tallying up of the enormous spoils won at Dorylaeum. For a Norman, Sir Charles was slight in build and deliberate of speech.

During the march from Nicea Sir Charles again and again had been summoned to attend councils as a scribe in the interests of his slothful lord, derisively known to the Cross Bearers as "Robert Short Breeches" or "Cut-Hose." In much the same capacity Sir Edmund had represented the interests of Bohemund and his tempestuous nephew,

Tancred. The latter, however, appeared to be losing a measure of his headlong ways and truculent manner.

It was the pen of Charles de Coffre-Fort which, with an exactitude unparalleled for that day, described the events following that first hard-won battle. For some unfathomable reason the Chronicler steadfastly refused ever to set a name to his accounts and so they were destined to survive the ages simply as the work of the Unknown. Often Edmund would encounter him employing a saddle for a desk and straining his eyes by the light of a smoky campfire in order to set down some event worthy of note.

His pen made known the terrors and suffering that affected the Crusaders after leaving Dorylaeum in the blinding heat of July. He described plagues of flies, stinging gnats and endless clouds of eye-inflaming grit. He bespoke the barrenness of the countryside, told how fields had been burnt and how all livestock had been herded away from the path of the Frankish host. Quickly the effect of these afflictions made themselves felt upon the disorganized Christian multitude still numbering close on two hundred thousand souls.

The weak as usual died like flies while one noble Frankish lady after another wearily yielded up her soul into the Saviour's hands. The horses and other draft animals also suffered and died.

Unlike Sir Edmund de Montgomerie, Sir Charles de Coffre-Fort rode with the main body. Not yet thirty, he bore privations patiently while the armies toiled through a range of forbidding black mountains and left the passes white with the bones of those who had perished through thirst and starvation.

Struggling now, across a wide and always devastated series of plains the Franks came at last before a walled city called Iconium and rested there when the townspeople opened their gates. But they found little food in it. When the march recommenced more and more pack animals sank exhausted and could not rise. In desperation, the men in chain mail loaded the most essential items upon oxen, sheep and even pigs, but the backs of these creatures swiftly became raw and bloody and they died, too. Sir Charles wrote sadly about proud knights, their mighty destriers dead, reduced to riding oxen. Others less fortunate trudged along like common pikemen stolidly lugging bridles and saddles against that happy day when once more they might mount a horse.

By the time the Crusaders sighted the Taurus Range, looming blue and forbidding across their path, three quarters of those great horses which had come down from Europe had perished. Only the mounts of Sir Edmund's Band seemed excepted in that respect. Reduced now to twenty-two companions, the Band scouted ahead of the vanguard and thus were able to glean such pitiful stores of food and water as might have been overlooked by fleeing inhabitants of this sun-lashed terrain.

Once among the mountains, wrote Sir Charles, the Chronicler, the Christian host's sufferings diminished for here to be found was water and grazing aplenty. Best of all, a final supply of food from the Byzantine Emperor reached them.

Inspired by the fabled abundance of Syria the Cross Bearers trudged into the ancient city of Heraclea. Here the sunburnt multitudes lingered during several weeks, but neither Bohemund nor Tancred was content to rest. These mighty lords preceded the main body through a succession of steep valleys and gorges until at last they passed through the "Cilician Gates" and entered upon plains which stretched all the way to the seacoast and to the rich city of Tarsus.

Unexpectedly this Turkish stronghold fell into their hands after a tidy little battle which cost the grim and merciless Italian-Normans but a mere handful of casualties.

In the early Autumn, wrote Sir Charles de Coffre-Fort, the Christians toiled out of the Taurus Mountains and descended foothills sloping towards a land which verily flowed with milk and honey. Here the Cross Bearers were made welcome by numbers of bandy-legged and dark-faced men wearing armor dating from forgotten times. Slatting upon their breasts they wore crude silver crosses and explained that they were descended from mountain fortresses to which their ancestors had fled, generations ago, before the fury of the Seljuks.

And now talk about the campfires centered more and more upon a fabulously wealthy city called Antioch. It was described by the natives as being impregnable to everything excepting treachery or starvation.

One day the Band rode out from dark cedar forests shrouding the foothills to find themselves in a long, broad valley at the far end of which the whitish walls of a great town sprawled atop a high hill.

This, wrote the Chronicler, was the famed city of Antioch. Here Emperors of ancient days had passed much of their leisure time. Titus, and Diocletian had played important parts in its planning and King Herod had constructed a marble palace of surpassing beauty.

Ever a strategist, the Chronicler set down also that this metropolis represented the key to great caravan routes connecting with rich cities in Araby, Egypt and other strange lands. Through Antioch passed spices, rugs and artifacts from Aleppo, Damascus, Cairo and other Mohammedan capitals on their way to Venice, Genoa and Byzantium. But much of these riches remained in Antioch.

Starved and hollow-eyed Cross Bearers poured down from the mountains to pounce upon Syrian abundance with insensate eagerness. They captured great flocks of goats, sheep and herds of cattle and wasted more than half of what they butchered. Carelessly the warriors in gray-brown hauberks trampled gardens and plundered orchards after massacring their owners.

Once the Christian host had advanced until details of the city's lofty battlements and massive towers plainly became visible, frowns appeared and deepened on the faces of its leaders. Due to losses suffered since Dorylaeum and the siege of Nicea their numbers were insufficient completely to blockade and starve into submission this pleasant-looking city where groves of palms shimmered among red or white roofs.

Certainly within the circumference of its walls must exist many orchards and gardens and certainly the Turkish commander, one Yagi Siyan—a grandson of the all conquering Alp Arslan—long since must have received intelligence of the Frankish advance. He would have been mad not to have collected plentiful stores of food and arms.

Squadron by squadron, levée by levée, and mob by mob, the Frankish lords pitched their tents before Antioch and with them brought pestilence and lawlessness.

Notable changes had come over the Cross Bearers, both in bearing and appearance, noted Sir Charles. He wrote:

"The knights and barons, often dismounted, their warlike finery reduced to tatters and dented mail, no longer look with scorn upon honest serjeants, valorous men-of-arms and other good fighters among the common sort. Many of these last having sufficiently proved their worth, were given the accolade and granted the right to wear gilded spurs. So amazing a thing could never have chanced upon the battlefields of Europe."

On an early November evening the principal leaders gathered in council. Presiding over it was gravely courteous Godfrey de Bouillon, blustering Hugh of Vermandois, Bishop Adhemar, the Pope's Vicar and Raymond of Toulouse with the pointed silver-gray beard. The Provençal in ill-concealed malevolence stared fixedly across the pavilion upon Bohemund, that red-haired paladin who never seemed to tire and was one of the few Crusaders who seemed to recognize his aims and how to achieve them.

With each passing day, Sir Charles noted that this gigantic Norman's stature among the leaders increased, for all that Robert Guiscard's son led one of the least numerous armies.

Present also in this faded and oft-mended pavilion were the two Roberts, of Normandy and of Flanders. These generally inarticulate cousins seldom raised their voices during deliberations, probably because they were too slow of wit to cope with wily men such as Raymond, Bohemund or the Byzantine general, Taticius. This last, brave in scarlet and gilt armor, had remained with the Franks, ostensibly to command a few *turmae* of Turcopoles, for all that the Byzantine main body long since had retraced its steps under orders to subdue outlying castles and cities in the Anatolic Theme and to return them to the rule of Byzantium.

At the council it was determined first to besiege Antioch with all energy, on the understanding that the city should be assigned to him who first raised his banner above its highest donjon. With half an eye, anyone present could sense that Bohemund was resolved that none but his own crimson banner should flutter above this, the fairest city in all Syria.

The siege dragged on all winter amid scenes of indescribable misery. The Crusaders' hunger grew so great that even cannibalism broke out among the wearers of the Cross and desperate men broke open tombs in Turkish cemeteries and devoured their contents to the outraged horror of the besieged.

Seeing this, the Turcoman commander, Yagi Siyan, dispatched couriers throughout Islam rallying the Faithful to avenge such desecration so, with the coming of Spring, great armies of Infidels began riding up from the east and south. Hawk-faced emirs and sultans, glittering with jewels and gold, converged upon Antioch followed by swarms of hardy lancers and tough, mounted bowmen.

Among these rode Rudwan of Aleppo, whose white-caped horsemen covered the countryside like snow and drove in Frankish foraging parties, causing the specter of starvation to grow greater and grimmer in the Christian camps.

So desperate became the plight of the Cross Bearers wrote Sir Charles de Coffre-Fort, that, in the whole camp, could be found less than a thousand horses fit to support a saddle, and no more than seven hundred gentle men still strong enough to swing their long swords as usual.

This veteran handful was entrusted to the command of Duke Bohemund. Among them fluttered the gonfanon of the Silver Leopard now supported by only fifteen leather-tough Companions: the rest had died of disease or had perished in one of those sudden little skirmishes that killed a man just as dead as a great crashing battle like Dorylaeum.

In the opening battle Emir Rudwan's Saracens—the first to be encountered *en masse* by the Crusading host—proved to be far better handled, better mounted and much wiser in the art of war than the brave but barbaric Turks they hitherto had engaged. On the other hand the Saracens had not yet measured their war-like skill against this race of Western men with pale eyes, fair hair and the strength of Polyclitus. The Arabs simply could not credit their eyesight when the ironclad cavaliers rode them down, slashed through their mail as if it were gauze and beat them to earth with ponderous maces.

A terrible melee ensued when little bands of Frankish knights hacked swaths straight through masses of white-robed horsemen. Nothing, it seemed to the bewildered emirs could stand before the Cross Bearers for, ere the day was done seven hundred knights, chanting hymns of victory, had routed Moslem thousands who had ridden into battle under green horsehair standards.

Bohemund's surcoat as well as Drogo of Cetraro's and Raymond Pilet's had been ripped and crimson-stained to the shoulder.

It was during this struggle that Stormcloud took a Turkish lance in the shoulder. It severed an artery, therefore amid the turmoil the destrier stumbled and sank suddenly onto his knees to lie snapping at the enemy until the last of his blood had escaped among dusty grass roots.

It seemed impossible, yet against odds of seven to one, the Franks had routed the best of Emir Rudwan's Saracens. As usual the victors in weary satisfaction knocked off turbans and helmets ere they lopped the shaven heads from these dejected, dark-featured warriors and tossed the grisly trophies onto a bloody pyramid—a feast for jackals and vultures.

Many hundreds of Saracen mounts had been captured, small but swift and powerful beasts from the best strains of Shiraz, Hamin and Mosul.

Despite the repulse of Emir Rudwan's relieving army Antioch continued obdurately to hold out. As the Chronicler wrote, they merely tightened their cinctures over already flattened stomachs and offered still more urgent prayers to Allah. So the siege went forward with the Franks shivering, coughing and dying on the mud within their sodden canvas and leather tents.

A measure of help for the Westerners came from the not-distant port of St. Simeon where a small fleet of English seafarers had put in an appearance. Miraculously, among their passengers were certain knights reported to be skilled in the arts of siegecraft.

By the hundreds the Turks within the city began to perish of hunger and as many others died in the stubborn defense of their walls. They massacred all Christian prisoners when, once more, the ravening multitude without was forced to feed on Turkish corpses.

Early in June Antioch fell, but only through the consummate treachery of one Firuz, reputed to be an Armenian and a Christian by birth. He had entered into secret negotiations with Duke Bohemund to admit him and a picked band of followers to the city.

Bohemund, crafty as ever, made no mention of this to any other prince. Instead, as leader in fact, of the Crusading host, he summoned a council of generals at which he suggested blandly that the city should be attacked in a final, grand assault and belong to him who first raised his banner above its citadel.

On a velvety June night when the Syrian stars glowed like white-hot spikes hammered into the purple-black firmament the attempt was made. This was only after a feint was made by the Westerners towards the southwest, as if considerable Frankish forces were departing on a foraging expedition.

At sundown the Duke of Otranto retraced his steps and, leading a force of picked men, Sir Edmund and the Chronicler among them, approached the city opposite two great towers known as the Twin Sisters. Sure enough, they came upon two ladders of twisted ropes, whereupon the sinewy Italian-Norman immediately swarmed up it, with his followers hard on his heels.

They caught their breath whenever swords or armor scraped the masonry until Bohemund himself gained the summit and bellowed, *"Dieu lo vult!"* Swiftly long Norman swords cleared that section of the walls, then Bohemund's men dashed below and opened a postern gate through which swirled a tide of inspired knights under Tancred.

By sunrise on June third, 1098, only Antioch's great citadel remained in Turkish hands and the Pearl of Syria had fallen into Bohemund's eager clutches which never in this life would he relax although raged at by fellow princes and roundly denounced by Holy Church.

Somehow, a surprising number of Syrian, Greek and Armenian females survived an appalling massacre which ensued when the Turks threw down their arms, but there were no males whatever. Therefore the Westerners slaughtered without distinction Moslems of every age and condition. They burnt their proud and fierce prisoners, maimed them, even slashed open their bellies and then led them about by their entrails until they collapsed gasping out praises of Allah and Mohammed, his one and only prophet.

The Chronicler set down, in his fair and clerkly hand, that the victors expected then to enjoy a period of rest and recuperation, but such was not to be. Hardly had the besiegers penetrated those walls which so long had defied their attack than three huge Moslem armies converged upon Antioch and so the besiegers swiftly became the besieged and soon they were quite as hungry and miserable within the city as they had been outside of it.

Around Antioch the tents of Moslem hordes glistened like snow upon the ravaged countryside. Above certain splendid silken pavilions presently were displayed the standards of Kerbogha, Prince of Mosul; Dokak, Sultan of Damascus; and Rudwan, that same Emir of Aleppo who had been beaten off by Bohemund's seven hundred knights so much earlier in the siege.

The bulk of the besieging forces had ridden up from the south and west therefore their cavalry masses carried lances in place of bows. So great were the Unbelievers in number that they could accomplish a complete investment of Antioch's battlements.

Soon a new and deadly pestilence penetrated walls which Turks and Saracens could not, so, in sheer desperation, the Christian leaders once more appealed to Alexis Comnene, reported to be maneuvering on the further side of the Taurus Range, and watching, from that safe distance, all which occurred beyond the southernmost frontier he felt capable of defending.

The Emperor's spies, of course, dwelt at length upon the vast number of Moslems concentrated about Antioch and reported the Franks as doomed. No force possibly could bring them food nor might reinforcements reach Antioch from the coast—galleys out of Egypt were seeing to that.

To Alexis, that hardheaded and experienced campaigner, an attempt to rescue his allies suggested chivalrous folly of the sort he always had deprecated. He therefore dispatched an encouraging but quite noncommittal reply to Bohemund's appeal and with his army retreated leisurely in a northerly direction, rebuilding and garrisoning castles and watchtowers which had belonged to his predecessors.

The second siege of Antioch progressed amid conditions so indescribably dreadful that even the eloquent Sir Charles de Coffre-Fort could find no adequate terms to fit them.

Pestilence ravaged the besieged without mercy and among others carried off little Richard, the heir of Cetraro, during the first week of his brief but arduous life. Sir Drogo, raging like a madman over the loss of his son, led his company in a sortie from the city and left several hundred Infidels weltering in their blood, but it did not greatly assuage his grief. Somberly the Lady Rosamund welcomed him back into a palace pre-empted by the Lombard, but was encouraged to perceive that some of the despair had departed from her lord's vitreous dark eyes.

"Take courage, my lord. With God's blessing," she promised, "and so long as you remain constant to me, I shall bear you another son who will live to rule over the great domain your sword will conquer in this fair land. Verily, it is a country richer by far than the Campania of Italy."

Ever she was encouraged by her twin who, leaner and browner than ever, snatched a few hours of sleep under their roof whenever duty permitted. There was little cheer, however, in Drogo's palace. Every morning and night the principal lords and princes attended Mass in one of these edifices which, originally churches, had been transformed into mosques and now had been rededicated to Christian worship. Well might the Christian princes pray, for to join the besiegers came reinforcements from Mosul, Turk Tughtakin, a merciless Atabeg of the Kari Seljuks. Also the Arab, Sokman ibn-Ortuk who presently ruled in Jerusalem.

Just when it seemed that all was lost and that starvation would accomplish what the Moslem scimitars could not, a simple-minded peasant named Peter Bartholomew found the head of what he claimed to be the very lance which had pierced the Saviour's side as He suffered on the Cross.

The Chronicler, together with Bohemund and a few others, privately was convinced that this was no Roman, but an Arab lance which Bartholomew produced from a pit into which he himself had descended.

For every doubter however there were a thousand believers and a strange impulse of Faith lent strength to the sickened and decimated Christians. So, on the morning of June twenty-eighth, every man strong enough to hold a weapon and many who could not, marched out through the Bridge Gate after Adhemar, Bishop of Puis, to attack an enemy whose countless campfires nightly shrouded the whole plain in a bluish haze.

So very few horses were left that many a valiant knight was forced to trudge into battle beside jackmen armed with pikes, Ribalds carrying cudgels and all manner of common folk.

So inspired had these desperate men become through possession of the Lance that when the battle became joined they simply would not fall back before incessant waves of howling Moslems.

All through a scorching June day the Franks swung their weapons much as they had at Dorylaeum, and whenever they felt faint they raised eyes to a standard contrived of a Cross upon which had been lashed the spearhead found by Bartholomew the Simple.

Peter the Hermit, too, was present to urge on the faltering while monks and priests caught up weapons from the fallen and fought like Norse berserkers when the riders of Aleppo and Damascus in black-and-white *khalats* charged like demons through the silver-green olive groves. These men of the West stood fast, despite everything, and died where they stood, gasping out their confessions to priests who, often wounded themselves, crawled about to offer absolution and extreme unction.

In the late afternoon sounded deep Frankish shouts and a resounding clatter of swords upon shield rims as the beset Christians rallied for the last time to support a charge of Duke Godfrey de Bouillon and Bohemund's mailed horsemen. These constituted the Crusaders' final reserve.

"God wills it!" croaked the Franks through throats grown dry as parchment.

And God willed that the Cross should prevail. Sir Charles wrote about it that same night for all that his fingers yet were numb through the shivering shock of his sword impacting upon the followers of Mohammed.

Thus, incredibly, the Battle of the Lance was won and the confederated Moslems scattered in headlong, panic-stricken fright. Not in nearly a hundred years would Infidel princes again so unite to battle with the Cross Bearers.

CHAPTER IX

Before the Walls of Arkah

So exhausted and depleted had the Crusading forces become that they could proceed no further until reinforced and led by someone who really could lead, now that Bohemund had won his city and was not disposed to adventure further. Moreover the bitter enmity which had flared between Bohemund and Raymond had to be patched up or the Crusade was doomed.

Following the capture of Antioch, Normans fought with Provençals, while Lorrainers, French and Flemings, too weary to bicker, maintained a precarious neutrality.

During the Autumn of 1098 several leaders died, among them valiant Adhemar, the Pope's Vicar, and Count Baldwin of Hainault. Hugh the Mighty of Vermandois seemed very glad to depart on an embassy to solicit aid long since promised by the Emperor and other puissant barons, found occasion to depart on private campaigns in order to garner in this town or that castle for their tenure.

Now hardly fifty thousand Christians remained of the near-two hundred thousand who had advanced so confidently upon Nicea and even these had become divided into two camps. There were those who wished to linger in Antioch and recruit their strength with Bohemund, and other dedicated souls who listened to the pleas of Raymond. The Count of Toulouse together with the rabble, Tancred, Godfrey de Bouillon and a great majority of the poorer knights felt constrained to carry out their pledges and so continue the long march upon Jerusalem.

Many were the allegiances which became switched during these days for now a new social order prevailed. Memories of châteaux along the misty coasts of Britain, Normandy and Brabant, in the sun-warmed valleys of Provence and in the dense forests of Lorraine, were fading fast. It no longer mattered whose sire had accomplished what, or who had held how many fiefs. An excellent fighter was listened to and respected while an inept or sluggish landowner was not, no matter how proud his lineage.

Late in November the Jerusalemites—as those who adhered to their oath to free the Sepulchre were called—quitted Antioch, fanned out over the Western third of Syria and, paralleling the sea, recommenced an arduous progress towards their goal.

Great changes militarily had taken place within the Crusading forces—both as to tactics and armament. Now their squadrons moved less ponderously and more speedily through being less encumbered by baggage, non-combatants and faint hearts such as the eloquent Stephen of Blois who had gone home. Hardly an European bred destrier had survived so Cross Bearers bestrode the best and largest of captured Arab chargers. No longer did the Franks persist in wearing chain armor on the march; such was much too hot to be endured and, for another thing, the lighter-boned steeds they bestrode could never have supported the weight. Shields, hauberks and helms now were slung on led animals.

In departing Antioch the Band of the Silver Leopard wore flowing white robes bearing a red cross at the shoulder and pointed helms so, saving their great physical proportions, might readily have been mistaken for Saracens departing on a *razzia*. They had learned also to wear *khoufies,* or light cotton gowns over their mail and so reduce considerably the sun's searing heat.

Now Sir Aethelm, Bras-de-Fer, Arnulfo of Brindisi and the rest carried goatskins of water sloshing from their cantles and from a distance were indistinguishable from Toraug. It was perhaps significant that of the original band all three Byzantine serjeants had survived to ride under Sir Edmund de Montgomerie's tattered blue and silver gonfanon. Steadfastly the former Earl of Arundel had refused to replace his standard because of its associations with Dorylaeum and the Battle of the Lance.

Two Italian-Norman serjeants remained and Rurik the Norseman; now "Sir" Rurik, thanks to prodigies of valor during the siege of Antioch. Of the men-of-arms only two Saxon and three Norsemen still dangled long legs from captured steeds and cracked ribald jokes on the march.

New faces had appeared among the veteran Companions, for the most part they were tough Armenians and Syrians, hawk-featured fellow Christians and mountaineers. They were all big men since Brasde-Fer would enroll no candidate slighter than the heaviest Saracen. As Edmund astutely had foreseen, their knowledge of this terrain already was proving invaluable.

Far off to the right of that road which the Jerusalemites traveled lay the Mediterranean, incredibly blue and cool appearing in this early Spring season. For a space this shore road wound through a verdant countryside where humble straw-thatched huts stood among fig and pomegranate groves. This land was bright with poppies, anemones and all manner of blooms which magically sprang out of barren earth whenever even a little rain fell.

Almost every rise or hill was crowned by the tumbled ruins of a fort or watchtower built long ages ago by some Phoenician, Greek, Macedonian, Egyptian, Persian or Roman commander.

Below Margat the coast of Syria became almost treeless, denuded of vegetation and proved to be inhabited only by wary nomads who wore rough gray *abbas* or brown cloaks of camel's wool.

The Band's special mission, assigned by Count Tancred, was to discover a Moslem port, weakly held, yet capable of receiving and discharging casual galleys fetching supplies—generally of the wrong sort —from Genoa and Pisa; not from Venice. The Venetians had remained the firm allies of Alexis Comnene.

Several such ports existed, Syrian companions of the Band reported; notably Botroun, Giblit, and, much further down the coast, the ancient haven of Jaffa, reputedly abandoned in favor of better situated ports like Gaza and Acre. Such strong ports as Tripoli, Tyre, and Sidon were not to be won without a siege.

Considerable urgency attended the finding of such a haven for, during the siege of Antioch, ships had come out all the way from "Angle-Land" as Continental Franks called England and with them

had sailed reformed Danish pirates and sea rovers, together with a
number of Frisian merchantmen, all of whom had heard The Word
and were sailing East seeking salvation for their souls.

The Jerusalemites, therefore, preserved in being a small fleet
which sorely needed a base of operations.

One mid-March afternoon after the Band had reconnoitered the
ruins of a large once-walled town, Bras-de-Fer turned in his saddle
and raised a brow in inquiry.

"We have ridden far enough," Edmund announced, wiping a sunburned brow. He then gave orders to head back to the Frankish army
busily besieging a town called Arkah, an outpost of the famous port
of Tripoli. The latter town was entirely surrounded by water and
could be reached only by a causeway the defenses of which had
defied all assaults by the Cross Bearers. The countryside was rich
and so, for several weeks now, the thirty thousand-odd Jerusalemite Franks had lived high.

Baron Drogo of Cetraro for the time being had installed his stately
wife in a minor stronghold situated beside a slow-flowing stream and
a garden rendered surpassingly beautiful through Arab imagination
and industry. Contemptuously, however, Drogo refused to consider
this pleasant spot as a permanent fief in the Holy Land.

It was here that for a space appeared hearty young Sir Robert of
Sanseverino, to recuperate from a wound sustained in the Battle of
the Lance. He had trouble quickly to avert his gaze from the tall and
once more supple figure of her he had fallen in love with so long ago
in Italy. But he did so. Rosamund was Drogo's wife.

Several times, Sir Robert referred to the departure of a second
levée from Sanseverino. Sir Toustain, however, had sent word that a
Pisan shipmaster had warranted to set this new levée ashore in Palestine no later than the month of May. The reason it had not long
since arrived was only that certain Sicilian mariners who had agreed
to transport these reinforcements had accepted a richer offer to enter the service of Byzantium.

Word, too, had been received from the Lady Alixe. She reiterated
that her every prayer included Edmund de Montgomerie whom she
hoped to join, if God so permitted, before Jerusalem was taken.

Many a fine early Spring evening, when it remained so cool that
fires had to be kindled indoors, Edmund, Robert, Drogo and Rosamund would speak of Alixe and of that fierce old campaigner, Count
Turgis.

"And have you never learned who dispatched that armiger in the
night to seek me?" Edmund inquired on one occasion.

Sir Robert hesitated, glanced across the chamber at Drogo methodically sharpening his dagger before the fireplace but the Lombard at that moment raised his eyes and gazed intently, searchingly, at Alixe's brother. "No. The craven who contrived that foul deed has never been discovered."

From an antechamber sounded the sudden laughter of Chloë and deep-throated merriment from Gerth Ordway. The young Saxon loved lazily to tease that lively, big-eyed girl and remained pathetically blind to the adoration in her look. Frankly, the Saxon marveled that, by cleverness or by good luck, Chloë thus far had escaped death, disfiguration or ravishment.

As usual the young Saxon's attention remained fixed upon the Baroness of Cetraro although Rosamund, like most of the few remaining gentle women, had obtained dispensation from practical prelates to don male clothing when in the field. Only when a halt such as this, afforded opportunity did the ladies undo certain bundles, and assume shimmering, multicolored robes originally fashioned for some Saracen female. European garments long since had worn out or fallen apart and there were here no seamstresses to fashion new ones.

The innate nobility of Rosamund's aspect had become accentuated and her beauty refined by faint lines about mouth and eyes which hinted at, rather than betrayed, her sufferings and grief over the loss of her infant. As a rule the Lady Rosamund remained preoccupied in superintending the preparation of whatever might be brought in as food for her household, or in cheering the sick and the wounded and accompanying them in prayer.

The burly Franks quartered at Drogo's holding spoke often and favorably of that *turma* of Turcopoles which, commanded by Count Leo Bardas, was all that remained of the superb Byzantine array that had effected the capture of Nicea. This *turma* had proven itself of inestimable value in screening the Jerusalemites' left flank and in detecting ambushes. Also it had brought in food and remounts and had encouraged fearful native Christians lurking among the hills to assist the campaign.

With these mercenaries it was learned, still rode the Countess Sybilla, a strange, silent figure who, on the march, occupied a camelborne howdah lined with silken bolsters.

Rosamund, incredulous at first, heard that Sybilla was as an angel of mercy among her uncle's heathen troopers. Also to her ears came word that the Countess of Corfu was seldom disposed to absent herself from revels held by Count Leo's officers whenever a stronghold was taken and the loot was piled high.

Never by any chance, however, did the lovely raven-haired

Countess visit a Frankish camp. If the big Westerners beheld her at
all she would be riding a fleet racing camel on the outskirts of their
encampments and escorted by twice-ten devoted Turcopoles.

Everywhere it was said that when Sybilla chose to sing beside the
campfires she put to shame the liquid melodies of bulbuls, the night-
ingales of Western Asia. Time and again simple Frankish pickets reported hearing her clear voice in the distance and, mistaking it for
the song of some angel, devoutly had crossed themselves and in
shaken accents had reported a miracle to their fellows.

When the first of such reports reached Edmund de Montgomerie's ears he recalled, with a sense of surprise, a prophecy called down
from a column in Byzantium. How curious that, until now, he never
had known that a bulbul and a nightingale were one and the same
bird.

All through the campaign and during Drogo's slow convalescence
a rough but genuine camaraderie had sprung up between Edmund
and the Baron of Cetraro, but as for Sybilla, that exquisite creature
might have existed a thousand leagues distant for all that he was
affected by her nearness.

Often, as the former Earl of Arundel lay in his blanket listening to
the eerie, bubbling complaint of hobbled camels and to long-drawn
calls of sentinels he wondered why she continued to ride with Count
Leo. Why had Sybilla not returned to Syria and the arms of Bohemund the Mighty? The Duke of Otranto, now titling himself Prince of
Antioch rapidly was becoming a most puissant Christian lord. Having
attained his stated objective he firmly refused to adventure further,
for all that Tancred, Raymond of Toulouse, Godfrey de Bouillon and
the rest abused him for a perjured knight who had fallen by the
wayside on the road to Jerusalem.

Unruffled, that red-haired giant had declared that he better
served the Cause by guarding their rear and keeping open communications with the Emperor, now safely returned to his marble palace
above the sky-blue Sea of Marmora.

Often Edmund pondered concerning the happiness of his sister
and about her feeling towards Drogo and Robert of Sanseverino.
Could it be purely in his imagination that while Rosamund appeared dutiful she was growing increasingly aloof towards her fiery
husband? Was she aware of this? Was she speculating over Sir Robert's lingering glances in her direction? Certainly young de Bernay
was being both inept and artless in his efforts to conceal that devotion first expressed in his father's castle.

Inevitably on such nights Edmund's last conscious thoughts revolved upon Alixe. Was she well? Was her love as constant as his?

Where might she be? Had she received any one of the several missives he had dispatched?

As for Drogo, that turbulent individual was acting astoundingly unaware or else indifferent concerning his wife and the handsome young knight who, whenever possible, was attendant upon her.

No matter what his marital attitude there could be no doubt that the Lombard not only had proved himself a magnificent fighter but also an excellent and a farsighted general; in fact, his levée invariably was to be found in the thickest of a battle—also foremost about the business of plundering a Saracen camp or town.

The Band of the Silver Leopard fared equally well, but fought more often, riding as generally it did leagues ahead of the army. Day after day Sir Edmund employed its special skills in scouting out the presence of hostile forces, in predicting the state of supplies to be found in a given region and in arousing such scattered remnants of Christian communities as still survived in the countryside.

To everyone's surprise the siege of Arkah dragged on and on through the early Spring. On one occasion the Turks besieged in Tripoli sallied forth, only to be beaten back in a savage little battle which proved that the charge of Frankish chivalry remained more than a match for fanatical but lightly-armed swarms of Moslem forces.

Now spiritual leaders among the Crusaders began to complain. Why were the barons tarrying thus on the road to Jerusalem?

Arnulf, Chaplain to the lethargic Duke of Normandy, and Daimbert, Archbishop of Pisa, he who had succeeded the well-beloved Adhemar as the Pope's personal representative, railed with such fury that Sir Charles de Coffre-Fort's fingers quivered when he set down their bitter diatribes in council.

The poorer knights, especially those forced endlessly to forage for themselves and their followers were among those who favored the dedicated leadership of Raymond and Tancred; Bohemund's yellow-haired young nephew ranted like a wounded lion against the suggestion that Arkah must at all costs be captured. Angrily he pointed out that every day the already scant ranks of Christian fighting men were being thinned and argued that the march on Jerusalem must be undertaken at once—or never.

In May the grain fields would begin to bear and all manner of vegetables could be garnered along the route. Most important of all, even minor water courses could be expected to be full, while by the end of June, they would dry up and the Christian host might expect again to suffer as it had outside of Antioch.

So it came about that early in May, 1099, the Cross Bearers struck their tents and loaded their scant remaining baggage upon transport camels and asses fetched in from pasture. They took heart to see how sleek and frisky their remounts had grown through long repose.

CHAPTER X

Saturnalia

In a pavilion carpeted with the finest of Persian rugs and walled with hangings looted during the sack of Antioch, Tancred sat at table. Many famous knights were gathered above him, men such as the great soldier of fortune, Raymond Pilet, Richard of the Principate and that celebrated military engineer, Sir Gaston of Béarn. Their harsh and scar-seamed features had been darkened to a deep red-brown by a sun every day growing more pitilessly torrid. Save for their gigantic proportions it would have been difficult to distinguish these Frankish leaders from Saracens so thoroughly had they adopted native dress.

Followed by Sir William Bras-de-Fer and Ahab, a Syrian Companion of the Band who claimed to be intimately familiar with the terrain south of Tripoli, the former Earl of Arundel strode up to the council table. He bowed briefly once to Count Tancred then to Count Raymond of Toulouse who sat with grizzled head tinted gold by the light of several beautiful Turkish lamps slung from tent poles.

The Bishop of Puis, a big-well-set-up prelate with piercing jet eyes, a dense black beard and heavy brows that met above the bridge of his nose, spoke first and swiftly made it clear that this Council had selected the Band of the Silver Leopard for a most hazardous duty. It was to detach itself from the Jerusalemite main body and reconnoiter the seacoast southward—all the way to Ascalon below Jerusalem, if necessary.

Not only was the red-headed Anglo-Norman to resume his search for an easily won port, but also he was to conduct a survey of the best routes practicable for the advancing Crusaders, with special attention to the location of water points. Further he must gauge the disposition and number of native Christians—if, indeed, any survived so far to the southward.

When the Bishop of Puis at length fell silent Tancred raised his leonine head and stared intently upon his tall henchman.

"We are informed reliably, I believe," said he in his harsh and guttural voice, "that your route swarms with enemies and that many long stretches of the seacoast are deserts lacking water, food and fodder."

"I believe I can safely guide my lord," promised Ahab the Syrian, vitreous black eyes lighting. "From my ancestors I have learned where are supposed to be hidden certain cisterns, ones forgotten for generations. Also I speak every dialect of the Holy Land."

"You *have* a glib tongue, it would seem," commented Richard of the Principate, fingering a sun-bleached brown beard. "So glib I find it difficult to trust you."

The Syrian bowed humbly, hands held on a level with his ears. "I regret that, my lord Baron, but I cannot restrain my eagerness when I think that my feet soon will press the soil of that same land in which our Saviour lived and died for our redemption."

"Every few days you will send back reports to us through Greek and Syrian members of your Band," Raymond directed somberly. "And they must win through else many of us are like to die of thirst or hunger."

Although Godfrey de Bouillon remained titular head of the reduced Armies of the Cross, it was Raymond the fiery old Provençal and Tancred who not only made most of the decisions but implemented them.

"With God's help," Edmund promised earnestly and touched the cross on his shoulder, "I shall accomplish all that you ask or yield up my soul into God's hand."

In quitting the council tent he recognized Sir Robert of Sanseverino's stalwart figure lingering outside a tent from which issued the querulous moans from the fevered, sick and wounded.

"The Lady Rosamund ministers within," explained Alixe's brother, "and will here remain until morning. A new malady has seized certain Flemish knights who drank from a polluted well. Shall we repair to Drogo's camp?"

After a brief ride among the campfires where Franks labored to repair broken harness, oil mail and to sharpen weapons, the two knights approached the mansion selected by Drogo of Cetraro as a temporary abode.

Abruptly Sir Robert reined in and bent forward among the shadows for, distinctly to be heard, were sounds of loud laughter, of shrill singing and that weird and wailing but seductive music played in this part of the world.

Apparently a detachment of the Lombard's levée must just have returned from a raid upon some nearby Saracen town for several dozen bound male prisoners squatted dejectedly about the courtyard amid piles of plunder and tethered camels. From the feasting hall escaped such floods of light and food-smelling smoke that Edmund and Robert peered in cautiously.

Seated on piles of gaily-colored pillows and swilling wine lolled the victors. Half dressed and more than half drunk they were watching the sinuous gyrations of a band of terrified and stark naked Arab girls. Of all ages between twelve and twenty they were being forced to dance under the threat of riding whips and belts ready to deal laggards a stinging blow.

Other maidens wept and pled, slim brown bodies gilded by the torchlight as they struggled upon a series of divans in the arms of Drogo and his principal knights. The dark-haired Lombard was preparing actually to force the act of love upon a young girl when he noticed those two figures in white surcoats rooted on the great hall's entrance.

Head drunkenly a-sway, Drogo stared owlishly at Sir Robert and his brother-in-law, then beckoned them on before sinking back on the divan and, roaring with laughter, resuming his defloration of the shrieking Arab girl.

"The smoke is thick. I—I have seen nothing," Edmund muttered, and, turning on his heel, he stalked back into the courtyard. Remounting, he sought his own camp but Robert of Sanseverino continued to gaze in disgusted astonishment upon a saturnalia which did not conclude until the stars paled and jackmen commenced to drive in horse herds and baggage camels.

Shortly before dawn the Band's principal Syrian Companion used a writing brush to paint Count Leo Bardas' name in curious, flowing characters upon a short strip of vellum. This he tucked into his cincture and wandered away from the Band's watch fires until he came upon a fellow Syrian muffled in a black and brown *abba*.

"You will find the *Strategos* encamped near the village of Daraba," he informed the shadowy figure. "Go with Allah but die sooner than permit this scroll to fall into the hands of any Frank."

CHAPTER XI

The Dry March

Throughout the first week in May the Band of the Silver Leopard reconnoitered the rocky Syrian coast between Giblit and Beirut with skill. During the past year of campaigning in this strange land Edmund de Montgomerie had modified very considerably previous military tenets and had done so with a readiness unusual among the unimaginative Frankish barons. No longer did he stupidly insist on defying the shattering impact of the sun's midday rays but, whenever possible led his men into whatever shade presented itself, be it a wood or a gully deep enough to cast a shadow or some ruin.

Always Ahab rode at Edmund's elbow. His advice generally proved to be sound but was a trifle too readily proffered to be accepted without support from the Byzantine Serjeant, Theophanes, or Jonathan, a generally silent and dark-faced Lebanese recruit.

By custom the Band broke its fast and saddled up during the second hour before dawn or even earlier when moonlight revealed the countryside in all its empty, pallid splendor. If there was no moon, myriad stars created a radiance only slightly less effulgent.

Rapidly long leagues passed under the hoofs of horses that grew visibly thinner and less sleek and which had to be cold-shod with distressing frequency because of the rocky ground they traveled. Soon the Band left behind Giblit—a pretty little port but with no docking facilities for more than a few coasters or fishing vessels.

Then it became necessary to follow a detour deep inland in order to avoid contact with inhabitants of the important town of Beirut. Again and again the Band cut across the fresh tracks of heavy caravans.

One evening Sir Edmund planted his sword Cross-like in the ground and led his liegemen in prayer of thanksgiving for, according to the Syrians, the Band had passed over an unmarked frontier and were treading the Holy Land at last!

As they rolled up in their mantles after gnawing cold shanks of greasy mutton—Toraug and Ahab had counseled against lighting even a single campfire—the Band heard not very far away the gurgling complaints and squeals of camels stabled in a caravanserai situated beyond a row of nearby hills. They heard also the yapping of dogs and many voices.

Fingers laced behind head, Gerth Ordway stared fixedly up into the sky and for once did not see there the beauty of Chloë's almond-shaped eyes. How inspiring it was to reflect that these very stars, a millennium and a century ago, had shone down upon this same land to light the Saviour's path on His journeyings.

Vanished were the Romans who then had ruled here, also gone, save for a scattered few, were the Jews who had persecuted and betrayed Him. All that remained as before was the glory of His name and the wonderful beauty of the desert at night.

Twice the Band, reduced to twenty-five through detachment of messengers carrying logistical information back to the Jerusalemite columns, massacred parties of robbers who had fallen into the cardinal error of mistaking this handful of hard-bitten horsemen for merchants somehow strayed from the caravan routes.

Once they had circled around Sidon and Tyre the country became more barren, deserted and waterless. They had beheld both cities but only from a distance. Prisoners, interrogated and then slain lest they betray the scouting force's presence, however, had disclosed that these ports, ancient as time itself, were being strongly held by Turkish garrisons; also that occasional European vessels such as the Companions had descried from time-to-time plowing along the coast, like lost sheep seeking their fold, could find no haven yonder.

At dawn late in May the Band pulled on loose white robes both to conceal the flash of iron mail and to ward off the sun's blasting heat. They were leaving behind the last wretched mud-and-thatch village where water mills creaked and groaned as blindfolded camels circled endlessly to raise the life-giving fluid from the depths.

At Toraug's behest the Cross Bearers drank deep, filled to bursting their goatskin water bags and allowed their mounts to drink until they would only snuffle at the water and gaze mildly at the bright blue sea sparkling in the far distance.

Hereabouts this sun-blasted stretch of coast proved devoid of trees or grass. The only vegetation were thickets of acacia thorn and great clumps of spiny, gray-green cactus.

"We should be riding camels," complained Ahab when, on the third day of the Dry March, the horses went hungry. "Those cursed creatures out of Sheol will eat cactus as readily as a child devours sweetmeats."

Searing, blinding heat beat up from beneath the horses' hoofs and was reflected off reddish-black rocks too hot to be touched. Fine dust enveloped the little cavalcade like a suffocating miasma, set eyes to smarting and throats to aching. When more and more sand dunes began to interspace ridges of rock and sun-baked clay certain horses commenced to fail so Edmund ordered riders of these weaker beasts to dismount and lead.

Long since the Band had abandoned their coifs and, on the third day of the Dry March they left off their hauberks since there seemed to be no evidence of life in the vicinity. Toraug and Theophanes counseled abandonment of the Band's heavy Norman shields, a course most unwillingly approved by Edmund and Bras-de-Fer, but the horses now shuffled along during the early and late hours with heads hung low, lackluster eyes half closed and showing long-dried sweat as silvery ripple marks on their coats. No one ever spoke unless it became unavoidable, their mouths were too dry and throats too swollen. They all knew that the last of their water, for all it had been doled out in miserly quantities, would be sipped that night.

Disaster befell the Band on the fourth day. Jonathan, the Lebanese and Ahab the Syrian who had never yet been proven wrong concerning the existence of cisterns and water holes earlier along the route, led their cruelly desiccated companions and beasts up to a little ruin and, on lowering a pot into a hidden well heard no resultant splash—only a dull *clank!* Gerth groaned and Sir Rurik soberly squeezed the last drop from his water bag for his horse's benefit.

Jonathan calculated that two more days would be required to reach a tiny oasis above Acre. During the night three men-of-arms died in delirium and only a dozen horses were able to struggle to their feet when the order to move on was given. No one mounted. What little strength remained to these gaunt beasts must be conserved. Lances, maces and every piece of unessential equipment were left at the campsite.

How paradoxical, mused Sir Edmund as, shivering, he once more set foot to a rough track paralleling the coast, that the Holy Land at night should prove so frigid whilst its days were such a torment of heat.

Of the twenty men who remained to follow his bleached and tattered gonfanon—he had detached two Lebanese the day before that they might return and warn that under no conditions must the Crusaders follow the shore route—three seemed in very bad case. Two Italian-Normans had become definitely lightheaded and Michael, a Byzantine serjeant, was talking very strangely.

Today it had been more than difficult to rouse the Band. Only Bras-de-Fer, Gerth—he must soon be made a knight—Toraug and Ahab arose with anything like readiness. The sick men fingered their rosaries and begged to be left behind. It would have been just as well had Edmund granted their plea since, during the forenoon two fell without a sound, slain by the pitiless sun, and the other suddenly uttered a weird war cry and lurched up a *wadi* never to be seen again save by vultures scaling ever lower and lower out of the burning skies.

Midday came with no hint of shade in sight and another horse gave out, its legs buckling wearily under it.

Toraug croaked through blistered lips, "We must keep going or we die."

Now the Band struggled along through the infernal heat reeling like drunken men and strung out over several hundred yards. They concentrated on the simple business of endlessly advancing one foot ahead of its mate. If only the sea were not there in the distance to mock their thirst!

At the head of the pitiable little column limped Sir Edmund tugging at the reins of his horse. He had jammed the gonfanon of the Silver Leopard into the cantle strap so it fluttered in the scorching wind at a crazy angle.

By now the Anglo-Norman's lips were split, his forehead raw with sunburn and his tongue so swollen that it filled his entire mouth. His eyes had retreated deep into their sockets.

On and on through this murderous heat. Water. Where was water? Surely, it was futile to continue? Was he never to see Jerusalem, never again to press the firm softness of Alixe? Oh, Alixe. Alixe. Each time he forced a foot ahead he thought her name, envisioned her just ahead offering an ewer of sparkling spring water.

Immediately behind marched Gerth, he guessed, then Bras-de-Fer, Ahab, Toraug and Sir Rurik. Following these, the last time he had looked through distorting heat waves he had seen Sir Aethelm and the Byzantine Theophanes—the other figures wavered along at wide intervals a few more leading horses but mostly they struggled on alone disarmed save for sword or axe—all else had been cast aside.

All that terrible day the Band tramped on, never looking back when one or another of the white-clad figures stumbled and proved too weak to rise. The heat hammered like invisible fists, scorched the skin, caused each breath to burn as if inhaled from a furnace.

At sundown only twelve of the Band straggled into the dry remains of a village. The rest lay scattered along the route, a feast for vultures. Even these would not have survived the next day had not Toraug's bow brought down a stray camel which appeared wandering ghostlike through the moonlight to browse on cactus sprouting among the huts.

The hollow-eyed, long bearded and half-crazed survivors lapped the creature's hot and sticky blood as eagerly as if it had been chilled wine and ate of its tender liver and lights—they needed no cooking. Somewhat restored, they hacked off chunks of meat against the morning. For the poor horses there was nothing, though their swollen tongues protruded between cracked and shriveled lips.

That night as the former Earl of Arundel lay shivering in his cloak he tried to foresee the future. Obviously to attempt to turn back would be madness; but to keep on? Well, the only hope was that Jonathan was correct in predicting that another day's travel surely would bring them to a small oasis lying inland and to the north of Acre.

While he lay with head pillowed on the hardness of his saddle listening to the heavy breathing of his liegemen it seemed that amid the blazing stars a radiance appeared and that down from it an angel floated earthwards. This angel was of a wondrous beauty and girt in shining mail. He smiled and pointed with a flaming sword.

"Not fifty leagues away lies your Saviour's Sepulchre so take courage. Remember your motto, 'In the face of Danger, rally!' Verily you have not voyaged all this way from England to perish within sight of your goal."

The angel then seemed to dissolve and in his place appeared a vision of Alixe de Bernay clad in blue and silver and wearing a chaplet of white blossoms.

"Keep on, Beloved of my Heart, keep on, for ere long I shall be with you."

Then she was gone and he lapsed into exhausted slumber.

Existence in Purgatory could be no worse than that sixth day of marching. The Band, after struggling to down a few mouthfuls of tough camel meat, staggered on. Curiously, the Franks remained the strongest. Sir Arnulfo, Sir Rurik, Aethelm, Bras-de-Fer and Gerth, though lean and withered as mummies, trudged on, leading their mounts while the Byzantines, the Lebanese and Syrians limped with heads bent and eyes vacant through this infernal, sun-drenched stretch of coast.

Anyone who chanced to touch a metal object suffered a burn, a scorch, rather, because not enough fluid remained in their bodies to raise even a small blister.

In the early afternoon Jonathan emitted a croaking sound and pointed southwest. Far, far ahead something shone as a glimmering white dot at the base of a sun-seared bluff.

"Oasis—Ramash?" queried Ahab and dropped to his knees.

Jonathan the Lebanese merely nodded but managed a faint smile and made drinking motions.

"May be warriors—in Ramash." The words fell thickly from Edmund's lips, so swollen was his tongue. "We so few—must wait until dark."

They glared at him, those tortured men.

"Water m'lord!" gasped Gerth. "Quickly! Water there."

"I know. Yet do we serve the Cross by risking death? We fall—how will our armies be warned?"

Never had anything been more difficult than for Sir Edmund de Montgomerie to restrain his fevered, semi-delirious followers. Yet he did so, even striking flat a Lebanese who croaked that he must drink immediately or perish.

The coming of nightfall and surcease from the heat lent a measure of strength to the ten remaining horses as well as to their masters. In silence the survivors advanced with swords drawn until they could discern a number of low black tents looming under some palms and grouped about a well-sweep which, in the imagination of the Band, shone as bright as the Cross of Redemption. The stronger men had to assist their feebler companions into the saddle and several mounts wavered dangerously under their weight yet once their riders were seated the poor, brave beasts seemed to discover some untapped source of strength.

A lone lookout was detected, alert and for some reason apparently uneasy. The Saracen kept gathering his *abba* about his shoulder, taking a few strides in one direction and then in another with bow strung and ready. His position had been well selected. None could approach the well and its few frayed date palms without being noticed.

In the shadows of a rock outcrop Edmund hesitated. Would it be possible to rush some fifty yards and strike him down before he could raise an alarm? A fresh man might do so but not these fevered scarecrows moving on legs that wavered like reeds. A hand descended on the Anglo-Norman's shoulder and Gerth's familiar accents breathed in his ear.

"Let me—I silence——"

Before Edmund could make reply the Saxon was crawling forward, flat to the ground. Every time the lookout faced his way he collapsed motionless among the stones of this starlit desert hillside. Foot by foot he writhed closer and Bras-de-Fer winced every time the starlight glinted on the broad blade of his *francisca*.

When the armiger was yet twenty yards distant the Saracen on guard apparently sensed something. Possibly a dislodged pebble had clicked against another. At any rate he wheeled, nocked an arrow to his string. It was then that Edmund despite his grinding fatigue sensed what must be done and quickly hurled a small stone off to his left.

Quickly as a cat the Saracen whirled and almost as fast Gerth arose to his knees. The *francisca* flashed back then was sent spinning over and over to strike the lookout between the shoulders and knock him flat, able to utter only gurgling gasps.

In a series of bounds astonishing for one so near the edge of collapse Gerth covered the distance to his quarry and locking fingers about the Infidel's throat prevented any outcry by him—forever.

In murderous silence the Christians charged at a jolting trot among the tents and that indomitable spirit which so often had retrieved Cross Bearers from disaster flared long enough to permit swords and axes to do their work. Some thirty sleep-drugged Saracens were slain or driven out into the desert and away from those blessed waters in the well.

CHAPTER XII

Sir Outcast

Aside from a few frayed and discouraged date palms and the incredibly smelly and vermin infested goatskin tents the Oasis of Ramash afforded no shelter from the sun saving a surprisingly well-built Roman guardhouse. Above its lintel the name of Tiberius Caesar remained incised in severely pure Latin letters.

Therefore it became necessary for the surviving companions and their horses to seek shelter within the guardhouse. The one exception was a lookout posted on the structure's stone roof for, during the morning, white-clad figures had been observed wandering dazedly and afoot amid the burning wastes of the coast. Certainly these luckless Arabs who had been driven from the oasis soon must perish. They knew, of course, that a quicker death at the hands of Franks awaited them beside the well.

It was Sir Arnulfo who, rousing from slumber, looked drowsily about then uttered a resounding curse. Then his fingers made the sign of the Cross. Edmund stared curiously upon the Italian-Norman and tried to forget a thirst which persisted despite water doled out a little at a time through the urgent warnings of Toraug and the other Asiatics. Too much water drunk at one time they claimed would kill men in their condition.

"Why do you thus curse?" growled Bras-de-Fer rolling over onto his side. "The heat in here is great but nothing as to what we suffered yesterday or before that."

"The devil fly away the heat!" snapped Arnulfo. "Count and see how many we number."

Swiftly Edmund ran his eye over the Companions. Of the Band's original gentle men only Bras-de-Fer and Sir Arnulfo, Sir Rurik and Sir Aethelm, remained. That made five, counting himself. Then there were Gerth, Sigurd, Toraug and the Byzantine, Theophanes, surviving from those who had enrolled at the abandoned barracks in the Galata quarter of Constantinople. That counted four more. Then there were the Asiatics: Ahab, Jonathan and another Lebanese which made in all thirteen men! Despite the heat a chill shot down the Anglo-Norman's spine. Thirteen! The most ill-omened number known to Christianity!

A grating laugh escaped Sir Arnulfo of Brindisi. "Thirteen Christian souls lost in the heart of an accursed, hostile country."

The scarred old Byzantine laughed and tilted a cup of water over his shaggy head. "Take consolation, my lord and reflect. Do we not now rest nearer to our goal than any Franks who are not prisoners?"

Jonathan the Lebanese nodded, arose, went out to refill a blackened iron pot and to collect dried camel's dung with which to kindle a fire since the Band had found food a-plenty as well as lances, shields and horses among their victims.

"By nightfall," Edmund announced hurriedly, "this evil number will be ended, for two of you, Ahab and Jonathan the Lebanese, must take your pick of the horses and make your way back—inland this time—and warn Count Tancred away from the coast road."

The two designated men grimaced, nor did any others evince eagerness to risk once more what they already had suffered.

Ahab quavered, "Oh, God, to fare out into the desert again—!"

"Let me depart, my lord," Gerth urged. "Mayhap I can explain the route better to Frankish ears?"

Edmund smiled and clapped his armiger on the shoulder. "Aye, I shall have to send you." There could be no real trusting of Asiatics so far as he was concerned. "But methinks the moment has arrived when, as Earl of Arundel and as your undoubted lord, I must knight so faithful a liegeman."

Curious was the ceremony which ensued in which bearded, sunscorched men in ragged *khalats* stood in a malodorous semicircle about the young Saxon. Gerth Ordway knelt and repeated those same rules of chivalry which Edmund de Montgomerie once had recited in Dover Castle. At the recollection sudden tears filled Edmund's eyes and his hand quivered when his sword blade touched the nape of Gerth's neck.

"Arise, Sir Gerth," he called in a great voice that caused the gloomy guardhouse to reverberate, "Arise and be proud!"

The other Franks beat him on the shoulders, even embraced the flushed and grinning Saxon. His prowess in battle and unfailing good nature had encouraged the Band during many of its darkest hours.

No golden spurs were available but Bras-de-Fer presented the new knight with a spare sword, a beautiful thing captured at Dorylaeum.

Suddenly the lookout hailed from the roof.

"A camel rider approaches!"

Snatching out swords, the Companions, blinking like newly awakened cats rushed out into the glaring sunlight.

"He rides alone?" Edmund called up. Lord! To be surprised like this was intolerable.

"So far as I can see, my lord," came the lookout's croaking voice. "He seems to follow our spoor and appears unafraid."

For all that the stranger must have noticed the Band running out of the guardhouse to stand shading their eyes the camel rider continued to approach at an unhurried gait.

Toraug jerked out his Turkish bow, nocked an arrow to its string then cast an expectant glance at Sir Edmund.

At the rapid, shuffling pace of a good *mehari* or riding camel approached a most singular apparition. The stranger's almost snow-white beard flowed midway down his chest and although he wore a turban twisted in the Saracen fashion and a ragged *khoufi* Edmund noted that his eyes were of the brightest imaginable blue.

A few spear casts short of the well, the weird figure pressed foot to his camel's neck, signaling it to kneel. Then straight as any lance the stranger advanced, continually making the sign of the Cross.

"Some Maronite hermit most likely," predicted Ahab. "Many such lurk about this wasteland."

He was wrong for the barefooted apparition called out in good Norman-French, "Greetings, my lords, and welcome to Palestine."

Challenged Bras-de-Fer, "Halt! Give your name and station."

"I was once a belted knight of Touraine. My name, I have solemnly sworn never to reveal." He advanced, brown, naked feet wincing not at all over the ground's furious heat.

Later the stranger revealed that once, many years ago, for his sins he had made the pilgrimage to Jerusalem, barefooted and unarmed; that he had quarreled with fellow pilgrims and had slain several. Overcome by remorse, he then had fled to this wasteland and had become an anchorite. Through fasting, meditation and prayer the Outcast was hoping to win redemption.

No amount of subtle prompting from the Companions could elicit the anchorite's name or title. But a gentle man he must have been so noble was his bearing and so intelligent his manner. Later Sir Outcast, as Sir Arnulfo dubbed him for want of a better title, explained that from a great distance he had observed the Band's tortured progress when, during the fifth day, they had passed the cave in which a hidden spring had made it possible for him to exist.

Sir Outcast sighed. "Indeed my heart bled; twice you passed close by cisterns known only to a few nomads and myself. The West Romans built them a thousand years ago I believe. During the rains they fill up."

The Anglo-Norman's sunken eyes narrowed. "How large are they? Enough to water a multitude?"

The gray head inclined gravely. "And to spare. You perhaps observed on your right yesterday a ruined town in which four tall columns remained standing? Well, one spring lies concealed beneath an ancient pro-consul's palace. I could not come up with you more swiftly," he apologized, "because I had to walk one whole day in order to borrow this beast." He nodded towards his camel, now crunching spiny cactus with as much enjoyment as if it had been clover hay.

"I scarce could believe my eyes when I thought to behold once more Frankish arms and mail. When I saw how big you all are I guessed that certain rumors must be true. Saracens fleeing from a defeat somewhere in the north——"

"Antioch."

"Ah, yes, Antioch—declared that a Frankish host, numbering as the sands of the desert are on the march to free Al Kuds."

"Al Kuds?"

"The Arab name for Jerusalem."

It was astonishing to witness how the long unfamiliar sound of Norman-French and the sight of mail forged in Europe stimulated Sir Outcast. He made it clear that he considered himself no real anchorite but a nobleman suffering self-imposed punishment for an offense against the code of chivalry.

Happily, the exile partook of food prepared in the Frankish fashion and smacked lips over a morsel of *zucra*, a delicious substance manufactured from very thick-stemmed reeds growing along the coast of Syria and tasting sweeter than the honey of Hybla bees.

The natives, Ahab once had explained, were given to pressing juice from these canes which then was set in the sun to evaporate, much as salt was obtained from seawater. The Companions stirred *zucra* into water and drank in honor of the new knight.

Sir Outcast borrowed a sharp dagger and with it joyfully shortened his gray, waist-long beard at a level with his throat, then trimmed yellowed and claw-like finger nails. He sighed and cast Sir Edmund a hesitant look.

"Do you mind, my lord, if I try the weight of your sword and see whether I have lost my skill?" The scrawny figure rose, filthy rags a-sway and eased the heavy blade out of its sheath. He then tossed his camel stick into the air and cut it neatly in half ere it reached the ground. Joyous laughter escaped him. "*Laus Deo!* A Saracen still might find cause to fear me."

Just before twilight, for the benefit of the messengers to the main Army, the former knight explained the route Sir Gerth and his companions must follow back up the coast to Sidon, upon which the Crusader army should now be casting covetous eyes. Again and yet again, he described the location of various cisterns, warning the messengers to make sure that they had not become emptied. Many had become damaged or dried by earthquakes which so frequently rocked this part of the world.

As promised, couriers were granted their pick of horses and equipment so before sunrise on their third day in the Oasis of Ramash they swung up into the saddle after having knelt and kissed Sir Edmund's hand, and started north—inland.

CHAPTER XIII

The Plain of Ramlah

"—And so," Sir Charles de Coffre-Fort wrote in his chronicle, "We, the Jerusalemites, following Duke Godfrey, Raymond of Toulouse and Count Tancred towards our goal, left behind the cool, pine scented forests of the mountains of Lebanon. At Giblit we were reinforced by a number of mariners—Angles, Danes and other seafaring folk who, in searching for us, had become wrecked upon this horrible coast.

"Numbering now less than twenty thousand fighting men we lacked either the power or the desire to besiege either Tyre or Sidon. Both of these cities are walled seaports of vast strength and firmly held by Infidel Emirs.

"It is truly marvelous," he wrote painstakingly upon precious strips of parchment, "to behold how excellent are the advices forwarded by my friend Sir Edmund de Montgomerie. If his messengers say that such-and-such a road will prove difficult, then indeed it is difficult; if he says our levées will discover sweet water even in the midst of a desolation, then water is there."

The Chronicler paused, annoyed by the bubbling complaint of baggage camels which, by now, the Cross Bearers employed as beasts of burden rather than asses, mules or horses. Despite everything, no Frank under any consideration would consider mounting himself upon such ungainly, ill-tempered and foul smelling creatures.

"De Montgomerie is right, also, in predicting that numbers of Maronites, fellow Christians, although of schismatic sect, would appear to guide and assist us on our way. These poor, misguided wretches wear curious copper or silver crosses upon them and observe rites which are as abominations to our good priests and bishops. Nonetheless these Maronites make admirable guides and willing laborers they so burn to avenge themselves upon the Infidels who, for

generations have exacted a tithe of their fairest sons and daughters
to enrich the brothel keepers of Islam.

"Slowly the leagues passed beneath our blistered feet and at last
we made camp somewhat inland from a rich and strongly-held City
called Caesarea. Here, exhausted by this heat which every day
strikes us down by the hundred, we were forced to rest beside a
river which, alas, fast is drying up."

The Chronicler licked dry and swollen lips then fell to sucking a
length of *zucra* cane. Truly it had a wondrous effect in quenching
thirst. Later he would fetch some back to Europe, as a marvel and
the first to be seen there since the Romans had disappeared.

So callused had the Chronicler's fingers become during the past
year and a half, he deplored the impossibility of handling his quill
with greater precision.

"—It remains to us all a mystery why a *turma* of mercenaries
employed by the Emperor Alexis not only are still with us but daily
prove useful and loyal beyond question. Why? Hardly a knight
among us but has suspected the Turcopoles and their *Comes*, a certain Count Leo Bardas, of treachery, come early, come late. But,
in sooth this affable general and his renegade Turks have guarded
our flank with skill and valor. Many of our strays and sick would
have been butchered save for the devotion of this crafty Byzantine.
Why does he persist in aiding us? Is it to spite his foresworn master?

"Many rumors center upon a fair young woman who rides always
with his *turma*. She is said to be Count Leo's daughter, by others
his secret wife, but most believe this creature of unearthly beauty
to be Count Leo's concubine. Certain it is, that whatever her station,
the Countess Sybilla is untiring in her devotion to the health of the
Greek Emperor's mercenaries. Not a whit more carefully does the
Baroness of Cetraro watch over the wounded among God's own true
servants.

"The guides swear that soon we shall be blessed with a sight for
which every one of us has pined, lo, these past three years; the walls,
towers and churches of Jerusalem! The Maronites among us solemnly
declare the Holy City to lie but a scant thirty leagues distant—a
thought which lends shoes to unclad feet and strength into backs and
arms wasted through hardships past imagination."

Sir Gerth and the handmaiden Chloë squatted comfortably upon
a pile of saddles outside a tent now occupied by Rosamund of Cetraro
together with Chloë and two weary French noblewomen widowed
during the long and futile siege of Arkah.

The sun now swung low, promising in a very few minutes to drown
itself in the Mediterranean's red-tinted waters.

"Tell me," Sir Gerth invited while rewrapping his new sword's grip with well waxed thread, "what chanced when my lady quit Drogo's bed and board?"

Chloë's smile faded. "When my lady heard of her lord's revels with captive Arab women and about debaucheries committed in Antioch she held a dagger at his throat as he awoke and forced him to swear never again to seek her bed."

"And she dared so to threaten the Wild Boar himself?" Gerth inquired incredulously.

"I was there," the girl insisted quietly. "His rage was fearful yet my lady's hand was steady and her voice like icicles. The point of her poignard drew blood ere my lord, cursing all the while, swore a mighty oath to do as my lady required. Sir Drogo has lived in a black fury ever since, for indeed 'tis said that he greatly loves the Lady Rosamund in his own fashion."

"Where is he now?"

"Why, noble sir, he now follows the Count of Toulouse. All the same when you rejoin your master bid him beware of Cetraro." Timidly her slender fingers stroked the back of the new knight's hand, still scarred by blisters acquired during the Dry March.

Sir Gerth looked up sharply from his work. "Why? What has Sir Edmund to fear? He has done the Wild Boar no disservice."

"My lord of Cetraro believes that Sir Edmund bore tales to his sister and so set her against him."

"But he did not. He would not. Besides, we quitted the encampment before Arkah the next morning at dawn." His jaw shut with a click. "Who then did betray Sir Drogo's lusting?"

"Lean closer." Fearfully Chloë glanced about at tents rising shadowy all about and then slipped a slim arm about his neck. "In sooth I believe it was——" She whispered a name which caused Gerth to start. His new knight's spurs scored the dry ground at his feet when he jerked them under him.

"Nay. That could not be! He would not!"

"I may well be in error and I do but venture my humble opinion. Still, I beg you to warn your lord against Drogo's wrath."

Earlier than usual on a day which promised to be fair, the Christian host broke camp and saddled up in less than a quarter of the time it would have required two years earlier. The sick, and the weak and the cowards all had vanished, and, saving that part of the army which had lingered with Bohemund in Antioch—to keep in communication with the Emperor, so they said—none were left among the Jerusalemites save the finest Frankish chivalry and the bravest common men.

The fair town of Ramlah opened its gates upon demand and so the Crusaders entered the first town to be captured in the Holy Land. How good it was to stroll its wide streets, to plunder *souks*, mosques and hostelries inhabited only by cur dogs, fleas and looters surprised at their work.

There appeared presently numbers of Samaritans in faded blue robes who smiled, but spoke no immediately intelligible languages. They showed these bronzed men from out of the West where to find cisterns, baths and granaries filled to repletion. Best of all, they declared that Al Kuds and the Holy Sepulchre lay not twenty leagues distant!

Sir Gerth, having attracted Count Tancred's favorable regard, overheard him explode in fury when Sir Gaston of Béarn rode in to report that the Saracens had burnt every beam or timber which might be employed in the construction of siege engines. This must be why, explained the engineer, so many of Ramlah's mosques and public buildings had been discovered in flames.

The Maronites particularly encouraged Englishmen among the army's land-bound sailors through declaring that St. George, patron Saint of England, lay entombed beneath the floor of Ramlah's principal mosque. They took this to be a good omen and, blaspheming as seamen always have, vowed to find the necessary timbers somewhere.

Sir Gerth Ordway, rolled up in a blanket among a pile of fodder near Count Tancred's tent awoke, hand gripping axe. Someone had touched his shoulder.

It still was dark but instantly he recognized a gruff voice. Sir Gaston of Béarn, his rugged features faintly outlined by the light of a dying campfire, was bent over him.

"Come but make no noise," he whispered. "Count Tancred does not wish the army to be aroused."

With care the Saxon knight then followed the famous engineer among sleeping men lying like the dead upon a stricken field. He guessed that shortly he would be dispatched for Jaffa where another messenger had reported Sir Edmund and remnants of the Band to be lurking among the ruins of that once important but long deserted port.

He was wrong. Twice fifty knights, shadowy in the half-light, were assembling behind Tancred's pavilion. Softly they cursed every untoward sound and held their horses' heads low lest they whinny. Sir Gaston and the new knight barely had arrived, cautiously leading their mounts, when a whispered order sent the hundred cavaliers swinging up into the saddle.

Moving at a walk and formed in a column of twos the company moved out upon its mysterious errand. At its head rode Count Tancred and the burly Bishop of Ariano. In silence they deserted the encampment to descend a narrow valley above which showed only a narrow strip of starlit sky. Swiftly, they walked out of earshot then took up a slow trot through foothills covered by the famous cedar trees of Lebanon.

"Friend, whither do we ride?" Gerth queried of the nearest *khoufi* muffled figure. He started at his reply and barely was able to suppress an exultant cry.

"To Bethlehem. Count Tancred will not risk that the Infidels put our Saviour's birthplace to the torch—as was the great Church of Ramlah. Besides," added the rider, "there must be found there beams and timbers which we must have."

Bethlehem. The name sounded tocsin-loud in Gerth's ears. Since his very earliest recollection that place had been the epitome of all things Holy. Just think. Right now his horse was, with each step, carrying him closer towards the birthplace of the Lord Jesus Christ!

While stars paled the brief Frankish column clattered as softly as it might through one village after another never halting or even drawing rein. Frightened faces peered out of windows and over rooftops but no one offered to fight. Dogs yelped and jackals answered them from among the foothills. At length the dim outlines of a sizable village built upon a little plain glimmered ahead. Gerth decided that, saving for a large white-domed structure near its center, this place differed in no way from hundreds of others the Jerusalemites had encountered south of Sidon.

Bethlehem! *Bethlehem!* Devout men among the knights crossed themselves repeatedly and bent helmed heads in whispered prayer when word was passed back through pale, shifting billows of dust.

Lances lowered, the Crusaders charged into the village just as day broke. They found no opposition so swarmed joyously through its streets drawing deep breaths of this surely sanctified air, then knelt beside their horses before the Basilica of the Virgin Mary to offer further prayers of thanksgiving.

A few terrified Christian monks, Syrians for the most part, ventured out of hiding to quaver greetings at these tall riders in white surcoats. Soon they ran back to their dilapidated little chapels and burst into hymns of praise.

For all that the countryside might at any moment swarm with Turkish and Saracen bands, Tancred and his company took time before completing their occupation of the place to accept fruit, honey cakes and meat from the villagers who clung, sobbing with joy, to their stirrup leathers.

Everywhere could be heard voices raised in joyous song, songs which faded when, after sunup, the yellow headed young nephew of Robert Guiscard ordered his followers to remount. The hard-bitten Cross Bearers exchanged quizzical glances. What was up? Tancred having won this Holy place, did not intend to abandon it. But the inhabitants need not have concerned themselves. It was southwards and not to the north that Tancred's yellow banner moved. He left, however, a strong detachment to guard the basilica before requiring that he be set upon the road leading to Al Kuds—Jerusalem the Holy.

A shortened column rode off at a canter since the day had not yet assumed the blazing heat of June.

Tancred's guide took their men in the long gray-brown hauberks along a dry gully then up and over a series of low hills along the sides of which dusty olive groves struggled to exist.

Just below the crest of a very steep hill, Samaritan guides held up skinny brown hands to indicate a halt. Cautiously then the big blond knights in flowing *khoufies* attained the summit and halted heavily breathing steeds. For a long while Tancred and his men sat in awed silence under the pennons fluttering from their lanceheads. Yonder, on the far side of a deep gorge, barely could be discerned a series of reddish-gray walls so much resembling the terrain in color that they seemed a part of it. Below, at the bottom of the valley, the Crusaders noted a square white structure and a smaller white edifice surmounted by a small and beautifully proportioned dome. Around these trees grew in profusion and wide green fields surrounded them. This, the Syrians explained in low and reverent voices, was the Garden of Gethsemene and the small church that of Mary the Blessed.

The less pious among Cross Bearers wasted little eyesight on that Holy spot, their attention being preoccupied by consideration of those tall walls rising about a third of a mile away. The one gate recognizable at this distance appeared to have been blocked up. Scattered over barren and rocky slopes leading up to the city on the summit could be seen the skeletons of palaces, temples and houses without number, and the minute figures of men and animals moving among them.

"Yonder, my lords," cried Tancred in a shaking voice, "lies our goal. We have come far, but *there it is!*" He swung off his horse, planted his cross-hilted sword before him and, pulling out his rosary knelt in prayer, an example eagerly followed by Sir Gerth and the rest.

The horses, too tired to stray, gazed with incurious eyes upon the spectacle of their masters bending brown, red or golden heads over joined hands and reciting half-forgotten prayers.

Gerth mumbled a *Pater Noster*—almost the only prayer he knew —but all the time kept his eyes fixed on Jerusalem lying over there under a sky of the purest azure. He experienced a sense of supreme exaltation. How many miserable, frozen, burning leagues had he and the men kneeling about him not traveled bearing the Cross on their bodies and seeking the eternal salvation which now seemed within reach.

If only Sir Edmund de Montgomerie could have been kneeling beside him Gerth Ordway's cup of happiness would indeed have brimmed, but the former Earl of Arundel probably lay at this moment some twenty leagues to the westward where, with the remnants of the Band, he was reported to be holding a deserted port called Jaffa.

CHAPTER XIV

Commander of the Turcopoles

By the light of one of the few candles remaining in his baggage chests Count Leo Bardas absently rumpled fine silvery-gray hair while his steely eyes traveled over Greek characters inscribed upon a scroll he held flattened before him. He read with care for the waxen seal he had just broken bore no less an important cipher than that of his august and imperial master.

With the harsh cries of Turcopole mercenaries riding picket duty sounding in the distance the veteran read and re-read a communication signed with that scarlet ink employed only by the Emperor of the Romans.

In substance the letter stated that while His Sacred Clemency rejoiced in this continued success of Christian arms, he felt it was, perhaps, not to the best interests of his Empire that the Frankish Barbarians should be permitted to capture Jerusalem. This opinion, averred the writer, was most emphatically shared by a number of anxious Moslem Califs and Emirs.

It would be far better for all concerned, wrote the Emperor, if the Franks contented themselves by establishing a number of weak little buffer states such as Bohemund's Principality of Antioch between the Empire of the Seljuk Turks and the realms of the Fatimite Moslems in Egypt. His trusted and well-beloved *Strategos*, Leo Bardas, therefore,

was, with great subtlety to obstruct and render a successful siege of
Jerusalem impossible.

"—Easy enough to command," Count Leo muttered, tugging at a
beard grown coarse and sunburned through long hours in the saddle,
"but what can twelve hundred Turcopoles accomplish against a host
which now counts thirty thousand swords?" Thoughtfully, the veteran
swallowed a draught of Cyprian wine and grimaced at its rawness.

At the sound of a female voice disputing with a guard at the tent's
entrance his handsome patrician's head swung slowly up. Count Leo
then arose and ordered the Countess of Corfu immediately to be
admitted. His niece stalked into the area of candlelight, her faintly
slanting eyes looking larger than ever. They were brilliant in excitement and her full lips quivered.

"I have just received word from one of your spies! 'Tis intelligence
of the greatest moment."

"Then in God's name lower your voice! Must you come dancing
in like some schoolgirl who has just won a prize?"

Thinner by far than she had been on crossing the Sangarius
Sybilla spoke in an undertone.

"A strong fleet of Genoese galleys descends the coast and is headed
for a deserted port near here. He did not learn its name."

"Jaffa," promptly supplied the Count. "What of that?"

"They fetch reinforcements for Tancred's men. Among them," her
breath rushed in with a hissing sound, "is a levée from Sanseverino."

"Ah! That *is* of interest. How many—?"

"Wait! With it travels the whey-faced wench upon whom my
loved one dotes."

"Alixe de Bernay?"

"Who else?" came Sybilla's chill query.

"And what of that?"

Sybilla's scarlet-tinted lips tightened and her breath quickened.
"If these miserable Genoese actually come to Jaffa they will expect
to discover it in Frankish hands."

"And so it is, but held by only a handful."

"The Infidels could wipe them out with ease and so ambush the
reinforcements as they try to land, could they not?"

Count Leo arose, refilled his wine goblet and stared into it. "I
grasp your meaning, my dear. This is indeed a rare bit of news,
especially because from those same galleys can be taken such timbers
as Sir Gaston of Béarn requires for the construction of his siege engines."

"Then, most respected Uncle, would it not serve the ends of justice
and avenge the insult to our house if Alixe de Bernay were slain or,

better yet, carried off to have her cold, Western blood heated in some Moslem's *haremlik?"*

"It might." The parchment signed in scarlet ink caught Leo Bardas' eye and again he tugged at his sun-bleached beard. How better employ the scant force at his disposal? How more seriously to hurt the Franks than deny them the construction of siege engines? Never in the world could even such ferocious fighters hope to storm those lofty walls defending the Holy City.

To starve the city out was not possible. There simply were not enough Cross Bearers to completely encircle Al Kuds; besides, soon the summer's heat would blast the land in earnest. Certainly the Westerners would be forced to retreat to the mountains of Lebanon all the while harried by masses of Turkish and Saracen cavalry already reported to be assembling for the relief of Jerusalem.

Sybilla's slim hands closed with passionate intensity over her uncle's forearm. "Allow these newcomers to come ashore and strike them once they stand, disarrayed upon the beach." Her eyes glowed like those of some predatory feline seen by firelight.

"And at the same time a fitting fate for Alixe de Bernay no doubt will be found?" the *Strategos* queried.

"Once she is lost my beloved will return to me," Sybilla cried fiercely. "Of that I am as sure as that the sun will rise tomorrow."

"Be that as it may," the old patrician mused, "I could perchance alert a certain Emir among the Saracens; his name is Moussa. With him I have had previous dealings. He could assault these reinforcements from one side whilst my Turcopoles," he said with a bleak smile, "displaying, for the occasion, the banners of Islam, strike from the opposite direction. Thus galleys newly drawn up on shore should fall to us and burn so handsomely that never a one of their timbers could be used against Al Kuds."

Briefly he patted Sybilla's hand, smiling to himself. "Yes, I venture such a maneuver lies well within the realm of a successful conclusion."

"Thank you! Thank you!" Radiant, Sybilla flung arms about her uncle, seized his wine cup and gripped its stem so tightly that her knuckles whitened. "Death to Sanseverino!" she whispered then drank deep.

CHAPTER XV

Port of Jaffa

In the pursuit of orders issued by Count Raymond of Toulouse, Baron Drogo of Cetraro departed together with the famous Raymond Pilet from the Crusader main body encamped along the road to Jaffa. His gonfanon showing the black boar's head on an orange field fluttered at the head of thirty knights and twice as many serjeants and bowmen, all well-mounted and seasoned campaigners.

Like everyone else who had managed to survive the arduous march from Constantinople the Lombard had lost so much weight that his hauberk swung in loose folds about his middle.

Now that they were nearing the end of their journey his company moved at a slow trot. They rode closed up because swarms of white-robed horsemen had been descried watching from various hilltops. These, however, had made no hostile move but appeared content from a distance to observe the progress made by these foreigners in chain mail.

Early on the morning of their second day away from the Jerusalemite camp Drogo's men halted on the crest of a hill in order to study the terrain ahead. What principally attracted their attention was a large, red-brown castle the keep of which had been partially demolished. Below it, crumbling walls connected this fortification with a trio of stone piers jutting well out into the Mediterranean's brilliant blue surface. Although rubble cluttered these piers, from a distance they appeared to be usable, moreover a short but wide beach suited for the beaching of galleys stretched away beyond vacant warehouses and the tumbled masonry of this abandoned port.

Drogo's followers then noticed a banner of some sort fluttering from the ruinous tower's summit but the day was too bright and the flag's colors were too faded to permit quick identification. Flashes as of sunlight upon metal warned the newcomers that this ancient port was not completely deserted.

Drogo vented a grunt of relief and, tugging back the cowl of his *khalat*, wiped sweat from his forehead.

"Praise to God we are in time!" called out a Gascon knight. "That surely is a Frank who rides out to greet us."

In a double column the Provençals clattered along the silent, weed-grown streets but halted when out of the castle's valueless gate strode a figure which caused Drogo's jaw to tighten.

Since having joined Raymond, Drogo had heard only the vaguest of rumors concerning Edmund de Montgomerie's whereabouts. Well, there stood his brother-in-law, tall and broad-shouldered as ever, and smiling in friendly fashion while he strode forward with hand outstretched.

Only with difficulty was the Lombard able to restrain an impulse to strike down this tale-bearer. Um. But how much sweeter would it be to allow the Anglo-Norman to perish in a manner devoid of honor. Certainly an opportunity must ere long present itself?

Cetraro therefore called out a greeting and rode forward to strike hands as if they were on the friendliest of terms.

Edmund, for his part, also was cordial, all unaware that, not long ago his twin had aimed a dagger at her husband's throat.

"Welcome a hundredfold welcome, Raymond Pilet and you, my lord of Cetraro," cried Edmund, "I had begun to think that help from Count Tancred might come too late. Only eleven of my Band remain, together with some thirty Syrians, who have joined me."

Sir Outcast next appeared to undergo the jaundiced gaze of Drogo and his Provençals.

While the new arrivals busied themselves with half-hearted efforts to block as best they might the worst breaches in the castle's walls, Sir Outcast joined the former earl atop the citadel's battered keep.

"My lord, a bevy of Saracens prowl those hills to the south and I have spied also many green standards advancing towards Jaffa from the north and east, but none of them seemed prepared to attack." The former anchorite's red-rimmed and deepset eyes swung towards the sea. "My lord, do you observe specks upon the horizon?"

"Ah, yes. What do you make of yonder sails?"

"They come from the direction of Cyprus but are too distant to identify. They may well be Infidel galleys out of Egypt, but I do not think so."

"Why?"

"The twenty-odd sails we have noted are brown rather than yellow so they may indeed be the Genoese galleys you were warned to expect."

During the afternoon Sir Outcast's prediction proved accurate when in loose formation, twenty-one Genoese galleys came threshing slowly along the coast. Protected by little castles built high at the stern and bow but lacking cabins of any description these clumsy craft headed all-too-trustingly for the red-brown port broiling under the torrid sun of late June.

Although Drogo and Pilet ordered their command to stand to horse and Edmund de Montgomerie posted his handful of motley followers to best advantage about the castle's walls nothing yet was to be seen of hostile forces, either to the north or south, nor yet upon that ancient Roman road winding inland to Jerusalem.

This circumstance bothered Sir Outcast no little. Stalking, tall and scarred about the camp, he tugged his shortened beard in anxious perplexity. "This is not like those hounds of Mahound. Why do they withhold their onslaught?"

To a blaring of trumpets and loud shouts of joy the Genoese ships came splashing into the little port and as many as possible at once beached themselves; others anchored or tied up to the crumbling piers.

"Would it not be wise to throw a screen of pickets well out into the country?" demanded Sir Outcast, after bowing deferentially first to Edmund and then to Drogo. "I have observed these Infidels and their ways too long not to suspect a stratagem."

Therefore as the ships commenced to discharge numbers of sea-worn Crusaders already burning immediately to join the Frankish host—Edmund de Montgomerie led his experienced veterans north of the road while Drogo, dark eyes glittering under an inner turmoil, led a part of his force to the south and left the rest to hold the castle.

Neither knight therefore witnessed the arrival of a Genoese galley which, aside from the baggage and armed men it contained, discharged also onto the beach a number of pilgrims, priests and a few women. One of these last however attracted the attention of all who could spare a glance from the toil of unloading horses, arms and supplies.

Refreshing as a cool breeze blowing on a stifling day Alixe de Bernay, indescribably fragile and lovely in her blue robes was lifted down onto the trampled reddish sand of the beach there to fall upon her knees and utter prayers of thankfulness that at last her feet were pressing the Holy Land's soil. Everywhere new arrivals likewise were making their gratitude known.

More galleys were poled in until reinforcements to the number of nearly four hundred men, unfeignedly thankful to escape the cramped and stinking horror of the galleys, became crowded in utter confusion upon the beach.

Sir Toustain, as commander of the largest contingent, cast his one eye over these bare hills crowding in so close to Jaffa and advocated immediate departure from the beach and onto the plain above. All too easy it would be for a shrieking wave of Infidels to sweep his disorganized levée off the beach and into the sea.

Hubert, Count of Catania, a tough old veteran of many a campaign against the Moors of Sicily, concurred. Therefore the newcomers streamed inland beyond the ruined port and left the ships which had brought them helpless as stranded porpoises and guarded only by a handful of drunken mariners who would stand no chance whatever of repelling a swift rush of Egyptian galleys such as came pulling into Jaffa at dawn, howling praises of Allah and of his Prophet Mohammed. Swiftly they butchered all boat guards then applied the torch to the Genoese ships and, by soaring firelight, rowed back out to sea all the while taunting such Christian dogs as came pelting back down the Jerusalem road in a vain effort to salvage what they might from the holocaust.

When his pickets reported the leaping glare of flames in Jaffa Edmund de Montgomerie, in an agony of indecision, debated whether he should abandon reconnoiterers sent on to the north and ride back to Jaffa but Sir Outcast, in his dry way, urged him to stand fast.

"My lord, we are much too few in any way to affect the dispute in Jaffa. Far better that we remain watchful here. There are the best of reasons."

"Why so?"

The emaciated knight uttered a snorting laugh. "Have you noticed the depth and the shape of those hoofprints we discovered at sundown?"

"I was otherwise occupied." Edmund swallowed a mouthful of rank water from a goatskin. "What of the prints?"

"Only that they were larger than those of Arab stallions, my lord. Moreover several of them were shod in iron."

"Large? Iron-shod?" Edmund's eyes, red and inflamed through these long weeks in the wasteland, blinked. "Would that not indicate the presence of Byzantine forces?"

"It would. But we beheld no Imperial standards when these forces scouted in the distance; only green horsetail ensigns!"

"But—but—what does this portend?"

"In a word—treachery."

"Impossible! The Emperor, too, is a Christian."

"Forgive me, my lord, but it is *not* impossible, although I cannot understand what the Greek Emperor intends. Show my lord that arrow you fetched in, Jonathan." His gnarled hands, deeply stained by great freckles, revolved the shaft. "This is not Saracen made but a Turkish arrow. These horsemen who have been reconnoitering us are from Aleppo. Dikak's hordes ride far to the south of here."

"What kind of Turk rides big, iron-shod horses?" rasped Bras-de-Fer. "I'll tell you! 'Tis those infernal Turcopoles commanded by the Greek General who forever is spying upon us. He and that purple-eyed strumpet he calls his niece."

CHAPTER XVI

Rear Guard Action

Because a cloud of arrow shooting Turcopoles—they undoubtedly were such despite the counterfeit green standards displayed by them—kept feinting at them and then withdrawing, the
Band of the Silver Leopard could not immediately perceive what
was chancing on the Jerusalem road.

The blow fell during midmorning when the reinforcements had
toiled some five miles inland. Howling, scimitar-brandishing Moslems
by the hundreds appeared from nowhere and charged down denuded hills. They attacked from either side of the Jerusalem road
shaking horsehair standards and burning to annihilate this straggling column who yet were seeking to regain land legs and a
semblance of discipline.

In a shallow, dry and narrow valley gouged out of the hills by
winter watercourses that paralleled the road, the reinforcements
neatly were halted by a swirl of Saracen lancers. Horse archers
among the Turcopoles, indistinguishable amid the whirling dust
clouds from their co-religionists, emptied their quivers into a screaming, struggling mass of Crusaders who, new to this mode of fighting
kept attempting to close with their hopelessly elusive persecutors.

Near the end of the assailed column still toiling painfully eastwards, Sir Toustain and Baron Drogo performed such prodigies at
arms that the new levées became inspired again and again to charge
back towards Jaffa against these dark-faced horsemen who kept
swarming in, like bees about a beer pot, and stinging just as viciously.

"Can we but beat off these swine until we near Lydda then the
Lorrainers there should ride to our rescue," the Lombard panted to
his second-in-command.

There must have been some topographical reason, Baron Drogo
suspected, why the enemy could for the moment attack only from
front and rear. Nevertheless the age-worn Jaffa road soon became so
dreadfully encumbered by dead horses and fallen combatants that
progress inland was slowed to a tortoise's pace.

It came as a particularly savage blow when Count Leo's heavily
armored and well-mounted Turcopoles suddenly took over the attack from the Emir Moussa whose Saracens, badly punished, had
begun to draw aside.

Still, the valley's very narrowness hampered the mercenaries' effectiveness. The Turcopoles were launching the last of their arrows—being Turkish they favored the bow over the lance—when a sudden shout arose and into their rear charged the Band. Surprised and not aware of the Band's scant numbers because of dust clouds, the Moslems raised startled howls and went streaming off in a northerly direction, granting the hard-pressed Christians a momentary but welcome respite.

Immediately Sir Edmund's men joined the rear guard, miserably aware that, somewhere along the center of this tortured column, the Saracens must still be striking shrewd blows.

Sir Toustain, his destrier from Italy killed under him, slung forward his kite-shaped shield, bellowing, "For the sake of our dear Lord stand firm." And ran heavily along the column towards the conflict.

Luckily Saracens reappearing to attack the rear guard were in no great hurry having delayed to despoil and behead those who had fallen along the line of retreat.

Drogo cast a hurried look up the Jerusalem road, then rode over to smite Edmund on the shoulder and so attract his attention despite the roar of fighting now approaching a new crescendo. "When we reach the narrow space 'twixt yonder two great rocks," he panted, "we will halt and check Infidel advance. The new people will be able to escape at better speed."

Edmund, scarlet-faced and arm-weary, nodded and, over the hissing sigh of Turkish arrows, ordered Bras-de-Fer to collect the Companions for a stand. When the gap between the two boulders loomed ahead he ordered the Band to halt and form a double rank before the Lombard's supporting force. By now half of the Companions were dismounted, armed only with swords and were protecting themselves with shields snatched up from fallen new arrivals.

Again the green standards were shaken on high, a few kettledrums roared and the high-pitched screaming of "Il-il-Allahu!" beat through the whirling dust towards the brazen sky.

Over his shoulder the Anglo-Norman glimpsed Drogo riding back and forth and pointing with his sword as he marshaled his men. Edmund was astonished to see that they were being formed up into a column rather than into line. He was granted no opportunity for conjecture for shrieking Moslem lancers in flowing varicolored *khalats* and *khoufies* again were thundering forward at an extended gallop.

Under the first onset Edmund's horse was borne reeling backwards and, tripping, fell heavily. He stepped free and jerked out his sword as the thin line of Companions was forced back between the two rocks. They fought confidently for in a moment now they should enjoy the support of the Lombard's men and would stay this slow retreat.

Bras-de-Fer, fighting furiously at Edmund's left, shot a glance over his blood-smeared shoulder. "Hell's fire! *That Lombard dog has left us to die!*"

It was true. Well down the corpse- and debris-littered road Drogo could be seen trotting amid the rear guard of his Provençals. To cut off the handful thus abandoned between the two huge boulders appeared a swirl of Saracens led by a huge officer in gilded mail. Count Leo's Turcopoles, it seemed, had deemed their treachery complete; no more was seen of them that day.

"Back-to-back!" Edmund roared and with Sir Outcast on one side and Sir Arnulfo on the other, commenced the fight of his life. Backed up against him were Bras-de-Fer, Sir Aethelm and Sir Rurik, the axes of whom wrought fearful execution.

The Band survived the first furious impacts because their flanks were protected by the two tall rocks and they could not be assaulted from the side but then commenced a struggle the duration of which seemed eternal. Over and over it was slash and stab, raise shield and cut, parry and swing again.

Gurgling groans and grunts arose. Several fallen men lay limp, their sprawled limbs a hazard to the devoted little Band. Edmund's arm felt as though weighted with lengths of iron chain. Sir Outcast tall and commanding, superbly restored through again wearing helm, coif and hauberk, must, in his younger days, have been a truly formidable champion, so tirelessly did he hack and thrust at the billows of men and horses which kept roaring in.

All at once, and for no perceptible reason, the attackers rode away from that stubborn handful of blood-drenched, breathless and glassy-eyed Franks. They left behind a high breastwork of Moslems fallen to attest the effectiveness of those long Norman swords. Gradually the hot air stilled save for the sobbing gasps from the sorely stricken and the hard breathing of those Companions who yet remained on their feet. Tall as they were, they seemed even taller because of the robed figures lying so flat about them.

From up the road no longer came sounds of combat.

"Satan fly off with those Provençal rumble-guts and that treacherous dog of a Lombard!" wheezed Bras-de-Fer. He was extending a gashed forearm that Theophanes might bind it up, he having acquired considerable art in such matters.

Slightly wounded and riderless horses were wandering aimlessly about so the survivors caught and mounted a sufficient number but delayed long enough for Edmund de Montgomerie to close the dust-glazed and sightless eyes of Sir Arnulfo of Brindisi. He then crossed the fallen knight's arms over his sword handle once Sir Outcast and Toraug had tugged the body into such a position that it faced towards Jerusalem.

Stiffly, because most of the remaining Companions were either wounded or had lacked sleep for nearly a day and a half, they mounted, and commenced to follow the retreat of the new arrivals. Along the road all manner of battle debris was visible while in the ditches and on nearby slopes lay scattered the stripped and headless corpses of sailors, priests and men-of-arms. The naked, ravished bodies of a few women lay beside the way, draining the last of their blood into dusty puddles.

The sun's rays now began slanting closer to the horizon so vultures and jackals took flight less readily at a rider's approach. In the distance wood smoke could be seen climbing into the windless sky, such a smoke as might be caused by numerous cookfires.

"A little walled village lies there," explained Sir Outcast. "No doubt we will find the fugitives encamped there, and, I hope," he added somberly, "that base, black-browed dog who left us in the lurch."

A little further on a considerable scattering of dead horses and human corpses indicated that here the Saracens must have attacked in force.

"Why, my lord," demanded Bras-de-Fer after spitting upon a Moslem body, "think you that those dog-delivered Infidels drew away and abandoned their attack upon us just when we were about to be overcome?"

"Belike they were recalled in haste to Jerusalem," was Sir Outcast's opinion. "Possibly the siege suddenly goes ill with these worshipers of the Fallen Angel."

Of a sudden Edmund's new mount, a nervous little stallion—the Arabs and Turks never rode mares—pricked its ears and the former Earl of Arundel, casting about for some reason, noted how the branches of a clump of acacias moved gently. At once he spurred forward with lance lowered and ready.

"*Au secours!*" a weak voice moaned. "*Au secours!* Water, for the love of God."

Au secours. That cry forever would remain associated in Edmund's memory with the courtyard of a sordid little stronghold called Agropoli.

Dismounting, the Anglo-Norman shuffled forward and parted the foliage until he saw a pair of mailed feet. They belonged to Sir Toustain, helmetless and all-but dead from a terrible lance thrust in his side. His single eye was sunken and glassy but a flash of recognition shone in it when Edmund bent his red head. He even summoned a faint smile.

"Now you—succor me," whispered Sir Toustain. "Thank God you are here ere I go to breathe the smoke of Purgatory."

Sir Edmund dismounted and bent to examine the wound. He straightened at once, shrugged and then turned aside to pull a morsel of food from his pouch. Solemnly he fell to chewing it.

"Edmund old friend, I—I fought my best, but—but——"

"The dead lie thickest hereabouts. You have won much glory."

"But—but I could not save your lady."

"My lady! *Alixe arrived in those ships?*" Edmund swayed on his knees.

"Nothing could restrain that gentle soul from seeking your side."

"But—but, *she was not slain?*" Sickened, he recalled those nude female bodies tumbled by the roadside. Had any of them been blonde? He could not recall.

"No. In—final charge—Saracens won through—slaughtering—sailors. Led by—tall Infidel in gilded mail." The veteran's voice faded and when he coughed bright scarlet spray dyed his grimy Crusader's surcoat. "Wore a heron's plume in his turban. I saw him sling your beloved across—saddle bow—bear her away. Couldn't prevent——"

A crashing fatigue engendered by the arduous past weeks suddenly drained Edmund of all strength and the earth seemed to reel while he bent lower over the one-eyed veteran.

"Is—priest among you?" gasped Sir Toustain. "My sins—many and heavy."

"Alas, no." Sir Aethelm and Sir Rurik then carried the dying knight out of the thicket and Sir Outcast placed a folded mantle beneath the battered head. He relapsed into the past and spoke brokenly, feebly of great, crashing battles fought long ago, the storming of towns and great deeds of valor he had witnessed.

"Of these," came his ever-fainter voice, "none surpassed duel—*l'outrance*—betwixt—English knight—and a Lombard. Aye, that was —greatest of all. *Ah, Seigneur Dieu*—receive the soul—humble knight."

The veteran then sank into a stupor and while little white stars commenced to blink amid that brazen dome above the Holy Land Sir Toustain de Dives came to the end of his campaigns.

CHAPTER XVII

The Beffroi

Jerusalem sat upon its hill of stone, its ancient walls soaring defiantly towards a sky which blazed like a fiery furnace from dawn until dusk. The Crusaders by agreement had occupied three strategically located positions. To the north of Al Kuds, Duke Godfrey de Bouillon and the two Roberts—of Normandy and Flanders—made camp agreeing, when the time came, to assault the Holy City from that direction. Count Tancred's forces lay astride the old road to Jaffa while stubborn old Raymond, Count of Toulouse, pitched his tents to the west upon the Hill of Sion.

It made no difference where they camped, the Cross Bearers suffered equally from the summer heat, dust, winds and myriads of stinging flies.

From the start water had been scarce for the simple reason that Infidels had filled or defiled all wells within a range of several leagues. No water at all remained in the course of the River Kedron. Now it became as jewels and fine gold—a kidskin of fetid water brought five silver pieces. Horses, cattle, goats and sheep died of thirst. Their carcasses smelt horribly and sickened the strongest Franks. It was with more faith than wisdom that these parched Men of the Cross harkened to a wild-talking anchorite who appeared amongst them. With staring eyes and ragged beard, the rag-clad holy man prophesied that, if all the Franks would take heart and attack *à l'outrance* before the ninth hour of the following day then, surely, the Holy City would fall into their hands.

The prophecy flew through the camps and grew as it traveled until a great multitude, largely of the humble sort, shouted with joy and begged to be led immediately to the assault. They paid no attention to less impressionable characters who pointed out that no scaling ladders were yet available, nor were there any battering rams or any siege engines whatever to assist such assault.

Partisans of the zealot won out, so wrote Sir Charles de Coffre-Fort, therefore during the night makeshift ladders were improvised and a few heavy tent poles converted into battering rams of the most elementary sort.

Next morning the inspired Christians attacked with such an impetuosity that despite hideous losses they carried a low and crumbling outer wall. A few zealots gained footholds briefly upon

Jerusalem's real defenses but soon were flung back, painfully scalded
or shot through by long, reed shafted arrows launched by Nubian and
Egyptian archers. As was inevitable the Cross Bearers' spirits after
this repulse sank to abysmal depths, especially when the wounded
died like flies and the appalling lack of water became ever more
evident.

The remaining animals moaned night and day until, finally, the
majority died and raised a mighty stench. The rest were to be driven
off to wells among the hills where they were subjected to continual
raiding. All were lost.

The Chronicler, writing during the middle of July, made a wry face
after paying two silver shillings for a sip of foul-smelling water from
a goatskin bag.

"Our Princes discovered," he wrote while the noises of hammers at
work upon a beffroi or rolling tower, beat maddeningly in his ears,
"that, due to an attack upon the Genoese ships at Jaffa, not nearly
enough timbers survived among the burnt vessels to furnish wood
for our mangonels, trebuchets, petrarias and the like. Therefore
Count Tancred, ever the most forward of our Princes, did dispatch
axemen to a forest lying thirty long leagues distant and told them
to hew down and shape trees of a suitable size."

Days passed before the first timbers, painfully hauled by men and
oxen, descended into what was coming to be known as the Valley
of the Damned. But then the accomplished engineer, Gaston of
Béarn, set to work constructing all manner of siege engines the most
important of which were to be a pair of great, rolling towers built
tall enough to overtop Jerusalem's main wall at its lower points. One
of these points Béarn located near the City's northeastern corner and
the other opposite the camp of Raymond and his Provençals.

"Verily," wrote the Chronicler, "these beffrois are imposing structures. Each is of three stories. The lowest level will shelter those men
who will push the engine up to the wall. The center story is the
largest and will stand level with the rampart tops. When the time
comes, a drawbridge will be lowered over which Christ's warriors
will attack while, from the uppermost level, archers and javelin
throwers will hurl missiles upon Infidels seeking to repel our swordsmen.

"Everywhere officers skilled in siegecraft superintend the construction of petrarias—stone and iron dart throwers—trebuchets and sows.
These last are long sheds open at both extremities under cover of
which battering rams and other stone-breaking devices are manipu-
lated."

A drop of sweat fell from the tip of Sir Charles's nose and stained the parchment smoothed out upon a chest. He heaved a sigh and cast a longing look at his almost empty water bag. Today a hot wind was blowing steadily in from the baking deserts to the east, nevertheless through the flap of his threadbare tent the Norman scribe could watch gangs of workmen hammering and sawing to build a *ballista*, a portable catapult which could hurl a big boulder many hundreds of yards.

A file of moth-eaten baggage camels shuffled by bearing faggots from which unskilled labor would fashion mantlets—or rough shields of willow and other light wood. Absently the Chronicler's gaze then wandered over to the two mantlets and ladder required to be furnished by every knight.

A dust cloud shook the tent and stung Sir Charles's already badly inflamed eyes. He had cause to be anxious; many Cross Bearers were going blind these days, their eyes grown pus-filled and ulcerous through the unrelieved irritation.

"Our greatest lack," he wrote, "is that of a real leader, such as was Bohemund at Dorylaeum and Antioch. Last week when the greatest lords and princes assembled to select such a man, the bishops forbade it, saying that it was not meet for a single mortal man to reign over that Holy City in which Christ had suffered and wore His thorny crown.

"So this council came to an end leaving Duke Godfrey, Count Tancred and Count Raymond of Toulouse free to follow their own dictates. Indeed, these princes quarreled and abused one another until swords were started out of their scabbards and it seemed that internecine strife was unavoidable.

"A miracle however occurred to prevent this. It was a visitation by the saintly Bishop Adehmar of Puis, he who had died of plague after the fall of Antioch to be mourned by all for his wisdom and piety.

"His ghost clearly was seen and heard by the quarreling princes. Sternly the shade of this good old man bade them make peace among themselves, then to humble themselves and do penance for their quarrels by marching barefoot all the way around the Holy City's walls. This our leaders promised to do after embracing each other and begging forgiveness."

So intense was the brotherly feeling, so sincere was a desire for reconciliation that if Edmund had encountered Drogo of Cetraro surely he would have forgiven the Lombard his inexplicable treachery on the Jaffa road.

Once the penitential march had been decided upon spirits rose and the same religious zeal which had started so many Cross Bearers on this long and tortured road, flared brightly.

On the night before the penitential march all the Crusaders fasted and confessed sins to priests who, untiring, until dawn moved from campfire to campfire. In the morning the Franks assembled barefooted and bearing palm fronds in their hands and long swords at their belts.

A surpassingly strange sight, this, reflected the Lady Rosamund, as with Chloë by her side, from a low hilltop she watched proud princes raise heavy crosses aloft and start a slow circuit of the walls. Before them moved priests who chanted, swung censers and held monstrances, reliquaries and golden crucifixes on high—to the shrill obscenities from Unbelievers crowding Jerusalem's walls.

Everywhere one heard the *Miserere* being recited. It was a hard tortuous path the penitents followed. It led over jagged stones, down rocky gullies, up sun-blasted slopes. Many fainted in the overpowering heat.

Meanwhile, on her knees, Rosamund of Cetraro begged that this penitence might earn God's forgiveness. Passionately Edmund's twin recited prayers some of which she had not repeated in years. Kneeling about her with bent heads the handful of gentle women remaining in Count Tancred's camp followed her example.

On the walls the jeering Infidels continued to spit, to wave crude wooden crosses in mockery while their women and children screaming insults, hurled excrement and other foul things towards this long line of bareheaded and barefooted madmen. But their commanders made no effort to send cavalry sallying forth from the gates although they might well have shattered that dismounted, half-armed and over-extended Christian column.

Just before dawn of July fourteenth, 1099, Count Tancred's oliphants commenced to bray without pause. Everyone knew what this meant and ran to his appointed post. Engines were manned and set to work some flinging heavy stones high into the air, others to raining iron darts at the parapets of Jerusalem. Constrictor ropes were wound so tight they screeched before manipulating the long armbeams of mighty catapults.

Swarms of sunken-eyed bowmen, sheltering behind mantlets of osier, aspen and willow, kept up a continual arrow fire at the wall. Others sweated and cursed to roll forward the sows and the battering rams within them. Still others used pinch bars in urging selected boulders towards the trebuchets.

The blaring of Frankish trumpets was answered by the confident, shivering clang of Arab cymbals and the rumble of kettledrums. In long columns ranged in the lee of the great beffroi, impatiently waited the pick of those knights who followed Count Tancred's banner. All about scaling ladders awaited use—when the siege tower should traverse the ruined outer defenses and on their rubble come to rest before the forty-foot main wall.

The beffroi advanced with agonizing slowness and many fell among common men who were throwing rounded logs as rollers before the great moving tower. These liegemen worked behind mantlets held by others but still Infidel arrows and javelins cut them down by the score. The beffroi shuddered, commenced to inch forward along the path laboriously cleared for its progress. Somewhere nearby could be heard the rhythmic *thud-thud* of an iron headed ram which, beneath its protecting sow had begun to gnaw at Jerusalem's red-gray walls.

Further away could be heard a confused clamor and the sounding of many hunting horns.

"The Provençals," grunted Bras-de-Fer, wiping sweat from his bearded chin, "are always noisy when not stuffing their bellies, but pray God, they are faring better than do we."

As a brazen sun soared higher men commenced to faint and lay on the baking ground, helpless and piteously moaning for water.

To Edmund it proved sheer torture to wait and wait in an agony of ignorance as to where Alixe de Bernay might be found beyond those walls—if indeed she had not been carried off into the interior.

Judicious questioning of certain prisoners on the part of Sir Outcast had elicited most disturbing information. The giant Saracen seen on the Jaffa road in gilded mail and wearing a heron's feather in his turban, had been a certain Moussa Habib, an Emir, a famous warrior. Aside from owning a palace in Jerusalem, this Moussa was lord over a small Emirate beyond the Dead Sea—a domain called Sazor.

Endlessly, Edmund with more or less violent persuasion, had questioned each and every prisoner who admitted knowing this haughty Emir. How was this Moussa disposed to treat his captives—female captives in particular? He obtained most information from a sullen, dark-faced young Arab princeling who, though chained hand and foot kept his head proudly raised and his gaze defiant.

"Speak true," Edmund had urged, "and you shall fear no harm. How does this Moussa Habib treat his prisoners?"

"The men he beheads with his own hand to test the temper of new scimitars."

"And the women?"

A flicker of amusement had relaxed the strained expression of this straight young Saracen. "Ugly females he sells into slavery but the beauteous he reserves for his own particular pleasures."

"Particular pleasures?" Edmund demanded sharply.

"Amusements too complicated and exotic for most tastes."

"Peace! Does he never hold such fair ladies to ransom?"

"Not ever. He reserves these Christian bitches for his most imaginative moments since such sluts deserve no better fate. He also——"

So shrewd were this Arab's insults that, flying into one of those red rages which had not overwhelmed him in many months, Edmund snatched out his sword and, with a single sweep, sent the princeling's small head bounding away down the slope. The Saracen's headless torso remained a long instant erect, spraying geysers of bright blood from the severed arteries then collapsed shuddering at Edmund's feet.

As the beffroi inched laboriously forward the Moslems shot at it until its forward side bristled with arrows like quills upon a hedgehog's back. When it creaked inexorably onwards, the defenders hurled bundles of flaming reeds and pots of oil upon it. Fortunately, theirs was not the secret of Greek fire, else surely the great beffroi would have caught fire and crumbled despite green hides nailed upon it to prevent burning.

During the afternoon a new and ever-popular ensign became displayed. Tancred, yellow head a-gleam and heedless of peril, ranged back and forth under the wall shaking in defiance a plain white banner marked only with a bright red cross of St. George.

Arrows of the Infidels whistled, glanced off the hard-baked earth, and often wounded in the legs those whose shields and helms protected them elsewhere but the tower advanced until it rested but two spears' lengths from the wall.

Then, joyfully, Count Tancred gave the assault signal. His men and those of Duke Godfrey toiled forward, lugging heavy scaling ladders but, no sooner had these been planted than Saracens used long, crotched poles to overset them, hurling the men on the ladders backwards to be broken upon the rocky earth. At the same time the beffroi took fire in several places, therefore all efforts were diverted towards saving the great tower so, when the sun swung low, the beffroi remained standing, still smoking gently amid heaps of corpses.

The baffled attackers then withdrew but not far for fear that the Infidels might risk a sally and so reduce their beffroi to ashes. Wearily the Christian forces made camp and assuaged their terrible thirst.

During the night Edmund and Gerth and other knights labored among jackmen to bring up fresh supplies of stones for the *petrarias*, iron barbs for the *ballistae* and ropes to replace those constrictors which had parted on the catapults and trebuchets.

Towards midnight a line of torches glimmered down in the Valley of the Damned. It was women bringing food and drink to those who had gone without sustenance since dawn. Rosamund of Cetraro and Chloë finally located the remnants of Sanseverino's levées toiling over a broken mangonel. They were working all the harder because on the wall above, could be heard the clink of arms, voices and heavy sounds as of stonework being replaced.

"—And where is my lord brother?" Rosamund demanded anxiously. "And Sir Robert of Sanseverino? Are they safe?"

When they stepped out of the shadows Robert de Bernay seemed aged by ten years since hearing of Alixe's capture. His gaze clung to Rosamund's erect, always gracious figure and fervently he bent to kiss her hand before gulping chunks of bread and cheese and washing them down with deep draughts of watered wine.

Chloë meanwhile wandered away all the while softly calling for Sir Gerth Ordway. She did not quickly return.

The besiegers ate almost in complete silence and when they had done Edmund fondly kissed his twin and stood a moment holding both her hands and gazing into her eyes.

"This may be farewell, sweet Sister, for if we do not carry Jerusalem's walls tomorrow, there will be no other day for us."

No need to point out that in a few hours now, the Cross Bearers' supreme effort would have to be made. Should it fail then the starving and depleted armies of the Cross must dissolve to flee headlong before more Moslems hastening up from Egypt.

CHAPTER XVIII

Jerusalem Victum

Just before dawn the Chronicler wearily laid aside his pen, tied up his now voluminous manuscript and placed it in a strong box. After donning coif, hauberk and helm he knelt before his sword planted in the earth, once again confessing sins and praying for strength in the ordeal ahead. Slinging his shield from his shoulder he tightened its guige and sword belt then strode forth to join a dimly seen mob of knights collecting behind the siege engines. Grimly, these were again being prepared for action.

Hearts sank whilst through the half-light they viewed the height of the soaring towers and lofty curtain-walls they were soon to assault.

During the night certain nobles led by Baron Drogo of Cetraro had circled the walls from Count Raymond's position to the northeast and learned that the Provençals also had broken down an outer wall, then had filled the ditch between it and the main wall thus furnishing their beffroi a path right up to the ramparts. There, also, the Infidels during darkness had mounted mangonels on the summits of towers. Now the enemy waited with plenty of inflammables such as bundles of reeds soaked in oil and bound with green hides or chains; sheaves of arrows and javelins lay ready to hand. There, too, weary Cross Bearers were drowsing beside scaling ladders tall enough to top Jerusalem's forty-foot walls.

To the former Earl of Arundel's chagrin Count Tancred and the Duke of Normandy were detached to deliver a surprise attack on the weakened Gate of St. Stephen, therefore Duke Godfrey de Bouillon took command of the grand assault by the beffroi.

"My lord of Toulouse," reported Drogo, "will launch his attack the instant he hears your oliphants." His somber gaze clung to Duke Godfrey's handsome features lest his eyes encounter those of Edmund de Montgomerie and his knights.

Both Sir Edmund and Sir Gerth, with bitterness seething like acid in their souls, recognized this dark-browed messenger but restrained themselves. No time, this, to avenge private wrongs! But was the Lombard not entirely responsible for the capture of Alixe? Surely, if his force had remained to reinforce the Band's rear guard action the Emir Moussa Habib's disastrous charge would not have taken place.

The assembled knights, as dawn brightened and drew the battlements above them in sharp silhouette knelt in prayer while priests commenced a chant which ended in a great cry of "*Dieu lo vult!* God wills it!"

Down from the battlements sounded defiant shouts of "Allah-il-Allahu" and "Allahu Akbar!" From the semi-darkness behind the great beffroi thousands of voices picked up the Crusade's battlecry.

Duke Godfrey lowered a gold-encircled helm over his coif then signaled his trumpeter whereupon dozens of the battered oliphants sent a heart-shaking clamor winging through the gray morning.

From the parapets those mangonels which the garrison had mounted during the night commenced to creak and whine while showering missiles upon the attackers. When these drew closer timbers and stones were dropped upon the inspired men struggling to cross the rubble filled ditch between the two walls. Bundles of com-

bustibles then were hurled at the beffroi which again had commenced to inch forward although swaying and groaning in its every
timber.

Through gathering daylight Edmund saw Sir Aethelm's long yellow hair glimmering like a golden shawl when he bent to heave upwards a ladder with the help of Gerth Ordway and a dozen other
Normans. Sir Outcast had joined Sir Rurik, the surviving Byzantine
serjeant and some newly recruited men in advancing another such
structure while Bras-de-Fer, roaring like a bull in battle helped the
Band's leader, Toraug and a few others to place their ladder.

Never before had anyone heard such a din created by the cheering of the Franks, and the shrill ululations of Saracens and Turks
defending the parapets, the crash of falling missiles and the jolting
creak of siege engines hard at work.

Along the parapet a glare of fire suddenly showed. For some
strange reason the defenders during the night had placed sacks filled
with straw upon their wooden embrasures; possibly they had hoped
to conceal the extent of damage done the day before?

In any case Frankish archers stationed on the uppermost tier of
the beffroi commenced to shoot flaming arrows which soon ignited
the straw and created gusts of choking smoke which hampered attackers and defenders alike. More ladders were carried forward and
yelling Crusaders swarmed up them.

From a corner of his eye Edmund perceived that now the tower
had come very close to the wall and watched the drawbridge rigged
on its second story crash downwards.

"At them! For St. Michael and Montgomerie!" yelled the Anglo-
Norman when his ladder's top came thudding to rest against the
parapet. He headed a drive up its swaying, buckling length.

Twice Edmund felt javelins glance off the shield he held high to
protect his head. God above, how long this ladder was! He began
panting harder and harder as pungent straw smoke stung his lungs.
Screams and shrieks from the ditch below attested that too many
Moslems missiles were finding a mark.

Alixe! Somewhere behind this wall she must lie. In—what was the
name? Moussa. That was it! The Emir Moussa Habib's palace if,
indeed, she had not long since perished or been carried away to
Sazor by the Dead Sea.

The ladder to Edmund's right now had been shoved in place and
two famous Lorrainer champions, a certain Lethold and his brother
were scrambling up its clumsy rungs. An indescribable energy activated these men panting upwards towards the flame-crowned bat-

tlements and a realization of their dedicated dream. "God wills it!"
they gasped. "God wills it!"

Edmund gained the summit, beat aside a number of jabbing spear
points and found himself slashing, cutting down enemies appearing
wraithlike out of the smoky gloom. Almost, but not quite, they over-
threw him when men on the ladder to his left broke and sent the
men upon it crashing back in a deadly parabola to lie stunned and
broken upon the rubble. Fresh streams of ladder-bearing Crusaders
swarmed over them and mounted to the assault.

By sheer physical power, the Anglo-Norman fought his way onto
the wall-top and swayed there under the impact of swords upon his
shield. His body ached under the thrust of spears probing, but not
penetrating, his hauberk.

"St. Michael for Montgomerie!" His family's war cry seemed to
lend him strength. Room must be won for men still on the ladders so
Edmund dropped his shield and grasped his long sword in both
hands. He swung and swung again with a deadly power that literally
clove in two several unarmored Turks. He advanced a foot and
swung and swung again. Then putting forward the other, he heard
Sir Gerth's Saxon war cry "Yutch, hey! hey!" ring out as the axe which
he still preferred to a knightly sword, cut a swath deep into the Infidel ranks.

Ha! Now another forward step became possible. Then a fallen
Saracen jabbed upwards and his iron-shod foot kicked the Arab's
face in. Swing and swing the great sword at that yelling wall of dark
faces.

Bras-de-Fer, cursing in an inspired fashion, just had gained a foothold when a mass of Egyptian swordsmen charged and drove the
attackers back to the very lip of the ramparts. They knocked Sir Rurik
over its edge. Only the blood-dimmed swords of Bras-de-Fer and
Edmund de Montgomerie and Gerth's and Aethelm's terrible axes
remained to defend the ladderhead until fresh swarms of Cross Bearers could mount Jerusalem's walls.

To the right an equally fearful struggle was raging about the
beffroi's drawbridge. The shivering sound of steel on steel, the shrill
howling of Turk and Arabs rent the sky. Abruptly, pressure upon
the hard beset four defending Edmund's ladderhead lessened.

Toraug, Theophanes the Byzantine, and Sir Outcast, having
cleared a foothold of their own, had charged along the wall to fall
upon Edmund's attackers from the rear. To beat these down proved
easy because now the defenders' attention had become diverted to
Cross Bearers fighting to clear the beffroi's drawbridge. There, God-

frey de Bouillon, beset on all sides, was raging like a Dark Angel
of Death.

Struck down from behind, the Saracens were driven from the wall
or fell off it as the two groups of Christians became united. This aid
was barely in time for heavily armed contingents of Saracens headed
by a tall figure in gilded mail appeared howling war cries and brandishing spears. So determined was their rush that again the Franks
were forced back step by step towards the beffroi. Edmund, refusing
to fall back, became contained by a ring of shouting, stabbing Asiatics.
Although his swordplay was magnificent the ring gradually tightened. The big Saracen in gilded mail then sprang in with scimitar
raised. Edmund, engaged in warding off a slash delivered by a sable-
featured Egyptian, knew he could not avoid his blow.

"Cetraro!" yelled a voice and a figure as great as his own sprang
forward to deflect a cut which must have felled the Anglo-Norman.
The tall Emir, squalling disappointment, would have come on again
but his men would not face the fury of those two deadly blades.

Edmund leaped forward, swordpoint aimed at the Saracen noble's
gleaming teeth and frenzied eyes, but a fallen Arab grabbed his
ankle, threw him off balance and down onto one knee. Then, surely
would the former Earl of Arundel have perished had not Drogo of
Cetraro interposed his shield. But in so doing the Lombard momentarily exposed his own left side whereupon a Turkish lance, driven
with all the impetus of a heavy body behind it, pierced Drogo's
hauberk and all-but transfixed him.

Even so, Drogo smote down his assailant ere he lurched sidewise
with blood gushing from his mouth. He then reeled and fell. Edmund and his men charged, whereupon the warriors in flowing robes
broke and ran off along the smoke-veiled ramparts.

The Anglo-Norman had started after them but paused while Sir
Gerth, Sir Outcast and Bras-de-Fer plunged by him. Sweat-bathed
and breathless, he bent over Drogo's gore-drenched form.

"I am spent," gurgled the Lombard. "Soon my soul will fry—Hell.
Forgive—I—mistaken."

To hear over the tumult of battle was difficult but Edmund caught
the words: "For—love of God—forgive my base action in tricking you
and Sir Hugues into combat in the Lady Rosamund's chamber."

"Trick?" It was hard to hear over the din of combat. Edward bent
low. "You sent that armiger?"

"Yes. First to Hughes and then to you. Later thought you—not Robert of Sanseverino—turned—ever-beloved wife against me. Convey—
her—eternal devotion—unworthy though I be."

"Pardon granted!" wheezed Edmund. He had to fight to force out his next words. "Farewell, my friend."

Then, mailed fist taking a fresh grip on his sword's handle, he pelted along the battlements at the head of a new group of Crusaders, who, having scaled the walls now joined with a stream of armored figures pouring like an angry torrent across the great moving tower's drawbridge.

By tens and hundreds Cross Bearers surged up the scaling ladders, to beat down or hurl the garrison from the walls. Then they pursued the terror-stricken Moslems down stone stairs and into Jerusalem's narrow streets.

When taken in the rear by Duke Godfrey's men, Turks defending St. Stephen's Gate, raised wails of despair and wavered long enough for Tancred's Normans to break down the portals and admit columns of mounted and quite berserk Franks.

At nine of the morning Count Raymond's Provençals broke into the Holy City from their side and fell to slaughtering everyone they encountered regardless of age, sex or condition. Thus perished many native Christians, pitiably unable to identify themselves as such.

Memories of long, hunger- and heat-tortured months, the loss of friends, the countless tales of outrage and a deep-seated religious hatred for these polluters of the Holy Sepulchre combined to incite the victors into an orgy of killing.

Like starving bears bursting into a vast sheepfold wild-eyed Cross Bearers raged throughout Jerusalem. Howling, the Franks smashed doors and dashed in to cut down desperate male defenders, then drove dripping swordpoints into the soft bodies of women who shrieked until life escaped through hideous wounds.

Basques, Lorrainers, Flemings, Rhinelanders, Provençals and Normans brought maces smacking down upon the uncovered heads of children and babies to splash their brains across floors of cedar or of gorgeous mosaic.

"God wills it! God wills it!" bellowed the victors as, laughing, they disemboweled gray-beareded patriarchs and mocked their dying agonies.

Somehow Toraug, Sir Gerth and Sir Outcast managed to keep pace with Edmund's furious progress along the once-pleasant Street of St. Stephen.

"Where lives the Emir Moussa?" the Anglo-Norman shouted whenever swordplay permitted and, at his behest, Sir Outcast repeated the question in half-a-dozen dialects.

At length the former earl entered a large, well-appointed house to pause blinking in this sudden contrast from the sun-drenched street. The sound of many voices intoning Mohammedan prayers issued from a lovely patio in which a sprightly little fountain still played. Here two armed Saracens waited, erect and defiant, amid a bevy of women and children huddled weeping about their knees.

An *imam* with a long gray beard had been reminding these people of the Glory of Allah—the One God—but at the ringing sound of armored feet he broke off, then pulled aside his robes to bare a bony brown breast. "God is Great and Mohammed is his prophet!" he screamed whereupon the women wailed louder and children whimpered like frightened little puppies.

Spattered with crimson from helm to spurs, their red-brown faces streaked with the same hideous pigment, the three Franks advanced like doom Incarnate. One of the wounded Saracens bowed, offered his scime's ivory handle then bent his turbaned head patiently awaiting the final blow. The other remained statue still—staring before him with unseeing eyes.

To Sir Outcast Edmund panted, "Tell them I will spare their lives if they will tell us where lies the Emir Moussa's palace."

Into this palm-shaded court beat the horrible death cries of folk being killed in the street and dying in the house next door.

"This Emir you seek," cried the younger of the wounded men, "dwells further down this Street of David. His palace lies close by the Pool of the Patriarch."

Edmund's blood injected blue eyes swung to Sir Outcast. "Do you know where this pool is?"

"Yes. 'Tis not far away."

"In God's name let us speed thither!"

The four Companions ran back out in the street to be almost trampled by a party of frenzied Catalan knights engaged in riding down a mob of fleeing Moslems.

Some Rhinelanders ran up and, raising fierce, triumphant cries, plunged into the house Edmund just had quitted and made short work of the dumbly resigned group awaiting death beside that pretty little fountain in the courtyard.

Smoke from burning buildings now commenced hanging low over the Street of David. Heaps of bodies partially blocked the street as they lay draining scarlet blood over the cobbles. These rendered the footing so treacherous that Sir Gerth slipped and fell. When he arose he limped badly. Everywhere houses were being battered open and then indescribably horrible sounds beat through their windows and doors.

"There! There! There is the Emir's palace!" yelled Toraug.

To Edmund's sharp dismay it instantly was apparent that a party of Crusaders must already have invaded this pleasant white-walled structure; its portals sagged on their hinges and the nude body of a lovely young girl lay sprawled across the threshold with crimson threads crawling from under her sprawled limbs to drip down the steps. Judging by the pallor of her hair she must have been born in Europe. Deep shouts, screams and the clatter and clang of swords hard driven against shields attested the fact that, on this palace's second floor, a fight was raging.

"Alixe!" Edmund's throat strained while running along a marble floored hall splashed with blood and strewn with bodies, he roared out her name. "Alixe de Bernay!"

Never in its long and blood-stained history had the thrice Holy City of Jerusalem witnessed so savage and insensate a massacre. The Moslems, knowing themselves doomed, fought with the ferocity of despair and in the end defended the city house by house. From rooftops they showered darts and shot arrows into Crusaders grown careless through the lust of killing and tasting the heady wine of victory.

Like blue-eyed, fair haired demons, the Franks raged through Jerusalem's streets hurling from windows corpses to be added to those mangled heaps which already were filling the street ankle-deep with blood.

Somehow Edmund forced himself to quit his senseless racing about this palace's dim corridors and to try to decide what best to do.

He deduced that Moussa Habib and what retainers remained to him must have made an effective stand at the base of a broad marble staircase leading upwards for Frankish shields, helms and weapons littered the yellow and black marble flooring and several big, yellow-haired Rhinelanders lay dead or dying on the treads.

"Alixe! *Alixe!* ALIXE!"

At a run Edmund led his handful of followers to the upper story where his coming turned the tide of a bitter struggle taking place at the head of the staircase. The intruders were being forced back by a band of Saracens in silvered chain mail and pointed helmets. These, it appeared effectively, had been defending access to a door of cedarwood bound in brass.

Like reeds before a scythe these defenders went down under Gerth's axe and the swords of Edmund and Sir Outcast. Little love ever having been lost between Turk and Saracen, Toraug, too, worked havoc among the Emir's men.

Making sure that no Arab remained alive the Anglo-Norman hurled himself against the door. When its panels resisted he and his former armiger picked up an iron-bound chest and flung it against the portal with such violence that the lock burst and it crashed back.

Near the entrance lay sprawled the bodies of several bejeweled and very lovely dark-skinned girls. Fixedly, their sightless eyes stared up at the invaders. One and all these maidens had been stripped to pantaloons alone then had been stabbed beneath the left breast.

Hysterical screams rang from the far end of this vast, carpet-hung room gay with alabaster screens and a floor of blue-and-yellow mosaics. A group of females, undoubtedly the Emir's surviving concubines, cringed upon a wide divan, their heads concealed beneath brightly-colored pillows. Others tried to hide behind gorgeous draperies while still others darted about in terror-stricken confusion. Some of these females wore filmy, rainbow-hued robes, others pantaloons of gauze and zones of cloth-of-gold, but the majority were nude save for jewel-studded anklets, bracelets and ropes of pearls twisted into long and lustrous tresses.

As in a nightmare Edmund watched a tall figure in gilded chain armor pounce upon a girl then deliberately drive a dagger beneath a swelling, rose-tipped breast.

Laughing the mahogany-faced Emir Moussa sprang to one side and captured another of his *haremlik* by her red-gold locks. He pulled her, screaming and squirming, from the group of women just as a butcher might select a fowl from a crate of chickens.

Edmund glimpsed beyond the divan and its tragic occupants a lone figure clad in a gown of transparent pale blue. Although she awaited her fate with face buried in hands Edmund instantly recognized Alixe de Bernay.

A noise such as some great beast might emit in battle escaped Edmund. It caused Moussa Habib to wheel once he had stabbed his latest victim and had dropped her, spurting bright streams from an ivory-hued side.

Whipping out the scimitar at his belt the Saracen strode forward. "So, Christian dogs," he called out mockingly, "you find few of my lovelies left to rape."

His weapon flashed as the Emir charged Sir Edmund.

Employing both hands the former earl countered, then whirled his sword high over head. The Emir's blade swung to ward the blow but better might he have hoped to divert a falling thunderbolt. The Anglo-Norman's weapon descended with such fearful violence that Moussa Habib's blade, though Damascus forged, was shattered and an instant later Edmund's sword bit so savagely into Moussa Habib's gilded mail that it parted and allowed his torso to be split from shoulder to belt.

"Alixe! Oh my Alixe!" The blood-spattered figure leaped over his fallen enemy and surged forward.

So bemused was Count Turgis' pale-haired daughter that when Edmund seized her she could only scream and stare in wide-eyed terror. Alixe de Bernay's over-tried nerves suddenly gave way and she went limp within the security of her lover's arms.

CHAPTER XIX

Christus Regnat!

By the fourth day after the First Crusade had been won, the air in Jerusalem's streets smelt sweet and a semblance of order had been restored to the conquered city. Everywhere small churches which had been converted into mosques were being freshly white-washed to conceal the flowing Arabic inscriptions which had defaced them. Then, to reconsecrate them, Holy Water was sprinkled on floor and walls while incense filled the air and candles glowed once more upon their altars.

Already, the barons were quarreling bitterly about partitioning the conquered Holy Land. With the approval of Count Tancred, Duke Godfrey de Bouillon who had never forgotten him who had led that charge to his relief, granted Sir Edmund de Montgomerie the fair domains of Sazor and all other possessions of the Emir Moussa Habib.

When evening came survivors of the Band of the Silver Leopard attended a solemn thanksgiving mass in the Church of St. John the Baptist. Bras-de-Fer was present, although his sword arm was supported by a sling and forever would be useless because of tendons severed by a Turkish battle-axe. Sir Outcast, gaunt as ever, was there still concealing his identity but in every other way a valiant Norman knight.

After Mass Sir Aethelm, despite a crown of bandages, exchanged rough jests with Toraug and Theophanes; the latter now wore gilded spurs, thanks to Duke Godfrey's gratitude for the Byzantine's valiant part on the ramparts. Sir Gerth, slow-spoken as usual, but with a merry twinkle in his blue eyes, chaffed Sir Edmund over the prospective ownership of a *haremlik* at Sazor.

Later on, the Companions collected upon the flat rooftop of Moussa Habib's palace and so enjoyed an excellent view of the city over which once more climbed the cook smoke of twice a thousand homes. Laughter again sounded in Jerusalem's crooked and winding streets.

For a while they spoke of the departed Companions: Sir Gaston of Beaune, Sir Rurik, Sir Arnulfo and Sir Reynard of Benevento who had perished so very bravely at Dorylaeum. They recalled also those brave serjeants and men-of-arms who had fallen during the long march south from Nicea and murmured prayers for the repose of their souls.

On a staircase leading to the roof sounded feminine voices and presently appeared those ladies who, on the Mount of Olives, had waited so anxiously while the battle for the walls had raged. With them stalked Sir Robert of Sanseverino, bigger and brawnier of appearance than ever.

He was handing along his sister but his eyes were only for the Lady Rosamund. Following them came Chloë, a diminutive figure in whose great dark eyes shone a tender gleam. On the rooftop appeared other ladies temporarily sheltered in the Emir Moussa's lovely marble palace.

Illumined by a golden sunset the Cross Bearers and their ladies lined the roof's eastern edge. Alixe de Bernay, surpassingly beautiful in blue, wore in her silvery tresses a chaplet of golden laurel leaves which, encrusted with diamonds, had been discovered in one of the Emir's well-filled treasure chests.

Upon the not distant dome of that great white structure called the Palace of Solomon considerable activity was taking place. A golden crescent which previously had adorned the dome's summit had been missing since Jerusalem's capture.

Edmund had placed an arm about a waist so slender that wherever Alixe de Bernay appeared folk made mention of it, and drew her close. Gerth cried suddenly, "Look, my lord! Look at the dome!"

Silence descended upon the roof while the knights and their ladies peered over intervening roof- and treetops at a black knot of men scrambling up the palace's freshly white washed dome.

Something glittered, then from crowds standing awe-stricken in the streets arose a great glad shout as a huge golden Cross was raised into place to shine in magnificent purity against the deep blue sky of evening.

Alixe de Bernay's lovely eyes swept upwards to meet the gaze of her own true love whom she loved so much as, in a nearby church, monks raised a joyous cry, *"Christus Regnat. Christus Regnat Semper!"*